THE THRESHING CIRCLE

ALSO BY NEIL GRIMMETT

The Bestowing Sun
The Hoard

THE THRESHING CIRCLE

Neil Grimmett

LAKE UNION
PUBLISHING

Text copyright © 2015 Neil Grimmett
All rights reserved.

Published by Lake Union Publishing, Seattle

www.apub.com

Amazon, the Amazon logo, and Lake Union Publishing are trademarks of Amazon.com, Inc., or its affiliates.

ISBN-13: 978-1477829332
ISBN-10: 1477829334

Cover design by bürosüd° München, www.buerosued.de

Library of Congress Control Number: 2014920771

Printed in the United States of America

To Lisa Danielle Teresa Grimmett.
For more than words can say.

'Beauty is merciless.
You do not look at it,
It looks at you and does not forgive.'

—*Nikos Kazantzakis*

PROLOGUE

May 17th, 1942, Cretan Mountain Village, Marianna

Kapetanios Michaelis crept through the village, blending with shadows, listening to sleepers snoring, dreamers murmuring, another young widow weeping. He used all his skills to leave unnoticed, yet knew someone would have seen him. 'These villages have a thousand eyes and ears,' he whispered to the owls; 'and even more tongues!' He imagined the old men later in the kafenion sipping grainy coffee and gossiping: 'Did you see our great freedom fighter last night? Not in the mountains with his men killing Germans, but here with his English tart spawning another half-breed bastard!'

Michaelis looked down at the lonely stone house and tried to touch a moment of warmth from the candle flame dancing in the night, but could not. He was too afraid for her, too ashamed of himself. He wanted to return and warn her. He'd tried before leaving. Now it was too late.

Instead, as he moved towards his men, he planned what he would tell her after the war. 'I lied because I loved you, had to have you, and like Zeus, adopted a disguise to seduce you. Then as my lust grew into something pure, I used another lie to keep you and sanctify our child.'

Those words stopped him. He had to go and tell her. But how? Marianna had been so excited. 'Look,' she'd cried, holding out her gift, tears welling, 'I think more of the villagers are beginning to accept me. Even like me. You'll never believe who gave me this!'

Marianna named the woman and read the look of shock on his face as pleasure instead of dread.

'I knew you'd be surprised. I told you I'd win them over. Even my friend Kyria Despina seemed stunned—babbling in her few words of English something that I couldn't understand.' Marianna had pushed the red silk gift under his nose and wriggled seductively. Then looked unhappy at his unwillingness to respond.

He felt the weight of his heavy black boots, which refused to move. How could he tell her that now she must not trust any of that family, without revealing everything? That even the embroidered symbol she'd admired so much—Gorgona, the two-tailed mermaid—implied a loose woman. Then leave her heartbroken and abandoned as he returned to the fighting?

He trudged on, trying to convince himself everything would be fine. What could they really do to her? Whisper or shout the truth about him? They'd already tried that and failed. Perhaps it was a genuine gift and an apology. Maybe the war could pull people together. Maybe it was possible to forgive and forget. Even on Crete. He touched the photograph of them he always carried in his pack, strengthened by what lay hidden behind its image.

Kapetanios Michaelis moved quickly along the path through the brooding Lefka Ori, the White Mountains, his fantasy blinding him to the German patrol moving below.

∾

Marianna began to write in her journal. A memoir she was composing for her parents and child, without knowing why. She put everything in without modesty or inhibition, every name and detail she could catch. And though her Greek was poor, her artist's eye more than made up for it.

༄

May 17th, 1942

A dream come true. I'd just put Athena to bed and got set for another long lonely night when a tap on the window startled me. Then there was a quiet knocking on the back door. I reached for the little derringer pistol that Michaelis had given me. Then the knock repeated and added our secret code. I rushed to let my husband in.

He was through the door and I was in his arms and being kissed with such intensity that I could have melted. My love, my life, had come home for a few stolen hours of passion, comfort and talk.

Michaelis told me a few of the things the Resistance were doing and made them sound safe, even comical. But I knew he was keeping all the dangers and horrors locked in his hero's heart. I saw, before he bathed, some of the blood; smelled the smoke and cordite, sensed the death that surrounded him like a shroud. He carried it as he carried his weapons, proudly.

After olives, bread and wine, served with him saying his usual grace of 'If good Cretan bread, village wine and our olives can't cure you, then God had better!' we made love. 'Another child,' I prayed, 'to make up for those we are losing to this stupid war.'

After we'd finished, Athena stirred. I watched with pride as Michaelis picked her up and stood, naked in the moonlight, our beautiful child quiet and easy in his arms. I tried, but could not shut out the terrible vision of her growing up without him. Then he kissed her and laid her back down with such gentleness it would not have disturbed a feather.

As he turned to me, I remembered my gift and news. I skipped naked across the room and opened the top drawer of my chest. 'Look, Michaelis,' I said, holding out a red silk chemise. 'It was a gift. And in a million years you'll never guess from whom.' I told him and saw the look of surprise at how well I'm learning to be a good Cretan woman. How even the family of his once betrothed were forgiving us for falling in love. I mean, a chemise from one woman to another! Their precious silk in this time of shortage? Knowing who I would share it with? It had to be an acceptance.

It is beautifully made, and very sexy with an intricately designed symbol which I've managed to convince myself is a fertility charm. I wriggled provocatively and dangled it under his nose and was surprised to see a look of shock cross his face. Maybe my foreigner's fantasy was too much for my Cretan warrior!

We went back to bed and talked about all our plans for the future. One of the things we decided is that when the war is over and we have won and Crete is liberated, we will go to England. I know what my parents must think of me and how worried they are. And there is a pile of unsent letters on my desk. But once they meet Michaelis and see their granddaughter, all will be forgiven.

When he went silent, I wanted to ask him if something was troubling him. Because, although the second time had been passionate and satisfying, it hadn't been the same as the first. A barely perceptible shift that only true lovers could sense.

Then it was too late to worry him with any of my newlywed's nonsense. He began dressing, strapping on his pistols and that terrible knife. Outside the window, stars were filling the night sky, stretching our little room to infinity. He brushed a kiss on Athena's head but refused to let me wake her.

I knew he feared her crying—as I'd sworn I wouldn't. And I didn't, at least not until I saw his figure pass into the shadows of the mountains.

*Now the tears fall and blotch the page, and one day I'll show him.
See, I'll say,* these were the real emotions of the woman who refused
to let you see her cry that night as she watched you march off to war.

*The strength of his goodbye kiss bruised my lips but it was his part-
ing words that have left the deepest mark. He started to say—after all
the goodbyes and sweet love promises—something strange. He said . . .*

෴

Lieutenant Meissher's BMW R12 sidecar motorbike raced through
the village with his sergeant and a storm trooper aboard. The rest
of the patrol followed, held up because Oberleutnant Link's staff
car had 'conveniently' blown a tyre. 'You go ahead and take her,'
he commanded. 'We'll round up the rest of the villagers when we
arrive. You'll be safe; all the young men are up in the hills, hiding.'

This intelligence makes me feel so safe, Meissher thought. They
were up there the other day, but still shot our execution squad to
bits before the first machine gunner fired!

Sergeant Hofner pointed to the house marked on the map,
detached from the rest of the village and identified by a huge tree
nearby. The bike skidded to a halt and they were off running before
the dust had settled.

Meissher registered a light burning and stood away from any
line of fire as Hofner hammered the butt of his gun on the door.
'Open up,' he ordered in German, then hammered again. A few
seconds later Meissher repeated the command in his thick, guttural
English. When there was no response, he ordered Private Schmitt to
use his huge body to smash down the door. It burst open and there
was a scream.

Inside, a young woman was moving away from a little writing
table towards a child's crib. 'Halt,' Meissher barked in English. 'And
turn around.'

She did. Sergeant Hofner sucked in his breath and even Schmitt's eyes widened. The Lieutenant had never seen a more striking woman—not just beautiful, but exotic and alluring. She was wearing a long blue dress, and though it was loose he could make out the perfect curves of her body and the shape of her long legs. Her raven hair was tied back, and he could imagine it being let down, falling like the softest night. He could also see that though she was startled she wasn't scared, and that excited him even more.

'What do you want?' she demanded. 'There's no one here except me and my child. Or is that who the brave Germans prefer to fight now they know they'll never beat the Cretan men?'

He marched over and stood very close to her. She was nearly as tall as him, and Meissher was over six foot. Her face was hypnotic and, though he sensed nothing but hatred coming from her, he would have given up the Iron Cross to have been kissed freely by her. Meissher held her gaze then moved quickly. He reached down and grasped the hem of her dress. Then, before she could respond, he raised it quickly up above her head. She began to struggle, and lashed out at him, raking his cheeks with her nails. Schmitt and Hofner had her in their grip and he kept the skirt raised, trying to ignore the pain from the gouges on either side of his smooth-skinned face. He kept staring and imagining what it would be like to touch her. He'd already confirmed that what they were searching for wasn't there, but still he couldn't stop looking at her thighs and the gap between them.

Lieutenant Meissher had worked his way through the ranks without wealth or family connections. He'd been decorated for bravery four times and was being named as one of the heroes in the victorious battle for Maleme Airfield. He'd never disobeyed an order, or even considered it a possibility.

Until now.

He knew as he continued to stare at this struggling temptress that he was going to. 'Why should some filthy Greek peasant have this?' he reasoned. She should be his by right. And would be. Now, before it was too late. It could only be one time, but the moment would be everlasting.

'Get out,' he ordered the men, letting her go, 'and leave us alone.'

They both hesitated. 'But, sir,' Sergeant Hofner protested.

'Get out,' Meissher snapped. 'Obey me.'

They released her and left. He pushed her towards the large Cretan bed. A wreath of dried flowers fell from the wall and he crushed her down onto them. Their scent awoke and filled his head as he tore her dress apart and began fighting with her.

She clawed him again, and Meissher slapped her so hard her head hit the wall. He struck her again and again and she stilled slightly, then resisted. He couldn't believe the shape and firmness of her breasts as he cupped them in his hand; he began frantically to tear off her panties. This revived her and he had to hit her twice more before he could remove them. Meissher stared at her vulva and longed for it to open invitingly for him. 'Why don't you scream if it's so bad?' he gasped, tearing at his own belt.

'Because of my child, you cowardly bastard,' she spat in his face.

As he began to get his trousers and pants down and she felt his erection sliding against her thighs, Marianna's hand closed against the derringer under her pillow. The moment she felt him touch the wetness left behind by her husband she drew it out and stuffed it into his face. His mouth opened wide and she was about to fire, when another mouth opened and emitted a voice colder than ice. That stopped her.

'Put that gun down. And get off her, you fool.'

Meissher leapt off the bed, his trousers around his jackboots and his penis shrinking rapidly. Oberleutnant Link stood in the doorway, Hofner by his side, observing them with indifference.

Hofner aimed the heavy machine gun at Marianna. 'Put that gun down,' Link told her softly. 'You're safe now and I don't want you shot.' She put it on the pillow and began to pull her panties back on and rearrange her dress as he carried on watching.

Link glowered at his Lieutenant in disgust, then smiled at Marianna. She noticed, though, that his eyes were devoid of mercy.

'Bastards,' she hissed as Athena began to wail. 'He would have raped me if you hadn't arrived. You've smashed down my door, petrified my baby. For what? There are rules even in war, I thought. Or don't they apply to fascists and Nazis? What gives you the right . . . ?'

Oberleutnant Link drew his Luger and aimed it first at Marianna and then at Athena's crib. 'One more word and I will blow that screaming brat's head off.' His expression didn't change, and the duelling scars on his cheeks added to the carved, rictus smile. 'Stand against the wall.'

She did, fighting the urge to comfort her child, but knowing that he'd do what he said.

'Lieutenant Meissher, get out and help round up the rest of these peasants. I'll consider tonight's performance, and see if a trip to the Russian front, maybe as a private, might not cure your ardour.'

Meissher slumped out.

'Search the hovel,' Link ordered. 'Tear it apart.'

Marianna stood against the stone wall, desperate to go to Athena as her screaming intensified. Hofner opened her bureau and began grubbing through her underwear. She heard plates smashing in the kitchen and the heavy jackboots of the storm trooper grinding them to dust. Outside, she could hear the villagers being herded into the square, and feared for them.

'Got it,' Hofner said, carrying the box containing Marianna's red silk chemise to Link.

The Oberleutnant took it out and began to examine it closely, making her flesh creep with foreboding. Then Link moved towards her.

'Is this yours?' he asked.

Marianna nodded, 'Of course.'

'What a clever little seamstress. So enterprising. So Cretan to recycle—even the remains of the dead can be used.'

'What are you talking about?' Marianna asked as he held the garment in front of her, stretching it across her face like a veil. 'It was a gift.'

'Yes, of course. A gift dropping from the sky. And paid for with loyal German blood.'

She looked at him. 'What . . . ?'

He gestured to the troops. 'Take her out and hang her.'

Marianna rushed to try to reach Athena, calling her daughter's name. They caught her and dragged her through the door. All of the women, children and old men of the village were gathered in front of the ancient plane tree—rumoured to have been a seedling when Christ walked the earth. Kapetanios Rossos, the head of the village, who'd been forced to stay down from the mountains while a bullet wound to his shoulder healed, was being held at the front of the crowd; blood was running down his face and he reached a hand out to Marianna as they dragged her past. She briefly held hers out to let him know she understood.

The whole scene was lit by flaming torches that the Germans had placed around the base of the tree. A white, unbelievably bright rope hung down from a branch and dangled, trembling, above a stool.

Back in the house, Oberleutnant Link placed the red silk chemise gently back in its box and closed the lid. He put it on the writing table next to her journal for Meissher to collect and, no doubt, fantasise over. The derringer was too good to waste, however, and he slipped it into his pocket. It briefly crossed his mind that maybe he should have waited a few moments more and let his common pig of a Lieutenant enter the English sow and have his brains blown out with it. The idea almost amused him. Almost. He looked dispassionately at the screaming child before walking to the door. 'Strip the woman,' he ordered. 'And hang her slowly so these swine can see what it is to dangle from a parachute with your life stolen by cowards before you reach the earth to fight.'

Marianna didn't resist the men as they tore her clothes off. She felt no shame as she stood naked, balanced on the stool, with the coarse fibres of the rope already cutting into her neck. She stared proudly and defiantly at the villagers and saw Kapetanios Rossos struggling to break free and the looks of horror on the faces of the women and children. 'Don't be afraid,' she called out in her best mix of English and Greek. 'My husband will avenge this. Save my child is all I ask of you.'

A huge cry of pain answered her and echoed into the mountains as Meissher jackbooted the stool over and Marianna hanged.

Link lit a cigarette and watched until the kicking death dance became a tremble, and finally stilled. He waited as his men began to drive the villagers into their homes before moving to Hofner. 'Tell Meissher to clear up and then follow us.'

'What about the child?' Hofner, a father of three, asked, gesturing to the house where Athena was still wailing.

Oberleutnant Link had his orders and knew what his part in this bargain was, but he didn't kill children for traitors and cowards no matter what they'd given in return. 'Leave it for Meissher. He'll enjoy taking his frustration out on it. Anyway, if he hasn't the stomach, it won't matter. These scum hate all foreigners. The child is a Frank to them; they'll loot the house before we're out of sight, and either smother it or let it starve.'

Hofner made his own decision after Oberleutnant Link left. He dimmed the light on the writing table, closed the broken door to the house with the baby still inside, and made sure his sadistic Lieutenant was kept amused with some of the young village girls until he tired of his sport and wanted to leave. Hofner felt good, and if he ended up on the Eastern Front with Meissher for forgetting to remind him of Link's orders then so be it. But there was no way he wanted to see that beautiful child follow her mother to the grave.

Later, after the last of the Germans disappeared into the fading darkness and Athena cried as her mother grew cold, shadowy figures began to move. One of them, silver-haired, tall and dressed in a flowing black robe, slipped stealthily into the house. She looked around and began gathering up what she could take, then moved towards the still-screaming child. Her long, thin hands closed around the baby and quickly silenced its cries.

1.

It was Kirsty's thirty-sixth birthday and one of her favourite old men, Valentinos, had nearly been killed rescuing a cat. The beast had cowered in the narrow street as a convoy of tourist Jeeps raced through. Valentinos had stepped into their path, scooping up the animal and flattening himself against the wall of Kirsty's kafenion as the vehicles brushed past.

Now he was sitting in the shade with four of his friends, sipping tsikoudia. It had been a quiet morning with just a gathering of English girls, married to Cretans who wanted refreshments and comfort.

Today, she didn't feel like giving any. Besides, she knew the stories. Their Greek gods either had them working twenty hours a day in the tourist trade, or had impregnated them and left them at home with the resident mother-in-law, while they returned to womanising now their family duty was done.

Kirsty saw these girls out of the kafenion window, holding up their bargains from the local market as their babies sat shaded in buggies. Normally, she'd have gone out and praised their efforts and given them a jug of wine on the house. Today, she carried on baking cakes, and knew that apart from handing them out, she was going to eat a couple herself, and to hell with the latest diet! Besides, she wasn't fat: just shapely, with a pretty, strong-featured face, intelligent eyes, and a mass of curly auburn hair that any man would want brushing his shoulder. So why no birthday cards except from ex-pat customers? Cretans didn't take birthdays seriously, so they were no surprise. But the men were.

There'd been two making overtures. And although she hadn't dated seriously since arriving on Crete four years ago following her divorce, it didn't mean she wasn't interested. She'd dropped enough hints about her birthday, October third, Bacchus's name day, god of wine, good times and revelry.

Kirsty decided to take a jug of wine and some glasses and join the old men at their table. Their tales and joy for life always cheered her up. Then, as she reached the door, Barba Yiorgos came shuffling across the square. Kirsty nearly dropped the wine as she darted back inside, praying he wasn't going to visit.

During the time she'd been running this place, there hadn't been many customers she didn't like. This one she detested.

He'd been away from Chania recently, staying in his house on the coast. Apparently he went there for his health—the city being too polluted in the summer for his failing lungs—and only visited his large town house to check on his other three properties (all rumoured to be brothels).

Kirsty watched him approach and heard the men calling out, 'Barba Yiorgos.' *Barba*, she'd been told by him many times, was the correct term of respect for a man of his years and wisdom. 'The great Kapetanios arrives,' one of them added. 'Yassou, Barba Yiorgos.' He was walking with a large, hooked and gnarled stick, a katsouna, the crook of Sfakian shepherds, often used by infirm old men for support, which he would place next to his seat at the head of their table and leave for everyone to see as he chain-smoked and drank more beer than the Germans.

And although Kirsty realised he was elderly, she was damn certain he wasn't as old as he acted, and that the katsouna was part of his games. He was dressed, as usual, in immaculate linen trousers, a spotless white shirt with a pair of thick, bright red braces, and sandals that looked as if the dust didn't exist. She had to admit that he looked striking: upright, broad and firm-figured.

And his face! He had a mass of silver-grey hair either flying loose or, more often, tied in a ponytail, a beard that most of the island's black-robed priests would die for, and blue eyes that sparkled with the light of the Libyan sea. He had a mischievous smile and a deep, booming laugh that turned heads.

Along with this went the worst personality and most spiteful nature she'd ever met.

For a start, he refused to speak Greek with her. Kirsty spoke it nearly fluently and could even cope with most of the village dialects. But every time she spoke to him, he pretended not to understand a word and answered in his perfect English, which the men found hilarious—even though they didn't know what he was saying.

Kirsty had tried to take it in good spirit and quiet her native Scottish temperament. But he always managed to awaken it and end up ruining her mood. But not today. She would be polite and sweet. Though she would never call him Barba.

One of the English girls poked her head in through the door. 'Kirsty,' she asked, 'could we have another bottle of retsina? And Barba Yiorgos said to bring him a jug of wine and a cold beer.'

'Got you running around already, has he, dear?' Kirsty whispered.

'Hey, English woman,' Barba Yiorgos shouted as she deliberately served the girls first, 'why don't you marry a Greek like these smart chicks? Then you could work for him all day and have sex at night instead of Ovaltine and cookies!'

Kirsty watched the four girls slump. She moved over to his table. 'The wine is on me, for brave Valentinos. The beer is not. And I'm not English. I'm Scottish.'

'And I'm not Greek. I'm Cretan, English woman. Ha ha ha.'

❦

Kirsty went back inside to toast her own birthday with a glass of wine. That's when she noticed the envelope propped up on the bar. Kirsty felt a thrill and opened it quickly.

Inside, there was an exquisite hand-painted card. It had to be an admirer, she decided. So artistic, so imaginative . . . So disgusting! Kirsty's mouth opened as she studied the scene. It was a Bacchanalian orgy. At the top of the scene was the god himself, bare-chested, cross-legged and holding a huge urn of wine. He was smiling a wicked smile, his beard dripping with wine, his eyes lascivious with desire for the woman dancing at his sandaled feet. She was clad in a diaphanous robe. Her hair was wild. And auburn.

Kirsty stared in disbelief as she saw herself dancing for Barba Yiorgos, both of them perfectly portrayed and unmistakable. She yanked it open.

'Marry a Greek, English woman. Marry me.
I may be getting on. And you'd be number four.
But there's life in the old dog yet.
That could make your lonely heart soar!'

Kirsty tore the card into pieces and rushed to the door. She was going to throw it in his face, then ban him. If the rest of his fan club decided to follow, they could. She stepped outside and, like the men at the table, the babies and their mothers, became transfixed by the light.

It felt as if she'd entered a film set for some psychedelic rock video. The sky, normally azure and endless, had closed in and changed colour, and not to the darkness of any approaching storm. Pinks swirled with a phosphorous yellow, boiling and roiling towards them at incredible speed. The lights from the taverna on the other side of the square, the bakery to the left, and along the narrow road leading to the seafront were glowing with an eerie ultraviolet intensity. A car that drove towards them appeared to have its headlights on fire with white heat.

'Earthquake?' she asked the men who were all still staring skyward.

'No,' Valentinos assured, 'mud rain. A sand storm above the desert in Africa has been caught in the clouds.'

Then Kirsty noticed Barba Yiorgos wasn't looking at the approaching storm anymore, but staring across the square to where the road bisected it. She followed the direction of his glare and immediately understood why. 'Dirty old goat,' she whispered, though for once she didn't blame him.

A young couple walked by, hand in hand, oblivious to onlookers or the sky. On this island of beautiful women, she was—even at this distance—one of the most beautiful Kirsty had ever seen. She was obviously Greek or Italian, with long glistening black hair and a figure that Kirsty would die for. She could only make out her face in profile, but that was enough.

'Po-po-po!' one of her old men muttered. 'Helen returns.'

'With Odysseus hanging off her arm, alas,' another added.

Kirsty looked at the man. He too had dark hair—though paler than his companion's. He was slim and moved casually in an expensive-looking linen suit. Then he smiled, and Kirsty couldn't help smiling back. An Irish look about him, she thought. Then they carried on their way.

Kirsty turned to tell Valentinos they were well matched, though in truth he was ordinary next to her. But then she saw Barba Yiorgos's reaction. He was still staring at the woman as the couple moved slowly towards the eucalyptus trees. This time, though, it wasn't with lust, but with shock. His reaction grew darker as he watched Kirsty glance over at the couple then back at him. It was as if he'd seen a ghost, but more than that. He was scaring her.

Then the first clap of thunder snapped her out of it. A spot of rain landed on a black Toyota parked in front of the kafenion. It immediately began to solidify into a sand-red encrustation. For the first time Kirsty was glad she kept the space clear for customers and parked her own car in Valentinos's semi-derelict garage, even though it was dark inside.

As the mud rain started to intensify, she thought of the couple and looked for them. They were under the densest of the eucalyptus trees, very near the adjacent taverna. The woman gestured to it; her partner looked inside, then across. He grabbed her hand and they ran through the rain towards Kirsty's kafenion. Kirsty gave another wipe to the table nearest the door and pulled a chair back as they arrived, feeling for some reason excited and nervous. The woman—even more stunning close up, yet with something deeper in her beauty than mere looks—accepted it with a warm smile. The man took the chair against the kafenion wall so that he was facing the storm.

The woman ordered two beers in perfect Greek. Kirsty went to fetch them and heard the man say in English, 'What fantastic auburn hair.' She felt herself glow slightly. Then again in English, 'I think it's raining blood.'

'Yes,' the woman said, also in English. 'And if that doesn't work there'll be a plague of locusts sent to drive us off!'

'What a strange thing to say,' Kirsty thought as she opened the beers. 'So what is it?' she wondered. 'Rich Brit buys himself a Greek goddess?' She knew this didn't fit, though, and sensed this woman would never be for sale. She took the beers out and noticed that the only person not still staring at the couple was Barba Yiorgos: he appeared to be glaring off into a different dimension.

The man thanked her in Greek.

'You're very welcome,' Kirsty replied in English, 'and I hope the mud rain won't ruin your lovely clothes.'

He looked at the marks on his suit, then at those on his lady's legs. 'It'll all come out in the wash,' he said, and a look passed between them.

'You're from slightly north of here,' he teased.

'Originally at least. Kirsty McIntyre from Inverness.'

'Patrick Sweeney from Belfast.' He shook her hand.

'And you're Greek,' Kirsty risked, turning to the woman and trying to hold her intense blue eyes.

'I was born in England but my mother's half Greek,' she replied. 'I'm Eleni.'

'Would you care to join us for a drink?' Patrick asked as Kirsty lingered.

'I'd be delighted,' she replied, and hurried inside to fetch her glass of wine and check on the cakes.

As she turned back from the stove, Barba Yiorgos was standing at the bar. Next to him were the remnants of his card. Kirsty waited for him to chide her about it. But he wasn't looking at it and hardly appeared to notice her. He placed a ten-euro note next to the pieces and turned to leave. He'd only had one beer—a small miracle in itself—which came to a euro.

'Yiorgos,' she called. 'Your change.'

'It's for you and the British couple to have a drink,' he said without looking back.

She watched him march, upright, through the tables, ignoring the men's pleas for him to stay. He walked out into the mud rain— torrential by now. His white shirt instantly became a mass of spots as if he were bleeding from a hundred wounds; his grey mop of hair and beard began to change colour as if he were growing younger with every quickening step.

She dismissed the strange juxtaposed image of death and rebirth from her mind and hurried out to join the young couple. Kirsty didn't notice until later that Barba Yiorgos had left his katsouna stick.

෮

Barba Yiorgos

That night, with the sea breaking on the beach along the Gulf of Kissamou and a moon shining a light—still strange from the mud storm—over the broken heights of Gramvousa Peninsula, there were two things Barba Yiorgos needed to do.

He'd just got rid of his son, Michaelis, who'd responded to his sudden request to be driven back to his beach house from Chania, even though he'd planned to stay for several days. He'd convinced himself he wasn't panicking; and yet for once his son's lunatic driving hadn't even seemed fast or reckless enough.

Barba Yiorgos went to the cedar chest and opened its secret compartment. He took out his US Army issue Colt .45 automatic and a full box of bullets. All good Cretans kept a gun even though it was illegal. All good Cretan parents showed one to their children: 'This is what waits for anyone who would steal someone's property or violate their life. This is what you may need if anyone ever tries to take our precious land again.'

He stepped out and, after first making sure his neighbour and cousin had fed his precious chickens and put them away, fired three shots into the sea, to let everyone know the Kapetanios had returned.

He went in and laid the gun on the ancient sofa, which he liked to sleep on these days. His favourite lyra player was on the television, but he could not listen. Barba Yiorgos's hand trembled as he reached into the chest for the second package, unopened now for so many years. He undid the silk wrapping from around the document and photograph. That was how he'd discovered them among the things he'd inherited after his father's death.

The document, which had been cleverly concealed inside the picture frame, had been another act of betrayal by his father: a will, leaving everything he'd owned, including the land Barba Yiorgos was now sitting on and struggling to keep out of the hands of the avaricious property developers, to Marianna and her child, Athena. Cutting his mother, brother and himself off completely. It had been witnessed by two of the Resistance's finest and most honourable men. Yiorgos often wondered what had been in their minds when they signed it. Had his father persuaded them his 'real' family would be safe, knowing that his wife would leave all her side of the property to her sons? Or like him, had they been so bewitched by the English woman that they'd not cared?

Barba Yiorgos had known instantly who'd been caught by the camera's lens, and vowed to destroy the image along with the will. Every time he tried, he found it impossible. Not only had her beauty captivated him; but the thought of what her loss had done to the proud handsome man next to her made it feel like sacrilege. And the will? She and her daughter were just more blood in the already-saturated Cretan soil. It was all that remained of them. And maybe, for a few living souls, their memory. Now he wasn't so sure.

He placed the photograph on the shelf so that the light fell on it. He sat hunched on the sofa, meticulously cleaning the gun and examining every detail of the woman. It was impossible, he knew it. 'And yet,' he asked himself, 'who was ever cursed with a better eye for a pretty woman than you, Yiorgos Casanova?'

But this woman and the one today were not merely pretty. They were . . . otherworldly.

'Are an old man's eyes playing tricks on him?' he questioned. 'Is it the start of a fever? Should I drink a glass of water laced with wine vinegar and lie in the dark with a poultice of it to drive it away? In the morning will she be just another tourist?'

Or had Nemesis really arrived? Had the Cycle of Blood, as vendetta was known on Crete, begun to flow again? Or had it ever really been assuaged? And how much of it would really be about honour?

He knew the answers. And where this confrontation would lead, as answering gunfire to his earlier shots rang out from the distant hills, confirming the inevitable.

2.

October 12th, 2004, Chania, Kirsty

Kirsty was feeling low. She'd had a lovely dream. Her ex-husband, Robert, in their Edinburgh flat, playing classical guitar. Through the window she'd seen the sun burning the mist off the castle, making it rise like Camelot, and shining magically into their room. She'd been dressed in a black silk negligee, reading the Sunday morning paper. The image was frozen to frame. Kirsty woke, expecting to hear Robert finish practising before bringing her toast and tea in bed.

She'd lain there, not wanting to face the loneliness that memory stirred. Luckily, her cat, Diego, landed on the bed, demanding his breakfast. In the distance, a broken-clock cockerel began announcing another false dawn, and she trudged into the day.

Kirsty was determined to snap out of her mood before the regulars or visitors arrived. 'We were just too young,' she whispered to the empty cafe. 'No one else to blame.' It was seeing how much Eleni and Patrick were in love that had awakened such sweet nightingales, nothing more, she decided.

Kirsty had seen them twice since their arrival. Eleni said they were staying for at least a month for a long-overdue sabbatical, though she hadn't said from what. Patrick was also evasive when she tried to pin him down.

Kirsty was by nature or nurture inquisitive, and loved to get to the bottom of any mystery. Mostly the things she investigated were easy, and even the more difficult were ultimately solvable and safe. These two, though, were deliberately keeping something hidden and it was driving her mad —and, for some reason, worrying the hell out of her.

Patrick enquired where they could hire a good 4x4, as they wanted to get to know a bit of the 'real Crete'. Kirsty pointed them to her very good friend Stavros, who had the best. She'd also invited them to a night's lyra music and Cretan dancing. But without their having outright refused, something in their manner told her they'd never be taking part in any of her evenings.

Stavros turned up shortly after and said they'd hired his most powerful vehicle. 'Took it for at least a month. A real off-the-road beast,' he'd stated. 'Strange, because they didn't seem the sort. I hope they know what they're doing. These mountains . . .'

A few days later, Eleni drove into the square, handling the Jeep like she'd been driving it for years, and Kirsty's slight nagging worry about them faded—almost.

'Been doing some sight-seeing?' Kirsty asked.

'Just trying to find our way around. Soak up the sun,' Patrick replied.

'Well, I've got the *Rough Guide to Crete*, plus some tourist maps if you want to borrow them,' she offered.

'That would be great,' Eleni said. 'It'll save us getting lost again.'

Kirsty sneaked a look inside the vehicle and saw a map on the seat. It was one of a series done by the Hellenic Military Geographical Service. She knew how hard they were to obtain and wondered how they'd managed it, and why. Kirsty also noticed there were lots of red circles drawn on it, all marking out-of-the-way places.

On their next visit, three days later, the vehicle was filthy. Eleni looked tired, Patrick angry. 'Do they always shoot the road signs to pieces?' he snapped.

'Only in the more remote areas,' Kirsty explained. 'It's to stop any invading Turks from finding their way around.'

They'd laughed at that and stayed at the kafenion for more than two hours.

Kirsty had discovered that they'd taken a villa called Jessica's at Pano Stalos, a short way from Chania. 'Do you like it at Jessica's?' she asked.

'How do you know where we're renting?' Eleni demanded.

Kirsty was surprised by the harshness in her voice. 'Ah,' she confided, 'everyone knows everything around here.'

A reaction close to panic passed between Patrick and Eleni, which left Kirsty wondering what she'd said.

She was puzzling over them again, letting her thoughts drive away any lingering strains of guitar music, when a huge tourist bus pulled into the square. It parked across the front of Cristos's taverna opposite, blocking its light. Kirsty smiled and knew that whatever was playing in her mind, she could forget about it, at least for the time being.

Andonis, nicknamed 'The Gorilla', had arrived. Kirsty adored him. She watched as Cristos came hurrying out to remonstrate, took one look at the towering physique of the driver and scurried away.

She filled a jug with village wine. Andonis always had the best stories and adventures to share.

The week before, he'd arrived while Kirsty had a kafenion full of British tourists. He'd climbed onto the roof of his coach, and, with the megaphone he wore around his neck during his guided tours, begun to regale them with his Zorba the Greek excursion speech, including the rumour that the Americans had hollowed out the mountain from the movies for storing atomic bombs.

Now she heard his voice through the megaphone again, reciting with a perfect Scottish accent, 'My luv's like a red, red rose, that's newly sprung in June.' Then just before she saw him, it stopped. Kirsty carried the tray to his usual table and watched, puzzled, as he walked backwards towards her. When he reached her he turned and held out a gorgeous puppy. It had a soft blond coat that shone with health, its eyes were dark and sorrowful and, though it was small, its feet were large and its bones thick.

'Belated birthday present,' he said. 'A rare, real Cretan dog. But for you, anything.'

Kirsty had been talking about getting a dog for ages.

'Andonis,' Kirsty cried, cradling the dog, which immediately began kissing her, 'he's stunning.'

∾

Some way through their second jug of wine, they watched as a large black Mercedes pulled up with a screech of brakes and bumped hard into a couple of her planters. Blood-red bougainvillea petals fluttered onto their table.

A man got out, walked onto her terrace. Kirsty vaguely recognised him, either from the local newspapers or from television. Someone important, someone not likely to be in her kafenion. He sat at the table farthest away from them and folded his arms arrogantly. Kirsty let him wait for Andonis to finish his protracted story before going over.

'Do you have any good wine?' he asked in a harsh Cretan accent.

'We only have good wine,' Kirsty retorted.

He smiled contemptuously. 'I mean a quality wine in a bottle. Not village plonk.' He gestured to the carafe on her and Adonis's table.

Kirsty went to fetch him a bottle of her best red wine. Before returning she studied him through the window. He made her uncomfortable. He was, she estimated, in his late sixties. And though he was dressed immaculately in a lightweight brown suit, with expensive leather brogues and a flashy silk tie, there was something of the mountain man about him that he couldn't hide. She could see him more easily with the traditional black sariki wrapped around his head, baggy trousers and high black boots. He was large, with coarse features over a thick neck that looked awkward in the constraints placed around it. *All for show*, she thought lightly, then, more coldly, *or disguise.*

Kirsty poured him a glass and turned to leave before he could taste it and comment.

'You can leave the bottle,' he said. 'This is a nice little spot you've found. Someone could really make something out of this.'

'I am,' she said, beginning to get more angered by this man than she should, sensing he was deliberately goading.

He looked at a table of four girls sharing a small bottle of retsina.

'Do you get a lot of English customers?' he asked.

Kirsty gestured to the girls. He made an attempt to laugh. 'I mean tourists, not our resident Shirley Valentines.'

'We get all sorts in here,' she retorted in a broad Scottish accent.

She made a face at Andonis when she got back and he whispered, 'Later.' Her new puppy, whom she'd christened Burns, gave her an excited greeting and curled about her feet. 'Come on, Andonis, tell me a story. I need a good laugh.'

'Well, I've got one fresh off the press. It'll be on the news later, though I don't think it will make you laugh. Early this morning, a couple in a large four-by-four went up into the mountains. They were well off the beaten track, looking, they said, for a remote, nearly abandoned village.'

Kirsty felt herself grow apprehensive and looked across at the man who had just come in. He still hadn't touched his wine and appeared to be looking or waiting for someone to arrive.

'They parked, got out, and were offloading all this fancy photographic equipment when a man, clad in black, came sliding down the mountains. The man from the truck pointed one of the cameras at him, but before he could take a picture, he got shot.'

'What?' Kirsty had a vision of Patrick crumpling in front of her eyes.

'Yeah, this mad mountain man raised his shotgun and peppered him through the thighs, then shot the woman in the back. He reloaded as they were rolling around on the ground, shouted out in Greek, "Crete is for shepherds!" and shot all their gear before bounding back into the hills. The man managed to get his wife into the vehicle and drive to the hospital, though they were both badly hurt. They're there now and the police are investigating.'

'I've got to go and see them,' Kirsty burst out, pushing away from the table and getting to her feet, scaring the puppy and nearly spilling the wine.

'You know them?' Andonis asked, looking almost as startled as Burns.

'Yes,' Kirsty said. 'I even helped them get the truck. I knew I should have said something. Now it's too late. They were such a beautiful couple. I can't believe it. They were only sight-seeing, for Christ's sake.'

'They certainly weren't. They were looking for a plot of land to build a house, or an old village one to restore. Typical Germans.'

'Germans! Are you sure?' She gripped the edge of the table.

'Of course I am. My cousin's heading the investigation.'

Kirsty couldn't keep the smile off her face as she sat back down. She was about to explain to the puzzled-looking Andonis what her outburst and relief were all about when a shadow fell on their table.

The man had moved across the porch without either of them hearing him. Kirsty wondered how long he'd been there and what he'd heard. He dropped a twenty-euro note on the table. 'Keep the change,' he said. 'The wine was excellent, as was the service.'

Kirsty noticed Andonis didn't look up to meet the man's eyes.

'I'll definitely be back. You can count on my custom from now on.'

'Thank you,' Kirsty managed.

He looked at the puppy. 'Nice to have them young,' he said. 'They soon become part of the family that way.'

He reached down and smoothed Burns, who put his ears flat and cowered. 'And there is nothing,' he continued, ignoring the dog's timidity, 'more important than the family. Except its honour.'

He turned and walked slowly back to his car. The puppy began to bark as he drove off.

'Good boy,' Kirsty encouraged. 'Brave Burns, you tell him. Who was that creep, Andonis? I know I've seen him around but can't think exactly where.'

'Everywhere,' Andonis replied. 'Everywhere there's a major property deal or political opportunity, that is. His name's Diomidis. A very dangerous man from a very dangerous family. They've been waging feuds for decades. Vendettas. Still are. Though, of course, these things are hushed up so that it doesn't put the tourists off. He owns a vast amount of land in Western Crete, plus the construction company to develop it, and wants a lot more. Especially the land Barba Yiorgos owns on the coast at Kissamou. That's the prize he and apparently a legion of rich Arabs want.'

'Sounds right,' Kirsty interjected. 'That old goat sat on a mountain of gold . . .'

Andonis ignored her and continued. 'Now he's down from the hills trying to get power in local government. So, I imagine, he can grant himself, or anyone who pays enough, building permission on his land regardless of any historical or conservation laws. And if you think he's bad, you should meet his two sons. Not that he lets them down from the mountains very often, thank God.'

Kirsty went to serve some tourists and cleared Diomidis's table at the same time. She saw that the glass was still full, the rest of the bottle untouched.

'Andonis,' she asked, 'do you know Yiorgos well?'

'Barba Yiorgos?' he corrected.

'If you say so. Do you like him?'

'No, I don't like him.'

'Good.' She gave a sigh of relief.

'I love him. He is a pallikari, a kapetanios. When my father died, he gave my mother money to raise the family and has never asked for anything in return except friendship. He'll help anyone in trouble. All those stories about brothels are lies. They're hostels run by his cousins, often for women brought here as prostitutes who managed to escape. That's why the rumours get spread. He's a fine, honourable man. But also sad. I think he does it to make amends for something, but I've never had the courage to ask.'

'Well, he certainly goes out of his way to upset me,' Kirsty said, feeling Andonis was letting her down.

'Maybe he's got a crush on you. He was a devil for the ladies once, you know.'

'Thank you, Gorilla.' Kirsty smiled, trying to keep the picture from the birthday card out of her mind. 'Isn't it time you were off showing some tourists the cache of atomic bombs in Zorba's mountain?'

He kissed her on both cheeks. 'Look after that dog,' he said. 'And remember what the women whisper about Barba Yiorgos and the fair sex: "The devil reformed is still the devil!"'

3.

October 12th, 2004, Kissamou, Barba Yiorgos

Barba Yiorgos was angry. He sat on his terrace, watching the sea and brooding. His walkway down to the water needed sweeping. In places, the logs were almost buried by the ever-shifting sand. He would make his son, Michaelis, clean it and do any repairs as payment for the other night.

All Barba Yiorgos had asked was to be picked up and taken to his friend's wake. He'd had reasons for going other than paying his respects. A man would be there, a former Resistance fighter and friend of his late father, whom he'd wanted to speak to without raising the old fox's suspicions. A perfect opportunity missed because his son was unreliable. Barba Yiorgos had told him he could go and sit in the nearby taverna and eat and drink for free. But even that hadn't enticed the son who claimed to worship him. And by the time Barba Yiorgos had realised Michaelis wasn't coming, it was too late to send for a taxi and arrive at a respectable time.

He opened another Mythos beer. Earlier in the day he'd fought on the phone with his younger brother, Nikos, in Athens. Nikos was nagging him to consider the huge offers—especially from one party—for his land on the Kissamou coast. Then, when he refused, he'd retaliated by blocking everything Barba Yiorgos wanted to do with their jointly held properties. Always with the same excuse: the family and its precious heritage. Barba Yiorgos nearly said, 'I'll tell you something about our great family history you don't know.' But he'd promised his father. And that was one oath he *could* keep. 'You're the same as our witch of a mother: unforgiving, pious and weak,' he'd yelled instead, and slammed the phone down. Then wished he hadn't.

Last week, Barba Yiorgos had cut his favourite cockerel's throat, then eaten him, slow-cooked with onions and herbs. He'd done it because the bird was failing to perform. Now he looked at the new one strutting around his hens with its fancy plumage and huge spurs but without jumping on a single one.

'By the gods,' he said, 'if I had wings I'd fly down there and impregnate you all, then beat up that cockerel for good measure. Ah,' he sighed, 'if only someone knew what fires still burnt inside me.' He thought of the letter the real Zorba had written to his friend, Nikos Kazantzakis, from his deathbed: 'Men like me should live for a thousand years. All the things I haven't done!'

But there was only one thing he hadn't done. And if this was the time to do it, then shouting at relatives, cutting birds' throats and drinking beer would not help.

Five times since he'd left Chania, Barba Yiorgos had waited until dark and then climbed into his old car, the one he kept for pottering along the seafront to the taverna. He'd started the engine, determined to drive the thirty-odd miles to the outskirts of a village that wasn't marked on any tourist map. To park in a spot that was even less known than the village itself. To walk through some ancient temple ruins that many people had tried to find and never would. On a little farther to a shrine, next to an unmarked grave. Neglected for so long it could be crumbled. If so, he would rebuild it. If not, he'd fill the lamp with oil and let its flame burn again.

On each occasion, as the sound of the old engine rattled through the broken exhaust, and the one beam had shone, Pharos-like, across the waves, he'd managed to convince himself it was all nonsense. He'd gone indoors and drunk ouzo until sleep came.

And every morning, he knew he'd been cowardly. 'Like father, like son,' he would hear the waves whispering over and over.

Then he'd seen her again, and knew he must do something.

His cousin Stelios and his young son came to visit. Stelios took Barba Yiorgos to his village, Pano Stalos, for dinner and afterwards suggested they should go and see the latest venture of another cousin, Dimitri: a cocktail bar with a roof terrace that offered panoramic views of Chania Bay.

The three had sat at Dimitri's enjoying a Campari and soda, looking across at the island of Agii Theodori and convincing himself that he'd seen the silhouette of one of the rare Kri-Kri goats.

'Do you know,' Barba Yiorgos told Stelios's young son, 'legend says that Agii Theodori was a sea monster who emerged from the depths to swallow Crete, but was turned to stone by the gods.'

As he finished saying it, the young couple from the day of the mud rain at Kirsty's appeared and Barba Yiorgos became as petrified as the island. He watched open-mouthed as Dimitri greeted them warmly and led them over to the table next to his.

'Are you all right, Barba?' Stelios asked as he kept staring.

When they left, Dimitri said they were honeymooners, who liked to travel and often came for cocktails, and that they were staying at Jessica's.

Afterwards, Barba Yiorgos kept seeing the young woman in his mind, dressed in a short, tight-fitting dress of black silk embroidered with red flowers, unconsciously bending to fuss over a cat as the men stared at her.

He'd placed her again and again next to the woman in the photograph. Their beauty and likeness were exact. But it was more than that. He sensed it coming from within her: a deep sadness and anger. Also, they hadn't arrived in the kafenion that day by chance. They were playing a role, cleverly.

Next, he'd changed his mind again, told himself he was seeing ghosts, ones best left buried. Then every time he looked at the photo he was off again. It was driving him crazy.

Now, he decided, he would do something about it. The grave and flame could wait. He would pay his respects to the living first.

Barba Yiorgos called a taxi and told the driver, Vassilis, yet another cousin, that he wanted to go to Maria's taverna in Stalos. It did the best lamb and cheese pie in the world. Besides, if you were staying at Jessica's villa, Maria's would most likely be a number one choice for dining out.

Vassilis dropped him off at Maria's. Even this late in the season the place was crowded. The large main room was mostly full of tourists, but it took him only a brief glance to see that the British couple weren't there. He sat in the section of the taverna reserved for Maria's family and friends, as the head waiter, Pavlos, rushed over. Soon Maria would arrive, with her damn mother in tow.

He was trying to think of some way of asking them about the young couple staying at Jessica's. The trouble was, Maria and her mother came from his village and shared the same crafty, suspicious nature.

He made a plan. When they arrived to join him for a tsikoudia after his meal, he'd mention he had a small house for sale.

Most of the foreigners visiting at this time were property hunting. Every old uninhabited village house was being sold and restored with no regard for either history or the future. In some villages the foreigners outnumbered the locals. And even though, if his brother would allow it, he wouldn't mind selling off some of their land and properties, he'd not let anything special go. Or even consider joining in with the practice of burning vast tracts of land to rid them of any wild trees that by law prevented them from being developed. Unlike one person, in particular, who seemed determined to cover the island in smoke and concrete!

'Ah, Barba Yiorgos,' Maria said, breaking into his thoughts, 'you're looking fit.'

'Yiorgos,' her mother crowed. She was clad in black, older than Methuselah and as bent as her stick. 'Come for my lamb and cheese pie again?'

Much later, with a full belly, but no information, he decided to play his hand.

'I hear the young couple staying at Jessica's are looking to buy a village house.'

'I don't know,' Maria replied, her eyes narrowing a fraction. 'But aren't they all?'

'I heard it was somewhere special, though. Our village, Kotsiana.'

'Kotsiana!'

'It's what Vassilis told me. He said he'd spotted them looking at some of the empty houses. Said there was no way he could mistake that girl.'

'There's not. But Kotsiana?'

'I only asked because I've got this place I might let go for the right price. Full of features: Venetian arches, cedar wood ceilings, old fireplace. Make a nice little love nest.'

'Barba Yiorgos.' Maria winked to her mother. 'You're a wicked man. They've been in quite a few times and they did ask Pavlos, when he served them, about some unusual places. But Kotsiana never got mentioned. They may be looking, but my instincts tell me they're on a honeymoon. In fact . . .' Maria broke off and pointed out of the window.

Barba Yiorgos turned in time to see a large 4x4 pull away. He caught a glimpse of the girl, and she appeared to be looking straight at him.

'Oh,' Maria said, sounding a little disappointed. 'They must have changed their minds.'

The mother chuckled, looking at the expression on Barba Yiorgos's face.

A little while later he said he fancied going up to Dimitri's for a cocktail, and Maria insisted that Pavlos must take him. After he dropped him off, Barba Yiorgos slipped into the shadows near Dimitri's and waited.

The night was hot and thick and cicadas fret-sawed the air into lumps. Then, as if a tap had been switched off, they instantly went quiet. All he could hear for the next few minutes was the gentle 'poo poo' of a Scopps owl, then in the distance the answering call of another.

Music began to come from the bar, alien sounds of US and British rock filling the olive groves and spilling down into the village. Finally, it stopped, and he heard the voices of departing tourists. He tensed as they passed, but the couple were not among them. He cursed softly. He'd been certain they were there. There'd been no lights on in Jessica's, though the vehicle was outside.

The sound of a lyra being played from one of the village houses made him wish he was home lying on his sofa listening to it, not skulking about in the undergrowth. 'You're going senile, old man,' he whispered, preparing to move. Suddenly, they were nearly upon him. He blended silently back into the cover of a deformed olive tree.

They were hand in hand, walking slowly along the drive to their villa.

'Did you see him?' the woman asked just as they passed.

Her voice sent a chill through Barba Yiorgos. He inched farther into his camouflage, thinking for a second he'd been discovered.

'Yes,' her companion replied. 'I thought he might come up to the bar.'

'Then that's three times,' she said. 'What was it you used to say—"Once is happenstance, twice is coincidence, three times is enemy action"?'

Barba Yiorgos heard the gate swing open and footsteps on the gravel but couldn't make out the man's reply. He tried to imagine who they meant, not wanting to believe it might be him. Or even—the thought made him grow colder—someone far worse. He dismissed that frightening thought and began to sneak back along the drive, slipping past the bar and into the gardens of the hotel. A short way from the swimming pool there was a path that led to the back of Jessica's.

It was possible to get very close to the main bedroom window, where a cover of orange trees touched their leaves against those of the night flower to mingle and give the sleepers sweet dreams. Barba Yiorgos positioned himself there and waited. He was determined to find out, by whatever means, if there was anything he needed to worry about. If eavesdropping on pillow talk was the only way, then so be it. A breeze moved the leaves, then died. All he could hear, after the lights in the house, bar and most of the village had gone out, was the gentle soughing of the distant sea.

Then he heard them.

An unmistakable noise that almost made him hurry away and leave them to their intimacy. But he couldn't stand any more doubts, not if they could be quelled.

The bed was sending out a powerful rhythm, and the woman began to moan gently. On and on it went.

He carried on listening, and felt a longing for a few more nights of good loving. It helped take his mind off the fact that he was desperate to go and water a thousand-year-old olive tree and was craving a cigarette.

Their lovemaking became even more frenetic. He could see shadows moving wildly through the curtains and her screams made the Cretan cats sound tame. There was a slight movement on a leaf and, with reactions that were still lightning fast, he caught the tzitzikas. Barba Yiorgos held it gently cupped in his hand, letting its good-luck vibrations tremble towards them as he heard their painful, joyous ending.

He released the creature and crept off to find a quiet spot to call a taxi. They would have no words, troubled or otherwise, after that performance, he assured himself. Maria was probably right; they were honeymooners.

And if the girl was related to the woman in the photograph, what was so strange about her coming here to visit? She'd been English; she may have had some relative in England who'd passed her looks and some of the story onto her. And what could they find out anyway? Even he himself had only ever managed to find out parts of the story. How could they hope to discover more?

'Take yourself home, Yiorgos,' he whispered. 'Go back to your peaceful existence and forget about this girl.'

And yet as he pulled the cell phone out of his pocket, he couldn't wipe the nagging doubt off the face he saw reflected in its screen.

'Why,' he asked for the hundredth time since Andonis had told him about the shooting incident, 'would he, of all people on this island, have one of his lunatic sons take pot shots at some Germans?' It didn't make sense. 'Unless he thought . . .'

Vassilis answered the phone.

'Come and collect me,' Barba Yiorgos gasped. 'I'm a tired old man and I need my bed.'

4.

Eleni and Patrick invited Kirsty to dinner at their villa. She spent an age getting ready, finding a nice wine and buying flowers. Then wished she hadn't bothered. Not because of the food or company, but because she'd been lied to. Also, she realised their only purpose in inviting her was to question her.

Kirsty hadn't seen them since they'd arrived more than ten days ago. She'd been worried since the incident with the Germans, and hurried over with Burns at her heels. She was relieved to see they looked well and were getting tanned.

Maybe relaxing at last, she thought.

'Well, I see the Cretan climate is agreeing with you,' she offered.

'Oh,' Eleni replied, 'we've taken a couple of days off to recover from our travelling.'

'You look like you've been doing some sailing or island hopping.'

'What?' Patrick said. 'How do you know?'

'There's a beach look, and there's an on-the-waves one.'

'You're very observant,' Eleni noted. 'We hired a boat for a week. It made a change from the mountains. And we're both good sailors. And . . .'

'Anyway,' Patrick interrupted, 'we've come to ask you to dinner.'

⌒◯

Eleni cooked Greek. And excellently, though definitely not Cretan: too many spices and even some hot chillies. Kirsty brought a bottle of wine, though not from her kafenion's limited selection. Patrick poured and waited for Eleni to take the first sip.

'Nice,' she said. 'From Santorini. Is it a favourite of yours?'

Kirsty was impressed. 'Well if I was rich or being indulged by a wealthy lover, I'd prefer a Chardonnay from Katsaros. But yes, it's a favourite.'

'To wealthy lovers and being indulged,' Patrick proposed.

Kirsty was glad that she'd made the effort to look good, as they were dressed stylishly.

After the food and light easy conversation, they went out to sit at a stone table under a vine dripping with red grapes. 'Well, what exactly brought you to Crete?' Patrick suddenly asked, catching her off guard.

'Divorce.' Bitter. Then, 'Romance, adventure, sun and sea. Have you ever tried to spend a winter in Scotland!'

Then she fired one back at Eleni: 'And where did you learn to speak such good Greek?'

'As I told you, my mother was half Greek. My parents bought a house on Naxos and I spent all my summer breaks there.'

'And you, Patrick? You don't do too badly.'

'Eleni taught me, and we've spent a lot of time on Naxos.'

Then he came straight to the point.

'And what do you know about Kolimbari?'

'It's a nice fishing village at the base of the Rodopou Peninsula with an interesting monastery a short way up the hill—though the

29

monks are very fierce: one glimpse of a woman's knee or bare arm and they'll drive you off.'

They laughed.

Kirsty looked at Eleni, in her short, backless dress, and pictured a monk dropping dead on the spot. 'We know all that,' Eleni smiled. 'We've been to the monastery, even saw the Turkish cannonball lodged in the wall. I mean something else. An old story that you might have heard. Maybe *someone* who visits your kafenion might have told you.'

Kirsty shook her head and stared into Eleni's eyes, noticing for the first time how blue and sparkling they were, trying to picture where she'd seen them before.

'A young English girl, an artist,' Eleni continued, 'who came over just before the outbreak of World War Two and fell in love with a Greek.'

'I've heard it,' Kirsty replied. 'Or something similar. English girls do it all the time.'

'But a lot different then, surely,' Patrick stated, sounding frustrated.

'Probably,' Kirsty agreed.

Eleni tried: 'According to this story, the girl fell in love with a man who was already married. They fled to another village, got married and had a baby. Then the war broke out and she disappeared.'

'I've heard something similar, but can't recall where.' Kirsty thought hard for a moment. Nothing came, except for the puzzling question of what exactly they were looking for. 'Sorry.'

They were clearly disappointed, and Kirsty slipped off to the bathroom feeling awkward. On the way, she looked into the bedroom. On a little table near the door there were two ferry ticket stubs to the island of Gavdos. Then on the bathroom shelf she saw a half-empty bottle of Dramamine. *Rented a yacht? Good sailors?*

When she walked back out, Eleni was in the bedroom and the stubs were gone. 'I've something to show you,' Eleni said. 'I'll bring it out in a minute.'

'We've always been fascinated by stories and local legends when we travel,' Patrick told her. 'We collect them like most tourists take home holiday snaps. I guess it comes of having boring jobs in the city that we enjoy playing amateur detectives. So I hope you don't mind our nagging questions.'

Kirsty nodded and smiled, not believing a word of it.

Eleni placed an old box on the table and gently opened it. Inside, there was white tissue paper, which she reverently peeled back. Kirsty looked at a red silk chemise, noting the exquisite stitching and embroidery. She recognised the symbol of Gorgona, the two-tailed mermaid, and smiled at its naughty connotation. Kirsty guessed they must have visited one of the women's cooperatives, where such crafts were kept alive. Yet, this looked too skilful for what was usually sold to tourists. And, though it appeared unworn, she felt it was old.

'Beautiful,' she said. 'And such an unusual design. I've never seen such fine needlework. It must have cost a small fortune.'

Eleni hesitated briefly. 'It did, far too much. But do you know anything about it?'

'I don't know what you mean.'

'I just thought,' Eleni persisted, gently stroking the image of Gorgona with her finger, 'it might be something traditional, or have a significance. We noticed that you had a lot of old Cretan objects and linen on the walls of your kafenion.'

'That was before my time, I'm afraid. They belonged to the previous owner.' She realised neither was paying any attention now, so she decided to change tacks. 'You were spotted driving in Omalos, you know.'

Stavros had told her he'd seen his 4x4 racing through the place as he'd been having a drink.

'As you said,' Patrick replied curtly, 'everyone knows everything.'

'On your way to visit the Samaria Gorge?'

'Yes,' Eleni said, before Patrick could answer.

'The "I survived the Samaria Gorge" T-shirt is a must to take home,' he added.

Yes, she thought, along with your local legends. 'So you did the walk?'

'We did. Not as bad as everyone makes out. But then Eleni and I do a lot of hiking.'

And, she understood, a lot of lying.

Kirsty knew the gorge normally stayed open until the end of October. So on the day they were seen, just over a week ago by Stavros, it could have been open. But early and late season floods were always possible and their power was not to be underestimated. Especially since 1993, when a number of walkers had been washed out to sea and drowned. There were early rains this year and she knew, from a group of disappointed German tourists, that it had been closed for four days before Eleni and Patrick's visit.

The evening felt strained and soon petered out. As she was brooding over it in bed, she recalled where she'd heard the story about the English woman.

It was in Kolimbari itself. She'd been helping a Cretan friend, Aliki, at a party. At the end of a long night, as they'd sat recovering, Aliki had shown Kirsty a small painting that had belonged to her grandmother. It was good and had caught the Cretan colours.

'This was done by an English artist who was touring the island. She was staying at the time with a family who owned a taverna and guest house in the village and much of the surrounding land. Then she caused a scandal by running off with their son, who'd married into another of the most powerful families on the island.

'My grandmother befriended her and said she was beautiful and innocent. I think that's why she kept the painting.'

Kirsty knew now exactly who Eleni and Patrick were searching for. After their lies, she decided not to tell them anything but to do a little digging of her own.

She recalled something else that night as she was listening to Burns, who'd suddenly decided to become a good Cretan dog and bark non-stop: she recalled where she'd seen those sparkling blue eyes before, and a picture began to form in her mind, a frightening one that made her deeply afraid for Eleni and Patrick and determined to get to the bottom of this mystery.

∾

October 27th, 2004, Chani, Kirsty

Kirsty was trying to console an English family who'd nearly been run over by a lorry as they strolled along what they presumed was a donkey track behind their hotel. As she did, the 4x4 arrived. It swung fast into a gap, narrowly missing the hire car. Kirsty saw the tourist couple flinch. She was shocked herself. Not just by the state of the vehicle, which looked as if it had been to Hades and back, but by Patrick and Eleni, who looked as if they'd been farther. They ordered village wine and two glasses of tsikoudia instead of their usual beers, and Kirsty wondered what had happened.

'Been off-roading?' she asked.

'Yes,' Patrick said nonchalantly. 'Wanted to get our money's worth out of the old beast.'

'I shouldn't let Stavros hear you call it that!'

'It's great,' he said. 'We're so glad you found it for us.'

Kirsty looked over at Eleni, who said nothing, but just kept staring at the distant peaks of the Lefka Ori.

'They'll be covered in snow soon,' Kirsty said, following her gaze. Neither responded. They were so wired that even Burns noticed and was shaking. Kirsty wanted to tell them the Greek expression, 'Siga, siga': slowly, slowly. But she sensed it would be a waste of time.

'I'm glad you turned up,' she tried, 'because I wanted to return your hospitality and invite you to dinner at my house.'

Eleni smiled but didn't speak. Now Patrick was staring at the peaks.

'Well, I'm not *that* bad a cook,' she said in her broadest Scottish accent.

'We've got to go deeper,' he sighed.

'I beg your pardon?' Kirsty asked.

'We'd love to,' Eleni said. 'What night?'

'I'm easy,' she said, suspecting an excuse waiting for any night she named. But Eleni continued smoothly.

'Well, as Patrick just mentioned, we do want to explore a little *deeper* in the mountains, but we'd be free on Thursday.'

Kirsty wanted them on her ground, so she played a trump card: 'I may even have some news for you.'

'What?' Patrick asked, returning to reality.

'Well,' Kirsty lied, 'after dinner the other night I did some enquiring, and the family of one of my friends knew the English woman in Kolimbari you were asking about. Or certainly a likely candidate. This friend is coming for coffee tomorrow and I'm going to quiz her.'

Now she had their attention. 'Brilliant,' Eleni enthused.

'You're a star,' Patrick added. 'Dinner sounds great. We'll bring the wine—and a special one!'

The three of them clinked glasses and they left after Kirsty pointed out her nearby house.

October 29th, 2004, Chania, Kirsty

Kirsty had been preparing food all day. Stifado bubbled on the stove. Dips waited: hummus and taramasalata and a special tzatziki for the dolmades. A Greek salad with the best Kalamata olives. She put a tray of potatoes doused in olive oil, lemon juice, garlic, oregano and sea salt to slow-cook in the oven.

Next, she scrubbed the house and laid the table with her finest Cretan linen. Burns got a bath, Diego a groom. Finally, she concentrated on herself. Kirsty brushed her hair until it glistened. She put on her favourite white flowing dress, a pair of gold-coloured shoes and a handmade necklace of Cretan silver and tiger's-eye jewels. She studied herself in the full-length mirror, pleased with what she saw.

By eight o'clock everything was ready. She poured herself a glass of ice-cold retsina and sat down to wait. When it reached eight-thirty she decided that at the very least they weren't being very English about punctuality. By nine, that maybe they were being a little too Cretan about time.

At ten, she knew they weren't coming.

'Don't they know what it's like to be a person who lives alone?' she moaned, forgetting all about her motives in inviting them. 'To be excited about something special happening and then be let down?' Kirsty looked at all the food, the place mats and napkins in their rings of Cretan silver, and nearly swept the table clean.

Instead, she changed into jeans and a smock top. She got in her car, then changed her mind. She went to her old Norton Featherbed instead. Her father's passion had been to restore vintage motorcycles. And from the first time she'd ridden on the back of his Matchless Twin, she'd loved them. She fired up her own beauty and raced towards Stalos.

'Who do they think they are?' she raged as the wind made her eyes water as if she were crying—or maybe she was. 'I'm going to give them a piece of my mind!'

She calmed as the road touched the coastline. The sea was balmy and at peace and made her anger feel pathetic. The beach was moonlit, and even this late in the year people were taking a night swim. And they were all couples. Her loneliness kept her driving on against any reasoning.

Kirsty passed Maria's and slowed. If they were in there, she'd walk in and sit at a table on her own without saying a word. They were not. She gunned the bike up the steep hill and parked outside Dimitri's. It looked empty and there was no noise apart from the slap of Tavli counters.

She walked down the drive to the gate and paused. There was a light on in the house and she saw a shadow slowly pass one of the windows. So they weren't even out, she thought. Couldn't claim to have broken down, got lost or anything. She pressed the intercom bell and waited, her breathing getting heavier as she did. Nothing. She did it again, this time for a long while. When she looked up the lights had gone out.

'You inconsiderate swine,' she hissed. 'I hope I never see you again.'

She stormed back down the drive and up the steps to Dimitri's.

'Ah,' Dimitri said. 'The Rose of Scotland. If only I wasn't a happily married man.'

'Dimitri, I came to visit the couple staying at Jessica's. Only I don't think the bell's working. Do you have the keys for the gate?'

She knew he let the gardener in when the place was unlet.

'I do, but they're not in. I saw them leave early yesterday and they haven't come back. You can't fail to hear that great tank roaring its way past here.'

'But the light was on.'

'I expect it's one of those automatic security systems that switch them on and off to make out someone's home. You can see into their courtyard from up here. Their truck's not there.'

He was right. She was about to mention the shadow but suddenly felt foolish and desperate. She accepted a Campari and soda on the house and sat down to contemplate the view.

Kirsty left Dimitri's when other people began to arrive. She took a slow drive home, feeling low and used. She pictured herself clearing away the food, then washing the pots and pans.

If they turned up at her kafenion again, she vowed she'd give them a display of Scottish temper they'd not easily forget!

Yet, as she turned into the narrow, moonlit street, a voice deeper than any anger whispered that they never would. And the shadow that had moved across their window had been real. She tried to see it again as she parked the bike in her garden and picture which of them it was. Suddenly, though, it seemed to have been too tall, and had something dangling from its head. She felt an ice-cold shiver ripple through her body and hurried inside.

5.

L yra music swirled from Barba Yiorgos's. The sun was setting over Rodopou, turning the sea from indigo to a burning pool of magenta. The new cockerel was performing like Don Juan and his precious chickens were as happy as brides. Everything in his life was back in order.

He raised a cold bottle of Mythos, took a long drink and went to sit outside. He thought he might call a taxi and go out to eat. He had a sudden craving for octopus, marinated in vinegar and cooked until it melted in the mouth. And someone he could share his high spirits with. It was the Cretan dancing night at Kirsty's. He'd get changed and show her a step or two.

The phone started ringing just as he was deciding what to wear.

'Barba Yiorgos,' Maria, from Stalos, said. 'I've been meaning to call you for over a fortnight, but Mother took a bad turn.'

'I'm sorry,' he said. A feeling of apprehension began to seep through the phone. He wanted to hang up and almost did before she could say any more.

'Only, I wanted to tell you that you were right.'

'Right?'

'Regarding the young British couple.'

He had nearly managed to shut them out of his mind. The photograph was back in its resting place. He'd wanted to believe they had gone home. And that he'd been mistaken about the girl.

'They're definitely house hunting. And, as you said, in Kotsiana.'

Barba Yiorgos felt the first chill of the coming Cretan winter drift in from the sea. 'They came in the day after you'd been, ordered your favourite pie and sat at your table. The woman asked Pavlos, when he served them, if they could speak with me. They were charming, but fishing. I played along, remembering what you'd said. Finally, they got around to it. "Who was that man sitting here with you yesterday?" she asked casually. I tried to look puzzled. "You know," she said, "the one with the incredible hair and beard?"

'"Ha," I said, "that's the famous Barba Yiorgos."

'Then the man chipped in. "Yes," he said, "but what's his family name?" I guessed they wanted to contact you about the house you mentioned, so I told them.

'Then they asked about your father. They even ended up talking to my mother and giving her a couple of glasses of wine. Well, you know what she's like with a drink inside her. So what do you think?'

Barba Yiorgos couldn't speak for a second.

'Well,' he finally managed, 'I better get the property tidied up.'

'There was one other thing. When they left, the girl came over to say goodbye. "Please," she whispered, "don't tell him we were asking about him. It was just that he looked so striking and we were curious."

'Clever little thing, I thought. You mean you'd hate for him to know how interested you are in case the price goes up. More than half Greek, I'd say.'

'Half Greek?'

'Yes, or her mother was—gave her looks and brains, all right. You'll have to watch yourself with her.'

◦◦

Barba Yiorgos waited until nearly midnight. He strapped on his shoulder holster and made sure the gun was loaded, then ran his finger along the edge of his father's saita—the knife named for the split wing of the hawk its handle represented—and slipped it through his belt. He dismissed the thought of the police stopping his beat-up old car and finding him armed like some andartis taking to the hills. There was only one thought, only one place to begin.

This time, as he turned out of his drive, the single headlight lit up a storm-tossed sea; waves reared up like wild horses and sent their spray over the car. The windscreen wipers didn't work and he was already struggling to see. But nothing, he vowed, was going to stop him. He drove on past the other beachfront houses and the closed tavernas, into the first village and then up into the hills. It had been a long time since he'd made this trip, but he remembered it only too well.

The light shone on an old church. Once, he recalled, there had been a stream flowing through its grounds. Its water was so cold that they used to lay a large melon in it, then after the service, take it out, give it one tap and it would explode into segments. 'Chilled red flesh to sweeten the blood of Christ,' his father once said. That memory made him shudder.

Finally, after what felt like one of the longest drives of his life, Barba Yiorgos pulled off the road and killed the engine. Then he waited, listening and watching. He stayed until he felt certain his arrival had gone unnoticed, then slipped silently into the darkness. He began to weave his way through the first of the olive groves, keeping the torch off until he was well away from the road, even though it was hardly used. But soon he was forced to turn it on because there was no easily discernible path. He reached the first of the derelict houses and an owl burst out as he illuminated one of the windows. He crossed himself, then flicked his long thumbnail three times off his front teeth to ward away the evil eye.

Barba Yiorgos was still thinking about the owl, and the one that had come to visit his father on the night he died, when a light flickered in the distance. He killed his torch and crouched down behind some rocks. He waited for whoever it was to get closer or move again, his hand sweating against the coldness of the gun.

No one stirred; there was only silence and darkness. He started moving again and saw the glow once more. It was faint and tremulous, and made him think of some will-o'-the-wisp trying to lead him astray. Then he knew what it was, and where it was coming from, though he didn't want to believe it.

He climbed over the stones of a low wall and shone his torch on the columns of the fallen temple. They were mostly buried and dissolving back into the earth, but still recognisable. He ran his fingers over the marble and felt its warmth. This place, which only he and a few others knew, had once been used by a cult dedicated to the worship of Aphrodite.

He stepped out of the ruins and onto the slope leading down to the small shrine. He stared at it, then slipped, landing hard on his back. He gasped for breath and tried to rise, but could not.

The shrine was glowing golden. Two oil lights burned inside, illuminating a scene he found almost impossible to conceive. The whole area around it had been cleared. The shrine itself looked as if it had just been set in place to mark a new death. But worst of all, there were fresh flowers on the unmarked grave: a huge carpet of lilies, spread like a blanket over the full length of the body below.

He began to hyperventilate and wanted more than anything to rise and flee, to take a sweet breath from the raging sea, uncontaminated by the sickly sweetness of the flowers he felt engulfing him.

As he managed to get to a half-comfortable sitting position and slow his breathing, a memory, not forgotten, but deliberately obfuscated, came alive as clearly as the day it had happened.

He was sixteen years old. His father, Michaelis, had come in after a night out. He was partly drunk—but then he always was.

'I want you to drive me somewhere,' Michaelis said.

Yiorgos could never refuse his father.

Michaelis had climbed onto the back of Yiorgos's motorbike and told him where to drive. When they reached the grove, Michaelis began gathering wild flowers from the roadside. Then he led Yiorgos to the temple ruins and told him what it was. He sat on one of the pillars and took his bag off his back. It was his army rucksack, and Yiorgos had waited for the bottle of wine or tsikoudia to appear. Instead, he took out a package, unwrapped it and handed over a framed photograph without speaking.

Yiorgos saw his father, young and handsome. Very much as he'd always pictured and vaguely recalled him: the great kapetanios who'd led his men with such courage.

Only, in the picture that Yiorgos had stared at, his legendary father stood with a beautiful woman who was definitely not his mother.

'What I'm going to tell you now,' Michaelis stated, 'is for your ears only. Your brother must never know. I promised your mother that *he* wouldn't if I could help it.

'Two years before the war, I met the woman in that photo. Her name was Marianna. She was an artist and had come from England to do some painting. Well, fate makes puppets of us all, and we were destined to be together from the moment we met.'

Yiorgos peered into the picture, hardly able to grasp what his father was telling him.

'Nothing could keep me from having her. Not the fact war was coming, or that I was married and you were only eight and I adored you. Nor that I knew we'd be despised by everyone in the village, and have to live as outcasts. Or even that I may have been putting her in danger. I loved her; still do.'

Yiorgos saw the tears in his father's eyes, but was too shocked to speak.

'We lived together in a village near to here. It was the happiest time in my life.'

Yiorgos remembered his father vanishing and being told he was off the island with the Greek army. Then, when the war came and Crete was occupied, that he was in the hills with the Resistance. He'd been proud of the stories. How his father had saved so many of the allied soldiers, smuggling them off the island as the enemy took control. How he'd been a hero of the spectacular kidnapping of the German commander, General Kriepe.

His father had returned home after the war. And though he was a shadow of the father he'd known and worshipped, Yiorgos had believed everything. He'd put his father's coldness and drunkenness down to the terrible things he'd witnessed.

Instead, he'd been with some English whore, while his mother had struggled to keep them going through those terrible years. And he'd always thought her hard and bitter and blamed her for his father's decline. He'd felt his anger begin to mount.

'A few months before the Battle of Crete, we had a daughter. Oh, she was the most wonderful baby.'

'Do you mean,' Yiorgos snapped, moving aggressively towards Michaelis, 'that I've not only got an adulterous father, but a bastard sister strutting around the island?'

The punch had come so hard and fast that Yiorgos was on the floor without having even seen it.

'She wasn't a bastard. I divorced your mother in my heart and in the sight of God, who knows the purity of a man's actions. What do bits of paper and the church know about love? Why do you think Cretan men hold their balls when a priest walks by? Your mother and I had been married by an arrangement. One made by two wealthy families that would end a vendetta between them. We never loved each other. I returned out of duty and my love for you.

'And I'll tell you something that only one other person still living knows. I did marry Marianna. The ceremony was performed by a holy priest in front of a thousand-year-old icon of the Blessed Virgin. That man is probably less holy now, but I know the icon still blesses our union, though it too carries the scars of German bullets.

'And Marianna was innocent. She didn't know I was married. So you see what your father is: an adulterer; a liar; and worst of all a coward, while she was the opposite.

'Now I will show you something.'

He'd led Yiorgos through the ruins to the shrine and a pile of stones neatly arranged on the ground.

'That is where my love sleeps. In that cold, unmarked grave. While I was in the hills fighting, the Germans were taking terrible reprisals. They took Marianna and hanged her from a tree and left her for the birds. Some of the brave villagers cut her down and carried her here. They told me the Germans had taken our daughter and I've never been able to find out what they did with her, though murdering children was nothing to them. And I searched for her until there was nowhere left to look. As did others. Even one I had believed might have despised her. But nothing. The Germans even took Marianna's journal, where she'd recorded our lives. So I had nothing left but the photograph I carried in my pack, and its . . .' Michaelis had paused then, before shaking his head and continuing. 'But that's worthless now. Like the man who wrote it.'

Michaelis had placed the wild flowers on the grave and poured oil in the lamps and lit them.

'At the time I had my doubts that the Germans had murdered my wife and child, because I was a leader of the Resistance. Why hadn't they taken them hostage and demanded my surrender or worse? And God only knows what I would have done to save them!

And there were other things that happened, questions that needed answering.

'But I was too broken to try. I was no longer even a man. Haven't been since that night, even though for your sake I wanted to be. Instead, I am a coward who, even though he knows the spirit of Marianna is not at rest and the blood in this ground cries out for revenge, has done nothing but pray to join her.' Michaelis had begun to weep.

Yiorgos had moved reluctantly to his father's side by the grave.

Michaelis pulled himself together slightly. 'A month ago, I went to Frangokastello with some friends. We sat playing our sad music and drinking. At dawn, as my friends slept on the sands, they came: the Drosoulites, "the Dewy Ones". The ghosts of Dalianis and his army marching from the castle.'

Yiorgos knew the story about the hero, Dalianis, and his men, who'd made a stand against the Turks and been massacred. And how, on or around the night of May 17th, their spirits were said to appear, and to vanish if anyone approached them.

'They were marching out of the mist towards me, and I knew they wanted something. Then each one of those heroes, from the humblest Epirote soldier to the great Dalianis himself, walked up to me and spat at my feet in contempt for what I'd failed to do. I know now that I will take my dishonour to the grave, as I have carried it with me since Marianna's death. And that I will never be by her side in eternity unless something is done. It's too late for me, but maybe not for you.

'Since that night, I've been haunted by vivid dreams of Marianna and my dead friends. I have a premonition that some evil is still alive and will come to you one day. That's why I'm telling you this. If it does, you must not back away. You may even have the chance to redeem your father's lost soul, if that means anything to you.'

45

A big part of Yiorgos had cried out for him to hug his father and swear he would never fail him; but another part couldn't easily forget that his father had betrayed them and dishonoured the family. That part, and the feeling that he wasn't getting all the truth, had won the day and he'd remained silent.

His father had clung to him on the drive home, sobbing like a child. After that day, he'd never mentioned it and had hardly spoken to his son again.

Yiorgos had been fighting with the Hellenic forces in Korea when his father died. He'd just started working in a New York hotel, a year later, when his mother had passed away and had been unable to return for her funeral. Then, after he finally returned to Crete, he couldn't bring himself to visit their graves. The idea of his father lying beside his mother, and knowing where he wanted to be, made it feel impossible. For many years, he'd been driven to visit Marianna's grave and try to understand what his father must have felt.

That day had changed and tainted his life.

Because, although Barba Yiorgos didn't have all the facts, he had enough to believe that his father had been as much the deceived as the deceiver. And that the evil he'd referred to was not only still alive but getting stronger and moving with purpose.

Now, sitting on the sodden earth, staring at a vision that could not be, the memory of that day returned to him with a hammer blow of shame. He got to his feet and hauled himself to the top of the slope, then looked back, hoping that the image might have faded like a mirage. But if anything, it had intensified. The glow from the shrine was radiating until Barba Yiorgos felt its heat. The flowers seemed to bloom again, their scent becoming so powerful he nearly gagged. He fled, almost spearing his eye on an olive branch, and stumbled on the hard floor of Aphrodite's temple. He was shaking so much when he finally reached the car that he could hardly get the key in the ignition. The drive home was endless, but he was determined that, at last, he would carry out the duty he owed to his father. No more hiding, he vowed, as a shooting star seemed to celebrate his courage.

Then, as he reached the narrow track running along the now-quiet sea, he began to reason things through. *Bend the truth, you mean, so you do not have to act the way you know you should, in other words*, a voice whispered before he quietened it.

Barba Yiorgos tried to find solace in imagining it was probably one of the old yiayias, who'd once lived in the village where Marianna had been executed, who was tending the grave and shrine. Not some young girl hell-bent on dragging him into a vendetta that could hardly mean anything anymore. These black-robed hags lived forever. And lamentation was their song of life. There was bound to be one or more of them who'd probably known Marianna and her story. His father had told him they'd carried her body to the place. What would be more natural than for one of them to attend the grave? Or even pass it on as a duty? The whole island was dotted with shrines and hidden graves, and there was usually a light kept burning by someone.

Surely, he reasoned, as the tears in his eyes at his weakness began to extinguish the passing brightness of that shooting star, the fact that Marianna was still being remembered and mourned was enough for her soul to rest. And if this Eleni was, as he suspected, in some way connected to Marianna . . .

Barba Yiorgos paused in his deliberations. He drew in a deep, empty breath as he pictured the photo of Marianna with his father and then Eleni when she'd first arrived at Kirsty's. He recognised clearly the same beauty and dignity in both their faces, saw the sadness and expectation in Eleni's as she'd looked briefly at him. And something else that he refused to consider a real possibility, with all its implications, both personal and financial.

He wiped his eyes dry and returned to the darkness.

If she was trying to find out the truth behind some distant family tragedy, then perhaps, if she sought him out, he would help her. In fact, he decided, he might anyway.

Barba Yiorgos sat on his terrace with a large glass of milky-white ouzo and a cigarette. He looked out to sea. There were nine fishing boats bobbing close to the shore, their lights swaying like a parade of penitents walking upon the water.

'Yes,' he said to himself, 'the mind can change anything it sees into what it wants to believe.'

Tomorrow, he'd go into Kastelli and buy fish. Time to purchase fresh fish when you see plenty of boats out. Not like some who buy when they've seen only one or two. Or the English and Germans who visit restaurants and pay for fresh fish when there's been a raging storm for three days and all the boats are chained in the harbour or sheltering in the lee of an island.

Barba Yiorgos laughed his booming laugh as loud as he could. He'd been told once by a wise old Turk, and had repeated it many times, 'It takes two smart Jews to fool a Greek.' And he was one smart Greek. He went to bed and slept well and without dreams.

But with his gun loaded and on a chair next to his sofa.

6.

Kirsty woke far too early after going to bed far too late. She decided to take Burns for a walk to the harbour. She strolled through the deserted streets and past her own kafenion. The fourno was already open, its olive-wood fire heating the oven and the smell of fresh bread filling the square. She felt good and tried to forget briefly about Eleni and Patrick, who'd continued to haunt her since their failure to show for dinner. Because no matter how hard she tried, she couldn't dismiss them from her mind until her fears were proved unfounded and she knew they were safe.

She'd reminded herself over and over that they'd not been particularly friendly, that they'd lied, stood her up for dinner, but it made no difference. In fact, it added credence to her worries. Their behaviour fitted in with her theory that they were looking for something or someone and it was dangerous and they'd just not trusted her. Their failure to show that night was the last time she or anyone else had seen them. The general feeling was that they'd gone off to another part of the island to finish their vacation.

Kirsty wanted to believe it. But she did not. And that shadow she'd seen moving across the window that night seemed to grow taller with each recall.

So why did she care?

The morning's other insistent voice had answered that: her father's, which had been quiet for decades but now seemed to be gaining in strength. It reminded her again of her broken promise, chided her for running away, and whispered that in some strangely connected way, this was a chance for redemption.

Kirsty reached the seafront and walked along to the harbour, enjoying the crystal clear water breaking on the rocks. One small ouzeri was already open and some fishermen were drinking and sharing mezedes.

Kirsty loved the labyrinthine Venetian streets with their old, wooden-balconied houses and the occasional crumbling palace. And the harbour, especially when the lighthouse and the Mosque of the Janissaries weren't swarming with tourists.

At the end of the quay, a group of fishermen were working in their colourful boats. She watched them for a minute.

'Kali mera, Kirsty,' Spiros, the captain called. 'You better watch out for my brother today.'

'Stavros?' she asked. The boat's engine thrummed into life and it began to turn towards the open sea.

'He's as mad as a wild cat with you. He rang to tell me . . .'

Another of the fishing boats started and she struggled to hear what he was yelling back. Something about English drunks.

It spoiled her walk back, trying to figure out what he'd been talking about and what on earth it could have to do with her. She was still puzzling over it mid-morning when an open-top car pulled up and Stavros jumped out and sat angrily at a table.

Kirsty hurried to take some beers over to where he was sitting.

'Do you know what I was doing all yesterday afternoon?' he snapped.

'Kali mera to you too,' Kirsty said, sitting down.

'I was with the police and a tow truck retrieving my brand new Jeep Grand Cherokee. You know, the one I rented to the couple *you* sent. My very best vehicle. Or it was; now it's a lump of scrap metal.'

'They had an accident?' Kirsty asked, feeling her concerns founded.

'They sure as hell did. The police found the Jeep at the bottom of a ravine, about fifty feet below the road. A total write-off.'

'What about Eleni and Patrick? Were they hurt?'

'Well, if they were, they managed to climb back up the side of the mountain and do a pretty slick vanishing act. A good thing my truck had roll bars, airbags and the best seat-belts in the world. Good job for them anyway, bastards!'

'What do you mean, Stavros? I'm not following you. People have accidents in those mountains all the time.'

'I'll say it slowly for you then. Sometime last week, they drove my new Jeep off the side of a straight road, with no sign of any skid marks, or a collision. Then they got back to the road, must have called a taxi on their cell phone and did a fucking bunk.'

'Are you sure? They might have been hurt. Did the police check the hospitals or anything?'

'Of course. Anyway, I went to Jessica's last night to try to find them. Dimitri hadn't seen them since last Thursday morning.'

Kirsty registered that this had been the day they were due to visit her.

'So I got him to open the gate. The place was empty. No suitcases or clothes. The doors wide open, the keys to the villa tossed on the floor!'

'But it doesn't make any sense,' Kirsty reasoned, trying, but failing, to envisage them behaving in such a way. 'They must have been insured to drive your vehicle. Jessica's would have been paid for in advance. So why run away?'

'Because they were drunk and couldn't risk calling for assistance and having the police turn up. Or me coming out and finding them pissed. I've only ever had good customers recommended by you before. You've been in this business long enough to know what a lot of tourists are like with drink.'

'Stavros, they seemed classy and sensible to me. And how do you know they were drunk?'

'Well, there was one empty bottle of tsikoudia, and another half-empty in the vehicle. The proper mountain stuff. And I'm talking about two-litre plastic bottles.'

For the life of her Kirsty couldn't see Patrick and Eleni driving in the mountains with tsikoudia in old Coke or lemonade bottles.

'What do the police think?'

'That *your* friends went up into the hills for a little off-roading fun. Found some village, bought a couple of bottles of hooch and had a high old time. And basically, tough titty on me for hiring it to them in the first place. The insurance company's already acting suspicious, and probably think I pushed it over the edge to get their money. Thank you very much.'

Kirsty really liked Stavros. He'd always sent his customers to her kafenion and been one of her first friends.

'Stavros, I'm really sorry. I cooked them a great meal last Thursday and spent most of the night waiting for them to turn up, and they didn't even have the decency to call. If it's any consolation, they had me fooled as well.'

'It's not. And I'm glad.'

He got up and tossed the money for the drink on the table.

'Stavros,' Kirsty pleaded, 'the beer's on the house. Sit down, please.'

'No, thank you. And no more customers either way.'

He stormed off as a group of embarrassed-looking tourists stood watching them.

Kirsty spent the rest of the day trying to forget it. She worked hard at baking cakes. Tonight was her Cretan dancing class and she was going to let her hair down.

The afternoon was really lively. All her old men were joining in with high spirits as the local priest blessed the new barrel of wine and drank more than all the rest put together. Kirsty was sitting with them whenever she could.

What could make it better? she wondered, as another cake turned out perfectly. Maybe one of her two suitors turning up and offering a belated birthday date? What could make it worse? That was easy: Yiorgos turning up and taking over. She looked across the square, half-expecting her thought to have evoked the old devil.

It was deserted, and she realised she hadn't seen him since the day of Eleni and Patrick's arrival. That started all the unwanted thoughts again, and she hurried out with a jug of cold retsina before they could spoil her mood.

∾

The Cretan dancing evening had been a great success, though marred by a strange incident. The musicians had given it their best, and the dance instructors, Dora and Eftichis, had responded in kind. At one time everyone in the kafenion had joined arms and formed lines and circles, trying to follow the intricate steps of the different dances. Right or wrong, it hadn't mattered.

After a well-earned break and food, the musicians had started up again. Kirsty, who was getting to be pretty good, had taken the floor with Eftichis to attempt the steps of the sousta, when the door had burst open and a man Kirsty had never seen before sprang into the kafenion.

He stood for a moment, studying everyone present. The musicians carried on playing, but Eftichis stopped dancing and led Kirsty aside. The man snatched up a glass of tsikoudia from one of her tables. He drank it in a gulp and banged the glass back down hard, then signalled to the musicians to pick up their playing.

He stepped proudly into the centre of the kafenion. He was at least six-foot-four, very powerfully built, and dressed from head to foot in traditional Cretan clothes, starting with the tasselled head-dress and ending with high, black boots.

His first movement was to raise his arms and glower at the audience. His eyes were as black as his clothes and long moustache. He stood rock still as the lyra music swirled around him. Kirsty thought he was either drifting into a trance or had become frozen, maybe through a sudden attack of nerves or stage fright. Then he began.

Nothing she had witnessed so far had prepared her for his display. It was brutal, but at the same time complex and precise. With each swirling turn, heel-clicking leap, or series of intricate steps, there was an arrogant toss of the head and snap of the fingers to emphasise the perfection of what he'd achieved.

He started to move faster and faster, and the musicians were playing as Kirsty had never heard them play before, though she sensed they were struggling to keep up. Then he began to leap higher and crash his boots together so that it almost seemed he was defying gravity. All of Kirsty's customers, and the dance instructors, appeared to be either mesmerised or petrified by his performance.

Suddenly, he jumped onto one of her empty tables. Then, using his heavy heels, he began to control the rhythm of the music, slowing to find the exact time he wanted. It became more Eastern, as sensual and hypnotic as a snake-charmer's pipe. He sprang and landed in front of the table where Kirsty had sat to watch. He stared at her and the people sitting, then stretched out his huge arms for them to join him on the floor as the music continued. No one moved, and after a moment he laughed contemptuously.

Kirsty gasped as he crouched and bit the edge of the table as if in anger at their refusal. Slowly, with his arms still stretched out for any willing takers, he lifted it from the ground. It was loaded with glasses of drinks, bottles and plates of mezes. Kirsty was only too aware of how heavy the kafenion tables were, even empty, and could hardly believe what she was seeing.

Next, the unbelievable became the impossible, as he began to dance with the table held perfectly balanced, the drinks steady in their glasses. The musicians carried on the slow music as he swayed, turned and undulated. Finally, he rose on his tiptoes, then raised one leg and held the position without the slightest discernible movement. He snapped his fingers and brought both arms down, slapping them against his belt and immediately silencing the music.

Everyone in the room, except Kirsty, started applauding and cheering. She could not, because of the way he was looking at her, and, it seemed, only her. He lowered the table and moved close. The stench of sweat and musk coming from him was overpowering.

'Would Madame care to dance?' he asked in guttural, village Cretan.

Kirsty could only shake her head in refusal.

He laughed the same mocking laugh, and the look of malevolence in his eyes intensified for a moment. Then he turned, reached into the pocket of his baggy trousers and tossed a handful of coins at the feet of the musicians before marching out.

'Who, or what, the hell was that?' Kirsty asked when her composure returned.

'Leonidas,' Eftichis informed her. 'He's from Sfakia and judged to be one of the best dancers on Crete. I've seen him dance before, but only with other men at a paniyiri in the mountain villages. I can't believe that he would come in here and give you a display like that. I think you were paid a great honour and compliment.' She saw a look of doubt on Dora's face as the musicians joined them.

'Maybe he just heard the music,' Manousos, one of the lyra players, said, 'and he couldn't resist the chance to show off.'

'Maybe Barba Yiorgos told him about your Cretan dance nights,' the other musician suggested. 'They're related in some way, I think.'

'That figures,' Kirsty said, trying to shake off the feeling of intimidation he'd inspired. 'He stank like an old goat!'

'That's because he spends most of his life in the hills living with them,' Manousos said, bowing his lyra. 'The melancholy knolling of goat bells and the wind are his only music and company for most of the time. Apart, of course, from his equally charming brother.'

Manousos deliberately struck a bad note and made a grimace. 'Now he really is worth avoiding.'

They started playing before Kirsty could ask why.

Later, after everyone had left, Kirsty was trying to recall something important, but could not. The reason she wasn't able to concentrate was simple: she was afraid. From the moment Jane, Kirsty's part-time help, had finished clearing up and left, it had been mounting. Each time she glanced up from doing her accounting or sipping a glass of wine, into the darkness beyond the kafenion's glow, it felt as if someone were looking back. Burns had growled and barked several times, and had refused to go out when she'd opened the door for him.

In a minute, she was going to have to shut off the lights and walk down the narrow, shadowy road to her home. Kirsty couldn't get Leonidas and his dancing out of her mind. Some-how, she felt there'd been a deliberate threat in it, and it had been aimed at her.

Cretan dancers did not pick tables up in their mouths. And asking her to dance? She recalled Manolis, a friend and widely travelled computer expert, telling her how just a short time ago in the mountain villages, to ask an unchaperoned girl to dance would have been taken as an insult to the family, a suggestion that she was 'loose', and very likely the man would have been found dead in a ravine the next morning. Had Leonidas been insinuating that Kirsty had no family here to protect her?

Kirsty was shocked out of her questioning by a blaze of light. A row of halogen spotlights filled the kafenion and a vehicle stopped outside. A figure jumped out, and a second later the door flew open. Kirsty nearly dropped her glass.

'Kirsty,' Stavros said. 'Did I scare you? You look terrified.'

'A little. I was daydreaming.'

'I've come to apologise. You've been on my mind all day.'

'There was no need,' Kirsty said, thinking she'd never been so pleased to see anyone in her life. 'Sit down and have a nightcap.'

Her hand was shaking as she took a sip of her tsikoudia.

'One of those nights?' Stavros asked, watching her. 'Too much raki with the dancing?'

Kirsty looked out and sensed that whatever she'd believed was there had now gone. She laughed with relief. 'Let's just say a little too much dancing!'

'Anyway, I was out of order and beg forgiveness.'

'You have it, unreservedly. And I don't blame you for being angry. It was disgusting how they behaved.'

'And weird.'

'Weird?' Kirsty asked, feeling something stir inside.

'Well, we get a lot of vehicles back after crashes, and you usually know from the inside what the driver and passengers were up to. Empty beer tins, bottles, cigarette butts and burns, spills and spews. You name it, we get it!

'But I've been going through the Jeep with my boys to see if there's anything we can salvage, and apart from the obvious crash damage, and those two bottles of drink inside, it's spotless. Empty ashtrays, no stains. And no glasses or cups. So what the hell were they drinking from?

'And another thing: Dimitris said he saw them leave on Thursday. Well, that truck had a very sophisticated set of instruments including a date and clock. They stopped that day. So it had been lying there for some time before it was discovered.'

'I don't understand what you're getting at,' Kirsty said.

'Well, just this. I'm a big drinker, and, from the sessions we've had, so are you.' He poured two more shots into their glasses from the small bottle of ice-cold tsikoudia. 'The Turks had a saying about this liquor when they conquered the island: "One glass is a gold coin; two glasses, two gold coins; three glasses, a farthing." I grew up on this. How much could you drink?'

Kirsty shrugged and drank her second gold coin's worth in a gulp.

Stavros did the same. 'This isn't bad, but the stuff left in the bottle I've got would make this taste insipid. So you tell me, how the hell, if, as the police say, they bought it in the hills that day, they could have drunk a two-litre bottle, and half of another!'

'So what are you saying?'

'Just that I don't think they could have consumed that much alcohol. Or that they would have, as they seemed to have been going somewhere special that day. As I said, it's weird. Anyway, they've gone: we'll never know.'

Stavros got up to leave.

'Somewhere special?' Kirsty asked, following him to the door.

'Well, I guess so. When we opened the boot, there was half a crate of very expensive wine and a stunning bouquet of flowers gift-wrapped in it. Of course, all the wine bottles were broken and the flowers trashed, so I couldn't drink the one or give the other to my mistress. No justice in this world!'

They embraced at the door. As he reached the Jeep a memory came crashing into her mind.

'Stavros,' she called, knowing and dreading the answer. 'Tell me the name of the wine and I'll buy you a bottle.'

'Too expensive for the likes of us,' he laughed. 'The very best Chardonnay from Katsaros.'

7.

November 7th, 2004, Sfakia, Kirsty

Kirsty sat on her terrace, sipping coffee and ruminating. Why, she asked for the hundredth time, had they come? Why had they lied about the Samaria Gorge? And about hiring a boat, when she'd seen the ticket stubs to Gavdos? Kirsty had always been considered observant. 'Moochers will be poochers,' her Granny used to warn.

And she'd seen something else the night of her visit to their villa, something she'd only recalled in the early hours. In the box with the red silk chemise there'd been an old journal, a pile of letters still in their envelopes, and what appeared to be a letter on old parchment, written in Greek. Collecting stories? 'Amateur detectives with boring jobs'! Who did they think they were fooling?

Kirsty swirled the dregs of her coffee. The brown, grainy paste smeared the cup, clinging in a random pattern of collided particles. Some of the Cretans claimed to be able to read your future from them. Valentinos had done hers once, gypsy-style with tall, dark strangers and untold wealth. Then he'd spoilt the joke by announcing that Barba Yiorgos could do it for real, and had.

'What do you mean?' she'd asked.

'He did yours one day when you left your cup and hurried off to serve some customers. He swirled it around then stared hard into the white cup for a long time. We all waited, knowing he has the gift. I had my fingers crossed that it was going to be good.'

'And?'

'He wouldn't say. Not then, not since. But I'll tell you something for certain. It was good.'

'Huh. I bet.'

'It was. He seemed amazed at what he'd seen in your future.'

Kirsty imagined he'd probably seen her marrying a Greek. Now she wondered. Had he seen something far worse waiting for her? She recalled how strangely he'd reacted when Eleni had first arrived. Had he foreseen this? Kirsty stared into the cup again and saw the drying grains begin to fall. Like the sands of time running out, the notion struck her, and she hurried to open the kafenion.

By mid-morning, Kirsty had made up her mind, and was just waiting for the right people to share her fears with. The Gorilla arrived and began bellowing across the square. But he'd do for a start.

'You're a crazy woman,' he said, after she'd finished telling him her fears. 'We love tourists. Kidnap? Murder? On Crete? Impossible!'

'What about the German couple a few weeks back?'

'A madman. Probably an Albanian.'

'Andonis, Eleni and Patrick *were* searching for something, and they got too close. I know they're in trouble.'

'Bah! Tourists are always in trouble. None of them can hold their drink. They sit in the sun for hours until they fry their brains. Then go off wrecking cars.'

'You know that their "wrecked car" was found very close to where your mad Albanian had his shooting accident?'

'That's a bad area. Unsafe and wild. What's the matter with the beach? They should have come on one of my tours.'

'Oh, bugger you, Ape Face,' she snapped, and stormed into the kafenion.

She had no more success with Jane and her new boyfriend, Stephen.

'You've been reading too many of those cheap thrillers,' Jane quipped.

'They were definitely coming to see me that night. Something happened to them.' She heard Patrick saying, "We have to go deeper," and saw him staring high into the Lefka Ori.

'But they got drunk and crashed their Jeep instead,' Stephen said, interrupting her thoughts. 'You told us.'

'Then hopped on a ferry and did a flyer,' Jane touched her arm. 'They're safe in England while you sit here worrying. You mustn't be so sensitive.'

'Or over-imaginative.' Stephen touched her other arm.

Kirsty shook them off. 'Why would a wealthy, sophisticated couple go to the trouble of buying half a crate of very expensive wine—and, incidentally, the exact wine I'd told them I loved—and a beautiful bouquet of flowers on the day they were due to visit, then go charging round the mountains, drinking enough raki to kill a donkey, before driving off the edge of a ravine and vanishing? Does it make any sense to you?'

Neither answered.

'They were here for a purpose. Something important connected with an English woman who disappeared.'

'Ah, *The Lady Vanishes*,' Stephen joked. 'I've got a great idea. Why don't you add an Agatha Christie night to your list of "special" evenings? Give all the customers a set of clues and send them off to find the missing couple? Be a big hit, I'm sure.'

His laughter drowned out what Kirsty suggested he could do.

She left them laughing, and put Jane in charge of the kafenion without telling her what she'd decided to do. She drove to the police station in Chania. The sergeant and his assistant chain-smoked, sipped their glasses of frappe and seemed intent on every detail. Then laughed in her face.

'Go back to your kafenion,' the sergeant sneered. 'You make good coffee but a lousy detective. There's no crime. Except that Stavros probably took cash for the hire vehicle and is struggling to find a receipt for the tax office! Your "mysterious" couple are safely back in England, maybe with a few bruises. This is a matter for insurance companies, not the police.'

His assistant showed her to the door and gave her arse a squeeze as she was stepping through. 'Maybe, if you're so bored and frustrated, we could take a coffee together, or even go for a swim.'

'Frustrated! Agatha Christie night!' Kirsty seethed as she drove off. She sped through Chania in the opposite direction to the kafenion, not even conscious of where she was going. Then she knew exactly where: Sfakia.

Though in certain parts this area was tamed and tourist-friendly, it was still a region whose reputation for lawlessness and brutality held sway. Stealing, feuding and vendettas reaching the scale of those on Sicily had always been a way of life. And, according to a lot of Cretans, still were. A lot of the men clung to the traditional dress; most, it was claimed, carried a concealed weapon.

Nearly all of the great tales of Resistance fighters and mountain guerrillas originated in Sfakia. There had always been bandits hiding in the hills, unfindable and dangerous. Kirsty had read about two ex-Civil War fighters who were found still hiding in the late sixties—twenty years after the events.

She'd been told there was a village that had been abandoned because of the vendettas, which most believed would never end. She'd also been warned that some villages weren't safe, and to stay away. She was driving now with the intention of finding some of those.

As she started to enter the desolation and remoteness of the Lefka Ori Mountains, Kirsty tried to picture Eleni and Patrick doing the same, and where they might be now. After passing through a couple of villages that seemed too touristy to have been the ones they'd have been looking for, she pulled to the side of the road. She was close—according to her map—to where the wrecked Jeep had been found. Kirsty got out and stood, looking first into the ravine for any tell-tale signs of damage, then up into the hills on the other side of the road, half-expecting some black-dressed shepherd to come careering down out of the mist, gun raised and ready to kill.

But there was nothing except the endless expanse of the White Mountains, bare and craggy, with an aura of brooding, untamed hostility. It made her feel vulnerable and she drove off quickly to find another village.

The next one she came to felt right, and she pulled up outside the only kafenion she saw. Inside, it was dark and smoky. A few tables were full of farmers and shepherds playing cards, and two men in traditional black shirts, baggy trousers and tasselled headdresses leaned on the bar. They turned and stared, unsmiling, but not, she tried to assure herself, threateningly. The man farthest away from her looked to be over six-and-a-half foot tall and seemed vaguely familiar. But with his black headdress and moustache it was hard to be certain.

By the time she reached the counter, everyone was looking. It wasn't considered impolite to stare at strangers on Crete, she reminded herself. There was no one serving at the counter and she waited for over a minute before the slightly smaller of the two men moved behind it. He nodded his head to ask what she wanted.

Kirsty ordered a half kilo of village wine and stood defiantly there. As he filled the bright red aluminium jug from one of the old barrels, she looked around. It was a small museum to the history of the war, she realised. Guns and knives adorned the walls. Three of the table tops were actually mounted on the tripods of large machine guns, the gun barrels still on their mounts, belts of bullets dangling and coiled on the floor like golden serpents.

'Disarmed,' the man said, banging down the jug of wine and a glass, making her jump. 'Nobody's going to start letting off a few rounds. Don't look so scared.'

The man stood with him laughed as one of the farmers made a rat-a-tat-tat sound. Kirsty met his gaze, noticing that both men had green eyes and blond hair.

'I'm not,' Kirsty stated.

He gave a dismissive grunt.

'Do you get many tourists in here?' Kirsty asked.

'Some.'

'British?'

'A few, mostly lost.'

He turned his back on her and started muttering to the other man. Kirsty took a few sips of the wine. It was old, browning and, she knew, incredibly strong—probably fortified with tsikoudia. The thought of where that might have come from made her press on. She got up and began examining the photographs on the wall. She sensed him watching again.

'Are these war heroes from here?' she asked him flatteringly.

'There are only heroes from Sfakia,' he stated. There was some laughter.

'I can see that,' Kirsty said. 'But without the hospitality to serve a traveller a few olives or mezedes with a strong wine.'

She returned to her seat. Almost immediately, a curtain behind the bar opened and a dark-haired Cretan woman appeared carrying a tray. On it were slices of cucumber sprinkled with sea salt, large rounds of tomatoes drizzled with olive oil and herbs, a bowl of green, split olives and chunks of village bread.

'Thank you,' Kirsty said, wishing she'd kept her mouth closed. Both men were smirking.

'Nice bread,' she said to the woman who was watching her eat every mouthful. 'And olives.'

'All our own,' she replied. 'Natural and without any chemicals.'

'And the wine?'

'My son makes it.' She gestured to the man who'd served her.

'It's good. I wouldn't mind ordering some to sell in my kafenion in Chania. I bet my customers would love it.' She sensed him react to this, and he moved closer.

'You want to buy some wine?' the one who'd served her asked. 'Some olive oil, olives for your kafenion?'

'I might be interested,' she coaxed, 'and some good tsikoudia if possible. The stuff I get's okay, but not great.'

'You can't get good tsikoudia in Chania. Only Sfakia,' he stated.

'I've heard that,' Kirsty said. 'Two of my friends, a British couple, bought some when they were here exploring a week ago. It was fantastic.'

He nodded to his mother. She produced three glasses and a plastic bottle of clear liquid from the freezer compartment of an old fridge. The other man—even bigger close up—joined them.

'See how it won't freeze,' her son said, taking the tray of drinks and pouring three glasses. 'That's because there's so much alcohol.'

They brought their glasses together as the mother watched, 'S'yeia,' Kirsty toasted. They responded and swallowed the small glassfuls in a gulp.

'Phew!' Kirsty said, as the fiery heat of the tsikoudia exploded inside her. 'This is something else!'

He poured three more. 'My name is Vangelis,' he said. He stared deeply into her eyes, then raised his glass again.

'This is just like my friends found,' Kirsty said, sipping this one. 'They may have even bought it here.'

Vangelis appeared delighted. 'It's the secret mountain herbs we put in the still. Too much and it would poison you; just enough and it can open your mind.' He swallowed his and banged the glass on the counter for her to do the same.

'You might remember my friends,' Kirsty said after finishing her drink and watching him race to fill her glass again. 'They were driving a brand new black Jeep Grand Cherokee. A beautiful woman—very Greek-looking—and her handsome husband.'

'We don't sell raki to tourists,' Vangelis's friend stated harshly, speaking for the first time. 'Especially not British ones.'

'And we haven't seen your friends here,' Vangelis added, handing the tray of full glasses back to his mother. They both moved away without saying another word. His mother began clearing away Kirsty's wine and food, though she'd hardly touched either. Kirsty paid and left with no one bothering to acknowledge her thanks or return her goodbye.

Well, she thought, that struck a nerve. She felt both pleased and a little afraid as she sensed herself being watched on the way to her car.

Kirsty decided she would drive on and see if there were any other villages Patrick and Eleni may have visited. She began driving farther into the remoteness, aware that they could easily have left the main road in their Jeep, but still too curious not to keep going. In some places, she saw clusters of houses clinging precariously to the sides of the mountains.

A lot of the buildings appeared deserted, with gaping windows, crumbling walls and boarded-up doorways. She wondered if it had been the vendettas that had driven the inhabitants away. She tried to imagine one of the villages or settlements, silent and benighted, as figures stalked the pathways with revenge and hatred guiding their stealthy footsteps.

A large motorbike roared past, snapping her out of her reverie.

'Arsehole!' Kirsty shouted as it swerved tight in front, causing her to reduce her speed sharply. She was about to blast the horn when a second bike arrived at her side, and then another, from behind, so close its front wheel could have been only inches from her bumper.

The bikes were powerful and loud and their noise filled the car, disorienting her. The riders were dressed in the same fashion as the men she'd just left in the taverna, and it could have been them for all she knew, as they had black scarves around their faces. The passenger on the bike in front turned and pushed his hand towards her: palm first, fingers splayed. A Cretan insult: not a wave, which a tourist might imagine. The passenger on the bike at the side did the same, flattening his open hand against the window so Kirsty could see his calloused fingers with broken, filthy fingernails clawing to get in.

Something thumped against the rear of the car. She stared in the mirror as the driver kicked out his long, booted leg and the car juddered. The man behind him held out both hands and, even though she was beginning to panic, Kirsty registered what he wanted her to see. A small, deformed digit on his right hand was waggling independently from the rest of his fingers as he repeated the insult.

The road was narrowing and dropped away steeply at the side one of the motorbikes was on. Kirsty started to inch towards it and also accelerated so that she was getting closer to the bike in front. The driver of the bike at her side got so near to the road's edge that his wheels were kicking up dust. Then just as she knew he was about to fall, he threw the bike into a wild wheelie and shot away with death-defying bravado. He joined the other bike; it too reared up on one wheel and they raced away together. A hard bump from behind distracted her from their antics and she looked in the mirror. As she did, the man with eleven fingers was pointing a sawn-off shotgun at her, gesturing for her to get over from the edge and keep driving.

The bikes ahead had slowed and let her catch up, then one dropped back to the side. The man riding pillion was aiming a pistol at her now. He also waved her on.

They sped her along the winding mountain road, faster and faster until she was struggling to stay in control, and even though her car was a high-performance one, the temperature gauge was climbing into the red. Her heart was pounding and sweat was pouring from her head and arms. Then the bike in front began to slow them down to a crawl. This snail's pace continued for what felt like hours, then suddenly the bike wheelied off again and she was forced to race to keep up once more.

Kirsty felt her anger outgrowing her fear. 'They're herding me like one of their goats or sheep,' she realised. 'Well, any second they're going to find out this one has horns!'

Before she could act, however, a village appeared from out of nowhere. It had an ancient, surreal quality about it, as though they had stepped back in time. They entered a square, with a huge monument depicting a woman carrying a gun, towering above two equally aggressive-looking men. The lead bike swung round it and raced back past her. Kirsty was about to do likewise when she noticed the other two bikes had disappeared. She watched in the mirror as the first turned off onto a dirt track and was quickly out of sight.

Kirsty carried on driving straight, not knowing where she was but determined to get away from them. The village quickly petered out, but she kept moving, expecting all the time to hear the returning roar of the bikes. After another long stretch of wilderness with no signs of civilisation, Kirsty came to another village, and realised it was the one she had visited. Outside the kafenion, Vangelis and his mother stood watching her as she passed, smiling at the look of shock and distress they must have witnessed on her face. Kirsty registered that the other man was not there and was sure he must have been on one of the bikes.

For the rest of her journey home, every noise made her jump, and she couldn't stop the angry tears glazing her eyes.

Back in Chania, she went straight to the police station. Halfway up the steps, she changed her mind. She went back to the kafenion instead, and, over a long cold beer, told Jane and Stephen what had happened.

'Drugs,' Stephen told her. 'There are hidden plantations of the stuff growing up there. The best in Greece, if you're interested.'

'What?' Kirsty exclaimed, incredulously.

'It's true,' Jane assured her. 'Some friends of mine went up there and got driven off. They didn't say anything about guns, but there were definitely men on motorbikes who made it clear they were not welcome.'

'It was the moment I mentioned the British couple,' Kirsty tried, watching a look of scepticism pass between them.

'It's a dangerous place,' Stephen said. 'Even the police stay away if they can. There was a story on the news last week that the police went up there to investigate a crime and a whole lot of villagers blocked the road to stop them entering. They stood there with clubs and other weapons. I saw the pictures of it. I know what you think, but it's about drugs.'

'It is, Kirsty,' Jane assured her again. 'Take the rest of the day off. You've had a scare.'

'No, you two bugger off. Go and smoke some pot if it's that good!'

Later Valentinos came and sat with her. She told him what had occurred. 'They do grow drugs up there and can be pretty aggressive,' he confirmed. 'At least from what I've heard.'

'I was on the road at the time, not near any drug planta- tions. It happened because I questioned them about the missing British couple.'

'Missing British couple?'

So Kirsty went through the story again, waiting for the same response, or some variation. Instead, he listened until she'd finished, stopping her now and again to ask for details.

'Well,' he said, 'if you're right—and there was something about them, especially the woman—then you're going to need help.'

Kirsty smiled for the first time that day and put her hand on his. 'Thank you,' she said.

'I don't mean me,' he said squeezing her hand in return. 'I wouldn't have a clue where to start. You need someone with con- tacts and knowledge. There's only one person I know who could get to the bottom of this, if he was willing to try.'

Kirsty didn't need to be told who.

'But how?' she asked. 'He wouldn't do anything for me. Oh, apart from marry me, that is!'

Valentinos dismissed this with a shake of his head before con- tinuing. 'By going and seeing him and being honest. Don't phone. Just drive up to his house and tell him all the things you've just told me. Be brave for their sakes and you might be surprised at what he'd do.' Valentinos got up, then paused as if looking at something far away. At length, he added mysteriously, 'Or what reasons he may have for doing it.'

8.

As a child growing up in Inverness, Kirsty's best-loved toy had been her dolls' house. It had been built by her grandfather on her father's side, a cabinet maker and her favourite relative. He'd built it out of scraps of exotic wood from his workshop floor, and brought it over on Christmas Eve. It had looked more like a fairy-tale castle than anything from a Victorian nursery. But that hadn't prevented Kirsty from peopling it with her ideal of the perfect family. Which, whenever she looked back and thought of her parents, made it seem like a bigger fantasy than any witches or wizards she could have invented.

Now, she was looking at her fairy-tale castle again. She stopped as soon as she caught sight of its turrets, out of both shock and a reluctance to continue. She'd often heard the men in her kafenion say that Barba Yiorgos lived in a wooden shack on the beach. And that was the picture she'd conjured of him: a cross between The Old Man of the Sea and Robinson Crusoe. One look at his house and the image crumbled.

Valentinos had given her directions, and she'd known the beach. It had some of the cleanest water on this part of Crete, and the advantage that it was never crowded. Kirsty was surprised to learn that she'd swum and sunbathed, sometimes topless, so close to where he lived. In her mind she envisaged him leering through binoculars at her.

That notion seemed now as untenable as calling his home a shack. It was a vast, Gothic folly, made out of intricate layers of carefully cut timber. She crept a little closer and saw a beautiful front garden with sea grass stretching down to a large steel fence. Kirsty sped up, more intrigued now than nervous. As she got closer to the gateway, the scene changed again. To the side of the landscaped garden, there were a couple of old cars, one a total wreck, the other close to being. Patches of vegetables and herbs were scattered everywhere, with an old railway carriage in the middle that was home to a flock of wild-looking chickens.

Kirsty turned into the drive and, sitting at the top of a large wooden stairway, not appearing to see her, was Barba Yiorgos. She parked behind the old car and crossed the lawn to the path leading up to his doorway. As she did, she spotted, under its own shelter, a motorbike. She knew bikes well and had ridden many, but this was the first Brough Superior SS100 she'd seen outside of a showground. It had been painstakingly restored by someone and she had an instant craving to drive or be driven on it—and for a moment sensed that one day she would. Then she remembered who owned it and quickly changed her mind.

Kirsty reached the bottom of his steps. He still hadn't noticed her and she thought he might be asleep. She glanced at her watch to make certain she hadn't arrived during siesta—the height of bad manners on Crete. She hadn't. Kirsty was determined to be acknowledged before speaking, already regretting that she'd placed herself in this position.

A chicken moved out of some vegetation and headed straight towards her. It was a large, brutish-looking creature and she shooed it away, certain it intended to peck.

'Ahhhh,' Barba Yiorgos gave a long, pained groan, 'what did you do that for, English woman? You've scared my favourite hen away.'

'I thought it might peck me. I'm sorry.'

'Peck you! My chickens don't peck. It was coming to lay an egg.' He made a tutting noise, something he often did at her in the kafenion that annoyed the hell out of her. 'Tut tut tut tut.'

It was louder and faster than ever and seemed to go right through her.

'Look,' Kirsty said, climbing the stairs and struggling to keep composed, 'I need to speak. And besides, chickens lay eggs in coops, not on stairs.'

He made his tutting noise again and pointed to a cosy little box positioned next to his chair. 'I've trained her. She comes every evening, talks to me, climbs into her little nest and lays me a beautiful egg for my breakfast. I'm an old man; I can't go mooching around chicken coops. Now you've gone and frightened her to death!'

Kirsty drew a deep breath. 'I'm sorry. I'll go and collect you some eggs before I leave. How's that?'

'Huh!' he scoffed, getting to his feet and staring as if he was undressing her.

Kirsty glowered back. He was wearing a pair of three-quarter-length canvas trousers, held up by his usual colourful braces, and nothing else. Kirsty couldn't help noticing that his naked chest was firm, powerful and covered in soft hair. His beard seemed darker than when she'd last seen him, as did his ponytail when he turned his back on her. He opened the large wooden door to his house and stepped inside. She waited for it to be slammed in her face. When it wasn't, she followed.

She heard Barba Yiorgos moving plates and cutlery. She followed the noise along a hallway, passing a spiral staircase that appeared to have grown out of its wood surround. Kirsty took a glimpse through an open door into a large room. It was artistically and expensively decorated, and made her wonder about the man behind it, and her opinions of him. Then she entered the kitchen and had them reconfirmed. It looked like the Cretan bedsit from hell.

Barba Yiorgos was slicing bread on a kitchen counter, next to a sink that had about a month's worth of washing-up filling it. 'Take a seat,' he ordered, without looking round.

'How?' she nearly asked. 'And where?' Kirsty peered at a huge Cretan sofa, covered with ruffled blankets, pillows and discarded clothes; two leather armchairs, piled high with books and newspapers; and some hand-carved wooden chairs around a table with enough empty beer bottles, used glasses and full ashtrays to sink a raft. She picked the least cluttered spot and sat down.

'So, English woman,' he sneered, placing a plate of bread and olives next to her, 'as I didn't order a kafenion takeaway, what brings you here?'

Kirsty waited as he went and fetched a jug of wine and some glasses.

'Thank you for the famous Cretan hospitality,' she said, raising her glass after he'd filled it.

He touched his gently against hers, breathed a quiet, 'S'yeia,' and sat the other side of the table.

'I need some help. Or at least some advice.'

'I've already given you some good advice. Marry a Greek. Marry me. If you think I'm too old, I'll fix you up with one of my worthless cousins. Most of them stay in bed all day and raise hell all night. You'd be good for one of them and it would keep you warm in the winter.'

Kirsty forced a smile as he grinned, poured a shot of beer into his wine and lit a cigarette. She sensed he was being deliberately provocative and as curious as a cat.

75

'Do you remember the young British couple that came into the kafenion the day you were there?'

'The British are always coming to your kafenion. Most of them are too scared to go to one run by a Cretan, in case they have to eat something not out of a tin. Ha ha ha.'

'On the day of the mud rain. The beautiful woman you couldn't stop staring at. She was part Greek, you know.'

Kirsty thought she might get a reaction at the last part, but got nothing.

'I always stare at beautiful girls. Do you know, once, I had a job as a bellhop in New York. Some of the prostitutes working outside the hotel were so stunning I thought I'd go blind, but I never stopped looking! You better believe it.'

'Yiorgos, will you listen to me? Valentinos told me you would help. He suggested I should come.'

'Valentinos is a good man. And it's Barba Yiorgos, to you. But for his sake, I'll listen.'

Kirsty told him everything she knew. To her surprise, and delight, he did listen. Sometimes he asked questions; other times he reacted as if he already knew what she was telling him, or as if he were surprised at learning something he didn't know.

'You say the man who eloped with the English girl was married?' he asked.

'That's what they said.'

When she mentioned the photograph, his eyes had left hers and focused at first on a collection of pictures and icons on the wall, then on a chest. He noticed her watching him and quickly turned back.

'Gavdos! What were they doing on Gavdos?'

'They didn't tell me. In fact, they lied, and if I hadn't seen the ticket stubs I wouldn't have suspected they'd been there.'

'What a clever detective you are,' he said.

Kirsty waited for another Agatha Christie quip, but instead he'd drifted away and mumbled to himself, 'Gavdos. I wonder if . . .'

'What?'

'Nothing. Carry on. You made me remember someone I haven't thought of for a long, long time.'

Kirsty didn't believe him, but continued anyway. At the mention of the silk chemise, he looked puzzled and shook his head. But when she told him about the journal and letters, he said, 'Journal? Did you read it?'

'No.' She thought he looked relieved.

'And they didn't mention any other documents?'

Kirsty thought he asked it a bit too casually and definitely looked more than relieved when again she said no.

She described to him where the vehicle had been found and his eyes darkened.

Then she told him about her visit to the village nearby and he shook his head again, and made his tutting sound, only this time it had sounded soft and concerned. When she mentioned the tall blond man in the kafenion, Barba Yiorgos tensed; as she described the one with eleven fingers he got to his feet and stared out of the window as if almost expecting to see him.

She finished, knowing she'd been believed and full of excitement over what he would say. 'Well? What do you think?'

He poured more beer into his glass and took a long drink. Kirsty saw that his hand was shaking.

'Tourists crash in the mountains all the time; it's a wild and dangerous place for inexperienced drivers.'

'What?' she cried.

'Lots of bends, poor roads, bad drivers. It happens all the time.'

'They were on a straight road, with no signs of skid marks or a collision.'

'And drunk, according to what you say the police believe.'

Kirsty felt her temper mounting. 'They weren't drunk,' she snapped. 'They were looking for information about that woman.' She paused, remembering suddenly. 'And I think a man, too, because I glimpsed a photo in the box. An old one of a couple.' Once again she saw Barba Yiorgos's eyes dart towards the chest.

'Maybe she was looking for her Greek roots,' he scoffed. 'Or maybe house hunting. Because I've just recalled something, too. There was a British couple staying in Pano Stalos, asking about properties. They asked in Maria's taverna. She called and told me.'

'I think she was looking for a lot more than that. And for some reason you don't want to accept it. You know what I said is the truth. I saw it in your eyes. Now you're unwilling to help.'

'*If* they have been kidnapped or murdered, it's by the fucking Albanians. There's either a ransom letter in England for some piffling amount, or their bodies are in a ravine, raped, robbed and murdered. The culprits are back home and will live for a year on their pickings.'

'Albanians! Do you Cretans always blame them for everything?'

'They're bastards. They cut an English couple's throats on Cephalonia because they saw them driving a new car. Wise up!'

Kirsty sighed resignedly. 'And what about me? What happened when I asked some questions? Wise up, huh?'

'Your friends were right: it's about drugs. There are bad men there who will do anything to keep their activities hidden. You strayed too close, that's all.'

'The man with eleven fingers—you know him, don't you?'

'I've never heard anything like it. Maybe you miscounted.'

'You're lying to me,' Kirsty yelled, getting up.

'Calm down, English woman. And don't you dare speak to me like that; I'm old enough to be your father. The police are right: they got drunk, wrecked an expensive truck and did a bunk. And I think I'm right: you need a Greek husband.'

'If I fucking well did, you'd be the last man on earth I'd pick,' she screeched, grabbing her bag off the back of the chair.

'I've told you,' Barba Yiorgos said, 'calm yourself. Go into the bathroom and take off your clothes. Sashay down my private walkway and take a nice cool swim.'

'You'd love that, wouldn't you? I just bet you swim naked and would be in the water next to me before I got my hair wet.'

She stamped towards the door.

'I never swim. And don't flatter yourself. My third wife, God rest her soul, used to carry a bowl up for me so that I could soak my aching feet. That's as close as I ever get to those widow-making waves. Besides, I've seen the sea waters turn red with the blood of my comrades so the likes of you can swim free. How could I ever soak in that?'

'Oh sure,' Kirsty said discarding the stories she'd heard his lackeys tell of his heroic military record, 'I believe every word. So I'll get one for you now if you want.' She turned away. 'And pour it over your stupid-looking, goat-brained head!'

His laughter, as deep, rich and mocking as ever, filled her head as she moved back out to the terrace. Barba Yiorgos followed her and stood watching as she descended the stairs.

'So what's really in it for you?' Barba Yiorgos demanded, catching Kirsty off guard. 'Not getting enough titillation from all those Penny Dreadfuls you read, or the corny detective flicks you make your customers sit through every Monday night?'

Kirsty felt herself flush, at both the insult and the fact that he knew, or presumed he did, what she read and watched. 'The books I read are by some of the finest writers in the world, and the films, which my customers happen to love as much as I do, are classics.'

'Ahh, so it's the man. You got the hots for that good-looking mick.

'I have not got . . .'—Kirsty was determined not to let him rile her—'got the "hots" for Patrick.' Barba Yiorgos snorted. She ignored him. 'I have very personal reasons for wanting to help them.'

'I can imagine just how personal. You need a man to take care of your personal problems. You better believe it. Ha ha ha.'

Barba Yiorgos turned his back on her and began to shuffle towards the door. Almost, Kirsty thought, as if he were reluctant to leave. 'I'll tell you my reasons if you promise to keep it a secret,' she tried.

He stopped moving and looked back at her. She felt his blue eyes burning into her. 'Ha,' he retorted. 'Who can keep a secret here? As my father used to say, this place has a thousand eyes and ears and even more tongues.'

'It's about my father,' Kirsty said before she could change her mind about telling someone something she'd last confided to her fiancé.

The word 'father' appeared to Kirsty to have struck a nerve, because Barba Yiorgos hurried back to his chair at the small table. 'I suppose my sleep can wait a few minutes more.'

Kirsty pulled out another chair and sat. She picked up a glass of tsikoudia she'd noticed earlier and swallowed it in a single gulp without offering Barba Yiorgos even the customary toast. She saw his eyes flash.

'I grew up,' Kirsty began, 'in Inverness. That's in Scotland, by the way.'

'Ahh, I know where it is. I don't need a geography lesson from the likes . . .'

'I was an only child. And though my parents didn't have a happy marriage, I had a great childhood. I loved my father, and he did me. We were incredibly alike and got on so well. He used to read to me every night he was home. All the children's classics and nursery rhymes. Then, as I got older, some of his favourites: Sherlock Holmes, Ellery Queen, Chandler and Hammett. He'd read them and we'd try to solve the mystery.'

Kirsty broke off for a moment, waiting for some sarcastic comment from Barba Yiorgos to sully the memories, but he was listening intently and smiling as if enjoying a shared experience.

'Then,' she continued, 'just as I was about to start my senior school he went out for his usual Sunday morning dram at the local and never came home.'

Kirsty waited for some reaction from Barba Yiorgos but got nothing.

'I was frantic, though my mother acted unsurprised. "Exactly what I'd always suspected," she kept telling everyone, including the police whom I'd insisted she call. "For him to run off and abandon me and the wain without a nickel. Gone off with one of his fancy women. I always knew he must be carrying on. All those nights out, supposedly working!"

'The police made some inquiries and quickly agreed with my mother. It was the blackest time in my life. I waited every minute of every day for news. Knowing it must come, dreading it would be the worst thing.

'Then a month later they found his body. He'd ended up in the river Ness and been swept into the Firth. The tide must have been flowing out, because his body had drifted all the way to a beach near Fort George. A sandy one amongst all the pebbly ones.'

Kirsty didn't know why that bit of information had stuck in her head or why it felt important to recall it, but the memory made her pause and struggle to keep composed.

'The police said it was either an accident, as he was known to have been drinking before his disappearance, or suicide. The Firth is still very popular for that, though they have a bridge over it now to jump from.

'My mother said drunk. Others, suicide. The Procurator Fiscal entered an open verdict as there were no signs of foul play.

'But I knew he'd been murdered.'

'Murdered!' Barba Yiorgos exclaimed. 'Why would you think that?'

'I felt it in my mind, heart and soul. He loved life and me. Besides, my father was brave and would never have taken his own life. Sure, he was fond of his whisky and beer, but he only drank what he could handle. Like you,' Kirsty added.

Barba Yiorgos smiled knowingly at her attempt to flatter. 'But murder?'

'His job,' Kirsty replied. 'And what he told me just before I lost him.'

'What did he do that was so perilous?' Barba Yiorgos asked, sounding intrigued.

'He was a crime reporter for a newspaper. But he often went freelance if he felt there was something more to a story, and some of his pieces exposed criminals who had escaped justice.'

Barba Yiorgos was looking quizzical and Kirsty sensed she had him hooked.

'My mother used to say he was just another sensationalist and a hack who did his best research in a bar. But I knew he was a man of integrity, and though he tried to make the things he worked on sound not too scary, even funny, I understood they were dangerous.

'Then, just before he vanished, he told me something that wasn't funny and it scared me. He came in late one night and I heard him quietly crossing the landing. I called to him to say goodnight and he came in and sat on my bed.

'I sensed that something was bothering him and that he was debating whether to tell me.

'"Kirsty," he said, "I don't know if this will frighten you, but I think you need to know. There are some people in this world who are greedy and corrupt. They will do anything to get what they want. Lie, steal, even kill. And all for money or power. Theirs are not crimes of passion but cold, calculated decisions based on profit. And they need to be stopped, whatever the price. Do you understand?"'

Kirsty felt herself begin to choke as the clear memory of her father came back, but wanted now to tell Barba Yiorgos as much for herself as anyone else.

'"But," he continued, "something you must be aware of. If you cross paths with one of these people you must be as brave as those heroes. It doesn't matter if these villains have guns or switchblades, or if they offer you gold, or threaten everything you love. You must always stand firm."

'"I will," I told him. "No matter what."

'"And always look for the truth."

'"Always."

'"Do you promise?" he asked.

'And I did. He kissed my forehead, whispered goodnight and told me he loved me. It was the last time we ever spoke.'

'Ahh,' Barba Yiorgos sighed, 'a very sad tale. So this is why you want to make sure Eleni and Patrick are safe, because of a promise to your father to always be brave and good?'

Kirsty sensed that she had him and that he was going to help her but still felt the need to drive home her real motive.

'No,' she stated. 'Because I broke my promise. I tried desperately at the time to convince everyone that my father had been murdered and make them search for his killers. But no one would listen. So I swore on my father's grave that when I was older I would find out who'd done it and bring them to justice.'

Barba Yiorgos had stopped smiling and appeared to be getting agitated. Kirsty pressed on.

'Then I went to college, fell in love, got married. All sorts of things that got in the way of my doing what I'd vowed. Then when my marriage failed I fled here to try to hide.

'But I've always been haunted by it and swore, if I got the chance to make amends, I would try. Because I believe that not to do our duty to those we love and have lost is a terrible betrayal of that love. And the worst form of dishonour to their memory . . .'

Barba Yiorgos sent the chair crashing backwards as he struggled to his feet. He was hyperventilating and gripping the edge of the table for support.

'Liar!' he bellowed at her.

Kirsty felt as if she'd been slapped and recoiled from the blow.

'Duty! Dishonour! What do you know of these words?' he raged. '*Revenge* is what you mean. Revenge and gain.' He thumped the table so hard the glasses flew into the air and viscous tsikoudia splashed everywhere. 'This is all a plot. That young witch has put you up to this, hasn't she? Your father wasn't murdered. All lies to make me . . .'

Barba Yiorgos stopped.

'What?' Kirsty cried. 'Make you do what? How dare you! You evil, self-centred bastard. I tell you my most guarded memory and . . .'

Kirsty was surprised by the speed with which Barba Yiorgos moved. Not towards her, but away. He darted in through his door and slammed it so hard Kirsty felt the wooden staging move as if another Cretan earthquake was starting. Tears began to stream down her cheeks as she got up. 'You . . .' she started to speak and moved towards the door. Then from inside she heard lyra music. Its volume increased until it swirled around her in a mind-numbing embrace.

'Bastard,' she yelled, and rushed to her car.

༄

Kirsty could still hear it playing as she lay in her bed that night. What had she expected from him, of all people? she asked herself.

But she couldn't rid her mind of the idea that he'd believed her story, and had known something about it.

She tried to dismiss it. Perhaps everyone was right. There was no mystery, and she was bored, and did need a Greek husband. Then the thought of Eleni and Patrick sitting under the vine with their box of clues came back to tell her she was right, and had to stay true to her instincts. And that they were in danger from someone greedy and corrupt.

The phone started ringing. Kirsty looked at the clock: three a.m. She hurried to it, dreading that it was one of the few remaining members of her family, with news of another death and more recriminations for how she never came and visited.

'Sleeping with a Greek yet, English woman?' a too-familiar voice asked matter-of-factly.

'What do you want, Yiorgos?' she growled, both relieved and angry.

'I've told you before, it's Barba Yiorgos to you.'

Kirsty took the phone away from her ear and was about to slam it down, when she heard her name called. She stopped.

'Yes? What do you want?' she said into the receiver. 'And I didn't think you knew my name, Yiorgos!'

'After you left, and even though my feet stayed dry—and thanks be to God, so did my head—I spent all evening up until now making a lot of phone calls. I've found some of the places they visited. And you're right: they weren't house hunting or simple tourists.'

'I knew it,' Kirsty burst in. 'What have you found out?'

'Well, they went to a famous monastery and questioned the priest so intently that he mentioned them to a friend of mine. Then they went to a fort at Aptera and tried to bribe my cousin, Nikos, who's the curator, to get them into the old prison opposite even though it's out of bounds. They visited a lot of strange places and met with some unlikely people.'

Kirsty felt sure he was holding back, and had already learnt something he didn't want her to know. 'So what do you think has happened to them now?'

'That they were scared off. They were digging up things some people would best forget and were warned to stop.'

'And then decided to drive their four-by-four into a ravine and leave a couple of bottles of booze in it to throw them off their trail! Are you trying to pacify me, Yiorgos? Or ease your own conscience because you won't do anything?'

'Tut tut tut tut,' he rattled down the line. 'I haven't said I won't do anything. I called to offer you the opposite. We'll track their movements and find out what they were seeking. And *if* something has happened to them, we'll work together to find out what, or even help if we can.'

'Thank you,' Kirsty managed, feeling a mixture of relief and shock.

'But there's a price. A small thing you have to do in return for my services.'

Kirsty sighed, thinking she'd almost known it was too good to be true. 'What?'

'I want to visit a few places I haven't seen for a while. Look up some old friends before I die. It's hard for me to get around these days. My relatives are always in a goddamn rush. So you could take me. You might even learn a bit about this island along the way. What do you say?'

Kirsty sensed he was being crafty, but decided to go along. 'You have a deal.'

'One thing, though. To track your friends might be dangerous. A bit like entering Daedalus's labyrinth to rescue someone, while the Minotaur stalks you. Are you brave enough?'

'I told you my reasons. You know I have to do it. And will.'

'Kali nikhta, Kirsty.'

'Kali nikhta, *Barba* Yiorgos.'

Kirsty heard his laughter bellow through the phone as she replaced it, and couldn't get the smile off her face as she lay in bed. As she drifted into sleep, the image of a black-clothed Sfakian came to her. He began slowly dancing, trance-like at first, then speeding up as he transmogrified into a half-man, half-bull figure, red eyes blazing and nostrils twitching as he scented for someone.

9.

November 10th, 2004, Village Panigiri, Kirsty and Barba Yiorgos

*P*anayotis moved out of the shadows and crossed the square as black and silent as a panther. He crouched in front of Kirsty's planters. His huge knife sliced easily through the stems of the jasmines, hibiscus and oleanders.

Normally, he loved this type of task—not as much as fire starting, but enough. Creeping down from the mountains, then returning, while the victims slept in their soft beds like newborn mice. But now he was too distracted; any pleasure was too fleeting to give satisfaction.

He longed to get back and see the woman again. Just to look at her and know that she was going to be his. Maybe only his. No matter what his brother thought. And he was thinking, all right. Panayotis could see it in his eyes, hear it in his breathing. He could feel it at night as he lay in the sleeping loft next to him, trembling and groaning until his release splattered on the straw.

Panayotis began to cut through the thicker stem of a bougainvillea. He tried not to imagine his brother, Leonidas, up there with her. He knew that he would definitely be looking, but not touching. Not yet. He'd probably demonstrate a few of his flashy dance steps to try to impress her. Maybe even look in through their spy hole and do what he did in bed.

That thought made Panayotis grasp the shrub harder, until the thorns entered his skin and blood trickled down his wrist, a crimson *paler than the petals falling and adorning his head. He gripped it even tighter and smiled. 'What were a few flashy, boot-kicking dance move-ments anyway?' he asked the dying plant. He knew what had impressed her. He pictured again how easily the foreigner had taken his brother out. One kick and a couple of blows and he'd been on his arse. Leonidas might be the best dancer on the island, but Panayotis was the best wres-tler. He'd saved the day and shown her his manhood.*

All the planters were destroyed, and he headed for the vine. It grew from deep under the kafenion and came out of stone as if nothing could have denied its right to light. Panayotis felt the thickness of its stem and stared up at the massing of tendrils, leaves and grapes covering most of the courtyard. It briefly crossed his mind how old the thing might be, and how many people it had given shade to, fed, or made drinks for.

He began to cut.

They'd been promised her when the moment came. Their bonus. He'd thought at the time he would take her first and that would be enough. Then, as feelings he'd never known began to gnaw away at his body and brain, that he did not want to share this time. The vine shook and a few grapes fell, bursting and spilling their seed impotently on the concrete. And, as his knife finally severed the vine, he'd decided. He would be the only one to have her. If not, perhaps his brother's body might join hers.

Panayotis took the paint can out of his jacket and tried to clear his head as he concentrated on spraying the strange symbols he'd been taught, and was now struggling to recall.

҂

Kirsty fought to keep calm. She sucked in a deep breath and climbed out of the car. She'd spent a good hour getting dressed smartly, doing her hair and make-up. She looked at Barba Yiorgos, who was sitting in exactly the same place he'd been on her first visit, dressed—or rather undressed—in exactly the same fashion. 'Probably,' she snarled to herself, returning his wave and smile, 'waiting for his precious chicken to lay its fucking golden egg!'

She didn't need another row after yesterday's two—first with the police, then with the taverna owner opposite. The police officers had tried to convince her that the vandalism to her kafenion had nothing to do with local youths. 'The writing's in English,' they'd deduced. 'Drunken tourists, as usual.'

'English!' she'd retorted. '"FUK OF HOM", "INGLSH WOR". I think even our "drunken tourists" could have managed better!'

They'd gone and sat outside Cristos's taverna opposite, under the shade of his still-living vine, sharing a joke and pointing at her. After the police left, Kirsty went across.

'I suppose you think this will bring back the customers you tell everyone I stole?' she'd snapped. They never spoke and she knew that Cristos resented her presence. 'I wouldn't be surprised if you'd put some of your yobs up to it, as they seem to be your only customers.'

'Actually, I was agreeing with the police opinion, that it was drunken English tourists,' he'd sneered. 'Or even, as they suggested, it was one of your customers who got short-changed!'

He'd laughed and left her standing in the shadows of the deformed, cropped trees that were as ugly and bare as she was feeling. Kirsty returned to her kafenion and spent the rest of the day answering a hundred questions about what had happened, wondering how the hell she was going to straighten out the mess. The thought of the dead vine, and trying to unravel it, made her head spin.

Then, to end her perfect day, Barba Yiorgos had called late again and dragged her, once more, in panic from her bed.

'I want to go to a panigiri tomorrow. At one of my favourite churches. We'll skip the early morning liturgy and get there just before the feast. You can pick me up at ten o'clock,' he commanded.

'I have a kafenion to run,' Kirsty had pleaded. 'I've also got a mess to sort out.'

'Mess? What mess? Get that funny-looking girl in. She's always glad to earn some cents. And don't forget, we made a deal. I've been doing my part, ringing everyone and making a plan. Now you do yours. You better believe it!'

He'd hung up before she could speak.

Now she was standing on the veranda next to him as he leisurely finished his cigarette.

'Are you coming or what?' Kirsty demanded.

'Coming or what?' he shouted, and was out of his chair quicker than Kirsty would have believed possible. 'Don't you talk to me like that, my girl! I've told you before, I'm old enough to be your father!'

His hand slapped her arse, and he was through the door before she'd registered it. Kirsty thought back to the other day, when the policeman had touched her and she'd wanted to claw his eyes out. Now, she found herself smiling and feeling, strangely, almost aroused by his touch and response.

In what seemed like seconds, Barba Yiorgos was back at the door, dressed impeccably, with his hair and beard glistening, and a sweet smell of expensive aftershave drifting towards her. 'What's the time?' he snarled.

Kirsty looked at her watch. 'Five to ten, Barba Yiorgos,' she admitted reluctantly.

'"Coming or what"! Now you've really pissed me off!'

He sulked for the rest of the journey, letting Kirsty struggle to find the village. When they finally arrived, the narrow streets were already crowded with smartly dressed pedestrians and an endless stream of cars. And, as Kirsty had feared, he insisted that they drive right up to the church, refusing every parking place she found along the way. 'I'm an old man. You can't expect me to walk up this hill, in this heat. You've already pissed me off; now you want to kill me!' After a torturous passage they finally arrived at the place where he 'always parked'.

A large procession was mounting the stairs to the church and all appeared to know Barba Yiorgos. She watched him push his way through the people in front.

Kirsty had lost him by the time she entered the gloom of the church. Small candles burned everywhere: beeswax, their yellow light not radiating enough of a glow to reach even the frescoed ceiling. People were moving through a haze of cloying incense, crossing themselves repeatedly and taking turns to kiss an icon. For some reason, though Kirsty had never believed, she did the same. She searched the crowd for Barba Yiorgos, whispering her own prayer that he'd not seen her do it.

Then she heard him. His deep voice had picked up the priest's litany and was following it word for word. The father looked annoyed, but Kirsty noticed several of the worshippers were beginning to titter, as if they knew what was coming next. Barba Yiorgos began to get louder until the priest was drowned out. Then he sped up, rushing through the list of petitions so quickly that the fixed responses were hardly finished before he was off again.

He brought it to a close and was out through the end door before anyone else had moved. Kirsty looked at the priest, who was gripping the pulpit and watching in shock as his worshippers followed Barba Yiorgos's speedy exit.

Outside, in a large courtyard, there was a makeshift kitchen and tables stacked with plates, glasses and bottles of wine. Kirsty made her way over to Barba Yiorgos, who already had a full glass in his hand.

'Well, that was different,' she said. 'When were you ordained?'

'Ha! Silly old fucker. We want to eat, not listen to his bullshit. If he can't get through it taka taka, best someone else does.'

He poured Kirsty a glass of wine, though nobody was drinking yet. She noticed one of the four women working behind the tables giving him a filthy look.

'I saw you kiss the blessed icon,' he said to Kirsty, his eyes brightening. 'What did you want to do that for?'

Kirsty felt herself blush. 'What are they cooking?' she tried.

'Goat pilafi. They've boiled the goat and cooked the rice in its stock. But the best bit's to come.'

As he said it, two men came through the crowd. They were carrying a large, steaming cauldron. She heard cries of delight.

'Staka,' he sighed and smacked his lips. 'The best goat butter.'

Kirsty smelled its pungent aroma as it passed, spitting and foaming next to her. The women moved aside from the vat of rice as the men poured it in. Then, after it was stirred by the priest, they began ladling plates with huge chunks of goat and mountains of glutinous, grease-gleaming rice. A disorderly queue began to form at the front of the table. Kirsty was about to join it when Barba Yiorgos shoved past her. He grabbed one of the largest plates. The woman serving tried to take it back.

'Join the line,' she commanded. 'You must wait your turn.'

'Ha!' he sneered, and handed Kirsty the plate. 'Save your breath, woman, to cool your pilafi.'

He snatched another plate, put his empty glass upside down on a full bottle of wine, took that and marched off. Kirsty followed him, trying to avoid the looks of anger and dismay.

A large area had been set up with long tables laid with white tablecloths, baskets of bread and cutlery. He made straight for one with a spot in the shade and was eating before Kirsty had sat down. She watched as he ate and drank ravenously, paying no attention to her as she picked at her food and sipped a little wine. All the tables were filling up, and on a stage musicians and dancers were getting set to perform.

'Do you want some more food?' Barba Yiorgos asked, pushing his empty plate away.

'No,' Kirsty said. 'Greasy goat pilafi, strong village wine and wedges of rock-hard bread at ten-thirty in the morning is not my idea of breakfast.'

'I suppose you'd prefer a wee dram of whisky and haggis, tatties and neeps,' he said, pulling her leftovers towards him. 'You could do with some feeding up, if you want my opinion. You're starting to look a bit scrawny.'

'Actually, I don't like haggis or whisky. But I'm glad the diet's working!'

Kirsty waited for some response, but could see he wasn't listening to her or interested in the food. He was also ignoring most of the greetings and attempts to start conversations by others gathering around. Instead, he was gazing at the small table set at the head of the longer ones. It was laid much more elegantly, and Kirsty guessed it was for the VIPs and that Barba Yiorgos was envious he wasn't there himself.

Then they arrived: the priest, a young attractive woman, and an old man flanked by two large men wearing dark suits and even darker sunglasses. The old man was dressed in traditional Cretan clothes and had an arrogance and power that immediately silenced the people nearest to him.

The women from the kitchen carried food over to them and Kirsty noticed that his food was served on a china plate and his wine poured from a glass carafe into a silver goblet.

'That,' Barba Yiorgos said, 'is Kapetanios Theodoros. A great hero of the Resistance. The woman is his new wife; not bad considering that he's eighteen years older than me, nearly ninety. You better believe it. The two monsters are the woman's brothers: probably there to keep other women away, ha ha ha.'

'Nice,' Kirsty said.

'I'm glad you think so, because as soon as he finishes eating, we're going to join him.'

The music started, and the dancers began thumping the wooden stage as they stepped into the irresistible grip of the swirling rhythms. Kirsty's feet began tapping along. Then she stopped and wanted to yell, 'We're supposed to be searching for people who I know are in trouble, not lounging here stuffing our faces while you meet old friends!'

'Right,' Barba Yiorgos said, getting up, 'come on. And, Kirsty, not a word about your British couple. Got it?'

She followed and felt like giving his swaggering ponytail a good tug.

'Ha, Yiorgos Americanos,' the old man said in a voice as mellifluous as Cretan honey. He stood, and the two men embraced and kissed each other's cheeks. Kirsty was ignored.

'Kapetanios,' Barba Yiorgos said, 'you're looking good.'

And Kirsty had to admit he did. Theodoros was short and broad. His hands and face looked as if they'd been sculpted from the rocks of the Lefka Ori, and his eyes burnt with the same blue fire as Barba Yiorgos's. But there was also, behind the hardness, a sense of calm and kindness that Kirsty warmed to.

'Boys,' he said to his brothers-in-law, 'take your sister and join in the dance. Sit, Americanos. The young should dance, and the old reminisce. Alas, but it's the way of things.' He glowered at Kirsty, daring her to take a seat. So she did.

'And shepherds,' he said, 'should go and attend to their flock.'

The white-bearded priest shot off, seemingly delighted to have escaped Barba Yiorgos.

Barba Yiorgos poured wine into two plastic glasses and handed one to Kirsty, giving her a sly wink.

'Ha,' Kapetanios Theodoros sighed, 'you shouldn't drink from such things, Yiorgos. It will bring you bad luck.' He made the flicking gesture to ward off the evil eye. 'I have never eaten or drunk from anything except bone china, glass or pure metals. Even in the mountains, I always carried my own cutlery, plates and glass. Once, when a German bullet shattered my bowl, I refused food until I could find a proper replacement.'

Kirsty spoke up. 'Were you in the mountains long? Do you know them well?'

Barba Yiorgos shot her a warning glance.

'I'm never out of the mountains, my child. I know them, I dare say, as well as any man living. Or dead, for that matter.'

He gave Kirsty a wicked look. 'So, Americanos, your taste in wives has changed. Beautiful, fiery, red-headed foreigners, instead of our Cretan angels.'

Barba Yiorgos replied quickly, 'There are no angels, Kapetanios. You recall what Kondylakis wrote in *Patouchas*? A father walks with his son, fresh from the mountains around their village. All the young women are out strutting their stuff. He warns his son: "They are all devils!" Then he shows him the kafenion, the restaurants and all the goods in the market. "So, son," he asks, "now you have seen everything, what do you want?"'

'"The devils, father, the devils!" he cries.'

Both men guffawed. Then they were off again.

Kirsty listened for a few minutes to their gossip about who'd died, what had been sold, et cetera, et cetera, but soon she began to drift. The music was in full flow now, and a lot of the villagers were dancing arm-in-arm in front of the stage. One couple were dancing together. The woman was striking, tall and sensuous in a skin-tight white outfit, and the man handsome. They made Kirsty think of Eleni and Patrick. *I'm being toyed with*, she decided, looking at the two men, who were drinking and yapping away. *Barba Yiorgos has no real intention of helping me. Never did have. Or if he did it was for his own purpose.*

'Kirsty?' she heard her name called a second time.

'Sorry,' she said, 'I was miles away.'

'I was just telling you,' Barba Yiorgos said angrily, 'that Kapetanios Theodoros was in the same Resistance group as my father, Michaelis.'

'Oh,' Kirsty sighed, thinking, Please, not a load of war stories. 'They must have all been so brave.'

'They were,' Barba Yiorgos stated.

'Your father was a fine man, Yiorgos Americanos,' Theodoros stated.

'Tell Kirsty about the day you rescued the villagers,' Barba Yiorgos coaxed.

'Ha, now that was a day to remember. I will tell it again, for you,' he said, touching Kirsty's shoulder.

She sat upright and smiled encouragingly.

'Every time we scored a small success against the Germans, they took terrible reprisals, usually against the innocent. Murdering women, old men and children. Burning villages. Anything to try to break our resolve. This day, they had lined up the villagers and stated that if the men did not come down from the hills and surrender, they would execute them. So we came and got in position. The German officer raised his pistol and the firing squad took aim. Our leader, Lefteris, gave us the signal and we shot. Not a single bullet missed its mark and the officer and his machine gunners were dead before their fingers had touched a trigger.'

He laughed at the memory, as did Barba Yiorgos.

'Fantastic story,' Kirsty said. 'You were heroes.' She gave Barba Yiorgos an impatient look. He registered it but carried on leading the man to tell another story. Then another.

And all the time he'd been pouring more and more wine in their glasses, ignoring hers. Now they'd started on the tsikoudia, without offering her a drop.

'He was a great man, Kapetanios Lefteris,' Barba Yiorgos said, as another tale ground to its bloody, triumphant end. 'My father often talked of him with pride. Also, with terrible sadness for his loss.'

'It was a terrible loss for us all, Americanos. One we could hardly bear.'

'The Germans caught Lefteris,' Barba Yiorgos told Kirsty, 'and the other members of the group. They took them to prison, at Aptera, and shot them when they tried to escape.'

'I often see Lefteris in my dreams as he was,' Theodoros sighed. 'So young, so courageous.'

'And cunning, my father always said. What was it you called him?'

'The fox. The white fox of the mountains.'

'I could never get my father to talk of his death, or how he was captured. I think the memory of it was too painful.'

'For all of us, Yiorgos. He was a man of grace and honour.'

'You know,' Barba Yiorgos continued, to Kirsty's growing annoyance, 'when I was a boy, I could never accept that the Germans were clever enough to have ensnared him. To have caught him and his men in one of their hideouts seemed almost unthinkable. I couldn't stand to see my hero being tricked by his enemies on his own ground.'

'Ha,' Theodoros confided, 'but Lefteris wasn't. If the Germans had tried to take him in the hills, they'd have been in their graves. He was taken in Chania. There was a house with a secret basement and a wireless to keep in contact with the Allies. It was also a meeting place for other leaders and fighters to gather and make plans.

'On this night, a group of the Resistance were there when the Germans arrived. They came quickly and with such force there was no chance to fight or escape. And, though I doubt he told you, your father should have been with them. Minutes before the Nazis arrived, a message came through and needed to be taken to me.

Michaelis was sent by Lefteris as the runner to carry it, though, as he told me, another man had repeatedly volunteered for this dangerous mission. So he escaped while others died. Fate? A blessing or a curse?'

'So now I know,' Barba Yiorgos said. 'I always knew that it couldn't have happened in the mountains and that my father carried some unspoken guilt in his heart.'

'Yes, Americanos, so now you do. But not all. And even though I know you're as crafty as a fox yourself, I will tell you what I feel you really want to hear.'

Kirsty was getting sick of this backslapping and 'reminiscing'. She could hear that Theodoros was drunk and guessed Barba Yiorgos was in the same state. 'Isn't it time to go?' she asked rudely, and got a kick under the table for her trouble.

'They were betrayed,' Theodoros said, grabbing Barba Yiorgos's wrist. 'I have never told anyone this before, though I've always carried it in my heart. A member of the Resistance was a traitor and sweetened his own life with the blood of others. There's no other explanation. But who? I've asked the gods a million times. Who?' He stared deeply into Barba Yiorgos's eyes.

Kirsty tried to see if there was anything in Barba Yiorgos's reaction that suggested he knew the answer to this, or suspected it had been his father. But there was nothing she could detect except the fact he hadn't finished gossiping.

Theodoros's wife and brothers-in-law arrived. They appeared disgusted by the state of Barba Yiorgos and gave him angry looks. He paid them no attention, but stood embracing Theodoros, who Kirsty saw was whispering something intently in his ear, not letting go, and with tears in his reddened eyes as he spoke.

She overheard the words 'will' and 'yes, as you say, witnessed and signed by Lefteris and Rossos. We all loved your father and would have done anything . . .' Barba Yiorgos embraced him even harder and asked if someone whose name she didn't catch knew of this.

'Yes,' Theodoros replied clearly. 'He found out at the time and was furious at everyone who gave any support to Michaelis, but we didn't care. We loved them, and just as I'd been glad at an earlier time to stand with Lefteris and witness their wedding . . .'

'What?' Barba Yiorgos demanded, dragging the poor old man away and carrying on for a minute out of earshot. Then it was all smiles and hugs and promises.

'Stupid, stupid old men,' Kirsty cursed as she drove home, getting faster and faster as Barba Yiorgos slept in his seat, his beard still glistening from the staka. She'd even had to fix his seat-belt around him, as he seemed too drunk to manage. She finally reached his house and jammed the car brakes on hard so they skidded to a halt.

'You can wake up now, oh great white fox of the food tables.'

'I wasn't sleeping,' he replied instantly, 'I was thinking. And you drove far too fast. I'm not quite ready to die yet! Now come in the house and calm yourself down.'

'No,' she said as he got out of the car. 'No, I've already wasted enough time on you.'

But he wasn't listening. 'Come in, hellcat,' he called as he reached the door.

Kirsty put her fingers on the ignition key, then changed her mind. She would go in. And show him her claws instead.

Barba Yiorgos was pouring two large glasses of ouzo as she entered.

'Don't you think you've drunk enough already?' she snapped.

He turned and smiled. 'I drink what I want. And, for your information, what I can take.'

Kirsty didn't reply. She was too shocked by what she was seeing in the kitchen. It was spotless and looked as if someone must have worked non-stop on the place in the few days since her last visit.

'Now I think I've pissed *you* off,' he said.

'Just slightly,' she snarled. 'I asked you to help me find some people I'm desperately concerned about. I've had my kafenion vandalised. And have had to spend most of the day, when I should be struggling to get things straight, listening to you bang on about the bloody war!'

'The man who led that Resistance group, Kapetanios Lefteris, has a monument erected in his honour. It is little known, and little visited.'

'I'm sorry. I know memories are important. It's just . . .'

'Your young couple visited and questioned someone I know about it. They took photographs and then went to a museum nearby to ask more about the events surrounding his death. I wanted to see if I could find out why. Or at least begin to understand what they were looking for.'

Kirsty took her drink and sat down heavily.

'And what do you mean vandalised?' Barba Yiorgos asked.

She told him what had happened as he tutted away in his irritable manner, before seeming to dismiss it as nothing. 'Ha, the wildness of youth.'

He handed her a framed photograph. It was of an incredibly handsome man. Errol Flynn or another Hollywood star. 'It's me,' he chortled, seeing the expression on her face. 'Me in my prime. I was wild and passionate with fires to consume the world. You better believe it.'

Then he became sombre and sad. 'He still lives. Do you know what is the worst curse of all? I'll tell you: to be a young man locked inside an old body with no chance of escape, and those fires consuming him instead.'

Kirsty got up as he lay down on the sofa.

'Next,' he said, as she started to leave, 'we're going to visit a monastery. And while we're there, we'll see if *you* are pure of heart.'

Kirsty walked to the door, shaking her head and trying to figure out what he was up to now.

'Kirsty,' he called, 'have you told anyone else about this?'

'No, not really.'

'Then don't. And one other thing: my son, Michaelis, will be round to fix your damage. It will do the lazy bastard good to do some work for a change. And if he makes a pass at you, or gets drunk, tell him I'll have his balls for souvlaki.'

'Like father, like son, then,' she whispered.

'So,' he said to himself as Kirsty drove off, 'someone *is* playing cat and mouse.' He looked around the tidy house and imagined Kirsty had thought he'd done it for her. He wondered how she would have responded if he'd told her that when he returned the previous night the place had been ransacked. Though nothing had been taken, because what the intruder had been searching for was safe in his hidden village house. And even more pertinent: how Kirsty would have reacted if he'd revealed what it was?

10.

The step turned golden the moment Kirsty's foot touched it. Just as Barba Yiorgos knew it would. Just as he knew that if he trod on it, its cold stone heart would remain unmoved, or possibly even darken a shade.

He watched Kirsty skip back down the ninety steps, her long white dress almost transparent with the blazing Cretan sun behind her. She looked vibrant and beautiful, and he wished he was thirty years younger and could rush up the steps to meet her. Then wished again he'd phoned her last night and confessed all that he knew.

He nearly had, before changing his mind. What, he'd asked himself, could he really say?

That the English woman the couple were looking for was probably his father's mistress—or, as Michaelis would have it, his wife. That she'd been executed. That there was a child who'd vanished. That Eleni was the mirror image of the woman in a photograph he had. But it wasn't just the vagaries of the story that had stopped him. Or Kapetanios Theodoros's words about Rossos and Lefteris signing his father's will while fighting in the mountains, which he knew. Or how Diomidis's father, Panayotis, had discovered this and been enraged, which he had not. Or even the fact that his father's unlikely claim about a wedding now seemed to have some truth in it.

He'd listened to the sea breaking and the night music of the land around him. His land. Barba Yiorgos imagined it turned into a concrete playground of flashing lights and booming music. He was its custodian and not yet certain where any of this might lead. Who, if anyone, could he trust?

Anyway, he'd decided—to appease his conscience—that if this led to where he suspected it might, it was best that Kirsty be kept as uninvolved as possible.

He'd spent a long time, then, watching the sea glisten in the moonlight and listening to the pebbles being worn to sand. *Sand*, he'd mused. It might as well be gold dust!

There were interesting facts about this stretch of beach running in front of his land. A few known, more being revealed. A lot of people knew it had some of the purest seawater in Crete. Most of them cursed the stony, pebbly beach that kept the tourists away. But there was apparently, just a short, pebble-biting stroll from the tide's edge, a massive sandbank. Soft, white sand under just three feet of water.

In recent years there'd been a rumour, one that had turned out to be a fact. There was going to be a new breakwater and harbour built across the bay. And an environmentalist had written a report stating that the tide flow would change its pattern because of it, and lift and dump thousands of tons of sand at a higher level.

The realisation behind this had dawned in many minds, and greedy eyes had begun to stare, blinded and driven by their own symptoms of gold fever. And one thing he'd learnt was these 'gold diggers' came in all guises and with clever tales to ensnare. 'All that glitters, indeed,' Barba Yiorgos had said as he'd pictured Eleni and Kirsty. He'd drawn the curtains and lay on the sofa with their images in his mind, waiting for his trip to a monastery with its own seam of hidden gold.

'Well?' Kirsty asked, standing in front of him, her hands on her hips and hair flashing in the sunlight.

'Well, what?' he asked

'I know the story. "Hriso skalitissa." If one is pure in heart, there is a step that will turn golden. Did it?'

'I could only see your hair burning my eyes, and that dress is see-through. This holy man we're going to meet spends more time with a telescope goggling down at the near-naked bathers than praying. So, as we don't want to distract him, stay in the shade!'

'Huh!' Kirsty said. 'Jealous that someone else might get a flash?'

She strutted off towards the monastery with Barba Yiorgos following, speechless for once.

The monastery was heaving with camera-toting tourists. They were either blocking the paths, queuing to get into the church, or staring the hundreds of feet down at the clear pink-tinged waters of the Libyan sea. Barba Yiorgos passed Kirsty and shoved his way through them. He led her to a door marked 'private', then barged in.

Inside the small, gloomy room a priest was seated on a throne-like chair behind an ebony and gold table. He looked magnificent. His beard was long and snow white. He was dressed in blue robes, with a tall hat and gold chain holding a huge cross. More like a wizard than a priest, Kirsty decided. And he was definitely casting his spell on the group of women and an old nun seated before him. They were listening intently and crossing themselves repeatedly as his rich voice preached.

Barba Yiorgos gave them a dismissive glance and sat down next to the priest, and beckoned for Kirsty to join them at the table. She registered the looks of surprise on the women's faces.

The priest quickly finished speaking, made the sign of the cross and gave an arrogant wave for them to leave. He followed as they trooped to the Dutch door and then closed it, blocking the bottom half with a chair.

'Yiorgos,' he said, his face lighting up. 'Like the snows! What news from the world outside?'

'Father Nikitas,' he replied, 'as resplendent as ever.'

Nikitas offered his hand and Barba Yiorgos kissed the ruby-red ring.

The priest looked at Kirsty for a moment, but kept his hand to himself. Then he darted off through a small door.

'Listen to me,' Barba Yiorgos whispered. 'Be careful. He's as closed as an oyster and as tricky as they come. And eat the cheese. Eat plenty or he'll eat you.'

Kirsty watched as the priest returned carrying a large silver tray. On it there were three small glasses, an ornate crystal decanter, slices of dark bread and a plate of oily-looking cheese.

He poured three glasses of tsikoudia before sitting down. 'S'yeia,' he said, then banged his glass on the table and threw the drink back so quickly that Kirsty hardly saw it go. Barba Yiorgos did the same and she followed.

'So,' Father Nikitas said, filling the glasses again, 'did you see that old nun they've sent to plague my life? All she does every day is nag and eat. Peck, peck, peck, until my ears are numb and all the cheese is gone.'

He took a piece and shoved the plate towards them.

'The monks make the cheese here,' Barba Yiorgos told her. 'Eat some!'

Kirsty did and listened as the two men chatted. Every few seconds another glass was banged down and drained.

'You, child,' Nikitas spoke to her for the first time. 'I've poured you drinks, Yiorgos has served you. While you just sit there waiting. What do you think we are, servants? Now serve us.'

They laughed as she did and a camera poked through the top half of the door to record the moment.

'Ha,' Barba Yiorgos sighed as the flash lit them up. 'Tourists!'

'So many, Yiorgos. Never a minute's peace to eat or drink.' He swallowed another glass and ate more cheese.

'My friend here, Kirsty,' Barba Yiorgos said, 'told me that her cousin and husband visited a short while back, and that you made them very welcome.'

'I always try to give. The blessed icon and golden step call them. I am just the tool of higher things.'

'My cousin,' Kirsty butted in, 'is a beautiful woman. Very Greek-looking. She and her husband were curious about some events connected with this place, I think.'

Father Nikitas reacted as if struck. He tossed his glass of tsikoudia down, not banging the table this time. Then filled another without waiting for them to drink theirs.

'My cousin,' Kirsty carried on, 'was particularly interested in a story about an English woman from Kolimbari. She fell . . .'

Kirsty didn't get any further as Barba Yiorgos reached under the table and squeezed her thigh so hard she nearly shrieked.

Nikitas got up and staggered back through the small door, clutching the empty bottle in his hand.

'Eat some cheese,' Barba Yiorgos snapped. 'Keep your wits about you. And your tongue still, or he'll be off like a mountain goat.'

Nikitas returned with the bottle full again. 'I do seem to remember them,' he said sitting down and pouring more drinks. 'A nice young couple. I gave them a blessing. I even allowed them to sign my special visitors' book.'

He went over to a shelf and carried back an old leather-bound book. 'Look,' he said to Kirsty and pointed at a name. 'He came here once and met me.'

Kirsty read the signature: Henry Miller. 'Yes,' she said. 'I read his book about Greece, *The Colossus of Maroussi*.' She heard Barba Yiorgos's fingers thrumming impatiently.

'Now, I have decided that you should sign it.' He handed her a worn Mont Blanc pen. 'Do it in Greek,' he said.

Kirsty scanned through the list of names and found very near the end, in disguised English, Eleni's and Patrick's. Eleni had written, 'I have a terrible feeling about being here. It's so disturbing to think it was all lies.' And signed it with another extra large question mark added after her name.

Patrick had written, 'I know. But maybe it was a young girl's fantasy rather than lies.'

She felt a chill run through her and was certain the message had been left for her to find.

'Father,' she said, as another drink was being poured, 'I need to use the toilet. Could you tell me where it is?'

The two men smiled.

'Follow the path outside,' Nikitas said, 'right to the end of the monastery.'

'You'll enjoy the view,' Barba Yiorgos added. 'And, Kirsty, on the way back, pop into the church and visit the blessed icon. You must see it, and be sure to light a candle.'

The toilet, in a stone building with a door that wouldn't close, was a hole cut through the rock. Looking through it Kirsty could see toilet paper and excrement coating the cliff sides and base some three hundred feet below. The narrow walkway had been crowded and she'd had to wait several times to allow tourists to pass. There had been two people queuing to use the toilet before her. Now there was a man outside, and she couldn't pee. Kirsty was desperate to get back. Finally, she managed to relieve herself and hurried away.

'*Go and visit the blessed icon!*' she sneered as she shoved her way along the crowded path. '*Light a candle!*'

When Kirsty reached the room, the top half of the door had been closed. She imagined she'd been locked out and marched towards it, determined to bang on it, with her shoe if necessary. Then the sight she glimpsed through a slight crack in the door froze her.

Barba Yiorgos had Nikitas on the floor. He was squatting on his chest and had hold of him by the sides of his beard. The holy man's robe had ridden up above his knees and his legs were thrashing around as he tried to get free.

Barba Yiorgos banged the man's head hard on the stone floor. 'For the third time, did you marry them?'

'No, he was already married. It would have been a terrible sin.' His head hit the floor. Then again.

Kirsty decided Barba Yiorgos must be raving drunk and was about to try to get in and rescue the priest, when she recalled those messages in the visitors' book, and waited.

'Listen to me,' Barba Yiorgos snarled, lifting Nikitas's head so it was close to his own, 'you hypocritical old sinner. If you tell me the truth, I won't go and see my friend the bishop and tell him about a young Russian prostitute staying at one of my hostels. You know the one I mean, the one who had to get dressed up as a nun and have her arse flogged until she couldn't sit for a week. Because, according to my cousin, who runs the place, she remembers you pretty damn well!'

The priest's head hit the floor again.

'I was a young priest then,' Father Nikitas sobbed. 'It was a sin, but he loved her so much. She loved him the same. I did it for love, I swear.'

'Bah!' Barba Yiorgos sneered. 'I'd like to know what you really did it for, but that can wait.'

'I swear, for love. Every time I look at the Blessed Virgin, I can still see them, along with their witnesses, Theodoros and Lefteris, standing there that night, bathed in a golden candlelight, and I have no regrets. She was the most beautiful and gentle person. I wept when I learnt what had happened. Have wept and prayed for them both, many times.'

'Maybe so,' Barba Yiorgos said, letting him go and standing up. Nikitas crawled to his seat.

'Did the British couple ask you this question?'

The priest shook his bruised head.

'Did they?' Barba Yiorgos shouted and moved towards him.

'Yes. Yes, the girl did. It was a terrible shock. I tried to reason how she could have heard about it. It was impossible, but she seemed to know all about it.'

'And you told them?'

'I told them it was a lie. And a blasphemy. Then commanded them to leave.'

'Huh! Sounds right for you. Did they know the man's full name?'

'Yes. They even knew about . . .'

Barba Yiorgos silenced him with a warning gesture and moved quickly towards the door. Kirsty fled.

She entered the church and walked over to the icon. She stood in front of it trying to figure out what had just happened.

'Saying a little prayer?' Barba Yiorgos asked, appearing silently next to her, eyeing her suspiciously.

'So beautiful,' she said, gesturing to the icon.

'It's a thousand years old,' he said, crossing himself. 'And very revered. Though that didn't stop the German troops putting a couple of bullets in it.' He pointed to some marks on its surface. 'Wait a moment, I must do something.'

Kirsty watched him go and put some money on a tray and then take two large candles and place them in an ornate, round tray of sand. His hand shook as he lit them and she caught a glint of a tear in his eye as he watched them start to burn. She went over to him and put her hand on his shoulder.

'Hadn't we better go and say our goodbyes to Father Nikitas?' she suggested.

'Ah,' he said. 'He sent his apologies. He's got a terrible headache and needed to go for a sleep. I think maybe he didn't eat enough cheese with his tsikoudia!'

'Glad I took your advice and did, then!'

Kirsty noticed an old nun sitting silently on a high-backed chair at the side of the church, observing them intently.

'Did he tell you anything about Eleni and Patrick while I was away?' Kirsty asked, keeping as stone-faced as she could. 'And why he acted so strangely when I mentioned their interest in the English woman from Kolimbari.'

'He said that they'd bothered him with a lot of questions he couldn't answer. And that he'd sent them away rather rudely. And that you'd made him feel guilty about his lack of Christian charity.'

'Nice to think he has such a good and charitable conscience,' Kirsty said pulling her hand away and turning to leave.

'I want you to promise me something,' he said.

Kirsty stopped, 'Yes?'

'When this is over, however it turns out, will you spend a night on a beach with me?'

'What?' Kirsty demanded. She heard the toothless old nun snigger. She had the strongest urge to slap him across the face before rushing off to her car and leaving him stranded. But he wasn't even looking at her, just sadly watching the two candles melt, their flames moving, melding and becoming one light.

'I might,' she said, knowing she had to have his help, whatever his motives were. 'But why?'

'I want to visit the beach next to the fort at Frangokastello on the night of May seventeenth and see if some people turn up. And if they do, how they will judge me.'

'If you're being deliberately mysterious, I don't need it. At least not until this one is solved.'

'Then we go next to meet a man who shines his light in dark places. A wise, kind man, who your friends went to visit. One who, with a shard of broken mirror glass, seeks to illuminate and unite the world.'

Kirsty shook her head and walked away. Outside the sun had lowered, the sea had changed colour and the sand appeared to be burning under the water. She looked down and tried not to imagine two lovers in a place too dark for any light to find them. But it was hard at that moment not to.

11.

*L*eonidas could kill a chicken with a needle. A single stab, expertly placed at the exact spot in the head, and its eyes would open wide for a moment, stare into his, then close forever. He'd done it many times, but still loved those seconds of limbo, created by his will.

His yiayia had taught him the secret along with many others, including, unlike his brother Panayotis, how to read. While his brother had wrestled and become as strong as a bear, he'd danced, learnt some of her magic, and the words of great Cretans.

She could take an emptied wine barrel and mix a concoction of herbs that, seconds after being dropped inside, would spontaneously combust, sterilising the wood ready for it to be filled again. No modern chemicals, no humane killers: just the cunning and skill of the ancient Greeks. He'd learnt well, delighting in the secrets of blades and fires.

The blade was to come; the fire was now. Over the last few years he'd lit many, usually with his brother. Cleansing the land for his father's improvements. Some of the conflagrations had been huge and complicated. This one was small and simple, but necessary.

Leonidas stepped from the shaded cover of the prinos trees. He moved quickly and stealthily onto the sand, but suddenly sprang into a dance. He couldn't resist it. The patch of beach was moonlit and looked like a stage. *The rhythm of the sea sounded to him this night as restless and inviting as any lyra.*

Leonidas danced and leapt, and pictured—instead of the white-bearded dummy he'd carried here—a woman watching him. She would be the beautiful Sfakian wife his family had found for him, in payment for what he was doing now and what he already had planned in his mind to carry out for their honour. He pictured her sprawled on a blanket with a bottle of his special red-tinged mournoraki, waiting for him to finish performing and join her under the stars. Then he saw his brother lusting over the English whore's every movement. As he did, his injured right leg went from under him and he hit the damp, gritty earth. Leonidas felt again the pain and shame of the kick that had landed so expertly, and felt the blows that had knocked him to the ground. But worse, he recalled his brother coming to rescue him from the puny-looking foreigner. He saw again his brother crush the man like an insect as the woman sprang to her husband's aid and ended up clinging to Panayotis's back, clawing him like they were already wild lovers.

Leonidas limped on towards the walkway, trying to shut those pictures from his mind and replace them with what he was going to do soon.

It was pouring with rain. Kirsty sat in the kafenion with about ten buckets, bowls and various containers on the floor surrounding her. The water was flowing through the roof as easily as if it had become a sieve overnight. She cursed the builders as she emptied another bucket. The roof had been repaired only a month ago. She saw the men again, drinking her wine and beer and eating her food for free, then charging about double what she'd originally been told.

Barba Yiorgos had managed to get her out of bed again to discuss today's visit to Kolimbari. Then, he'd hung up in the middle of the conversation and refused to answer when she'd called him back. For the rest of the night Kirsty had struggled to recall what had been said at the time, and what he might be trying to hide now. Or, more worrying, had something happened that had made him hang up and refuse to answer?

A black Mercedes pulled up with its headlights on full, illuminating the gloomy day and exposing her as she sat brooding, with raindrops falling close to her head. The blue-tinged halogens went off and she saw the smiling face of Diomidis beaming at her, apparently delighted at what he was witnessing. She waited for him to poke his head through the door, make some disparaging comments and leave. He climbed out of the car and then stood surveying the destroyed planters, the graffiti and dying vine, like some reporter sent to comment on a natural disaster. He came in.

'I told you I'd be back,' he announced, 'for some of that excellent wine, attentive service and, if you'd permit today, your company.'

Diomidis stepped gracefully through the buckets as if they weren't there and sat on one of the stools in front of the counter. He ordered a bottle of red wine and insisted on pouring Kirsty a glass. She felt trapped and wished someone would arrive or the phone would ring. Anything except being alone and less than three feet away from that smiling face, with the fear that his unblinking eyes were inspiring as they peered into hers. Most of all she wished Barba Yiorgos would come strolling in and drive him away.

'So,' he said, as he caught her glancing towards the square, and as if he'd read her thoughts, 'I hear we have a mutual friend now.'

'We do? Who?' Kirsty asked, already knowing the answer.

'Yiorgos Americanos. Yiorgos Casanova, or, if you're weak and foolish enough, Barba Yiorgos. He has many names and just as many faces.'

'I don't know him that well.' Kirsty stared at the door. 'He's just showing me some of the sights. I'm the chauffeur; he's the guide.'

'Nice idea. It's good to have someone leading you along to the right places. Did you know that we're related, your guide and I?'

Kirsty shook her head slowly and heavily.

'Oh yes! We go back a long, long way. My father and his were in the same Resistance group during the occupation. They were brothers in arms, and also brothers-in-law.

'He married into my illustrious family. A very advantageous move on his part, I assure you. Then just before the outbreak of war, do you know what his father, Michaelis, did?'

Kirsty watched as one of the buckets filled and formed a skin of surface tension that was about to break if she didn't move it, but she could not.

Diomidis saw her looking at it and started speaking much louder, as if she weren't paying attention.

'Do you know what the great Kapetanios Michaelis did?' he raved. 'What would turn him into a drunken waster, while my father became one of the most revered men of this country? At his funeral, hundreds of people lined the streets At Michaelis's, even his son, Yiorgos, did not attend. Do you know why?'

'No,' Kirsty said calmly, 'but I have a feeling you're going to tell me.'

Diomidis pushed the stool away and stretched over the counter. 'I will tell you,' he continued. 'And as a warning. Then you can judge for yourself who you should be guided by.'

As he spoke a big Nissan pick-up screeched to a halt outside. It was loaded with tools and pots of plants. A large, long-haired man jumped out and began shaking one of her planters before stamping towards the door.

Shit! Kirsty thought. What now?

'So,' Diomidis said, 'Michaelis. More of the devil's spawn.'

The man came in and looked up at the ceiling. 'Father told me I only had to fix the terrace,' he said. 'He didn't say anything about the roof. I'll have to go and fetch more materials.'

Kirsty smiled and felt a wave of relief: his voice and features were those of a younger Barba Yiorgos.

'Wouldn't you like a drink first?' she asked.

'Wouldn't I,' he replied, returning Diomidis's stare defiantly. 'But Father said if I did he'd have my . . .'

'I know' Kirsty said, smiling. 'He mentioned it the . . .'

'I must go and leave you to your work,' Diomidis butted in. 'I also have tasks that press. This island went from the donkey to the Mercedes in one leap, and needs men like me to keep working to make sure it doesn't return.'

He walked to the door and stopped a step away from Michaelis, daring him, it felt to Kirsty, not to get out of his way.

'Excuse me,' she called, 'but I think you forgot to pay.'

He moved back and took out a twenty-euro note. 'I always pay my debts,' he said, tossing it on the counter. 'Not like some.'

This time he passed Michaelis and touched his arm. 'Please give my regards to your father,' he said. 'Tell him he's in my thoughts a lot.'

'I'll be sure to tell him,' he replied, 'and be certain you are in his.'

Jane arrived a short while later and took over from Kirsty as Michaelis carried on working. Then he made her day as she was leaving to collect Barba Yiorgos. 'It's not dead,' he said, kneeling by the severed vine.

Kirsty went over to look, and as Michaelis scraped away some bark, she saw green wood underneath. He pointed to two little spots on the thick stem of the remaining vine. 'They're new shoots, and already starting to bud. We'll let them grow for a bit, then train the best. You'll have a cover and grapes again before you know it.'

117

'Thank you, Michaelis,' she said. 'This is very kind of you.'

'There's a lot of life and sap in these old Cretan vines,' he told her.

'In some old Cretan men, too!' she quipped.

'You better believe it,' Michaelis said, in a perfect imitation of his father's voice.

Kirsty was still smiling as she drove off. A black Mercedes coming the other way made her think back to Diomidis. What had he been going to tell her? Something bad about Barba Yiorgos's father? And what had he meant by 'a warning'? She was determined to tackle Barba Yiorgos about it as soon as she got to his house. But when she did, what she saw quickly changed her mind.

He was standing on the edge of the beach, oblivious to her arrival. Kirsty got out of the car and registered with shock what he was looking at. She hurried to join him. He turned to look at her and Kirsty saw tears in his eyes.

'Bastards,' he snarled, as she stood by his side looking at the still-smouldering remains of his walkway. The logs had been carefully arranged to make a wigwam-shaped fire, which had kept its shape as it burnt. Now it was a small black point in the middle of ripples of ash.

'Oh, Barba Yiorgos,' she said, 'I'm sorry.'

'I laid every one of those cedar logs myself. It nearly killed me. But I swore after I'd had this house built, I'd not let sandy feet traipse in and out. My child, wives, relatives and friends, even lovers, have all walked barefoot along that sweet-smelling wood, then back, clean and dry, to eat and drink with me. Now a lot of them are dead, or rarely bother to come anymore, but I could still see them. Sitting alone in my room, I could visualise them crossing that bridge to the water I would never enter, hear their laughter and be with them again. Now it feels as if someone has lit their funeral pyre.'

Kirsty gave his hand a squeeze. She pictured the damage to her kafenion. 'Someone is trying to warn us off,' she stated, as he carried on watching the plume of smoke drift on the gentle sea breeze.

'I was on the phone to you when it went up, boom! They must have piled the logs up, very quietly and craftily. Then poured petrol over them and set a detonator. By the time I got out, there wasn't a sign of the bastards, just the fire, fully ignited. With an effigy of me burning on top! It's a good job for them they'd gone or I'd have put a few rounds of buckshot in their arses.'

'I was worried about you. I called twice after you cut off.'

This seemed to cheer him and he gave Kirsty's hand a squeeze back. She decided not to mention Diomidis at this moment. 'I'll tell you what,' she said instead. 'You can borrow Burns for a week or two. He's becoming a great guard.'

'You,' he said, letting go of her hand, 'may need him more than me.'

He was walking off before she could ask him what exactly he meant.

'I have to get changed,' he called back. 'It's time to look into the light.'

Kirsty waited until he was inside, then she walked down onto the beach. The heat from the fire was still intense and had a strange colour in its heart. She stood looking for a moment, then noticed something peculiar. From where the logs had been taken and carried to the fire there was a confusion of footsteps, but there was only a single set leading up and down the beach, large, deep and wide-striding. Kirsty followed them a little way, then told herself not to be stupid. 'How could one man have moved all those logs in that amount of time?' she asked.

∽

Barba Yiorgos insisted they stop at a taverna at the end of Kolimbari village. He claimed he needed a cold beer and something to eat before visiting the Orthodox Academy. They sat outside, on the opposite side of the road, near the harbour wall. The owner, who'd treated Barba Yiorgos like he was a returning hero, kept crossing the road and bringing more plates of food, which so far Kirsty had only picked at. He came over and lit a couple of dainty little candles, even though it was still early evening.

Kirsty watched the flames dancing inside their green and red glass lamps. She listened to the gentle cadence of the sea as the sunset began. Romantic, she thought, and tried to picture this place sixty years ago, and the English woman who'd visited and fallen in love, abandoning everything for that passion, including, in the end, her life. She'd never really known a love like that, she suddenly realised. Kirsty nearly asked Barba Yiorgos, 'Do you think I'll ever fall in love? Is there still time? Did you see it in the coffee grounds that day?'

But he hadn't spoken since they'd sat down, and only grunted if she tried to start a conversation. Instead, he was staring fixedly at a couple of large buildings standing side by side; they looked like they had been boarded up for many years. 'The sound of those pebbles,' she tried, 'makes me think of the poem "Dover Beach": "Where ignorant armies clash by night."'

She got no reply. 'What is it, the company or food? Or are you scheming how you can buy and renovate those ruins that are so much more interesting than either?'

He slowly turned to her and seemed to come back from a long way off. 'Memories,' he said, 'of when those ruins were a lively kafenion, taverna and guest house. They were serving drinks when the Turkish ruled here. Think of the men seated outside drinking coffee and raki while some agha controlled their lives with a whip and sword. And before the Turks, the Venetians; before them, the

Arabs. All conquerors of this island at one time. But never conquerors of the Cretan spirit. The things endured here would have laid most nations grovelling on their bellies for an eternity. Here they couldn't even persuade a peasant to change his religion! So whatever happens and whatever you see, you mustn't judge the Cretans too harshly for their lies and treachery. It's ingrained as a defence as much as a fault.

'And I already own those buildings!'

'You think Eleni and Patrick are dead, don't you?' Kirsty blurted.

'If they're still on the island, I believe they're alive, though in great danger. Not yet dead. Of that much I'm certain, but very little else. Now I want to walk the rest of the way, past the Gonia monastery, and see the peacocks. They have a thousand eyes, just like the villages, my father used to say. Then we're going to meet a man with only one.'

12.

'The shells rained in that night. At first, to a child, it looked like fireworks and I started clapping. Then one hit the house and exploded.'

Kirsty and Barba Yiorgos were seated in the opulent library of the Orthodox Academy with its director, Telemachus. Kirsty thought he looked wise and kind. And though his face was dreadfully scarred, his hair longer than Barba Yiorgos's, and he wore a black patch over one eye, there was an intellectual sophistication that radiated from him.

'The house was ripped to bits as if made of straw. My grandparents were killed instantly, and their golden antique mirror they'd been so proud of splintered into shrapnel. One large piece took out my eye and embedded itself in my cheek. It stayed there as my mother dragged me from the rubble and we made our escape into the mountains.

'Over the next years, after the shard of glass had been very skilfully removed and my wounds tended by a wise old woman making her own escape—and carrying her own burden—I could never stop touching it. Every time I heard of another death or atrocity, felt the pain of my own loss, or saw these scars, I would grasp those jagged edges and let my blood mingle with what had been spilled for this island.

'Then I started working on it each time I needed to think. Patiently using my smoothing stone to wear down another edge as my thoughts grew and coalesced. When I finished my polishing, I had a perfect round circle of mirror glass. And along with it a mind and heart emptied of all hatred and bitterness.

'I decided to make it the eye I'd lost. I would let it catch the light and shine into any dark places I could find. That task has carried on all my life. This is how the academy came into being. Sponsored, to my delight, by German funding. They wanted to give the Cretans a sign of repentance and reconciliation. Especially here, a place that is so strongly associated with the Battle of Crete, the Resistance and so many countless and unknown victims.'

Telemachus paused and gave Barba Yiorgos a sad look.

'It is said that Cretans know how to neither forgive nor forget.'

Once again, Telemachus paused and stared at Barba Yiorgos, who pretended not to notice. 'Come with me, young lady,' the Director said.

Telemachus led Kirsty out onto the balcony. 'Look up there,' he said, pointing to some land and a cliff face a short way off. 'It's a mass grave of Cretans killed in the war. There,' he pointed through the pine trees and across the bay, with the sun, now red and bloated, turning it the colour of blood, 'is the German War Cemetery where more than four and a half thousand bodies are buried.'

Kirsty heard one of the monastery's peacocks give out a haunting cry. 'It's so very, very sad,' was all she could find to say.

'At night, two lights burn in remembrance of them. One on the cliff, the other in that cemetery. Sometimes, when I stand here at night, I see their beams meet and mingle as if dancing on the water. Joined in peace and harmony. It's my belief that if we can find reconciliation and forgiveness here, we can find it anywhere on earth.'

They returned inside where Barba Yiorgos had managed to find a wine decanter and pour three glasses.

'Telemachus,' he said, after they'd all touched glasses and taken a drink, 'Kirsty is concerned about a young British couple that came to visit you. They were looking for someone and some history connected with the events of that time.'

'And your interest, Yiorgos?' Telemachus asked, staring suspiciously at them.

'I'm worried about them,' Kirsty said quickly, as she sensed Barba Yiorgos was about to be tricksy. 'I think they've been kidnapped and are in serious trouble. We're trying to help them. You must believe me.'

'Must I? Let's see.' Telemachus reached into a small pocket of his waistcoat. He took out a silk pouch and slipped out a small, round mirror. It caught the dying light coming from over Kissamou Bay, then the crystal lights above. He transfixed the light so that it became a ray, then shone it first into Barba Yiorgos's face and eyes, then Kirsty's, so that she was momentarily dazzled. He held it there and she felt herself being examined.

'Yes,' he said, 'they were here. And I fear you may be right, that they're in danger. I warned them, but knew they would keep searching.'

'What did they want to know?' Kirsty asked, feeling she'd just passed his test.

'Many things.' He turned the mirror so it lit up Barba Yiorgos's face. 'While keeping many things from me. But with my bright Cyclops eye, I can see when people are hiding in the darkness.'

He kept the light on Barba Yiorgos as he stated this. Then he began to gently sway it between them, so Kirsty almost felt herself being hypnotised.

'They were, I believe, following a trail laid down many years before. And unfortunately, one laid in blood. Kazantzakis said, "Stick a spade in the soil of Crete and it will turn up blood." And they were digging deeply. They also had some unusual pieces of a puzzle they were trying to put together.'

'Like a red silk chemise,' Kirsty butted in, wanting to escape the light's movement.

Barba Yiorgos gave her a startled look, as if he'd come awake.

The mirror stopped moving and Telemachus smiled at her. 'Yes, they did. I'll tell you what I told them. When the Germans first tried to conquer the island, Hitler sent in his elite parachute regiments. The slaughter was terrible as the Cretans fought to protect their homes. Few Germans ever reached the ground. If they did, bullets, blades and stones were waiting for them. As one Resistance fighter put it, "Killing them wasn't the problem; counting the corpses was!"

'The Cretan women started using the silk from the parachutes to make clothes. When the Germans finally began to gain control they tried to prove that the material had come from their para-chutes, but couldn't, as white silk was made on Crete. So, as the fighting continued, they started dyeing the chutes red, and issued an edict that anyone caught wearing red silk would be executed.' He laughed. 'I remember my father telling me that at night the village washing lines were full of red undergarments.'

'So you think that the silk chemise they had was made during the war?' Kirsty asked.

'Almost certainly. And judging by the skill of the work and embroidery, I doubt very much by the English woman your friends were looking for.'

'Did they tell you how they got it?'

'I asked, and the girl lied. She told me they'd bought it in an old shop in Chania and she was just curious.'

'What else did they want to know?' Kirsty probed.

'About the Resistance fighters and the war. But really, though they skirted all around it, only one specific incident: the capture of Kapetanios Lefteris and his men in the basement in Chania.'

Kirsty recalled the old freedom fighter at the panigiri telling Barba Yiorgos that they'd been betrayed.

'And in particular, what had happened after their imprison-ment at Aptera.'

Barba Yiorgos sighed deeply at the mention of this, and began to skilfully manipulate his komboloi, the large, worn, yellow beads clacking rhythmically together.

Kirsty witnessed an almost imperceptible gesture pass between the two men. She had come to believe, since living on Crete, that it was possible for the trained eye to decipher a complete conversation between Greeks at fifty feet away, as they relied so much on body movement and facial expressions to convey meaning. This one clearly meant they both knew something she did not, and neither wanted to tell her.

'Okay,' Kirsty said, 'which one of you is going to tell me what happened?'

'I think it would be best for you to do it, Telemachus,' Barba Yiorgos cajoled. 'I'm getting old and my memory is failing.'

'Yes, Yiorgos,' Telemachus observed, 'I can see how old you think you are!' Kirsty watched the light catch a dark corner of the room and then begin its swaying movement again.

'After their capture, they were taken to the prison the Germans had set up below the site of ancient Aptera and the Izzedine fortress of the Turks. I see them often in my mind, looking up at those ruins, or staring across the blue waters of Souda Bay to the islands, waiting to die.

'Only they weren't. Unlike the Sirens, who cast off their wings after defeat and crashed into the sea forming those islands, these pallikaria were planning to fly. As the endless days went by and the Germans took and tortured different members of the group to try to find other Resistance members—including, as you know, Yiorgos, your father—they were digging a tunnel.'

'He never forgave himself for not being there the night they were caught,' Barba Yiorgos said. 'I think he thought he could have done something to save them if he had been.'

Kirsty waited for the beam to touch Barba Yiorgos's face and for Telemachus to look into his eyes.

Instead it carried on with its gentle movement.

'On a cold moonless night they made their escape. But somehow the plan was known to the Germans and they were waiting. In the shadow of those Minoan ruins, these new Greek heroes were machine-gunned to death. All, that is, except one: Kapetanios Panayotis, who miraculously escaped the shooting, made a leap from the rocks and swam to freedom. He carried the story of the defiance and heroism back to the Resistance to help inspire them to keep fighting. His tale is one of the great moments in the Battle of Crete. And, justly, it made him a hero.'

'And richer than before!' Barba Yiorgos snapped.

Telemachus stilled his polished shard at this exclamation, which to Kirsty smacked of jealous bitterness, and let its beam illuminate Barba Yiorgos's face. The men stared hard at each other. Kirsty saw a fire burning darkly in Barba Yiorgos's eyes, untouched by any of the hope or beliefs of the man shining the light.

'Did they want to know anything else?' Kirsty asked, as they carried on staring.

'No,' Telemachus said. He put his mirror back into its pouch and stood up.

'And did your beam of shining light point them anywhere else?' Barba Yiorgos asked, also getting up.

'Yes,' he said, then touched his scar and eye patch. 'To others who I believed would shine a different light into the darkness and offer a healing for the pain I sensed. Or so I hoped at the time.'

Barba Yiorgos nodded in understanding, as Telemachus bowed his head and squeezed Kirsty's hand to say the goodbye he seemed unable to voice.

❧

Another light began to glow as the night closed around them. Kirsty was seated on the sea wall a short way from the taverna they'd visited earlier. Barba Yiorgos was at a table with a jug of wine and some olives. Since leaving the academy, he'd hardly spoken. Once again, he just sat staring at the old buildings, as if they had cast some melancholy spell over him. When Kirsty had nagged him about what the information they were gathering meant, and where it was leading, he'd become cryptic and, Kirsty thought, deliberately illusive.

'They're like the pieces in a mosaic: until they're all set in place, there's no clear picture.'

When she pushed it further, he became irritable.

'Leave me to think,' he snapped. 'Go and sit on the wall and watch the beams of reconciliation shine on the water.'

Kirsty glanced back and saw him still staring at the buildings, with the wine and olives untouched. She turned away and saw a light, high on the cliff. It was coming from a small opening in what she guessed was a chapel of some description above the mass grave. At first it was weak, glowing like some candle in a Halloween pumpkin. Then it began to intensify, until Kirsty saw it touch the dark waters roiling and crashing against the rocks. She looked across the bay to Maleme and saw the other light, already as hard and cruel as a searchlight, cutting its path through the waves.

Then the two lights met. The golden, ancient light of Crete touching the stark ray of another would-be conqueror. As she watched, they seemed to meld, until in the middle of the ocean there was a glow of warmth. Kirsty imagined Telemachus looking down and seeing a world bathed clean in that water.

'So,' Barba Yiorgos said, snapping her out of her reverie, 'what do you think?' He gestured towards the lights on the sea.

'I think it's a marvellous idea. We should all learn to forgive and forget.' As she said it, Kirsty thought of her father gently kissing her forehead that final time and all the years of anger and regret. 'But it's . . .'

'So easy to say, so difficult to do,' Barba Yiorgos intuited. 'Some sins live on, and the deeds that brought them about cannot be pardoned. I want to ask you something now, before this goes any further.'

'Yes, what?'

'Do you think the weakness of a parent is inherited by the child?'

'No, of course not.'

'Do you believe the guilt of a parent and the reason for that guilt can be atoned for and put right by the actions of the child, however many years later?'

'Well, yes, I suppose it could.' Kirsty's mind was racing to try to understand what he was saying.

'And finally, do you believe in evil? A black-hearted corruption of the human spirit that can be passed from generation to generation as easily as the colour of eyes or hair?'

Kirsty looked at the sea, where the lights were still mingling and pulsing out their message of hope.

'Yes,' she said. 'I'm afraid I do.'

'Good,' Barba Yiorgos said, touching her bare arm gently. 'Then come back to the table. I have something for you.'

He poured her a glass of wine and pushed the lamp closer. He took a small box and placed it on the table. 'There are reasons I asked you those questions. They aren't easy to explain, but I'll try.

'My father died a drunk, living with a woman he'd come to despise, and a great debt left unpaid. But he'd once loved passionately, and a broken heart had destroyed his desire to live or act. So, I forgave him. And although he did some cruel and thoughtless things for this love, he was in his heart, and in many of his actions, a brave and honourable man.

'I, like my father, drink too much. I have loved passionately, though often not wisely. I, too, have an outstanding debt to settle. But I believe in life and living for today, in loyalty to family and friends. And, though many will tell you differently, I'm an honourable man.'

Kirsty bit her lip, recalling her conversation with the Gorilla that day.

'There are others, though, who aren't. The great hero you just heard about, for example. The inspiration of the Resistance, who, according to my father, never fired another shot against the Germans after his miraculous escape. Kapetanios Panayotis, the father of your new-found friend.'

'My friend? I don't understand.'

'Ha, but I think you do. He's become very fond of you for some reason. Though he's always hated foreigners, and only learnt to speak his crappy tourist English for business reasons. My dear cousin, Diomidis, the son of Panayotis.'

'Oh,' Kirsty said, 'him!'

'Him indeed. And he believes in only two things: money and power. As did his father.'

'Do you think he's done something to Eleni and Patrick? Is that what you're implying?'

'I don't know. Stones in our mosaic. It isn't his usual style. Burning land, intimidating, or conning people out of their property, yes, but kidnap and murder?'

Kirsty felt herself grow cold at the last word.

'At least, not by his own hand. Unless, maybe there was something too dark he was hiding. So I'm still trying to fit the pieces together. But I tell you, beware of this man and his sons, one of whom you've already met.'

'Met?'

'Leonidas. He came and danced for you and your students. A *danse macabre*, most likely, if you'd known the steps.'

'Are you spying on me?' Kirsty asked, feeling she was in some dance herself, and one step behind the beat. Also, thinking back to the reaction of Barba Yiorgos in the academy about Panayotis's wealth, that she might be being deliberately misled.

'Well, are you?'

'Watching over, shall we say.'

Kirsty thought it must have been Valentinos who'd told him, then realised it could have been any of the old men or women. 'So I'll have to be more circumspect.' She tried to sound jokey and mask her suspicions.

Barba Yiorgos grinned. 'For instance, I know Diomidis paid you a call before you came to me. I knew it before he'd got back in his car. And I bet he had some interesting things to tell you.'

'He didn't get the chance. Your son, Michaelis, came in as he was about to.'

Barba Yiorgos gave her a deep, questioning look.

'Now,' he finally said, after holding her eyes for a long while, 'I want you to have this.' There was a necklace inside the box on the table, resting gently on a layer of black velvet. Barba Yiorgos lifted it carefully and held it next to the light. The chain was made out of woven stands of gold and held a blue jewel. He turned it so that the lamp glowed through it and lit up a black stone embedded in its heart, perfectly centred, so that an eye looked back at her.

'It's lovely.'

'This is very old,' he said. 'It was my great-grandmother's. I was always going to give it to one of my wives or mistresses, but for some reason never could. Now I'm giving it to you.'

Kirsty felt a sudden charge of suspicion and pulled back from the stone.

'Why? What have I done to deserve such a favour? Or more likely, what am I expected to do?'

'Tut tut tut! You're going to piss me off again. I choose to give it to you because the time is right. It's a special piece. The symbol we call "mataki" to ward off the evil eye and protect the wearer. Is that good enough, or do you want me to throw it into the sea?'

'Yes, it's good enough, and kind. Thank you.'

'That's better. And one other thing: stop thinking I'm trying to seduce you. I've had women so beautiful you'd be dazzled by them. You better believe it!'

Kirsty felt herself blush.

'Now, allow me.' He got up and placed the chain around her neck. He closed the clasp and let the cold stone drop down towards her cleavage, which she sensed, regardless of what he'd just said, he was studying. Then, by accident or intent, his finger brushed across from the nape of her neck to her shoulder. Kirsty felt a charge of energy that made her shudder, then glow. She was certain she heard him sigh softly.

'Tomorrow evening,' he said, sitting and nodding in approval at the necklace as she stretched her head back to show him, 'we're going to a party in a remote village with two names, where a fire will be lit, a spirit released, and maybe another piece of our mosaic revealed.'

13.

Kirsty stood on the roof terrace of an old house. She had a glass of village wine in one hand and a bunch of keys in the other. They were on their way to the party, but Barba Yiorgos had insisted on a detour, and that she memorise the directions.

'This,' he announced, as they drove up a steep, rough track through olive groves and past the crumbling deserted houses, 'is my love nest, ha ha ha.'

They'd pulled up in front of a long white house surrounded by a high stone wall. The gates had opened automatically and lights came on to illuminate the building.

'Actually,' he said as they'd stopped, 'this is where my father came after the war to escape many things, and, I now understand, to die. See that there?' He'd pointed to a beehive-type oven. 'It cracked on the night he died. They often do. Such things aren't possible, you might believe. Mere superstition. But here on Crete they happen. On the night he passed away, an owl landed on those bars.' He gestured to the ones covering an upstairs window. 'My mother was awake and thought it had come for her. She was terrified and tried to wake my father and knew, as its silent white wings carried it away in the search for another soul, he'd never wake again.'

Inside, the house had been magnificently restored. Three Venetian stone arches made tunnel-like entrances into different rooms. The floors were covered in natural stone, and though the walls had been plastered, in places the stone had been left exposed, as had the ribs of old olive wood. The ceilings were constructed from large cedar logs and made Kirsty think sadly of the ones that had led from Barba Yiorgos's property on the beach. The whole house was furnished in traditional Cretan style with brightly coloured carpets on the walls and floor, and seemed to Kirsty more Eastern than Western.

'Nice,' she said, also noticing the many weapons and photographs of armed men.

'And private, my escape from the world. I restored this years ago and told no one. And I want it to stay that way.'

'Then why are you showing it to me?'

'Listen to that,' he said, changing the subject and tapping one of the beams in the wall, which rang like metal. 'Ancient olive wood, harder than iron. My team of Russian builders broke three chain-saws trying to cut them out. So they stay. Now pour two glasses of wine.' He pointed to a huge wooden barrel under the stairs. 'I'll join you on the roof terrace, but first, I have something to find.'

'These are the keys to the house,' he said, after joining her. 'The key ring is the control for the gate. Make sure you keep a fresh battery in it.'

'Why?'

'Because it won't work if you don't.'

'Very funny! I mean, why are you giving me the keys to your house?'

'So you have somewhere to bring your lovers. I'm a romantic at heart.'

'I don't have lovers. I have a cat and a dog.'

'But you're beautiful and intelligent. You'll find someone to love.'

'That's not what you told me at Kolimbari the other night,' Kirsty replied, dangling the keys in front of his face.

'When I was young, and before I left, this was a vibrant, thriving village. Look at it now.' Kirsty peered out into the darkening evening. All around them were derelict and crumbling houses. In one area a tower was falling apart and bats swirled around it like moths drawn to its cold fire. As she looked farther up the hill, she saw weak lights glowing from a couple of the houses, with two small shrines signalling back to them.

'Mostly, the only people who remain are old, sick or dying,' Barba Yiorgos said. 'The young have gone to Chania, or, if they have any ambition, Athens, London or New York. They knew there was nothing here for them and fled before it was too late. Some foreigners will buy these houses one day, I expect, and maybe save the village. Who knows? More likely it will send them crazy and their dream homes will be the next ruins.'

Kirsty rattled the keys again.

'We're being stalked. The Minotaur I told you about has been unleashed and has left the labyrinth. After you went yesterday, I did what I saw you doing, examining the fire and noticing the single set of tracks. Only, unlike you, I carried on following them.'

Kirsty rebuked herself silently for not realising that he'd been watching her.

'No other footprints joined them as they left the beach. I went and checked with the campsite owner, and he told me there's no one staying at the moment, but that he'd heard a motorbike arrive and leave, then saw the fire, which he guessed must have been a beach party! And whoever was strong enough, and stealthy enough, to have torn up those logs and make that fire without being heard is a force to be reckoned with.'

'The damage to my property? You think the same person did it?'

'Hmm. Possible, or a similar creature.'

'Then we must be on the right track, at least. Eleni and Patrick did find out something they weren't meant to. I'm not afraid. Are you?' Kirsty was determined, whatever her doubts, to play along for their sakes.

He laughed softly. 'Yes, but for you. That's what the keys are for. If you need to run or slip away, phone me, then flee.'

Kirsty put the keys in her pocket and patted them.

'Right, then let's go to our party. And when this is over, you can hang onto those keys for when you find that lover,' he laughed as she punched his arm.

❧

Barba Yiorgos got them lost three times. Though Kirsty noticed on each occasion when they'd turned off, there'd been car head-lights behind them. Then, as soon as the car hadn't followed, he'd announced *she'd* gone wrong again. Finally, after driving along some of the most narrow, convoluted roads and tracks she'd ever seen, and through two semi-derelict villages, they arrived at a large house on the outskirts of another settlement.

Kirsty parked behind a long line of cars. All of them, she saw, were new and expensive—'from the donkey to the Mercedes', she heard Diomidis saying again—and wondered how many of them would disagree with his plans for the island. 'Are you seriously telling me Eleni and Patrick came here?' she asked. 'I wouldn't have thought David Livingstone could have found this place!'

'Your young friends had a lot of information from somewhere, or someone. They came to see an old man. These are all his relatives. They've come to celebrate the lighting of his kazani. This is how they make tsikoudia – the proper stuff, which can be hallucinogenic and give you "raki dreams". Not like the tourist version that gets sold in some kafenions.'

He was out of the car before Kirsty could respond, not only to defend her tsikoudia, but also to tell him that she knew exactly how they made it, and had been to a demonstration on Chania harbour. Then, as she caught him up and they got closer, she was glad she hadn't. Because what she'd witnessed seemed to have been from another planet!

In the glow of a huge kiln-type structure, two men were heaving large logs of olive wood into the flames. Standing next to them, a giant of a man was moving the fire so it was roaring under the cauldron on top of the mound. He was stripped to the waist, glistening with sweat and smeared black from burning wood. Sparks danced around him like fireflies. To Kirsty, he looked like a figure out of Dante's inferno, or the devil himself.

A large crowd of well-dressed people were gathered in the light of the fire, warming themselves and watching intently. 'They only have a licence to run the still for three days,' Barba Yiorgos told her as they got closer. 'The fire will be kept going for twenty-four hours a day to make sure they produce as much as they can.'

The master of the kazani stopped shifting the coals as he saw faces turning towards them. He gave Kirsty a ferocious look, his eyes picking up the colour of the fire and his muscles tensing. Then he saw Barba Yiorgos and smiled. 'So,' he boomed to his audience, 'the great Kapetanios Yiorgos honours us with his presence. But who's he got on his arm tonight, dare we ask?'

'This, Alexis, is Kirsty. She's a government official and I've brought her along to make sure that the village clocks don't run backwards again!'

The crowd laughed as Alexis embraced Barba Yiorgos and kissed his cheeks. Then just about everyone greeted him and ignored her. She registered that they all called him either 'Barba', or 'Kapetanios'.

Someone brought a chair for him and placed it in the centre of the small semi-circle surrounding the fire. He took it without uttering a word of thanks, then sat there like a king, with his courtiers bringing him wine and food, while she was left without a drink or any of the mezedes that were being passed around. Kirsty made up her mind that she wasn't going to go over to him and stand like some lady-in-waiting. She moved as far away as possible and tried to concentrate on what was happening and ignore the feeling that the people resented her being here.

Two men appeared on top of the oven and began pouring the contents of a large steel drum into the cauldron. 'Kirsty,' Barba Yiorgos called. He did it again when she pretended not to have heard.

'Yes?' she said, arriving by his side. 'Aren't you getting enough attention?'

'Stay by me and watch,' he ordered. 'You may learn something.'

Two more men arrived and emptied another drum, of what she knew, from the demonstration on the harbour, was the fermenting 'must' left over from the wine pressing. Then an old woman arrived and began pushing handfuls of dried sticks and leaves into the liquid.

'Special secret herbs,' Barba Yiorgos informed her. 'Every village makes their own tsikoudia with subtle variations. All claim theirs is the best, the nectar of the gods. A few men, like me, can actually tell the difference. And the stuff that was found in your friend's car, which Stavros let me taste, didn't come from here. Instead, a stream of blood flows from this cursed place, and we must tread carefully if we're to follow it. As you can tell, they don't like strangers.'

More men arrived and placed a large lid on top of the cauldron. It looked like an elephant's head with a long, stiff trunk.

'If that gets broken,' he said, after handing her his glass of wine, 'it cannot just be substituted, and by law, they must apply and pay for another permit to run a still. Let me tell you, that elephant has had more lives than any Cretan cat!'

A young woman rushed over to replace the glass of wine he'd just given Kirsty, deliberately brushing against her and then strutting away provocatively. Kirsty ignored her and watched as the men began sealing the lid with what appeared to be clay and attaching a pipe to the end of the trunk. A short way off, a little boy set up two glass vessels and placed the other end of the pipe in one. Everybody went silent and waited. She heard a collective sigh as the first drops of liquid began to fall, then a cheer as it turned into a flow. Alexis put some of the spirit into a measuring jar and dropped a hydrometer into it. He smiled and gave a thumbs-up sign to Barba Yiorgos. A second later he brought two glasses over to them.

'This is the strongest part of the tsikoudia,' Barba Yiorgos whispered, as Alexis poured himself a glass and raised it to the crowd. 'Some of the men will only drink this, and it makes them blind.'

'Nice,' Kirsty said, looking at the viscous, still-hot liquid in her glass, and the expectant faces watching her.

'S'yeia,' Alexis cried, and swallowed his drink in one gulp. Barba Yiorgos did the same, and Kirsty followed. She heard a round of applause as the liquid sent a rush of alcoholic fire and energy through her.

'Now we go and eat,' Barba Yiorgos said.

Kirsty followed with the rest of the people as Alexis led them to the courtyard of the house. Three very long tables had been set up with candles and glasses for both wine and tsikoudia. Bottles of tawny, old village wine were placed strategically, and in front of each seat there were plates of china and silver cutlery. A large barbecue and oven had been lit and a group of women were gathered around cooking. Kirsty estimated the tables could seat at least a hundred people and, as she and Barba Yiorgos took their seats in the centre of the middle table, they were already nearly full.

Kirsty searched the faces of the people to see who it might be that they'd come to meet. As she did, the provocative woman from earlier made eye contact and gave her a filthy look. Kirsty held her stare as the woman got up and walked around the table to Barba Yiorgos, who was seated opposite Kirsty. The woman appeared to be about the same age as Kirsty, only dressed to look a lot younger. She had a mass of curly black hair and a hard face, heavily made up with a dark lip-liner exaggerating her sensuous mouth. She was wearing three-quarter-length red leggings that were so tight they looked as if she'd painted them on, and her large breasts were struggling to stay constrained by a deep-plunged bodice of white satin. Kirsty hated her on sight. And even more so when she forced herself onto the seat next to Barba Yiorgos.

'Yiorgos Casanova,' she cooed in a high-fluted voice, 'my hero.' She kissed his face and Kirsty saw a tinge of blood-red lipstick stain his beard and wanted to reach over and wipe it clean. 'How I've missed you.'

'Katerina,' he said. 'Nice to see you too. This is Kirsty.'

Katerina didn't even bother to look.

'Your father was in fine form on the kazani. Will your grandfather be joining the celebration?'

'Bottoms up!' Katerina yelled, banging on the table one of the glasses of tsikoudia that had been ceremoniously carried over from the still. She downed it in a gulp and waited, challengingly, for Kirsty to do the same. Which she did, and saw Barba Yiorgos give her a warning look.

Then Katerina began to flirt, touching Barba Yiorgos at every chance and whispering so closely that her thick lips were almost brushing his ear. And, to Kirsty's mounting anger, he appeared to be lapping it up.

Then the food started to arrive. Massive platters of meat—goat ribs, lamb, pork, village sausages and a steaming pan of snails—along with wooden bowls of Greek salad and potatoes glistening in olive oil, oregano and lemon juice, and baskets of brown bread, hot and straight from the family's fourno. The bottles of wine began to empty as the feast became more riotous. And all the time, Katerina was carrying on with Barba Yiorgos. She kept popping snails—which she expertly removed from their shells—into his mouth and letting her fingers linger afterwards. Every once in a while, she'd look at Kirsty, bang another glass of either wine or tsikoudia on the table and call out, 'Bottoms up!' as she downed it and waited for Kirsty's reaction. Which, to Barba Yiorgos's annoyance, Kirsty did every time. 'Probably the only fucking English you know, bitch,' she whispered to herself as she swallowed another shot and heard Barba Yiorgos make his tutting sound. But she didn't care. Why wasn't he talking to her? Kirsty asked herself. More importantly, why didn't he shoo the bloody tart away?

Kirsty realised something with a shock. She was jealous. She was absolutely seething with it. She wanted to kick the woman so she went flying off the chair. And then tip a glass of wine over Barba Yiorgos's stupid, goat-bearded head.

Suddenly, Katerina stopped her antics and everyone went silent. Two young women were positioning a very frail-looking man in a wheelchair at the head of their table. He had a colourful Cretan blanket covering his legs and another draped around his shoulders. Kirsty thought he looked like some mystic, and tried to picture Eleni and Patrick coming here when there was no celebration to lighten his words. Some foreboding of what he would say made her shiver.

The old man opened his eyes, deep and hooded, and stared at Kirsty as if he was reading her mind. He looked at Barba Yiorgos and smiled. One of the women handed him a glass of tsikoudia. He swirled it around, sniffed it, then said 'S'yeia,' very softly and drank it in one go. The toast was returned and the party burst back into life.

Music began and people started leaving the tables and dancing. Kirsty sat and tried to eat one of the hot chestnuts that were being carried over from the kazani's ashes. But really she was watching Barba Yiorgos, who was standing near the barbecue with Katerina in front of him. She was dancing. And, Kirsty had to admit, she was great. And all of it, the barely restrained sexuality, was aimed at Barba Yiorgos. He turned away from her and beckoned arrogantly for Kirsty to come over. There was no way, she decided, she was going to dance for him, if that's what he had in mind. Thinks he's the Shah of Persia, she thought angrily, burning her fingers on a chestnut as she did.

'Get that fucking woman off my back,' he snapped, the moment she reached him and before she had a chance to speak. 'We won't get a word out of her grandfather if she follows us over to him.'

'Maybe you shouldn't be so attractive, "Yiorgos Casanova"!' Kirsty mimicked in Katerina's voice, then marched over to her. She placed her arm on Katerina's shoulder, as she continued to writhe and undulate, so that it looked as if she was going to join her. Instead, Kirsty pulled her head close to hers. 'If you go anywhere near my fiancé again tonight, I'll kick your fat arse out of its supports,' she snarled in Greek.

By the time Kirsty reached Barba Yiorgos and looked back, Katerina had fled and was standing next to her father and looking very sheepish.

'Now we go and meet the ancient Rossos,' he said. 'And bear in mind that he's virtually senile—ga-ga, you understand? So if he says anything that sounds strange, ignore it.'

'Of course,' Kirsty said to herself. 'Only you speak the truth!'

They moved away from the courtyard towards a lemon tree surrounded by a low stone wall. Under its leaves and fruit, lit by the glow of two burning torches, was a small table laid with bread, wine and olives. The old man in the wheelchair was next to it and a very handsome youth was playing a lyra.

Barba Yiorgos sat down and pointed at a chair for her to do the same. The music continued and the old man seemed to be asleep.

'Yiorgos Americanos,' he suddenly said, 'with another beautiful woman on his arm.' His eyes opened quickly and he gave Kirsty a quizzical look.

'Thank you kindly,' Kirsty said.

'Kapetanios Rossos, this is Kirsty. We want to ask about . . .'

'I had a dream that you'd come. I've had many dreams and memories awakened in these last weeks.' Rossos silenced the music with a wave of his hand that also sent the youth scurrying away. 'Do you know, Yiorgos, there's a passage in Kazantzakis's great novel, *Freedom or Death*, where an old kapetanios lies under a lemon tree as a lyra gently plays, and all of his family enjoy their celebration. His eyes close, and he goes gently and peacefully to his eternal rest. I've sat under this tree a hundred times and always I awaken.'

'A man like you should live a thousand years,' Barba Yiorgos said.

'Sometimes, I think I have. Just like that tree,' Rossos said to Kirsty, pointing to a gigantic plane tree a short way off. 'That's perhaps the oldest tree on Crete.'

'It's magnificent,' Kirsty said.

'And also, for me, the saddest. Do you know why this village is called "Marianna" by some?' he asked her.

'No, I've never heard the name before.' She looked at Barba Yiorgos, who wouldn't meet her eyes.

'Pour some wine,' he said, 'and I'll tell you.'

Kirsty filled their glasses.

'A young woman of that name was hanged by the neck from those branches.'

'Was she English?' Kirsty asked.

'Yes, she was.'

A look passed between Rossos and Barba Yiorgos that made her sense either a deep pain they shared, or a secret.

'She was very beautiful and innocent. But the Germans took her in the night, while all the men were in the hills fighting. They stripped her naked and put a rope around her graceful neck. Then, as she shouted out her courageous words of defiance and expected promise of revenge, the cowards murdered her. And I could do nothing but watch. Though, as God is my witness, I tried. I had a bullet wound in my shoulder and could hardly move, yet I still fought until they beat me into submission.'

Kirsty touched the old man's hand as his voice began to break.

'Only a few people still call the village after her,' he told Kirsty bitterly. 'They prefer the original name, as it's not tourist-friendly to have such memories. They want to forgive and forget. But this is not the true Cretan way, is it, Yiorgos? Or have you learnt to forget?'

He glared fiercely at Barba Yiorgos. 'It's a sad story, Kapetanios Rossos,' Barba Yiorgos said. 'Did you tell it to the young British couple who came to visit you a short time ago?'

'Oh, what big eyes and ears you've still got! Yes, I did. And much more.' Rossos turned to Kirsty. 'On the night they killed her, they made all the women and children watch. I can still see the life draining out of her as she kicked on that cursed rope, and hear the screams of the villagers melting the snows of the distant mountains with their pain.

'But even that wasn't enough for those Nazi pigs. After she died, a young officer came over to me. "That carcass stays there," he warned. "It stays there until it rots, and then still hangs there for all to see. I'll have my men pass by to check. And if she gets moved, I swear, you and half this stink hole will take her place."

'They left, but I'd seen the loathing for her on that animal's face and knew he'd meant it. So that night, I cut her down and laid her poor broken body in a donkey cart. Then, as the rest of the village slept, two old widowed sisters sneaked her away and buried her where she would never be disturbed.'

'Where's the grave?' Kirsty burst in. She knew Eleni and Patrick would have visited it—or at least tried to.

'I don't know,' Rossos said. 'I told the sisters not to tell me. I didn't know if I could make my escape to the mountains, and I feared that if that German officer caught me, he might be able to force me into telling him where the body was. I made them pledge to keep the location hidden and tell only one man where she was buried. That man was her . . .'

Barba Yiorgos interrupted loudly and said something in a strange language. Rossos looked puzzled for a moment, then replied in the same tongue. They carried on for some time, oblivious to Kirsty. She recognised some of the words, but not enough to make sense of what was being said. She suddenly realised they were speaking ancient Greek.

'Alive?' Barba Yiorgos cried, reverting to demotic Greek. 'But she was old then; it's not possible.'

'Cretans live a long time, Yiorgos. Look at me. Those black crows go on forever. They put their men in the coffin, themselves in widow's weeds and become older than any olive tree. My grandson is working on getting an electric supply to the island of Gavdos. He was in the taverna there and said a tall, old woman came up to him. "So," she said, "you're the grandson of Rossos from the village of Marianna. Is he still alive? Then tell him Kyria Despina sends him her wishes and for him to be as strong as the islands."'

'Did you tell the British couple about her?' Barba Yiorgos asked.

'Yes, I did. But though I might be getting old and not as sharp as some, I think they already knew. And I tell you, sitting and talking to that girl was like being visited by a ghost.

'I thought Kyria Despina might give her the answers to much of what she seeks. Things only that witch knows, about what happened. And one secret she's kept all these years from everyone. They made me a promise they'd ask her for the truth, and bring me the answer. But they never came back.'

'We're trying to find them,' Kirsty told him.

Rossos spoke to Barba Yiorgos in ancient Greek again. Kirsty made out the words 'child' and 'deceit'. Then Barba Yiorgos got up. 'I think we're tiring you,' he said, and bent down to kiss Rossos's cheeks.

Kirsty said her farewells.

'Do you mind,' she stormed, after they'd finally managed to get away from the celebration, 'telling me why you suddenly decided to speak ancient Greek? And what exactly it was you didn't want me to hear?'

'It's the best language for expressing sorrow and grief. Our way of letting true emotions burst forth. The acts of a Greek tragedy can only be voiced in such words.'

'Oh, right! So what role are you playing in this tragedy? Hero or villain? And what exactly was expressed?'

'That there's an old witch, still alive and living on the remote island of Gavdos. She was one of the two sisters who buried Marianna. Your young friends went to visit her shortly before they disappeared. We must go and find out what she told them.

'I only hope that you're a good sailor; the crossing can be rough. If the weather gets bad, we might get stranded for days. There's very little fresh food or water, so pack plenty of peanut butter sandwiches and Dramamine. And my role in this? Hero or villain? You'll have to be the judge.'

'Are you being honest with me? Do you know more about this than you're telling?' Kirsty demanded.

'Am *I* being honest with *you*? Do you know what I received just before we left? A hundred congratulations on my forthcoming wedding! What did you tell Katerina that for? They're already planning a feast for the great day. This will be all over the damn island by the morning.

'Honestly, do you think I'd be crazy enough to marry a Scottish woman who can piss me off quicker than anyone I've ever met?'

At least he didn't say 'English', Kirsty thought as he went into one of his sulks. She drove through the thyme-scented night, trying to discern shadows from solids, truths from lies.

14.

Kirsty was clinging to the stair rail and sagging on a cold, wet, steel step. She could feel the water seeping through her jeans, and frankly didn't give a damn. At this moment, Eleni and Patrick could be hanging from that plane tree for all she cared. Nothing mattered except the rolling of the ferry and her wish to die, or to kill the old goat who was in the bar making eyes at some young woman and drinking beer.

Kirsty began heaving again, though there was nothing left to come up. 'Ha ha ha,' she heard Barba Yiorgos's laugh echoing in her mind as she'd fled the table. 'I told you to pack Dramamine!'

The 'fuck off' she'd wanted to yell had been choked by her seasickness. Kirsty had once sailed with a friend to the island of Santorini and got caught in a storm. She'd ridden it out easily. But this was something else. A simple fifty-kilometre crossing from Crete to the southernmost point in Europe, the island of Gavdos, and it already felt to her as if she'd travelled to the edge of the world.

'Only another hour to go and we'll be there,' Barba Yiorgos said, appearing suddenly.

Kirsty wondered how long he'd been watching her. 'Go away,' she said, 'and leave me to die in peace.'

He sat on the step and gently brushed back her hair. 'Drink this,' he said, handing her a glass of thick-looking yellow liquid.

'I can't.'

'Oh yes, you can. And must. It's a panacea. The captain, Yiannis, takes this medicine every time he makes this crossing, and I persuaded him to let you have a dose. So drink.'

Kirsty swallowed the sickly-sweet syrup and almost immediately felt herself get steadier, then calm.

'What's in it?' she asked. 'It's marvellous.'

'Alcohol and herbs. Secret as usual—but sure to include Diktamos, which the Greeks have always believed is a cure for everything. Captain Yiannis gets his supply from the witch we're going to visit. In return, he sells her love potions to the young and not so young.'

'What do you mean, "witch"?' Kirsty felt well enough to ask.

'Kyria Despina. She's a powerful white witch; she cures the islanders with her medicines and tells their fortunes. Yiannis told her that we were coming after I'd booked the tickets, and she said, "I know."'

'Look,' Kirsty said, pointing across the rough sea to a rocky headland.

'Gavdos. Climb up there,' he pointed, 'to the three-holed rock, and you will be at the end of the continent.'

'It looks so deserted and desolate.'

'It is, now. Once there were more than eight thousand people living there. Even had their own bishop. Now, apart from a colony of fucking hippies who camp on the beach in the summer, there are only forty or so islanders. Most of the houses are dissolving back into the rocks. Life was just too hard.'

Kirsty tried to picture what it must have been like to spend a winter in such an isolated spot. For some reason, she felt it would

149

have been romantic, with the storm seas cutting you off from the rest of the world as you held your lover and survived on whatever you could.

'I like it,' she said. 'I might come and stay here for a long holiday. I can sense something about it.'

Barba Yiorgos nodded. 'The Greeks lived here in classical times. Homer wrote about it. Some say it was the island of Calypso. Ha, one of the most wicked women in the world.' He made the sign to ward off the evil eye and spat three times into the sea.

'Wicked? I understood she was a goddess of love, and very beautiful.'

'Ha,' he scoffed. 'She tried to keep Ulysses for herself, when he was crossing oceans to return to his true love. Do you know what the worst sin is in this world?'

'No, not really. Murder, I imagine.'

'Bah! I'll tell you. To break up true love. Anyone who would come between two people who have fallen deeply in love is the most despicable person alive. To destroy God's greatest and purest gift is a crime that no atonement can pay for.'

Kirsty thought of her own weak marriage and knew she'd never come close to the love he was talking about. She also saw the deep sadness in his eyes. 'Are you telling me about something that you've experienced?' she quizzed.

'I've never been lucky enough to love like that; but I once loved someone who had.'

'Who?' Kirsty asked, thinking of Eleni and Patrick and what she'd recognised between them.

'Look, look!' he cried, getting to his feet. 'A dolphin! Now we're like Zorba in the movie. 'What sort of person couldn't love a dolphin?'

Kirsty had been staring at the same spot and there'd been nothing.

❧

After leaving the harbour at Karave, where Barba Yiorgos had insisted on stopping at the taverna for two glasses of tsikoudia, it felt to Kirsty as if they'd been walking for miles. He was perched on a dusty, black donkey, which a local had been delighted to lend, and she dutifully plodded, still slightly green from the journey, by his side. Everywhere, wild herbs burst out of the volcanic-looking landscape, their scent filling her every breath. In one place there was a strange, almost perfect circle of natural stones with a clump of bright red flowers right in the middle of the solid-looking floor. 'Look,' Kirsty said. 'How unusual at this time of year!'

Barba Yiorgos stopped his donkey. 'It's a threshing circle,' he said, seeming to ignore the flowers. 'An aloni.'

Kirsty didn't bother to tell him that she knew a little about the well-loved Cretan threshing circles. She had visited some, but guessed, as with the kazani experience, that what was on show for the tourists and what lay in the hidden heart of Crete were worlds apart.

'These were used for preparing barley and wheat for thousands of years all over Crete and here. Right up until the nineteen-eighties in some places. But that's not all these stone circles produced. Did you know that?'

'No.'

'Huh, I thought not. Flattening that floor took a huge effort by the whole village. Mixing the mud to coat it, then using donkeys and sheep to pound it down. I once saw fifteen beasts like this one used. Do you know the word for the process? Patoma. The same word used for the marriage bed. You better believe it, ha ha ha.'

Kirsty smiled and felt herself blush.

'In ancient times the circle dance originated inside them: the criss-crossing steps were used to separate the grain from the straw. Also, they were the birthplace of Greek theatre. Another thing you didn't know, hey?'

Kirsty shook her mass of hair and tried to imagine how this had happened.

'After the harvest, there were gifts to the gods and the celebrations. These became ritualised and evolved into the great tragedies performed in our ancient amphitheatres.

'Now you know. So much culture started on Crete. And do you know how the soulless bastards treat their historical alonia? They dig them up to grow more crap, or bury them under concrete for another fucking housing development! Always culture and corruption go hand in hand to keep Greece in the dark ages.'

Kirsty sighed and started to move.

Barba Yiorgos gripped her shoulder and held her. 'But they had another purpose once that's more pertinent to us. If anyone had a fight to settle, they would come and have it in the aloni after the harvest while the straw still padded the floor. This was the tradition and follows the myth in which the Cretan hero Digenis Akritas fought with the figure of death, Charon, in a marble aloni.

'Some think fighting to the death in threshing circles, alonia, is a Cretan tradition that pre-dates vendetta. Better than a bullet in the back, hey? I would gladly flee our enemy to this place, strip naked and sort our fight out in those stones with our knives drawn and the straw to soak up the loser's blood.'

'I only asked about the flowers,' Kirsty said, sensing that Barba Yiorgos meant exactly what he was saying and trying to lighten his mood.

'They are anemone,' he replied, 'the windflower. They were white once, until the blood of the dying Adonis, the god of desire, was spilled and they burst through the ground in the red you now see.'

'So much blood,' Kirsty said.

'And more to come if we stand here talking all day,' Barba Yiorgos snapped, digging his heels into the donkey's flanks and moving off.

Most of the houses they then passed were uninhabited and did appear to be dissolving back into the ground. Then they came to one that wasn't. This home was painted white with bright green shutters and climbing plants wrapping it in a flowery caress. A neat garden surrounded it with, Kirsty saw, many different herbs and vegetables growing.

Barba Yiorgos tied the donkey to the gate, and they went into the yard. Near the door a table had been laid. There was a pot of honey and a large bowl of yoghurt, some olives, dark bread and a jug of wine. Also, Kirsty noted, three glasses and three chairs.

Barba Yiorgos pulled one out for Kirsty, then sat down himself. After a few minutes, the door to the house opened and a woman stepped out. She was tall and stood straight-backed and firm. She was wearing a long, regal, black dress, and had silver hair plaited and hanging down the full length of her back. And though Kirsty knew she was very old, she was timeless. Ageless.

She made Kirsty feel safe and, at the same time, afraid. The momentary glance she cast over Kirsty had felt like a pulse of energy passing through her and exposing everything. Then she fixed her attention on Barba Yiorgos, who stared back defiantly for a moment, then began to wilt under the growing intensity of her gaze.

'Ah, Kyria Despina,' Barba Yiorgos managed, rising unsteadily.

'Sit down, Yiorgi,' she commanded, pointing a long, finger at him. 'I am too old and delicate-skinned to be kissed by bearded men. And if that filthy beast you've worn out carrying you here eats my favourite jasmine, I'll put a curse on you.'

Her voice was soft and alluring and immediately made Kirsty want to hear everything she had to say.

'So,' she continued, 'like your father, Kapetanios Michaelis, you have finally come to me. The last time I saw you, you were a child; now you're middle-aged.'

'Ha!' he snorted.

'And you are named?' she turned to Kirsty, her blue eyes burning intensely.

Kirsty felt something warm radiate through her as she whispered her name.

'Yiannis told me you were English, but I see you are not. You are Celtic.'

'I'm from the Scottish Highlands.'

'You'll find what you are seeking, in many things. I sense that strongly.'

Kyria Despina gave her a hard, penetrating look before continuing. 'I told Eleni and Patrick they had made a special friend, even if they were not yet aware of it. And I see I was not mistaken. Now you fear they are in serious trouble and are trying to save them, yes?'

'*We* are,' Kirsty said. 'Are they?'

Kyria Despina looked sadly at Kirsty and nodded affirmatively. 'First, I will tell you what they came here for. Yiorgos, stop acting so nervous and pour some wine.'

Kirsty watched as he filled the glasses and still wouldn't look at either of them.

'This is the most potent wine of all the Greek islands,' Kyria Despina said. 'So sip it slowly, my child.

'When the young couple walked into my garden, my heart, which has beaten for far too long, nearly stopped. Rossos had sent me a message about them, and even though I always knew someone would come, the notion that the time had finally arrived was almost impossible to believe. Then I saw Eleni and fantasy became fact. Before she even spoke I was transported back, over half a century, to the night when the Germans came and took her grandmother, Marianna.'

'Grandmother!' Kirsty interjected. She looked at Barba Yiorgos, who didn't appear even slightly shocked by this revelation.

'Yes. Such beauty and grace do not come to many, and she is the reincarnation of her grandmother, both in looks and spirit.

'They told me, though I knew, as soon as I saw her, what they wanted. Then Eleni read to me from the journal I once held but could never translate. She clung to the letter I'd sent back with her mother, telling the facts, voicing my suspicions, naming names. But most of all, warning the child never to return. As Eleni read, I was again in the village listening to a tale of joy and sadness. Marianna had recorded every moment of love—and, I'm afraid, hate and recrimination. I wept as I heard the things that had been said and done to her by those who'd despised her for falling in love and following her heart. But my tears were dried by how she had recorded her feelings of warmth towards me, my sister and Rossos.

'I made Eleni keep reading, as I didn't want to leave Marianna again. Then, as the final entries came, I heard what I already knew. That the family who'd despised her the most had invited her for a meal and given her a gift. A gift she was so delighted by, and one I sensed at the time was an act of treachery.'

Kirsty saw Barba Yiorgos and Kyria Despina exchange a cold glance at this.

'After Eleni had finished reading, I carried on with the story, saying a few of the things I'd not put in the letter.

'As Marianna had swung from that tree and the Germans left, I crept into the isolated house and took her daughter, Athena.' Kyria Despina stopped. And it seemed to Kirsty that the island itself held its breath, waiting for her to continue. Kirsty watched as Kyria Despina's eyes blazed with radiance then dulled and became moist.

'Athena!' Barba Yiorgos exclaimed, breaking the silence.

'Yes, Yiorgos, Athena. After the Greek goddess for wisdom and war. Appropriate for their lives and the times, I think. The Germans wanted the child dead and had left her to starve to death. I believe they'd been told to murder her, but unlike with Marianna, didn't know how to justify such an action and wanted to place the blame on the Cretan villagers. They'd stated, as with Marianna's body, that if anyone touched her they would be executed. While Rossos and my sister, Aliki, cut her mother down, I did my part. I also took the journal, a pile of letters and the gift she'd been so proud to receive.

'While Rossos made his escape, Aliki and I took the body and baby and held our solemn funeral. I knew I couldn't return to the village with her, so I carried Athena first into the mountains, and then to this island where my family had always lived.'

'Curing a boy's eye on the way,' Barba Yiorgos recalled from their meeting with Telemachus.

'A man who now sees clearer than most for my efforts,' she said, not acting surprised that he knew.

'Like Zeus, Athena was raised secretly in a cave. I loved her and whispered a greedy prayer asking the gods to let her be mine always.

'But I knew she had to go. There were far more dangerous and bitter enemies than any Germans to fear if she stayed. So with the help of the former Resistance fighters, we contacted the British. A young officer was sympathetic, and agreed to take Athena back to the address on Marianna's letters, which I knew were to her parents.

'I returned to Chania and left Athena at Souda Bay, being held by a stranger. She was calling out to me: "Yiayia, yiayia," until those words entered my heart and would stay forever. I told her grandparents in my letter never to let her return, or try to contact me, and that if she did, her life would be in danger. So I knew this was our goodbye.

'Now see her.' Kyria Despina took a framed photograph from the folds of her dress and placed it on the table.

Kirsty held her breath for a moment and heard Barba Yiorgos utter a long sigh. The woman was the spitting image of Eleni, though, if anything, even more stunning.

'Eleni brought this so I could see how my baby looked on the eve of her wedding. And it will lie in my grave, though I know my spiritual daughter will be there before me.'

'Before you?' Kirsty asked. 'What do you mean?'

'Athena is dying. She's in terrible pain with bone cancer. Oh, how I wish I could get some medicine to her, and pray there might yet be time.

'Eleni told me that Athena never stopped reading the journal and the translation of the letter I had sent. And, though she'd only been a baby at the time, she claimed that she never stopped dreaming of a kind lady in the cave. But more than that, she was haunted by what had happened to her mother and father and felt her life overshadowed by some terrible tragedy that had occurred and gone unpunished. Her pain, Eleni knew, was intensified many times over by this. And the strength she should have been reserving to fight her disease was being sapped by something beyond her power to resolve. And even worse, Eleni believed, her mother's spirit would never be at peace if something wasn't done.

'So her brave daughter came to find out the truth and carry it back before her mother died. Her mother thinks she and Patrick are taking a well-earned break, and only Eleni's father knows the truth about her mission, though he tried, according to Eleni, to do everything to dissuade her. And now?' Kyria Despina looked imploringly at Kirsty and Barba Yiorgos, waiting for one of them to speak.

'I think whoever was behind what happened so many years ago has kidnapped, and will, if they haven't already, murder Eleni and Patrick,' Kirsty said. 'I suspect it has to do with many things but I'm not sure. I also wonder'—she paused and looked directly at Barba Yiorgos—'who, if anyone, I should trust.'

Kyria Despina nodded her head. 'I can tell you that Eleni is still alive,' she said, 'at the moment. Though, as you suspect, the sands of time are running out. I cannot find Patrick's spirit and can only pray for him.'

She got up and walked into the house, then returned. 'This is for you,' Kyria Despina said, and handed Kirsty two phials. 'The yellow one is for your journey back. The other is to be sent home with Eleni when you find her. It will help my Athena and soothe her into her sleep. Now, Kirsty, I wonder if you would mind gathering some herbs while I talk to Yiorgos about a private matter.'

Kirsty felt herself flush, and was about to respond angrily. But she realised that she could—must—trust this woman, and whatever she was doing was for the best reasons, and not out of any duplicity.

'Of course,' she said, and left them.

The moment Kirsty was out of earshot, Kyria Despina spoke angrily to Barba Yiorgos. 'So why are you lying to this very special girl? Why does she not know about your father?'

'I swear, until now, I wasn't sure of the facts. I never knew about the fate of the child. My father said the Germans had taken her. How could I know Eleni was her daughter? When I saw her, and the likeness was unmistakable, though only in comparison to a photograph I'd seen, I couldn't, or maybe didn't want to believe the evidence of my own eyes. I even tried to convince myself that perhaps Marianna had a sister or other relative in England and the family likeness had come through. Anything, except face the truth. A coward, you see, like my father turned out to be. And a liar and stupid. But I promise I will try to put things right.'

Kyria Despina gave him a long, hard look. 'You deserve to feel this way, Yiorgi,' she said, then touched his shoulder gently, 'but there's still time for you. And your father told you the truth: nobody, not even Rossos, knew what happened to Athena. I kept her fate a secret and, until now, always have. I told you your father came. He was seeking her. I hid her and told him that she'd disappeared by the time we got back from burying her mother. I saw his heart break, but knew if Michaelis took her then—which he would have done—he wouldn't have been able to protect her. I swore to myself that as soon as Athena was safe in England I would reveal the truth to him.'

'But you never did!' Barba Yiorgos retorted. 'He went to his grave without knowing. As tormented by her loss as he was by Marianna's. How could you have been so cruel?'

'Because I told Michaelis something else that day. I told him Marianna's dying words: "My husband will avenge this."

'And after that, I waited for him to act. When he did nothing, my anger grew. I couldn't bring myself to tell him in case he still failed to act and the evil that had destroyed one innocent life took another. This evil, as you know, Yiorgi, has a long arm as well as a long memory. Believe me when I tell you that I agonised over keeping your father from his daughter, and his daughter from knowing the truth. But I knew I was right. Look what's happening now!'

Barba Yiorgos nodded. 'And you told Eleni and Patrick where Marianna's grave was?'

'Yes, and they promised to light a candle and place some lilies on it for me. I hope they did.'

'They did.'

She crossed herself. 'Some other things before you go, Yiorgi. Eleni hasn't come back just to find out the truth. You know that, don't you? She has the right to more than justice.'

He got up. 'Yes, but be assured in this: I will see this through, to whatever end.'

Kyria Despina stared hard at him. 'Beware greed, Yiorgi. It devours more than any hunger it has ever appeared to sate.'

'I've given my word,' he said, holding her penetrating gaze.

'Yiorgi,' Kyria Despina continued after a moment, 'the woman, Olga, who gave Marianna the gift that her granddaughter carries, still lives. She's returned to her family village in Sfakia. Now, I'm told, Olga is a widow and looks older than me. Aged by guilt, I suspect, over what she did. I sent Eleni and Patrick to find her, warning them that she may be watched and that it was a dangerous place. I see in my mind that that's where they were trapped.

'Olga needs to confess something. But not to any priest: to you. Or to Eleni, if she'd reached her. Now you must go and listen.'

Kirsty arrived back with a basketful of herbs.

'Well done,' Kyria Despina said, as Barba Yiorgos moved towards the donkey. She embraced Kirsty and said quietly, 'It was my words, not just those written, but those I sang from the cliffs, year after year for my daughter, that brought Eleni here. I am a seer, my child, as well as a siren, and you are in great danger, surrounded by lies and deceit. But much in this depends on you. I will use all my powers to try to help. Let your instincts guide you. And come back to me one day.'

15.

The phone kept ringing but Kirsty ignored it. She lay in her bed with the mosquito net trembling in the sea breeze. She knew it was Barba Yiorgos calling about tomorrow's visit to the remote Sfakian village, where the woman who'd betrayed Marianna lived. And where, if Kyria Despina was correct, Eleni and Patrick had disappeared. He'd told Kirsty that the woman, Olga, had moved there after the war, hiding with her dark secret. But then, thanks to Kyria Despina's warning, Kirsty suspected Barba Yiorgos had dark secrets of his own. And, worse, he was deceiving her.

On the voyage back, Barba Yiorgos said that he knew the village well. 'It's half-abandoned, dangerous and forbidding. I'm not surprised they got into trouble going there without a guide or protection. I wish they'd come to see me first.'

'Like me,' Kirsty replied cryptically. 'I just wonder why they didn't.'

Kirsty lay in her bed listening to the phone, recalling Barba Yiorgos's blue eyes staring back at the island with seemingly genuine concern and oblivious to anything implied in her retort. She wanted to answer it more than anything and have him assure her that everything was okay between them, but heard Kyria Despina warning her about deception.

She needed to think. As usual, she turned to the one person in her life who'd never willingly let her down: her father. She pictured him sitting on the bed and giving her advice. 'You must gather all the pieces together. Interview everyone and believe no one until you've had time to check their stories and balance the facts. Then, and only then . . .' Kirsty saw her father pause for dramatic effect before reaching inside his coat as if for a gun but pulling out his Mont Blanc instead, 'the top comes off and the moving pen writes . . .'

So tomorrow, Kirsty decided, she wouldn't go with Barba Yiorgos. Not until she had all of the facts and had done some balancing. There could, as far as she could figure it, be only one other person 'deceiving' her: Diomidis.

He'd tried to warn her about Barba Yiorgos and his father, and maybe she'd dismissed it too easily. What if he'd been telling the truth and, just because she—time to admit it, girl, she whispered to herself—really liked Barba Yiorgos, she had refused to listen? The facts her father would have collected stared at her: Diomidis's father, Panayotis, had made a daring escape from Aptera and was revered. Barba Yiorgos's father, Michaelis, had died a weak drunk and was in some way connected with Marianna and, therefore, Eleni. Barba Yiorgos might have his own reasons for wanting to find them—or for making certain she did not.

Had his father in some way been connected with the murder of Marianna? And with the betrayal of the other Resistance fighters on that day when he was 'sent' off to deliver a message and escaped being caught? Was this just another part of some ancient, unresolved vendetta between Barba Yiorgos's and Diomidis's families?

Kirsty ignored the phone and tried to draw a picture for herself before acting further. She was still a little undecided about who'd been Marianna's husband and Athena's father. But her first choice was the leader of the Resistance group, Lefteris. She formed a mental image of him: handsome and courageous. Kirsty imagined him gazing out across the turquoise Souda Bay, suffering from his torture wounds and waiting to die. She wondered if the Germans would have told him about Marianna. 'We have hanged your little English spy,' she heard them saying. 'But don't look so lovelorn: soon you'll be lying next to her again. In a lime pit!'

She couldn't help juxtaposing this terrible image against the expression on Barba Yiorgos's face that day at the church, when Kapetanios Theodoros had told him that he knew the men had been betrayed. She'd thought then that it was an expression of sorrow. But what if it had been one of surprise, that someone else might know of his family's treachery and dishonour?

Kirsty didn't want to believe it. The phone started ringing again and she almost ran to answer it and hear him deny everything. Instead, she picked it up and slammed it down again before he could speak. 'Some facts first,' Kirsty whispered into the dead phone. 'Then we'll talk.'

She stared at the mouthpiece, which was dangling just short of the floor like, she suddenly thought, a body hanging from a tree, and hurried, shivering, back to bed.

A short while later she heard her gate open and Burns greeting someone he knew.

'Kirsty?' Valentinos called. 'Kirsty, are you okay? Barba Yiorgos just called. He's worried.'

She got up and peeped through the window.

Valentinos stood in the middle of her garden. He was in his old-fashioned and very English-looking pyjamas with Burns in his arms. For a second, Kirsty's resolve nearly weakened. Then she remembered the saintly Kyria Despina's cold look at Barba Yiorgos when she told them about Marianna's joy at being befriended by the family who'd most despised her. What if it had been Barba Yiorgos's relatives offering the hand of friendship, so no suspicion might fall

163

on them? Maybe even Valentinos knew all about it—possibly the Gorilla was in cahoots, decrying Diomidis and telling her what a 'great man' Barba Yiorgos was, and having his son, Michaelis, doing work for her for free!

Kirsty opened the window. 'Valentinos,' she called, 'I'm fine. I've just got a terrible migraine. Please, tell Barba Yiorgos I'll have to cancel tomorrow's trip as these attacks usually last a couple of days. I'll get in contact when I feel better.' She closed the window before he could reply.

Kirsty returned to bed and thought over the conversation that night in Kolimbari when Barba Yiorgos had talked about the sins of parents, of atonement and revenge. 'What if you were still seeking revenge, and not atonement?' she asked sadly, stroking the blue eye of the mataki and praying it was not so.

∽

Diomidis hadn't seemed surprised by Kirsty's request for a meeting. In fact, he sounded on the phone as if he'd been expecting it. 'And about time,' he said. Then, sounding genuinely concerned, he asked if she wanted him to come to the kafenion or if she preferred not to be seen with him.

Kirsty wanted to meet him on his own territory, so went along with the latter suggestion. She'd been given directions to 'one of his homes' on the outskirts of Chania. She'd arrived at a neoclassical mansion that had been restored, ostentatiously, in her opinion. The views, however, were magnificent, and from the garden she could look down on all of Chania and the sea beyond to the horizon. A Filipino maid answered the door and led Kirsty through to Diomidis's study.

After she'd gone, Kirsty looked around the opulent room. The walls were plastered with paintings and old photographs of proud, regal-looking Cretan men in traditional dress. All of them heavily armed and clearly part of the countless struggles against occupation. One wall was dominated by a full-length portrait of Diomidis. He was also arrayed in a traditional costume, with two belts of shining, golden bullets crossing his black shirt and a large saita knife in his belt along with two pistols. In his hands he was holding a rifle engraved with scenes of heroism from Greek mythology. It looked, as did everything, brand new, and either hired or bought for this painting.

It made Kirsty feel a little sad for Diomidis, as she envisaged him struggling to live up to the reputation of his illustrious father. Something in his expression was mildly disturbing. Still, she decided, a little play-acting out of pride didn't make a person guilty of anything more serious. And yet, as she waited, Kirsty felt a huge pang of guilt overwhelm her and felt so disloyal to Barba Yiorgos that she almost fled. 'See it through,' she commanded herself.

Diomidis came in, greeted her warmly with a kiss on both cheeks and offered her a seat in front of his huge desk. As she sat, he moved and stood next to the portrait. He adopted the same pose for a moment. Kirsty watched as he then strutted to his desk and sat in a large antique chair, settling himself into what he obviously considered the correct attitude for this meeting. Kirsty wished again she'd not been driven to this.

'Well,' Diomidis said reassuringly, as if intuiting her feelings, 'I realise that you're deeply suspicious of me. So it's up to me to assure you that you've nothing to fear, unless you fear the truth.'

He raised a finger to prevent Kirsty from speaking.

'First, I will tell you something that you may not approve of. I have been watching you closely.'

Kirsty felt a shadow move across the room and the light and temperature lessen.

'But,' he quickly continued, 'only out of concern. Nothing else.

'I know far more about this matter than you do. But first, as a show of faith, I want you to tell me exactly what you've uncovered, or think you have. And let me warn you,' Kirsty heard his voice straining to make that word sound less threatening than it did, and failing, 'that I have more than "a thousand eyes and ears and tongues" working willingly for me. So if you've come here to play games, I'll know, and this meeting will be over.'

Kirsty swallowed before replying. She'd thought deeply about how much to tell Diomidis. Up until this moment her decision had been to keep quiet about most of it, but now she judged this as pointless. He undoubtedly knew their movements, and if he were behind anything that had happened to Patrick and Eleni, what harm could there be in telling him what he already knew? It might give her some information to help them. And, she reasoned, if he were innocent, then Barba Yiorgos was the deceiver.

So Kirsty told him most of it. Diomidis listened without interrupting, but was unable to hide his expression of surprise at several of the things she revealed, making Kirsty question her judgement and hold back some details after all.

'Well,' he said when she finished, 'you've been badly fooled and used, I'm afraid. I knew most of the story from my family's unfortunate involvement. I didn't know that Marianna's child had been saved and sent back to England. She vanished the night the Germans executed the woman, and no one, I believed, knew of her fate. And though I've fewer reasons than most to feel this, I'm pleased to know she survived. And also glad to know that my father's friend, Kyria Despina, is still living. I'll have to pay her a visit myself soon.

'I obviously couldn't have known about Marianna's granddaughter, or that she'd come here seeking some of the facts behind her parents' history. If I had, I'd have helped. Is she beautiful, as I'm told Marianna was?'

Kirsty felt the question was contrived and that he knew exactly what Eleni looked like. 'Yes,' she said, trying to keep the doubt from her voice. 'Stunning.'

'What a shame I never got to see her. When I learnt about this young couple straying into areas not suitable for tourists, asking questions about dangerous people, I was concerned. That's why I took the time and trouble to come and see you when I'd heard you'd befriended them. Then I saw, to my further disquietude, with whom you were sitting, and knew Andonis would be acting as Yiorgos's agent, poisoning your mind against me.

'After I was informed about the young couple's abandoned vehicle, I checked with my very close friend, the head of police. He was certain that they'd left the island and were safe. But when I heard about your enquiries and who you'd turned to for help, my heart sank. Both for the young couple and for you. Because I knew if he was mixed up in it, there had to be duplicity and crime involved. For gain or deception. An evil man from evil blood.'

Kirsty couldn't let this go. 'I'm sorry,' she said, 'but just about everyone I've met has great respect for Ba . . . for Yiorgos. He's troubled and wretched about a lot of things but not evil. I don't believe . . .'

'You are under his spell, one he has cast over many.'

Kirsty heard a real warning in Diomidis's voice and knew better than to contradict him, because he was doing something that Barba Yiorgos had never managed: he was scaring her. She looked past him at one of the pictures and saw the man who'd danced in her kafenion leering at her. She nodded compliantly.

'I came to see you once more, to warn you about Yiorgos, but I could tell, like with so many other unfortunate victims, he had you in thrall. I even questioned, briefly, if you might be in league with him. I was going to find out when you were without Yiorgos's thug, Andonis, or his spy Valentinos watching over you. But, of course, Yiorgos's son just happened to arrive and prevented me from doing so. However, I see you're struggling to break free. Better late than never—isn't that what the British say?'

Kirsty nodded again.

'Good. Then first I must disillusion you about several matters. This story is one that has, like so many myths on this island, a hundred versions. None of which is the truth. For Yiorgos has worked tirelessly and successfully to make sure that has been kept hidden. And I have been constrained by the pride and wishes of my late aunt, his mother, not to expose him. Even his brother, Nikos, doesn't know the facts about his father! But now, I am going to tell *you*. Your idea about Kapetanios Lefteris and Marianna is a romantic one, I agree, but the truth is not. Kapetanios Lefteris was a great and honourable man. He was also a faithful husband and devoted father. Marianna's lover—note I don't use the word *husband*—was not. Her lover was Barba Yiorgos's father, Michaelis.'

Kirsty felt the blow fall. And knew that this was the truth. And that Barba Yiorgos had kept this from her. Even worse, that instead of helping Eleni and Patrick, she'd undoubtedly put them deeper in trouble, maybe even cost them their lives. She felt devastated but carried on listening, sensing things were only going to get worse.

'Michaelis,' Diomidis continued, 'had, like his son would do later, lived for years in America. He was fluent in English, and so, when this beautiful girl arrived and stayed at his equally treacherous parents' guest house, he used his silver tongue to seduce her. Then he ran off with her, leaving his legitimate wife, my aunt, and his young sons, Yiorgos and Nikos. He managed to convince this innocent young lady that he was unmarried, got some drunken sot of a priest to perform a blasphemous ceremony, then tried to hide her away in a distant village where he hoped his lies would go undetected.

'My aunt was heartbroken. All my relatives were deeply shamed by what happened. But also, with their belief in loyalty and honour, they swore to right this wrong.'

Kirsty guessed Diomidis was talking about vendetta and was about to interrupt, when he changed tack.

'Some of my family lived in the village where Michaelis tried to hide her, and were so saddened by her plight that they tried to tell Marianna the truth. They had no English; she, very little Greek. Not that it would have mattered. She was young, in love, and by now pregnant. She put their kindness down to hate and jealousy.'

Kirsty couldn't keep a look of scepticism from her face.

'Michaelis was a liar!' Diomidis shouted, banging his fist on the table and making Kirsty jump. 'He even went to the trouble of making a will, convincing the poor girl that she would receive everything if he met his death. A will that would, if it still existed and came to light, disinherit Barba Yiorgos from the land he guards so jealously.'

The disconcerting expression that Kirsty had noticed earlier reappeared after he said this, and he continued quickly and loudly before something that sounded a warning in Kirsty's mind could develop.

'War was raging and Crete needed every good fighter. But my father, Kapetanios Panayotis, vowed that once the Germans were defeated, he would kill Michaelis for what he'd done to his sister and our family. And I promise you that if death hadn't claimed him far too young, he would have. He was a true Sfakian. As am I. And I will honour his pledge. But in my own way. I'm a modern man and we must learn to live in modern times. Soon, I hope to be mayor. When I am, I will pay Yiorgos back for his father's acts and for those he perpetrates now.'

Diomidis reminded Kirsty about what she'd told him of the meeting with Kapetanios Theodoros at the panigiri and what he'd said about a traitor. And how Michaelis had escaped the Germans.

'My father always knew that Michaelis had betrayed them for two reasons. One, like his son is, he was a coward, and knew the day of reckoning was coming and tried to get the Germans to kill my father before he had to face it. And two, he'd tired of his flirtation with Marianna and wanted to return to my aunt. He must have foreseen his life after the war, living with some foreign girl and their baby in a cold stone house, ostracised by decent people. He measured it against all the land and property he'd married into, and hoped to add to his own. More than enough motivation for a man like him to betray her, as he'd attempted to do to my father. As for his comrades? Nothing but sacrificial pawns.'

Kirsty sighed. All her images of this great love affair that had crossed decades and had been so treasured by Athena, and then Eleni, began to crumble as Diomidis's words wormed their way into her mind, which was already reeling from Barba Yiorgos's deceit over his father. 'What do you think has happened to the people I've been looking for?'

'Yiorgos is a very dangerous, evil man. He turned some of his family properties into brothels. He peoples them with teenagers from impoverished countries and keeps them fed on drugs. He has connections with the Russian mafia and has polluted Sfakia with drug plantations. If he thought your friends were getting too close to finding some damning evidence that might expose his father, or thought that that poor girl did have the will and a claim on his lands, he'd have no hesitation in dealing with them. Did Eleni mention that she'd any knowledge of the will when she had dinner with you and showed you her grandmother's journal?'

'No,' Kirsty replied. 'Could it help if she doesn't know about it?'

'It may, but I doubt Yiorgos will risk it.'

A worried look quickly crossed Diomidis's face and he looked nervously at Kirsty for a moment before regaining his composure. 'I suspect, sadly, that the young man may already be dead; the girl, probably not so fortunate,' he stated.

Kirsty shuddered. 'But why would he lead me along to meet the very people who might have revealed the things you're now saying? It makes no sense.'

'A smoke-screen, maybe. Or to see how much you knew. To cover his tracks and get rid of you or anyone else who might threaten him. I promise, soon I will put an end to his games, but now I must think of you. By coming here, and not responding to his calls, you may have alerted him. If so, he'll be desperate to stop you. He may even do something terrible to frighten you off. We have to decide on the best and safest plan of action.'

'Are you suggesting that I should go with him later today as planned, to visit the woman in Sfakia?'

'No,' Diomidis cried, getting up. 'That region is his lair. He has family and friends there capable of anything. His tribe's blood feuds and vendettas have torn the place apart and driven off half the population. I think you met some of them on their motorbikes the day you described to me. And that was just the periphery, a little taste of things to come. Incidentally, did he name the exact place and, more specifically, the woman you were due to meet?'

Barba Yiorgos had. But for some reason an image of Kyria Despina flashed into her mind, kind and wise, her silver hair let loose and blowing in the storm winds of Gavdos, repeating in a powerful voice the warning for Kirsty to trust her instincts. And she saw Eleni, and still couldn't accept that such beauty and grace had come from someone being portrayed as so evil. 'No,' Kirsty lied, 'he just said it was a woman whom Kyria Despina sent Eleni and Patrick to find. One who was connected with the death of Marianna.'

Diomidis's eyes burned into hers. 'There are a lot of villages and isolated houses, a lot of very old women in them. I'll have to see what I can find.' His look and voice softened, and he placed a fatherly hand on her shoulder. 'You have been very loyal, and your friends would be proud. Now I must do what I can.'

'So what is the safest way to go?' she asked.

'I suggest that you return to your kafenion and carry on as normal with *your* business.'

He raised his hand as she was about to protest. Kirsty noticed that next to the large gold rings and bracelets, his skin was as worn and gnarled as old olive wood.

'I'll get in touch with my friend, the chief of police. This time their tracks will be followed by *professionals*. And if we can't find them, or don't receive any news from my contacts in England about their safe return, I'll have Yiorgos behind bars for kidnap and murder. You've done your best. Now go and be patient.'

'Thank you,' Kirsty said, disliking this man as much as she liked his version of the truth.

'And when Yiorgos calls, tell him you've learnt all the truth about his deceitful father. Also, let him know you now have the protection of Diomidis. He'll be reluctant to cross me. I shall also instruct my sons to keep an eye out for you. They're brave and gentlemanly, not like the animal he raised. Now go and be assured that I'll do everything to find out what has happened.'

Kirsty thanked him again and went back to the kafenion to take over from Jane.

The moment Kirsty left his office, Diomidis picked up the phone and called one of his many relatives in Sfakia. 'Go,' he said, 'and give this message to my sons. Tell them the enemy is preparing to strike. To leave their little flock secure and come to Chania. There's someone here who's in desperate need of their protection.'

ॐ

Valentinos came into the kafenion later that day. Kirsty waited for the messages from Barba Yiorgos to be voiced, and had already made up her mind that she wasn't going to mention Diomidis.

'I hope your migraine is getting better,' he said.

'Much better. Completely vanished, in fact. And thank you for your visit last night. I thought your pyjamas were most becoming.'

'They were a gift from my daughter who lives in London—best quality, like the Greek coffee you make, and that maybe we'll drink together.'

Kirsty felt certain he was setting her up. 'Valentinos, I can't join you today. It's my classic film night and I must prepare food.'

'You British,' he said, as she hurried away after giving him his coffee, 'and your old films. So romantic, so sentimental.'

'Actually,' Kirsty called out from the little kitchen, 'it's an Agatha Christie murder mystery.'

A pulse of sadness engulfed her as she recalled all the things that had occurred since the last references to that author. Some great detective you turned out to be! Kirsty thought. Well, at least now she'd stopped playing the role, and if she'd done the right thing by going to Diomidis, matters were in the hands of the professionals. The 'if' echoed louder than the whispered thought, however, and a doubt grew on the periphery of her consciousness that she could make neither tangible nor quiet. Something about what he'd said didn't sit right.

'Murder mystery,' Valentinos said, appearing at the door. 'If only I understood English I'd come, eat popcorn and watch. There's nothing I like more than a good mystery. As does Barba Yiorgos.'

Kirsty waited for the inevitable messages and pleas.

'I imagine he'll be very sad that you couldn't accompany him today on the next step of the puzzle you were once so keen to solve.'

'He still went?' she asked, surprised and suspicious.

'Of course he did. Michaelis and Andonis have gone in your place; they're probably already there. Barba Yiorgos is a man of great resolve. That's why I sent you to him when you told me of your concerns. Still, I mustn't keep you from your film mystery.'

∽

The movie night was a relief. She'd sat at a table with some of her friends, eating popcorn in the crowded, darkened room, as the complications of the plot unravelled. At the end of the show Kirsty put on the lights. As she did, something from the movie—a clue that everyone had missed except for Miss Marple—flashed into her mind. Then it was gone again as everyone started babbling about the film.

A spark, though, had ignited a pale fire. It carried on burning after the last of her customers left. Something connected with a mistake—as in the film—that had betrayed the villain. It carried on smouldering after she went to bed, and was still there as her puppy started barking then went suddenly silent, and sleep finally came.

16.

After no replies from Kirsty, then Valentinos's report on her, Barba Yiorgos hadn't been able to sleep. He lay on his sofa with violin music playing as the sea sucked in and spat back the pebbles as if they were as unpalatable as the feelings he was trying to digest. As he clung to the photograph of his father with Marianna, he imagined Kapetanios Rossos supine under his lemon tree, longing to die. And for the first time in his life he wished the death owl would call on him.

Migraine attack, he thought; headache! He'd known plenty of women's 'headaches' in his life. But this one was a hundred times more painful than any sexual rebuff.

Barba Yiorgos guessed Kyria Despina had whispered the truth about him to Kirsty before they left Gavdos. Or that the history of Marianna and Athena she'd revealed was the final clue Kirsty had needed to see through his deception. He'd recognised Kirsty's intelligence from the start. So why had he tried to fool her? The only true answer he could find—though in his present mood he'd have happily accepted the more heinous one of greed—was shame.

How could he begin to explain the shame he'd felt most of his life over what his father had done and failed to do? To humble himself before a relative stranger and foreign woman by confessing that he'd been running for years to escape what was his duty? His excuse, 'I'm Greek, Cretan, Sfakian; you're not just from a different land, but in trying to understand these emotions, you might as well be from a different planet,' felt shallow in comparison to the trust Kirsty had placed in him.

He threw the photograph against the wall and heard the glass shatter. He thought of Telemachus shining his light on him and what he would see hiding in the darkness of his soul.

Dawn came: it was going to be a beautiful day on Crete. And as hot as hell where he was going.

Barba Yiorgos got up and looked at the table he'd laid, before Kirsty hadn't answered the phone. There was a vase full of flowers from his garden. His favourite hen had laid him two eggs and there was bread due to be delivered, fresh from the fourno. He'd planned to make a special breakfast for her before they set out. Now it looked desolate; worse, he thought, like a trap with pretty petals laid over a pit of spikes. The work of another would-be seducer like his father.

He went and sat in his chair and watched his beloved chickens. 'Kirsty,' he suddenly said aloud, 'I swear I'll bring Eleni and Patrick back if they're alive.' Then made another vow in silence before phoning his son and Andonis.

A short while later, a 4x4 Nissan pulled into his drive. Michaelis and Andonis got out. Both men were solemn as they approached. And, though cleverly hidden, as instructed, he knew they were carrying guns.

'Time to go,' Michaelis said, looking at his father, who was still in his canvas trousers, braces, and nothing else.

'What time is it now?' Barba Yiorgos snapped.

'Ten to eleven,' Andonis replied.

'I said eleven.' He stepped quickly into his house, touching with a slight joy the memory of when he'd done a similar thing with

Kirsty and heard her again demanding, 'Are you coming or what?'
He was dressed and groomed with a minute to spare.

❧

They drove in silence, quickly leaving behind the Crete most visitors
thought they knew. Barba Yiorgos understood that the real mystery
and heart of the place lay hidden beyond their reach. The ever-
expanding development was a thin carapace, no more intrinsic to
the Cretan spirit than were the Turkish forts, minarets or mosques:
just scars. The same as the Venetian walls and buildings: tourist
attractions. No one would ever conquer Crete: not with guns or
parachutists; not with cheque-books or velvet handshakes. Barba
Yiorgos had travelled much of the world and had seen that if most
of the countries had endured over the centuries what this island
had, they would never have got back up off their knees, let alone
be dancing.

He watched as the mountains began to rise and the ravines
deepened. Goats clung to the cliffs as if the laws of gravity did not
apply. Overhead a lammergeyer vulture floated in the thermals
looking for leftover bones to scavenge. Once, Barba Yiorgos had
liked nothing better than to spend solitary days in the mountains,
searching for herbs, sleeping under the stars, and marvelling at the
violence of nature that had created this landscape, and the stoicism
of the people who inhabited it.

Now he felt old and vulnerable. The place seemed barren and
hostile. He sensed the vulture's cold eye on him, and shivered.

'Turn that air conditioning off,' he ordered, 'I'm freezing to
goddamn death back here!'

'It's off, Father.' Michaelis looked nervously across at
Andonis. Not from fear of where they were going. Or what might
be necessary when they got there. But because both men sensed

177

Barba Yiorgos's anguish and anger and knew nothing was going to please him.

'Did you see the eagle?' Michaelis tried.

'It was a bearded vulture, you damn fool. Your mother would turn in her grave to see what we produced.' He cuffed his son on the ear, but lightly and playfully.

'When we get there, we'll have to move quickly, taka-taka, before that old bitch or any of her clan spot us. I want you to park at the bottom of the slope that leads to her home. I will go in alone. Andonis, you will stay by the truck and make sure nobody follows me. Michaelis, you will slip behind and guard the other way. If anyone tries to pass, stop them. If you see anybody in black carrying a gun, shoot them before they shoot you. But please, not a fucking priest. People are funny about killing them, even up here.'

'Is that where the British couple's car was found?' Andonis asked, pointing into a ravine. Michaelis pulled over and Barba Yiorgos looked down. He could see the scars left by the accident. The road they were on was straight and firm-surfaced. The only things that marked it were goat droppings and the stains of their urine.

'They'd have needed to be a little more than drunk to have ended up down there,' he stated. And a lot more than lucky to have survived and walked away! Barba Yiorgos suddenly chuckled. Andonis and Michaelis looked at each other, but knew better than to speak. Then he laughed loudly. 'They might still be alive. That stubborn, Scottish hellcat could have been right all the time.'

'Father,' Michaelis asked, 'how do you know?'

'They were never in that truck. If someone had wanted them dead, they would have been, with a nice little fire to make certain. And that "eagle" you just saw would have been dining out on bar-becued bones before they were found.'

He got back in the Nissan and they drove on. Soon they reached the village that Barba Yiorgos knew Kirsty had visited.

And he was absolutely convinced it was where Eleni and Patrick had stopped, and, probably like her, said the wrong thing to the wrong people. A lot of these villages were still as lawless as the Wild West. Once it had been rustling and gangs of bandits; now it was growing drugs and robberies with connections running from the corrupt local policemen to the Russian Mafia. Kirsty had just been luckier, he thought, staring at the kafenion and wondering why that might possibly have happened. He resisted the temptation to stop and give them some payback for what they'd done to her. 'Not yet,' he muttered.

As they climbed farther into the mountains, he got out his cell phone and kept playing with it, desperate to call Kirsty and tell her all his thoughts and emotions.

'I'm glad you've got used to the phone,' Michaelis said, watching him in the mirror, 'but it might not work here. The mountains can block the signal sometimes.'

'Then why did you buy the piece of crap for me?' he snapped, shoving it back in his pocket. But he was consoled by the thought that Kirsty might be trying to call him at this very moment and couldn't get through.

'Turn here,' he ordered a while later.

They left the road and began to follow a trail that might once have been an ancient highway but was now only the domain of goats, sheep and their shepherds. The first small settlement was quiet, with its dozen or so houses appearing closed for the winter. But Barba Yiorgos knew they weren't, and that they would have been seen.

The trail became what looked like the meanderings of a dried-up stream bed. But he knew it had once been well trodden, and still was by some.

'We're getting close,' he said, 'so be on your guard. If she's got wind of this, or any of her family have been forewarned, we'll have a welcoming committee. There are other matters that lie between us besides this. Ones still to be resolved. Look.' He gestured ahead to the village they were entering.

It appeared to Michaelis and Andonis as if some catastrophe had occurred without leaving the usual visible scars of its passing. No lava-encased corpses or layers of ash; no earthquake rubble with buildings torn apart by the belly-laugh of the gods of the underworld. Not even the modern, manmade version with bullet holes, burnt-out homes and the evidence of fresh-turned earth covering mass graves.

There were houses leading up from the track, melding and clinging precipitously to the mountains; others were on the flat ground, in rows of three and four, or detached. They ranged from small single-storey buildings to large wealthy-looking properties that might once have been merchants' houses or country retreats. Some were beginning to crumble; others appeared more recently restored.

All, though, had one thing in common: they'd been abandoned. Curtains hung, shroud-like in windows; furniture stood dustily inside. Outside, tables and chairs waited for another gathering as the bougainvillea and vines ran wild, entwining them in strangleholds and a thorny grasp.

'It feels like we've just boarded the *Mary Celeste*,' Michaelis said, peering into another empty house and almost seeing the family seated in the perfect still-life setting of their front room.

'More like Chernobyl,' Andonis said, as they drove on through the desolation.

'There are mysteries here,' Barba Yiorgos stated, 'stranger than any abandoned ship. And hatreds that will endure longer, and are more poisonous to life than any atomic particles.'

The pervasive gloom of the place held them in its silent spell as they continued through this heart of darkness.

Finally, the village petered out. Barba Yiorgos placed a hand on his son's shoulder and ruffled Andonis's black, curly hair with his other. 'Have I been a good father to you, Michaelis?' he asked in a quivering voice. 'And a good friend to you, Andonis?'

'What?' Michaelis questioned, as Andonis looked down sadly.

'Are you, even in a small way, proud of me? And no matter what I asked and did, would you trust it was right, and honourable?'

'You're my father,' Michaelis said. 'I worship you. I've never heard anyone mention your name without attaching due respect to it. And I would break their necks if they dared to do otherwise. I know I let you down sometimes, but it's out of weakness, not any lack of loyalty, I swear.'

'You've been a second father to me,' Andonis added. 'And I'd never question you or doubt anything you did.'

'Good,' Barba Yiorgos said, his voice back under control. 'Because there are many things to come and this is a good place to begin testing your resolve. Stop here.'

A narrow path led to a small cluster of houses. Smoke was rising from several chimneys, chickens ran around in yards, dogs began to bark, and the inevitable cluster of Cretan cats were milling about.

'Signs of life,' Andonis said.

'And the traditional Cretan welcome waiting, no doubt,' Michaelis added, trying to sound light.

'Get into your positions,' Barba Yiorgos ordered. 'And be doubly alert, because I feel we may have been tailed, or that someone already knows about this.'

Michaelis and Andonis looked surprised.

Barba Yiorgos got out and began walking towards the houses as Michaelis moved stealthily through the olive groves and Andonis stood on guard. Halfway there, Barba Yiorgos passed an old shrine, the light a mere jack-o-lantern flicker behind its smoke-darkened glass. Then he reached a second one, new, with a flame glowing clear and golden. He thought of the two lights shining across the Bay of Kissamou. 'Reconciliation,' he scoffed, tossing his head in contempt.

He entered the gate of the third house, sensing more than knowing that it was the right one. Jasmine and citrus pushed through cracks in the yard. The walls were painted in a fading pink that appeared to blush with shame in the afternoon sun. But, as he moved along the path, Barba Yiorgos smelled a sourness and felt a sadness that no amount of sweet scents or pretty colours could mask.

The door flew open just as he reached it and a woman he'd not seen since he was a child stood there. Then, he recalled, she'd been pretty; now she was, as Kyria Despina had said, badly aged. What should have been a sprightly old widow was a crone, bent double and wrinkled like a salt-dried olive. A bony, claw-like hand clutched a walking stick. She was dressed in thick black clothes and Barba Yiorgos knew that she would probably not take them off or bathe until spring came.

'You have your father's eyes, Yiorgos,' Olga said. 'It was Kyria Despina who told you of me, wasn't it? I've been seeing her in my dreams for weeks. What is it you want?'

'So many questions, Olga. But it's you who must answer mine.'

'I know,' she said, beckoning him into the house.

Inside, the only light was from a dull fire burning in a metal stove. It was a peasant's house, where once the animals would have wintered downstairs while the family slept above.

'Sit down, Yiorgos,' Olga said gesturing to a small table. She poured a glass of tsikoudia and put some split green olives in front of him before sitting close to the fire.

'I always knew that before my end, you would come,' Olga said.

He waited, knowing, as Kyria Despina had prophesied, that this was going to be a confession.

'I prayed for it so many times after my husband died. I begged, "Please don't let me go to the grave as he did, soiled and unpunished."'

'My sister passed away last month in the house next to this. She had a smile on her face the night before, played the mandolin and sang. She went to her grave with a heart full of love and purity. I could never tell her what I'm going to reveal, in case she despised me, or tried to share the burden.'

'Tell me then,' Barba Yiorgos said, half-expecting to hear the approach of motorbikes or the sounds of gunfire before the final pieces of this puzzle were revealed.

'When your father, Michaelis, and Marianna set up home on the outskirts of our village, there were some who resented them deeply. Especially my husband, Kostas. "You foreign whore, taking a good man away from his wife and child," he'd shout in his broken English every time he saw her. Then he would work overtime trying to turn others against her. I believed it was because he was related to your mother's family and, to my shame, I joined in.

'But Marianna didn't react. She just carried on smiling, trying her hardest to speak to us, and clearly deeply in love with your father and their child. My heart softened every time I saw her, though I dared not say anything. When Kostas went into the hills to fight, he'd warn me to keep up the hostilities.

'Then, one night after the Germans had occupied the island, Kostas crept back into the village. He was carrying a package. I briefly imagined he was bringing me a gift. Instead, he said: "Olga, I want you to befriend Marianna. I've been so full of hate for what I believed she'd done to Kapetanios Panayotis's sister that it blinded me to the truth. But now, after fighting alongside Michaelis, my eyes have been opened. I've seen too much hatred and death, and know there's more to come. I don't want to die, or see Michaelis die, and imagine that young woman and her child alone and unprotected."

'Yiorgos, I swear I believed every word. There were tears in my eyes, and I respected my husband for what he was saying.

'He handed me the package. Inside there was a delicate red silk undergarment with the most exquisite embroidery I'd ever seen. "A seamstress in Maleme made this," he told me. "Give it to her and say it's a gift from you. Then invite her to dinner on Friday, and I will do my best to see if Michaelis and I can slip back to join you." Then he kissed me before leaving. A Judas kiss, if I had only known.

'The next day I went to call on Marianna. She made me so welcome I could have wept for all the bad things I'd done and seen done to her. The house sparkled, the garden was full of pretty flowers and vegetables and her baby was beautiful and joyous. "For me! For me!" she cried in her poor Greek. I can still see her holding the red silk up to her cheeks and saying, "You're so kind, so sweet." Then, naughtily, "You wait until my husband, Michaelis, sees me in this!" And we laughed together.

'A few days later the Germans came and silenced that laughter forever. Nobody, I believed at that time, knew why. We presumed she'd been working as a British agent or that it was just another act of retribution against the Resistance, as she was with one of its leaders.

'Then after the war we moved and tried to make a new life. And though the baby I wanted so much did not come, things seemed fine. Then Kostas started acting strangely. He would mutter away to himself, or fly into uncontrollable rages and beat me, sometimes until I couldn't move. Other times he would disappear for days, then come back looking half-starved and refusing to say where he'd been.

'One day, after drinking heavily, he began sobbing and couldn't stop. I heard genuine sorrow, so I asked him what was wrong.

'"I saw Kapetanios Michaelis today," Kostas wept. "He was sitting in the garden that beautiful young woman made for him."

'I knew better than to ask him why he'd visited that accursed place, or why Michaelis was back there, as I already knew he'd returned to your mother.

'"Now the garden has become a jungle," he continued. "Michaelis didn't know I was watching him. Then, he refused to look up when I spoke."

'I said I understood, and we were all heartbroken by what happened to Marianna and their child. I assured Kostas it was the worst night of my life and I'd have done anything to have saved her.

'He began to laugh like a madman, rocking back and forth with his knees pulled up to his chin. Then he hissed, "Save her? You? But it was you who betrayed her."

'I screamed, calling him a liar and evil, risking any amount of beatings to deny what he was daring, even drunk, to insinuate. So he threw me on the floor and whispered his filthy-breathed tale, as if even the cats must not overhear the words.

'The Resistance were slaughtering the German parachutists. Shooting them in the air like pigeons, spearing them on pitchforks or caving their heads in with boulders. The women were taking the white silk to make clothes. So the Germans started dyeing the chutes red and issued an order that anyone found wearing it . . .'

'I know all this,' Barba Yiorgos interrupted, 'Telemachus at the Orthodox Academy told me.'

'But *I* didn't know anything about it at that time. I swear this on my dead sister's grave. In our remote village there was no silk, red or white. I believed I was giving her the hand of friendship, not the card of death. When Kostas told me, I was devastated and wanted to know why he would have made me do such a treacherous thing. "So you could help someone else give her to the Germans," he sneered.

'"Who?" I demanded. And his laughter grew even louder. "Someone you will never know; someone who gave other people away but without the need of your little silken gift."

'I couldn't even bear to look at him again. For the rest of his days, I would speak to him only if threatened. If he ever tried to touch me I went rigid.

'On his deathbed, he sent the priest to plead with me to go to him and hear something important that might make me understand what he'd done, and what had haunted his days. But I walked into the mountains, then to the little church, and lit a candle for Marianna, and didn't return until I knew he was burning in hell.'

'Did you tell anyone else about this?' Barba Yiorgos asked.

'Yes, the day after I heard this story. Your father. He was still, as I'd suspected, at the house where Kostas had found him. He looked terrible. I pictured him and Marianna as they'd been together and could hardly bear to disturb him. Then I saw the shadow from that ancient plane tree darkening the scene. It seemed one branch pointed a finger at me and I saw that poor, innocent naked body falling again and again and knew I had to speak.

'So I told him everything. He just sat in silence, his blue eyes burning with the same hate and loathing I now see in yours.

'I didn't ask to be forgiven, and knew that all my apologies and genuine sorrow meant nothing to him. How could anything, after what we'd done to his wife and child?

'I went back to my miserable life and waited. I knew he would come to honour her last words. Every step I heard in the night, every creak in the house had me preparing myself for death. My only wish was he'd kill Kostas first, so that I would know he had paid for what he'd made me do before I followed him to damnation.

'But he never came. And my husband died in his bed. Why, Yiorgos? Why did your father fail her?'

Barba Yiorgos couldn't answer.

'It would have been a blessing for me, because I've died a hundred times since. There have been many, many nights when the thump of her graceful body on that rope wakes me from my sleep, and I hear her laughter again, and see her sweet baby in her cot. Then, over and over, I hear the whispered words of my husband.

'That's how my days of remorse have been since he told me. I came to my old village to hide away and find some comfort with my sister. Now she too has gone. I suspect you have come to end my life. But every word I've told you is the solemn truth, and I will at least go to my grave with honesty on my lips.'

Barba Yiorgos got to his feet. The white handle of his father's large saita knife flashed red as it reflected the flames of the fire. The light caught Olga's eye and she bowed her head in readiness. He moved slowly towards her, then gently touched the back of her neck. He felt her stiffen and tremble and saw tears run down her wrinkled skin.

'I've not come to end your life, Olga,' he said, returning to his seat. 'I believe you. My father asked me to carry out the things he couldn't do, and I haven't done any of them yet. So I will do one of them now, and forgive you for any part in his tragedy. You have lived too long, paid too much already for someone else's sins. Also, although your husband was cruel and cowardly, he was controlled by a much stronger, more evil hand. I also believe if it hadn't been through your gift and the Germans, this person would have found some other way of getting rid of Marianna.'

Olga stopped crying and looked up.

'Marianna and Michaelis's child, Athena, was rescued, though,' he continued. 'She was sent back to England.'

Olga began crossing herself repeatedly and muttering a prayer of thanks.

'But there's more. Athena is very ill and her daughter and son-in-law came over to find out the truth for her. Now they have disappeared. A very courageous lady and I are trying to find them, if it's not too late. Kyria Despina sent them to see you, as she sent me.'

'But they never came. I didn't know. Who would hurt them now, after all this time? My husband is dead. I'm not afraid of the truth and would have told them.'

Barba Yiorgos pulled his chair close to hers and took one of her hands. 'Olga, this isn't about you or Kostas. I think the evil that moved then still moves, and *is* afraid of the truth.'

'Well, I'll tell it, then,' she said. 'If anyone has harmed Athena's child I will tell my story in any court they are taken to.'

'Olga, you're brave, but I don't think this will be resolved in courts. Now I must go. I sense things are moving rapidly and I have my own confession to make before it's too late.'

'When you find them,' she asked, 'will you bring Marianna's granddaughter to me, so that I can tell her in my own voice what I've just told you?'

'I'll do my best,' he said. He bent down and kissed her on both moist cheeks. As Barba Yiorgos reached the door, he stopped. 'Olga, Athena's daughter, Eleni, carried the red silk chemise with her, the same one you gave to her grandmother. She took it to Telemachus and asked about its history. He told her it was from the war years and had been made by an expert hand. I don't suppose you know who made it?'

Olga bowed her head again and breathed in deeply. 'Yes, Yiorgos,' she sighed. 'My husband was only too pleased to tell me, as I am saddened to tell you. It was your mother.'

❧

Later that day, as the first breath of darkness began to shrink the mountains and blacken the sea, another vehicle stopped near Olga's. A man got out. He was dressed in traditional Cretan clothes and blacker than the night. He needed no protectors to accompany him, and marched straight towards her house. On the way, as he passed the first shrine, he snuffed out its light, then did the same with the second. When he reached her door he opened it with a fierce kick from his heavy, black-booted foot.

Olga screamed and dropped the intricate, white lacework she'd been labouring on for many years.

'Olga,' Diomidis snorted. 'Two visitors in one day. It must be your lucky one!'

'Diomidis,' she said, 'such a long, long time.' Her voice quivered, but she was determined to be brave, as she had promised Yiorgos. 'Don't they knock doors in Chania, or have you just forgotten your manners since leaving the hills?'

'What did Yiorgos Casanova want? Not to pay court to you, now you're a widow,' he sneered. 'Or was it for a little family history? What did you tell him?'

'Everything I knew. And he told me a lot more.'

'Did he, now?' Diomidis moved closer.

'Something he didn't tell me, but I now know. The evil man who betrayed that girl to death was your father. He was a traitor and a coward.'

Diomidis clubbed her under the chin with the top of his fist. Her jaw broke and the sound of her mouth closing was as loud as a rifle shot. Olga collapsed onto the floor. He picked her up as if she were a rag doll and carried her to the top of the stairs. Then he held Olga upright with one hand and slapped her face until she revived.

'My father was a great man,' he raved, his eyes darting from side to side, spit flying from his mouth. 'A hero who gave everything to his family and country. You should have been as proud as your husband was, to serve and stay loyal. I even went out of my way to protect you a short while ago from unwanted visitors.'

'So it was you who took Eleni,' she slurred through a mouthful of blood, 'just as your father took Marianna.'

Diomidis looked into her dazed eyes. 'Old ladies, I always think, should have stair lifts.' He shoved her backwards and watched her spiral down the stairs. He descended and stood next to her crumpled body. A faint, wheezing breath rattled from her, then another.

'Damn,' he hissed. 'You tough old bitch.' Diomidis hauled her back up the stairs. This time at the top, he placed his hands under her armpits and heaved her upwards and outwards so that her head crashed onto the old beams and she fell to the flagstones without touching a stair, her black widow's weeds fluttering as impotently as the melted wings of Icarus.

Diomidis strolled into the early night. He stopped by the shrine, took out one of the oil lamps and relit it. 'Only fair to give you a decent send-off,' he said to the icon for Olga's dead sister, staring out at him wide-eyed and golden.

He returned to Olga's house and paused for a moment inside her door. He picked up the lace she'd been working on. 'Oh, the eternal web-weaving of these Cretan widows,' he gibed, laying it over her body, then tossed the lamp on top, igniting her funeral pyre.

17.

*D*iomidis's son, Panayotis, watched Kirsty's bedroom lights go out. He had been standing motionless, waiting for hours in the shadows. When he'd completed this little task there would be another long vigil, this time in the dark dampness of a garage, his brother, Leonidas, by his side. 'Go ruffle a little fur and feathers first,' their father had laughed, 'then we'll deal with the distraught owners. The two of you, bring Kirsty to our summer retreat. Then, when she's safe, I want you to take Yiorgos for a nice long swimming lesson.' And Leonidas had joined in the laughter. But Panayotis could not.

For the first time in his life he felt separate from his brother. They were watching each other day and night, neither trusting the other to be alone with Eleni. Both were waiting for the word, each desperate to make the first move. But Panayotis had already made it: he'd touched her as they locked her in one of the cells. Leonidas had been leading Eleni in from her morning toilet when she'd turned to try to run to another cell: she'd collided with Panayotis, who was tending to its inmate. As she did, he thrust his hand between her legs before his brother pulled her back. He was certain that his finger had entered her.

What was even more exciting, though, was that she hadn't shouted at him for doing it. Then, almost unbelievably, as he'd put her food out in the larger room, she'd smiled at him. 'Thank you,' she said, as he placed some cold meat, mizithra and salad on the table: her first words that weren't an insult or threat. Her look of defiance, arrogance and contempt was gone. He watched with delight as it returned when his brother arrived with some wine and got a toss of her head for his thanks.

Tonight, when he'd put her back in the cell, she'd deliberately stopped walking in front of him along the narrow tunnel, so he was forced to bump into her. As he did, Panayotis placed his large, six-fingered hand on her buttock and gave it a squeeze. Then, when she'd not pulled away or turned to claw him, he gave it a harder one and felt her quiver with excitement.

As Panayotis moved silently through Kirsty's gate, he recalled how firm Eleni had felt. Nothing like the Chania whores he and his brother usually visited on the last day of the month. Once, he'd looked forward to that experience for days. Now, the thought of their fat, blubbery bodies and hard, dead faces disgusted him. He knew the only thing that would ever satisfy him was Eleni. He even began to dream that he might steal her away and find someplace where they could hide. And if the wrath of his father and family followed them, then he would fight them to the death. He imagined the tears running down Eleni's beautiful face as he fell trying to protect her, and how she would follow him into the grave rather than let them take her.

The dog began to bark. Panayotis moved with lightning speed and stunned it into silence with a punch. He froze and waited to see if its barking had alerted anyone. When the lights remained off, he took one of the small nooses from his pocket and slipped it around the unconscious animal's neck. He tied the other end to the branches of Kirsty's pomegranate tree and dropped the dog so it fell several feet. The impact snapped it awake, so it began to kick and writhe as it died, the leaves and fruit shaking as if a strong gust of Cretan wind had entered the garden.

He'd wanted to kill the cat first, as they were always more of a problem than dogs and had too many bolt-holes if spooked. Once again, he waited and fantasised about Eleni. Then he sensed the cat coming, slowly, as if its instincts had already detected something wrong. Then curiosity really did kill the cat as it looked up at its friend and turned to flee. A minute later, another wind, a mere zephyr this time, stirred the leaves as Panayotis closed the gate, leaving a few drops of his own blood on the latch, and loped off into the Chania night.

While his brother was slaying pets in a cosy little courtyard, Leonidas was creeping along the sands again, but with no dancing and no effigy to carry: just his long steel needle and death in his heart and mind. He saw that the results of his last visit had been washed away by the sea. There had been a storm last night, he recalled, booming and bellowing in the mountains and through the rooms and tunnel of their hideaway. He'd wondered then if Eleni was sleeping. His brother had been pretending to snore, Leonidas knew, trying to lure him off his guard and sneak down to her. Now he sniffed the air, like any predator seeking its prey, and moved quickly to Barba Yiorgos's garden.

The chickens were warm and snug in their pen. Leonidas compared them to the ones they kept. Even in the dim interior of the railway carriage, lit only by a hunter's moon, they looked magnificent. For a second or two, he wished that for the first time he could disobey an order and take these home. But he knew he would never do that. Family duty and honour were everything to him. He was the true son of his father and grandfather, he knew, lifting the first bird.

It didn't move: he guessed they were used to being petted. It died with a tremble as light as its own feathers. Normally, he would have been disappointed not to have felt more of its pain. He loved that desperate, still-unbelieving struggle to cling onto what was being taken. But he knew it wouldn't have mattered however hard it had died. It would have seemed flat in comparison to what had been recently haunting him.

Leonidas's yiayia used to read to him from the works of Cretan writers, both old and new. One passage from all the books stood out. It was from Kazantzakis's Freedom or Death. The great Cretan fighter against the Turks, Kapetanios Michaelis, seduces the mistress of the ruling Turkish Pasha because she's been sleeping with another fighter and member of Michaelis's family. As she lies next to him on her silk sheets, he plunges his knife into the whore's heart. With each thrust of his long needle, Leonidas felt a frisson of sexuality and excitement pulse through him. Every day for the last week, he'd watched through his spy hole as this English whore washed herself. Her perfect body was exposed to him as she wasted more water in a day—though it was ice-cold and drawn from a well—than he and his brother used in a month. 'For what?' he whispered each time he watched her. 'To ensnare or seduce who?'

The last chicken shuddered and went limp. When that woman had to die, he desired more than anything for it to be by his hand. He wanted to lie next to her, having satiated himself fully and brutally first, then plunge his dagger up through her ribs into her heart, and feel her life drain away as she realised the depth of his contempt.

He hanged the chickens from the branches of a lemon tree, then went to collect his motorbike, full of determination, pride and resolve.

Strange fruit hanging from the poplar trees. The words from that song kept coming into Kirsty's mind as she drifted in and out of sleep and odd shadows moved slowly on her wall. She turned away and let the early morning sun wake her fully.

The phone began to ring. She looked at the clock: it was half-past seven. 'Time to get up anyway,' she sighed, and moved to the phone table next to the window.

'Kirsty,' Barba Yiorgos began, 'check your pets. They've . . .'

Kirsty looked through the window and cried out in shock. Then shouted into the phone: 'You bastard! You evil old bastard!' She dropped the phone, heard his dry voice crackling through the mouthpiece. She stood frozen for a moment staring in disbelief at the bodies of her pets, her children—the ones she could never have—dangling from a tree. 'Snap out of this,' Kirsty ordered herself and ran, still naked, into the garden.

After she'd cut them down and covered their poor broken bodies with her favourite tartan rug, Kirsty threw on a robe and went to the phone. Diomidis had warned her that Barba Yiorgos might do something terrible. And she had doubted him. Even held things back from him. 'Even phoning to make sure and gloat, you evil, wicked old man,' she cried out. The door! Kirsty suddenly thought, rushing to lock it, half-expecting his monstrous son, Michaelis, or the Gorilla to arrive.

She sat on the chair next to the phone trying to calm herself before calling Diomidis. He would come running to her rescue and have Yiorgos in prison before the day was out. She couldn't wait to see him in court. Kirsty began dialling. Then her finger stopped before it pressed the last button. The spark that had been smouldering all night since the end of the film ignited with a force that nearly threw her off the chair. She dropped the phone for a second time, with a shock even greater than the first.

Miss Marple had found the clue: something the guilty person had said that he couldn't have known.

Kirsty had heard it and missed it. Worse still, her stupidity had let the vampire in.

She'd always had a photographic memory for things people said, often to her regret, as when she caught them out in a lie and could no longer trust their words, or think of them as friends.

Now the memory of Diomidis's words shouted and echoed in her brain with a cold, undeniable reality. '*When Eleni showed you her grandmother's journal . . .*'

But Eleni hadn't shown it to her. Kirsty hadn't mentioned anything about the journal or letters she'd glimpsed when she'd been shown the red chemise. In fact, she didn't even know for sure that it was a journal. Or have the slightest clue it was her grandmother's.

Kirsty felt a hammer blow of understanding jolt through her. The only way Diomidis could have known about it was if he'd taken the journal when he had Eleni and Patrick kidnapped or murdered. It had probably been right there in his desk while she'd sat in front of it, betraying Barba Yiorgos.

She recalled the look that had crossed Diomidis's face when he'd said those words and asked about the will, and how quickly he'd changed the subject. He'd realised his mistake, and was clever and crafty enough to know that even though he hadn't been seen through then, eventually he might be. She imagined him brooding on what action to take, and the answer she judged he'd been likely to come up with made her shudder.

Kirsty stood at the window peering down at the two little bundles below, cursing herself. 'Your father would be ashamed of you,' she sighed. 'You played straight into his hands. You gave him all the information he'd probably been looking for. If Eleni and Patrick weren't dead before, you probably just signed their death warrant, as well as your own and God only knows how many more.'

Something else came to her as she stood there muttering self-recriminations. Everything Diomidis had told her about Barba Yiorgos's father had been a reversal of the truth. Panayotis had betrayed his comrades to take his revenge on Michaelis because he was a coward. He'd set the Germans onto Marianna. They'd let him escape that night in payment for the Resistance fighters' lives, no doubt with some bargain made about future deals. Or to make sure there were no claims on any property from Michaelis, Marianna or their daughter.

Kirsty remembered Diomidis fussing over Burns the first time he'd visited, saying there was nothing more important than the family's honour. 'Honour!' she'd sneered. 'Kapetanios Michaelis's will, building developments and greed, your only motive.' There was more honour in Barba Yiorgos's little finger. And she had no doubt that if the whole story were known, his father would have been the same. And she'd just called him an evil bastard!

Kirsty had to speak to Barba Yiorgos. She grabbed the phone, praying he'd still be there. It rang and rang. As it did, she thought of Eleni and Patrick. They must have had enough information to figure out who'd been behind Marianna's murder and had come looking for some justice for her dying daughter. Maybe there was information about the will in it as well. Clearly not the will itself, since Diomidis was still looking for it. They'd got too close and Diomidis had pounced.

He'd been playing cat and mouse with her and Barba Yiorgos ever since, biding his time. Some warning told her it had arrived.

'Yes?' Barba Yiorgos's voice sounded soft and sad.

'Oh, Barba Yiorgos, I've made a terrible mistake. I went to Diomidis: I told him everything. I now know it was him. He let slip that he knew about Marianna's journal. I've let us all down.'

'Kirsty,' he said, his voice firm. 'Thank the gods you're safe. I made the terrible mistake by not being honest. I suspected who was behind it all along. But on my word I didn't know. All I had were the bits of the story my father had given me. It wasn't until we followed the tracks of Eleni and Patrick that I had the pieces to complete the mosaic we once talked about. Yesterday I got the last piece. And I would have told you the truth if you'd been with me.'

'Barba Yiorgos,' Kirsty sobbed, both for his words and for what had happened. 'He killed Burns and Diego last night. Hanged them from my tree.'

'He had all my beautiful chickens slaughtered last night, too. Diomidis is trying to instil fear in us. Frightened people are easier to beat. And I sense he is ready to close the book. I believe that Eleni and Patrick are still alive, just. I think he's been keeping them hidden to see who would look for them, and what they might find out. As long as we're out of his grasp, they may survive. But time is running out. You must stay calm.'

'I will,' Kirsty said, feeling her strength returning as she heard the power in his voice.

'Do you remember the house in Kotsiana?'

'Yes,' she said, thinking back to that night and, even with what was happening, how easy she'd felt in his company.

'I'll be waiting. Then we'll make a plan. Also, there's an old map of my father's that I *must* find and a place, lost to my memory, that I pray is marked on it.'

'No.'

'What do you mean?'

'Barba Yiorgos, I must bury my animals first. I can't bear to think of them lying there with flies walking all over them.'

Barba Yiorgos snapped her out of her sentimentality. 'No! Move now! If not, you and your young friends will be feeding the flies shortly. Diomidis normally likes to keep hidden and we have forced him into the open. He's a sadistic coward who will happily see us, and Eleni and Patrick, suffer torture before killing us as payment for crossing him. Valentinos will bury your pets. There's little time left. So no more arguments. Just flee!'

Kirsty felt herself grow cold at the certainty in his tone.

She hurried, washing in cold water and putting on jeans, a thick shirt and a quilted waistcoat before stuffing a large bag with clothes and basic toiletries.

Kirsty called Jane and told her she had to fly to Scotland immediately to visit her mother who'd fallen ill. She took a final sad moment to bid her friends farewell, brushing their lacklustre coats. Her tears refused to flow and she was determined to stay angry. 'Sorry, babies,' she whispered and slipped into the narrow streets of the village.

A mist was licking its tongue up the road from the sea, shrouding and soaking everything with its salty kiss. The early morning sun had become a cold white glow, as if its fire was being extinguished and a new ice-age was coming. Kirsty hurried to get into her car.

Her parking space in Valentinos's garage area looked equally spectral, with all the usual dark corners more hidden than ever. The damp smell was heavier and holding some animal scent in its weight. Like a cave, Kirsty thought, as she entered. Or, the word came unbidden, a crypt.

She hurried through the gloom, put her bag in the boot and had just reached the door when a movement shattered the silence and made her leap with fright.

'I'm Panayotis,' a hard, grating voice announced arrogantly. An immensely tall figure, blacker than anything in the building, stepped from the shadows. The knots on his sariki hung down below his eyes and his moustache was long and drooping. Kirsty saw the cruelty and brutality in his eyes. She tried stealthily to push the button on the car door. 'Someone,' Panayotis mocked, watching like some raptor hovering over its twitching prey, 'thought you might be getting ready to bolt. Scurrying off to the arms of that piece of shit, Yiorgos. How romantic!'

Kirsty took her hand from the door and made up her mind to go rushing into the street, yelling her head off. She was a fast runner and could scream with the best of them. Barba Yiorgos had just said Diomidis liked to keep his crimes hidden, so maybe his son wouldn't follow. She tensed.

'Naughty, nosy girls, who tell lies about our family, must be punished,' another, similar voice hissed.

This one seemed to come from above and near to the entrance. As Kirsty looked, another huge, black-clad figure dropped from the roof girders, where he must have been clinging like a bat. The man landed with agility and spiralled a full circle before facing her.

He was a slightly smaller version of the man who stood behind her.

'Now we'll have that dance you refused me,' Leonidas sneered.

Kirsty fingered the keys so the ignition one was ready. 'Valentinos,' she bellowed at the top of her voice and stared past Leonidas. He turned with the speed of a snake and his brother rose even taller. Kirsty moved, opening the car door, leaping in and closing it in one movement. She had the lock down as Panayotis grabbed the handle. He yanked it so hard that the car rocked violently and Kirsty's head hit the side window. She swivelled elegantly to the right and confirmed the other lock was down before he could reach the other side. 'Thank you, Mother,' she whispered as he tugged on the other door, 'for all those pointless ballet lessons.'

Kirsty got the key in the ignition while the two men joined each other and stood in front of the car, as if their physical strength could stop it moving. It might, she thought, but she doubted it. It was a sixteen-valve powerhouse and she knew how to drive.

'Right, you murdering bastards,' Kirsty snarled, 'see how you like this.' She turned the key, her foot on the clutch, the gear engaged and ready to hit the throttle and wheel-spin through them.

Nothing happened.

She tried again and again. The ineffectual whirr of the starter motor sang a pathetic song. She looked out of the window. Both men were beaming with delight. Leonidas drew something slowly from behind his back. A set of spark-plug leads dangled down from the distributor cap. For some stupid reason it made Kirsty think of the octopus left hanging to dry outside the fish restaurants on the Nea Hora seafront. One of the fishermen had told her that they could escape from virtually anything. The smallest hole or crack and they'd squeeze through it.

Kirsty knew, as the figures began to move, that there was no such possibility for her to do likewise.

Leonidas tossed the leads away and dissolved into the mist, while his brother moved menacingly towards her. Kirsty cowered as he reached the front windscreen and leered in. She screamed as he threw a punch aimed at her face. There was an explosion and a hailstorm of glass crystals sprayed her with their cold sharpness. Kirsty tried to clear her eyes and face as she waited to hear the click of the lock opening.

Instead, a hand reached in and grasped the front of her shirt, squeezing her breasts together so she cried out in pain. Then he tore her back out through the opening with a series of brutal tugs, banging her hard against the steering-wheel until she was free. She felt the glass grinding into her and the bonnet as he swept it clean with her body.

Panayotis lifted her off the ground with one hand. He held her so their faces were only inches apart. For a moment she thought he was going to kiss her. Then he pushed her away and his other hand came into play, swinging with a roundhouse punch. The pain jolted through Kirsty like an electric shock and she tasted concrete. Then there was nothing.

18.

An atrocious place he'd once visited. Scarred by the madness of a family divided. Barba Yiorgos stood on his roof terrace at Kotsiana, anxious for Kirsty to arrive, and searching his mind trying to find it again. Some nagging voice told him he must. Downstairs, his house had been ransacked, not by any intruders, but by his desperate search for the map. He'd found nothing. And though the memory of his visit was still clear, its location was not.

His father had taken him. An early lesson, before the ones about an English woman, an illegitimate daughter, a grave, betrayals and dishonour.

'I want to show you something, Yiorgos,' his father had announced. 'So some day you might come to understand just how far people can grow apart, even when they're joined by blood and brick.'

Barba Yiorgos looked at the road leading through the village, then at his watch again. Kirsty should have arrived by now. He lived a lot closer to Kotsiana, and had double-checked she'd left by ringing again when he'd arrived. He'd even tried her cursed cell phone and got some stupid 'Caller unavailable' message, whatever that meant. So where was she?

'Keep calm,' he ordered himself, and returned to his search.

It was so long ago but he could still recall the lesson he'd learnt.

'See that bridge,' Michaelis had said, parking the Land Rover, after driving through a maze of tracks and through a fast-flowing stream. There was a narrow, arching bridge spanning a deep ravine. The middle had been destroyed. 'A German bomb did that and nobody will ever repair it.'

'Is that what you wanted me to see, Baba?'

'No. The Venetians built that bridge to lead prisoners to what is hidden in the cliff, as did the Turks after them.'

'A prison, Baba?' Yiorgos asked excitedly. 'In the rocks?'

'Yes. A gloomy set of dungeons and a torture chamber, with a secret tunnel leading down to the beach. Over the centuries it has tasted much blood and heard many cries of pain and anguish. The Resistance used it during the war as one of their hideouts and a place to keep German prisoners. Even General Kriepe spent a cold night there once. It's an evil place full of foul memories and bad dreams.

'But that's not what we've come to see. Look there.' He'd pointed down an incline to the bottom of a small cliff face. There was a huge pile of stones that appeared to have fallen from the cliff, but Yiorgos saw they'd been cut and shaped, and had once been a house. 'Your Uncle Panayotis has just bought that and is going to restore it, for some reason. And, unlike the previous owners, he knows what lies behind that house. So maybe he'll restore the prison too, and lock your poor old Baba in it!'

'But you know the tunnel—you could escape,' Yiorgos had said, understanding even at his early age that the two men loathed each other, and that behind his father's joke lay a bigger truth.

'Of course I could. Anyway, once a mother, father and two sons lived in that house. They kept livestock and grew olives. Then the parents died. The brothers carried on living and working in contentment. Until one day, after their usual visit to the market in

Chania, they went to their favourite taverna. Only this time instead of souvlaki and Tavli, there was a woman.

'Two silly goats and a cunning fox. Ah, it happens. But after she'd played her games and tired of the brothers, each blamed the other for what had happened. "She would have been my wife if you'd stayed away," one raged. "No, mine," his brother replied. "You ruined my chances with your jealousy."

'They fought with their tongues, then fists. But it resolved nothing. Then they went for silence. Even that was not enough. So they cut that house in half. A perfect split divided by a wall they built together, running right through its middle. Each stone laid in silent bitterness. They also stole bits of each other's half. A stone here, a beam of wood there, whatever.

'The brothers grew old and didn't care that they were a joke. "Hey," someone might yell as they sat in the taverna at their separate tables after market day, "what's it like to put your arse on half a toilet seat?" Or, "How many eggs can you get in half a frying pan?"

'Nothing mattered to them except their hatred. It was as tangible as the mountains, and just as unmoveable.'

Michaelis looked down, and Yiorgos pretended to know what his father was trying to tell him.

'One day,' he continued, 'with a storm thrashing the sea and turning it to the colour of squid ink, one of the brothers became ill. He lay in his bed, his heart flickering like the flame of a spent candle. "Brother," he called, tapping on the dividing wall. "Brother, I'm dying. Help me."

'His brother let him call again, just to make certain his voice was growing weaker and it was no trick.

'When he was certain, he replied. "Oh yes," he cried through the wall, "I'll help you!"

'He thought all the waiting had been worthwhile. He'd won, and couldn't contain himself, or even bother to step out into the rain. Instead, he grabbed a pick and began to smash down the wall they'd built and strengthened over so many years, shouting as he hacked his way through, "Now I'll be avenged for what you did. Avenged!"

'But suddenly, at the very moment he broke through and looked into the startled eyes of his brother, who saw not the Grim Reaper but his mad sibling coming through their sacred wall, the house fell, burying them both. With all the things they'd taken from each other's sides of the property, that wall had been the only thing of substance left.

'Under those dry stones are dry bones. Buried by the weight of a stupid hatred and revenge over nothing. So many killings on this island are about nothing more than trivialities. Sheep grazing on the wrong grass, disputes over property and inheritance. But sometimes there is nothing trivial about vendetta. Sometimes the cycle of blood must flow. Do you understand me, Yiorgos?'

'Yes,' he'd said, though he didn't, being far more interested in the prison cells and torture chamber. And most especially, the entrance to the secret tunnel, which he'd managed to nag his father into showing him before they left.

Now he was trying to find it again, and couldn't. He knew that if Panayotis had died before restoring the place, Diomidis would have completed it. It was an evil place once; and would be now. And he sensed that if Eleni and Patrick were anywhere, they were there. But it was so long ago. And he couldn't concentrate. 'Where is Kirsty?' he kept asking, as he tried in his mind to follow another road snaking around a mountain, or a track leading through an endless forest of olive trees.

The phone rang and he rushed down the stairs.

'Barba Yiorgos,' Valentinos gasped, 'I've failed you. I've failed Kirsty.'

'Tell me,' Barba Yiorgos snapped.

'After I buried Kirsty's pets, I went to my garage to feed the cats. Kirsty's car was still there, but the windscreen was smashed and there was blood smeared on the bonnet. They've got her. You told me to watch over her. I promised and I've failed.'

'No, you've not. I should have sent Michaelis and Andonis to collect her. I knew it. It's my fault.' Barba Yiorgos hung up.

He looked at all the things he'd thrown around in his search for the map—a montage of his history held together by memories, the one he most wanted missing from the picture.

'Where?' he shouted, more desperate than ever to find the location of that accursed place.

Nothing came. He sat down and could have wept. Then, against his will, his eyes began to close, and his head felt as heavy as a rock. He felt himself leave his body and float, looking down at the sleeping figure, then over an ocean. Kyria Despina stood in her kitchen stirring two large cauldrons of potions.

'One to inspire courage, Yiorgi,' he heard her say. 'One to clear the mind and aid the memory.' Two tastes touched his lips and he jumped awake. First, he saw Kirsty as she had been that day at the Monastery of the Golden Step. Then, he saw the pile of stones, heard the rushing of water, tracked the lanes leading from the road, and knew exactly where the place was. And exactly who was there. And exactly what he needed to do.

But then, like his father, he'd known what he had to do for most of his life and hadn't done it. He decided to at least come out of hiding and return to his beach house.

Then . . .

19.

Kirsty was in a coffin. That was her half-waking thought. They'd buried her alive. She was about to start shouting and clawing when she felt a shudder, then a jolt that bounced her upwards so her head hit the wood above. She tried to stretch out her legs, because they were hurting worse than her face. Only she couldn't, because this 'coffin' had been made for a dwarf who stank of goat.

Kirsty began to heave. She detested the smell of goats. Now, as the vehicle careered along, the cloying, musk-ridden stink was oozing into her clothes, hair and skin.

They stopped moving and she heard a door open. Kirsty tensed herself and waited to be exhumed and finished off. Then the door slammed and they were moving again. Faster and over rougher ground. She felt every boulder and hole in the ground, and the few seconds of smooth road began to feel as sweet as her favourite reading chair.

Kirsty heard a hissing explosion of water, felt its icy touch begin to seep into her crate, and imagined it rising and filling her nostrils and mouth. Then they were climbing so steeply she was thrown back as if experiencing the G-force of a jet plane. Next they dropped just as steeply, before the vehicle came to a halt with a vicious slamming jolt.

This time two doors opened, and Kirsty heard the voices of the brothers approaching. Her 'coffin' was opened roughly and she blinked, trying to adjust to the sudden shock of light, and get some understanding about where she was and what was happening.

Panayotis dragged her out of the crate, which she saw was in the back of the ubiquitous red pick-up truck, along with a motorbike and animal feed. He pulled her over the tail-gate and dropped her to the ground. The two men stood towering above her as she tried to get some feeling back in her legs and rise.

A short way from where she was wriggling—bloodied and bruised, but not broken, if that's what they imagined—there was a strange-looking house. It appeared to have grown out of the rock behind it. She saw that there were no electricity or telephone lines. And that there was a well, with a bucket roped above it.

'All the mod cons,' she whispered to herself, trying to stay brave and deny the pervasive feeling of gloom and despair emanating from the place.

'Come on, bitch,' Leonidas spat. He hauled her up by her hair. 'There's someone in our little parlour who's dying to meet you. Or maybe just dying.'

Panayotis opened the door and Leonidas shoved Kirsty into the house so hard that she went down on her knees. She used her hands to stop going farther, then wished she hadn't. The flagstone floor felt like flesh and she slid in its putrefaction.

'Jesus,' Kirsty said, getting up and not wanting to look at her hands or knees, 'you boys sure do keep a tidy home.'

Leonidas pushed her again, 'Sit,' he ordered, pointing to a long, dark, wooden bench that looked as if it might have been stolen from a church. Or a monastery, Kirsty thought, as she sat and peered at the other end of the room and saw two high-backed, partially enclosed, black stasidi chairs. One of those feudal orders where the brothers hate the sight of female skin and are more proud of cannon balls than of any icon. Against the end wall, next to the chairs, there was a huge Cretan sofa covered with goat hides.

She began to study the rest of the room as Panayotis opened the shutters. It was long and low; the walls were bare stone with not a drop of colour or anything hanging to break the starkness except two crossed swords. A short way from her, there was a table. Not the type where you might picture a gathering of ebullient Cretans celebrating another name day or festival, but a small, rusting metal one with three ill-matching chairs. Kirsty imagined Panayotis and Leonidas sitting opposite each other, eating in silence, and almost pitied them for what their lives must consist of. Or, more appropriately, she decided as they stalked around muttering in undecipherable grunts, what they existed for.

Slowly, as her eyes adjusted to the gloom, she noticed a tapestry on the other end wall. It was large and hanging from an ornate steel rail. On it there was a symbol whose name she recalled easily, as well as where she'd last seen it: Gorgona, the two-tailed mermaid. Only unlike the intricate one on the red chemise, this one was lascivious and vile: a massive white bull was mounting the female figure from behind with its huge penis spurting a release, portrayed in blood-red silk.

'The Minotaur is let loose,' Barba Yiorgos had warned her. And now she was in its lair. Kirsty wished more than anything that she'd managed to meet Barba Yiorgos and that they were together on his roof terrace. She saw him waiting for her; she prayed he wouldn't think she'd let him down again. Then, just as the pervasive spirit of the place began to touch her spirit, she knew he would not. He will come, she assured herself, and smiled.

Leonidas began emptying the contents of a box he'd fetched from the truck. Fresh bread, cheese, preserved meat and some fruit.

Panayotis put three plates on the table. They were white, new and clean, and looked surreally out of place. Then he went to the counter next to a large marble sink without any taps, and started to prepare a meal, delicately and painstakingly, as if he was doing something for the first time in his life.

Leonidas poured three glasses of wine and put the cork back in the bottle. The glasses also looked new. The wine was shop-bought, though there was a barrel dripping into a jug a short way off.

They finished their preparations and stood back, staring at the table as if it had just landed from outer space. Panayotis gestured to Leonidas, who marched over and helped Kirsty to her feet by gently linking his arm through hers.

Suddenly, he viciously tightened his hold, dragged her past the table and followed his brother, who'd lit an oil lamp and was moving towards the tapestry. Kirsty stared up as they reached a narrow ladder leading to a sleeping platform. Even in the gloom, and from this distance, the two cots looked disgusting. An icy chill touched her as she visualised herself being thrown on one of them and raped, their odour and filth joining the goat perfume to complete this perfect day.

Instead, Leonidas carried on marching her towards the tapestry where his brother stood mirroring the blood-shot eyes and wanton expression of the bull. As they reached Panayotis, he grabbed the heavy material and pulled it along the rail to reveal a large wooden door. He opened it, and Kirsty felt the air grow colder and danker with a scent of salty ozone, as if they were entering a sea cave. Panayotis handed his brother the light and let him lead the way. She followed him into an arched tunnel that sloped down steeply. A short way along it there were doors, and Kirsty was sure she heard some movement behind them: human or animal, she wasn't sure.

It's a prison, she realised. Something dating back centuries. Kirsty sensed the horror of the place, heard the chains and cries of pain, smelled the burning flesh of the torturer's irons, and felt a deep sense of helplessness.

Leonidas stopped at one of the studded cell doors. Kirsty stared past him and saw the tunnel disappearing into darkness. She looked behind her and saw Panayotis—blacker than any tunnel and far more threatening. He waved his hand for her to follow his brother, who opened the door and entered. For the first time Kirsty noted the extra finger on his right hand.

'The police know about you and your father,' she tried. 'I phoned them. I already told them about you and your little deformity after our first meeting. They'll know who you are, and where this place is, and will be searching for me. Also, someone was expecting me. He'll be on his way by now and not alone.'

'Even God doesn't know about this place,' Panayotis mocked, waggling his extra digit. 'And this is a blessing, not a deformity. It may even tickle your fancy if you're lucky. And as for your boyfriend, he's going for some swimming lessons shortly. Besides, you have friends here already.'

He pushed her into the room where Leonidas stood waving the light like some wrecker drawing a ship to its doom. He made a bowing gesture and stood aside for her to enter. As she did, Kirsty saw at the end of the arch-roofed cell a stone bed covered with more of those goat hides. And sitting there, arm in arm, were Eleni and Patrick. Kirsty could hardly believe her eyes. She felt a charge of warmth and rushed towards them. 'Are you all right?' she cried in English. 'Have these bastards hurt you?'

Leonidas grabbed her arm before she could reach them. 'We've brought you together for a reunion,' he said. 'Or maybe a farewell party.'

He let her go and placed the light on a shelf, giving it a shake so its rays made his and Panayiotis's shadows tower and move threateningly in front of her. Kirsty put her arms around Eleni's and Patrick's shoulders.

Eleni looked up slowly and smiled.

Still beautiful, even in this situation, Kirsty registered.

'No,' Eleni said, 'not me, anyway. They beat Patrick up the day they kidnapped us, but since then it's been nothing but threats.'

'Kirsty,' Patrick asked, 'what are you doing here?'

She looked at his badly bruised face and saw the suspicion in his eyes.

'We've been searching for you since you disappeared.'

'We?'

'Yes, we. Barba Yiorgos. I think you know him.'

Eleni nodded and her face clouded in doubt. Leonidas grunted in contempt.

'And now you've come to set us free,' she said sardonically, touching Kirsty's bruised face.

'He'll come,' Kirsty said in Greek. 'Don't you worry.'

Panayotis filled the room with his laughter at this. 'Come on,' he snapped, 'reunion over. Dinner time.'

Eleni and Patrick got up. 'They normally keep us in separate cells and in the dark when they're away,' Patrick told Kirsty quietly, 'so we wondered what had changed.'

'For meals, though, we're taken back into their house and have a chance to be together,' Eleni added. 'But, of course, we have to put up with their delightful company!'

Kirsty heard the anxiety in her voice. And she knew why. From the moment the brothers had got close to Eleni, Kirsty could sense their overwhelming lust. It was a raw longing and made the hairs on her neck prickle. She took Eleni's hand and walked protectively by her.

Eleni and Patrick sat at the table and ate in silence, though she could see neither of them wanted to. Kirsty pushed her plate and glass away.

'Food. Eating for,' Leonidas said, in an attempt at English.

'Nice try,' Kirsty replied in Greek. 'If you keep us prisoners long enough, you may even grasp the basics of grammar!'

'Eat your food,' Panayotis snarled in Greek, 'or we'll force-feed you.'

'They will,' Eleni assured her.

'Father said that our guests must eat,' Leonidas added. 'And they will.'

Kirsty's jaw ached from the earlier punch, and her head was throbbing after being thrown around in that stinking crate. She looked at her watch: half-past two. She'd left to meet Barba Yiorgos at about eight. Six hours! she thought. Travelling? Unconscious as they brought her here? How could she know where she was, or hope for anyone to find her? A feeling of frustration and anger began to grow.

Kirsty watched Eleni and Patrick in this filthy hovel mechanically chewing away. She turned to the brothers. They were seated bolt upright in those hideous chairs that would once have held monks. They were greedily watching every mouthful, and Eleni with a far deeper hunger.

Tweedle Dee and Tweedle Dum in prayer, she thought, but didn't want to dwell on what they were praying for. But then, something else came to her: Tweedle Dee and Tweedle Dum fought a great battle, and that had just been over a nice new rattle! She caught Eleni's eye. Eleni gave her a smile and wink as if reading her mind.

'Do you boys always do what your daddy tells you without questioning why?' Kirsty asked loudly.

Neither looked at her but stared at each other instead. Kirsty registered their puzzled expressions.

214

'I mean kidnap and assault. Imprisoning people. Murdering their pets and destroying property! Not the normal career a half-decent father would choose for his sons, is it?'

Still they wouldn't look at her.

'You're both good-looking men,' Kirsty continued. 'Strong and fierce. Good dancers, too. Shouldn't you have wives and children by now, and not be living together with your goats?'

This time she did get a response. The instant the word 'wives' had left her mouth, they'd both stared at Eleni and then at each other.

'But then, it might be that you prefer goats to women and that your father prefers to keep you chained up until he needs to let you off the leash.' Kirsty had been told once that there were families who bred sons for the sole purpose of carrying out a vendetta. 'They have no education or careers, nor will they ever marry,' Valentinos had said. 'They know their destiny and accept it without question.'

Now she knew she was seeing it for real.

Panayotis got up. He moved to an old wooden cabinet and opened one of its heavy drawers. He took out a wicked-looking pair of shears that Kirsty guessed were used on the goats and sheep. He moved slowly and menacingly across the room and stood next to her. 'If you say one more word about my father,' he snarled, 'I'll cut your fucking tongue out.'

'Then how would I be able to eat this meal you've so lovingly prepared?' Kirsty asked, defiantly holding his gaze.

His hand moved towards her face.

'Panayotis,' Eleni said sweetly, 'would you get me another glass of wine? It's delicious. Or if you're too busy, maybe your brother could.' Panayotis was over at the counter before Leonidas could spring out of his seat. Eleni glanced back over at Kirsty.

'And I need to use the bathroom,' Kirsty said, 'or whatever hole in the ground passes for one around here. Maybe you could show me,' she said to Leonidas.

He scowled at her, then at his brother, who was solicitously filling Eleni's glass. So, Kirsty realised, Eleni has them at each other's throats. Smart, she thought, but also very dangerous. Kirsty touched her arm as Leonidas barked, 'This way,' and gestured for her to follow.

They stepped outside, and Leonidas gripped her shoulder. 'If you get any fancy ideas about running,'—he opened his waistcoat and revealed the handle of a heavy revolver—'you'll get a bullet for your trouble.'

Run? she thought, as he led her across the yard. Run where? She didn't think she'd ever seen such a desolate location. Normally, there was the beauty of the mountains to look at, the big blue Cretan sky or the ever-changing sea. And though she knew the Lefka Ori were towering in front, could hear the sea a long way below, and feel the warmth of the sun, none of it seemed real. The whole island appeared to have dissolved into this gloomy, remote valley. Kirsty shivered and followed Leonidas.

The toilet was a small stone building annexed to the side of the main house. Kirsty didn't really want to go, but had two reasons for getting out. First, she wanted to try to locate herself. She knew the island quite well, and if she could spot some familiar landmark, that would be enough. She'd learnt a lot about knowing where you were by walking in the Highlands of Scotland with her father. But there was nothing—not even a tree with a vestige of moss to show which way the sun shone.

'In,' Leonidas commanded, dragging open the door. Kirsty heard and felt his annoyance at being out here, and sensed his urgency to get back to Eleni. She decided to take her time.

She'd expected the toilet to be filthy. Instead, it was clean and smelled fresh. Just behind the door there was a stand-up toilet with a hole in the middle. It had been cut into the rock, and a full bucket of water waited to flush it. Kirsty stared into the hole and sensed that it went a long way down to some cavernous chamber, unemptied for centuries. For a moment it made her think of the one at the monastery she'd visited with Barba Yiorgos, and she saw him once again banging the old priest's head on the floor. It made her smile briefly, then question what he'd really been trying to find out that day. A black thought came to her: perhaps now she would never find out.

'Come on,' Leonidas called. 'Move yourself.'

'I have to wash first,' Kirsty retorted. 'I have blood on my face and hair from where your courageous and handsome brother hit me.'

He snorted in frustration.

Next to the toilet, through an arch with some ancient hieroglyph-type symbols and dates from the seventeenth century carved in its surface, was another room. This one was larger, with two high windows that Kirsty noticed had been recently glazed with modern frosted glass.

In the corner there was another stone trough with its hole leading to Hades and a full bucket of water. There was also a sink, a large marble one with flecks of red running through its surface like the blood covering her skin that she saw in the mirror. Kirsty washed quickly and, as she looked for a towel, spotted two toilet bags. She peeped inside: Chanel No. 5, Lancôme make-up, et cetera, in one; Boss and an elegant shaving set in the other. Of course, Kirsty realised. They'd taken Eleni's and Patrick's luggage after kidnapping them. She recalled the shadow that had moved across the window at Jessica's.

Kirsty pictured how it must have been for them that night, and despised herself for how she'd reacted. She visualised them out here with buckets of cold water, determined to keep clean and sweet-smelling for the moments when they were close to each other, Eleni struggling to keep the toilet and bathroom clean. And each time she did, one of those two animals defiling it again. Probably deliberately. She could see the brothers rifling through their toilet bags, maybe even trying some of the exotic scents to cover up their foulness and impress Eleni.

These thoughts made her more adamant than ever. She slipped her mobile phone from its pouch. It was the latest model and very expensive, so she carried it inside a concealed pocket of her waistcoat, out of any thief's reach. Now she was extra glad that she'd kept it hidden, and prayed it would still work after her roughing up. It did. She found Barba Yiorgos's number. God, Kirsty prayed again, please let him have kept his promise to always keep his charged and on. She keyed in *Taken by Diomidis's sons. E and P alive. Strange house in valley. Old prison hidden behind. I need you.*

She hit send. 'Message failed' flashed up. She did it again with the same result.

Leonidas started laughing. 'They don't work up here,' he taunted, his voice echoing around the room. Kirsty stared up at the windows and then around the room trying to see where he could be observing her from. She saw nothing, but could feel his gaze upon her. The pervert must have a spy hole, she realised, and with disgust imagined him watching Eleni.

'That's why we let you keep it after we gave you a nice, long, probing strip search.'

Kirsty felt her flesh creep.

'Now, out before I tear the fucking door off and shove that phone down your throat.'

Kirsty hit send again, and was sure, as the noise of Leonidas crashing the door open filled the room, there had been the beep of a message being sent. She stared quickly at the screen and was shocked to see that it had gone into picture mode: a photo of Kyria Despina she couldn't even recall taking was smiling at her. 'Damn,' she said, hiding it as Leonidas loomed through the broken opening.

'Does your big brother know you've got a spy hole?' she taunted, trying to keep him distracted from the phone.

He cuffed her hard. 'Keep your mouth shut,' he snarled.

Kirsty looked at him with contempt. She pictured him glaring at Eleni as she went about her ablutions, his eyes bulging and his mind full of lust. 'I guess that means no.' She smiled through the pain of his blow. 'But then, maybe she likes to let Panayotis watch her without one.'

He hit her again, this time in the stomach, and winded her.

'Over here,' Leonidas ordered.

Kirsty followed him, doubled over and gasping, to the well-head. 'Look down.'

She leant nervously over the edge. He put his arm around her waist so she couldn't move, and peered down the shaft with her. At first it was just a hole fading into an infinity of blackness. Then, as her eyes got accustomed to the light, Kirsty made out the hewn, almost perfectly circular rock walls, with lichen and other plants coating the sides. Finally, she saw the steel shimmer of water.

'Now get that fancy phone out,' Leonidas said, tightening his arm around her.

Kirsty struggled to get her hand inside her jacket and reach the mobile.

'Does it take pictures?' he asked when she did.

Kirsty nodded.

'Then take one of us.'

She opened it and her heart soared. *Message sent.* Kirsty pointed it at them. As she did, Leonidas roughly kissed her, pushing his filthy-tasting tongue into her mouth, forcing her to let the phone record the moment.

He stared at the picture on the screen. 'Nice,' he said. 'Now drop it in the well.'

'Piss off!' Kirsty snapped, trying to break free. She looked at the phone. The expensive birthday present to herself that she couldn't really afford. She recalled Barba Yiorgos's delight at discovering they had the same model and her teaching him how to use some of its more complicated features.

Leonidas grabbed her trouser belt and started to heave her over the side. She struggled but he was far too strong. Her head went down into the well, then the rest of her torso. Kirsty tried to use her hand to get a purchase on the side of the well but the rock was too smooth and slippery to grip.

'Drop it, or you go swimming with it.'

Kirsty stayed calm and attached the photograph to Barba Yiorgos's earlier message and hit send, and then she released it. It fell, a cold blue light spiralling into the darkness. She heard it hit the water and saw its gleam fading in the depths of the well. And yet, she was sure it had beeped a drowning message of hope. It steeled her as Leonidas changed his grip and let her go farther down. He grasped her by the ankles. 'Beg,' he said, his voice booming into the void. 'Beg.'

'Fuck you,' Kirsty echoed back.

He let go of one leg and dangled her in even farther. Kirsty's courage held, though she'd never been so frightened. She sensed neither of the brothers could do anything too bad without their father's orders.

'Beg,' he said again, his voice already sounding ineffectual.

'Go and play with yourself, little boy.'

Kirsty felt his hand loosen slightly. Then she was hauled back into the light and dropped roughly onto the ground.

'You didn't really think I would contaminate our water with a piece of shit like you. Besides, there's already a deeper, colder place waiting for you, English whore.'

'Yeah, and neither you nor your brother can even spell it.' She got up and walked contemptuously towards the house, though her legs felt like jelly.

20.

As Kirsty was dangling, suspended between life and death, Barba Yiorgos was drowning in a deeper well. He reloaded and raised his US Army issue Colt .45 and fired his ninth bullet. For the first time, the shot missed cutting the cord and letting another of his chickens fall. It whirred its way across Kissamou Bay towards the Rodopou Peninsula. The sky was darkening, a storm coming, and though the sea was calm, he sensed, as always, its treacherous nature.

'I thought nine was your lucky number, Kirsty,' he slurred. He poured the last of his second bottle of tsikoudia into his glass and threw it down in a gulp. He had snap-top beer bottles of the drink lined up in his huge, blue American fridge. He kept it very cold, until it became viscous. Just the way he liked it. He went to collect another.

The phone rang while he was indoors. He ignored it, knowing who it was. Valentinos with another update. He'd had a whole series of them since his return, each one adding more harrowing details and attempting to increase the pressure on him to do something. The first one was to say that Jane had opened the kafenion, and when Valentinos had told her about the death of Kirsty's animals, the damage to her car and his fears, she'd called the police. They'd arrived, and stated that the car had been burgled. The stereo was missing. Windscreen smashing was the thieves' favourite method of entering. It happened all the time. This thief had clearly just been unlucky and cut himself.

Valentinos informed them about Kirsty's pets. The police were equally dismissive. 'These ex-pats don't know how to look after animals,' the officer told him. 'They let them roam; the animals steal and tip over bins. A dog should be kept chained. Cats are vermin. If we went around investigating every allegation by some foreigner claiming his pet had been shot or poisoned, we'd need fifty more officers.'

The next report had been about Kirsty's house. Jane had insisted the police go and check it. Finally, a detective and his sergeant arrived and did. They found the door open, and inside, that every drawer and wardrobe had been emptied. There were no suitcases, which to the detective was the most significant thing about the scene. 'Looks like your friend just up and went,' he deduced.

'Done a bunk,' the other added. 'We get a lot of this. Usually it's to do with fines and unpaid taxes. Maybe it would be a good idea for us to send someone to go through the books before you vanish as well.'

'Barba Yiorgos,' Valentinos had told him, 'they won't do anything. They've been bribed. You must act.'

Act, he thought, slamming the phone down. I've been doing nothing else for years, reinventing myself every day. Why should I change now?

Valentinos had called again as Barba Yiorgos was halfway through his second bottle. 'There are two people in Kirsty's kafenion,' he raved. 'They're going through all her papers with a microscope. I'm certain they're planting evidence to prove she had to run. I can't believe they've moved so fast. The bastards!'

'It all depends on who's bribing them,' Barba Yiorgos stated and hung up.

He'd taken his seventh shot then, cutting the cord hanging his chicken as cleanly as he had the first six. Its body had landed with a thump disproportionate to its mass, startling him.

The last time Valentinos called, he'd pleaded again for Barba Yiorgos to do something. 'You can't abandon her,' he sobbed. 'She gave you her trust, and more, I think. You're a great Kapetanios like your father.'

'I'm more like my father than you'd care to know,' he said, and hung up again.

Barba Yiorgos went and picked up the photograph, which was still lying in a pile of broken glass. He saw that his father's image had been damaged badly, with cuts zigzagging through his body. Marianna, though, appeared fresh and unblemished. The copy of his father's will lay in the ashtray, back from its hiding place and awaiting the flame. He stared at it for a moment, then dropped the photograph and hurried outside.

Just like my father, his mind raged as he poured another drink and made his eighth clean shot. A coward who crept back to his wife and let his enemy die peacefully in bed, then tried to force his son into acting in his stead.

Yet, his father was also a hero of the Resistance. And Barba Yiorgos had been a hero, too. He went back inside and carried out the Purple Heart and Bronze Star medals he'd won in Korea. He placed them next to the bottle and took another drink. And the girl, Eleni—she had his father's blood pulsing through her veins. She hadn't been afraid to come back to the island. He stood up, full of resolve, then sat down just as quickly.

He began to blame and curse other people for how he was feeling. First his father, for everything. Then Eleni, for coming and opening up this can of worms. And Kirsty, for poking her nose in and involving him. But finally and most of all, himself.

Then he'd fired his ninth shot and missed.

The phone stopped ringing and he took another drink from the third bottle and fired again. This time his aim was so far off, he actually hit one of his once-precious birds. The heavy .45 calibre bullet exploded the chicken into a starburst of feathers, blood and flesh. When it cleared, all that remained was the head hanging from a noose, its dead eyes open and looking at him.

'Oh, God!' he cried, dropping the pistol on the table. It was his favourite bird. He pictured her delicately climbing the stairs to lay an egg for him. Then he saw Kirsty shooing her away on their first real meeting. He couldn't stand it; he raised the pistol again and placed the muzzle in his mouth. Barba Yiorgos's finger started to tighten on the trigger and stopped. The barrel didn't taste of metal or smoke, but of the earlier tastes he'd experienced after dreaming of Kyria Despina. He put it on the table, staring at it in disbelief.

His head began to clear. Panayotis and Leonidas were coming for him, he realised. They'd already taken Eleni, Patrick and Kirsty. All dead by now, he suspected. He was probably the only one left alive whom Diomidis feared. His sons would have been sent to close the matter. Barba Yiorgos's hands were shaking so much he could hardly reload the gun, but he did. 'I promise you this much, Kirsty,' he whispered. 'I'll go down with a fight, even if I can do no more.'

The cell phone beeped twice. He pictured Valentinos's text message. *Please, great Kapetanios. Be brave.* 'Don't worry,' Barba Yiorgos said in silent reply to it, 'I'm going to.'

A short while later it sounded again and something told him he had to check it. Barba Yiorgos fetched it out and sat down, his vision almost double from the drink, his hands still shaking as he prayed that he could remember some of the things Kirsty had so patiently taught him.

He read the text from her. The words 'I need you' entered him with a stabbing jolt.

Then the message came again with a picture attached and he stared in horror at what was being portrayed.

Barba Yiorgos leapt up and grabbed his gun. He fired three shots rapidly and the last of the chickens dropped, softly this time it seemed, their bodies falling, almost simultaneously, to the ground. He spiralled the half-full bottle into the air, waiting until the moment it reached its zenith before firing. It shattered, showering the bodies below in his benediction of glass and alcohol.

The light was fading. Barba Yiorgos looked out across the roughening sea to the horizon where the clouds were beginning to broil and ball up as tightly as fists about to strike.

Then he went inside to prepare for what was coming.

He opened his trunk and gently placed the damaged photograph back in its box, swearing to restore it if the chance ever came. On top of that he placed the will, which might prove to be a bargaining card if there was time for that left. If only he had . . . Barba Yiorgos stopped such thoughts.

Next, he took out the traditional Cretan clothes his father had worn during his time with the Resistance. He stripped off, and for the first, and probably, he felt, the last time in his life, began to dress in them.

Barba Yiorgos pulled on the baggy beige trousers, looking at the mended bullet hole from a German rifle that had narrowly missed crippling the wearer for life, and the shrapnel scars and the dark stains of blood that would never wash out. The trousers fitted as if they'd been tailored for him, as did the thick black shirt, carrying its own marks of battle. 'Some coward!' he sighed, feeling the coarseness of the material and noting that there was no sign of anything having touched the back of either garment. He struggled to pull on the heavy, black leather boots. Needs a wife's helping hand, he thought. And then couldn't get the idea from his mind that the last time a woman's hand had helped his father with these, it had been Marianna's, on the night she'd been killed.

Barba Yiorgos placed the sariki on his head and the knots were the real tears he wept inside for that image.

Finally, he took his father's long, intricately engraved saita knife from the trunk. He withdrew it from the scabbard and touched its gleaming edge to test for sharpness. A pearl of blood immediately sprang from his thumb and ran down the part of the blade where his father's name had been written. 'How sharp is it, Baba?' he had once asked.

'I'll tell you something, Yiorgi. I've chopped Germans' heads off with this blade and they only knew it had happened when they nodded and something unexpected landed in their laps!'

Barba Yiorgos could still hear their laughter from that day as he slid the saita back into its scabbard and placed it in his belt. He checked himself in the mirror and smiled. Then, after making two phone calls, he stepped out to wait. He sat at the table in the twilight as the first distant rumble of thunder came, staring at the image of Kirsty on the cell phone. And nothing else mattered at that moment. Not family history, honour or vendettas. Not his late father's will. Or whether every inch of the surrounding land did end up covered in concrete. Just that look on her bruised face. And what was happening to her.

Some time later, bright headlights lit up the track to his house as lightning was beginning to illuminate the evening sky. The sound of the two approaching 4x4s was louder than the thunder.

He picked up his pistol.

The time had finally come.

21.

A flash of lightning flared through the gaps of Kirsty's cell door. It was the second strike and the only light she'd seen since being put in the room hours ago. She glanced around again, while counting out the seconds to detonation. There was nothing worth seeing anyway; just an arched room cut out of the rock, some messages and dates clawed into the walls, the soiled stone bench she was perched on and a rusty bucket of stagnant water in the corner.

She reached nine seconds and thunder arrived, crescendoing around her, amplified by the shape of the prison. The last time it had been thirteen counts. Getting closer, she realised, and asked the momentary calm the same questions for the hundredth time: What were those two evil bastards up to? What did he mean by 'your boyfriend's going for some swimming lessons'? And the answers came back in an aqueous and drowning voice: Barba Yiorgos, Barba Yiorgos. Over and over like waves breaking on a shore.

Kirsty knew they'd gone for him. And though she was desperate for his safety, she wanted more than anything for the door to open at this moment and him to be pushed into the cell with her. He'd solve everything then. She didn't know exactly how. But just to have him near one more time would be enough.

Kirsty strained her hearing; the storm paused as if holding its breath. Once again, all she heard was the sound coming from the tunnel. An eerie, haunting noise, like the faint roaring of a furnace or the sibilance of a distant sea. It made her skin prickle, especially as every now and then another cadence seemed to join in with an ululation of whale song or pain.

Also, there was a smell: mineral and elemental. A taste of the underworld, she thought; it had filled her mouth the few times she'd tried to get close to the door and shout, unsuccessfully, to Eleni and Patrick. The metallic tang seemed to have tainted even her words, making them sound tinny and ineffectual.

❦

When she'd first been led to the cells with Eleni and Patrick, Kirsty had presumed they were going to be put in together again. Instead, they'd been separated.

Earlier, they had been lined up on the filthy sofa as Panayotis and Leonidas sat at the table and tore their meal to bits, glowering at each other, then over at their prisoners, like two wolves ready to fight over the scraps.

'How close did you get to the truth?' Patrick had asked, ignoring another deliberately loud burp from one of the brothers.

Kirsty looked at their captors and put her finger to her lips.

'Don't worry,' Eleni assured her. 'No savvy English.'

'Don't you believe it,' Kirsty whispered, thinking how many tourists and ex-pats had made the same mistake. Then she decided it didn't matter what they heard now. 'We were close. And I know my friend has got even closer.'

'Barba Yiorgos?' Patrick said, sounding sceptical and suspicious.

'You know he's Kapetanios Michaelis's son, don't you?' Eleni stated.

'Yes,' Kirsty said. 'But I didn't. Not until recently, anyway.'

'Huh!' Patrick exclaimed.

'But I believe he had his reasons for not telling me. Barba Yiorgos had a lot less of the story than you did. He had nothing except a photograph and a broken tale from his father. Until he saw you and your incredible likeness to Marianna, he'd believed your mother had been taken and murdered by the Germans. Even after seeing you he wanted to deny it, but he was still willing to help. And still will—I know it.'

Eleni looked sad and Patrick took her hand.

'I've read my grandmother's journal a hundred times,' she said, 'and it's so heartbreaking to know that it was all a fantasy. She wrote two pages about her wonderful wedding ceremony, describing the monastery. She even wrote that Michaelis told her the Golden Step had glowed as her foot touched it after she was married.'

'We went to see the priest on our first day here, and he denied every word of it. He laughed in my face and told me it was all a fabrication. It was horrible and disturbing. I even wrote it in his wretched visitors' book.'

'I read it,' Kirsty said.

'But we *were* wrong,' Eleni continued, ignoring her. 'The priest told us about Kapetanios Michaelis and his true wife. He sent us to find his son, Yiorgos, if we didn't believe him.'

'And we did,' Patrick said. 'But he must have been forewarned and was skulking around and spying on us. We were convinced that he was behind this kidnapping.'

'How disappointing,' Kirsty said, praying there would be time for Barba Yiorgos to prove himself.

'Even Kyria Despina tried to keep up the pretence, insisting that my grandmother was "a perfect bride and mother". She'd written the same in the letter she sent with my mother all those years ago, along with so much other information. Just a lie concocted to make things sound better than they were. In some ways I'm glad I don't have to take this news back to England.'

Kirsty started smiling.

Eleni stared at her, angry and offended.

'I'm sorry,' Kirsty said touching her cheek. 'It's just that something has clicked into place. They were married.'

'What?' Eleni queried. 'Michaelis was already married.'

'I know, but all the same, he married Marianna in front of the holy icon in that monastery. The priest performed the ceremony. And there were witnesses. She believed it to be genuine and was innocent. Kyria Despina was telling you the truth. And, though I didn't know it, I heard the same from the priest's mouth. And he wasn't laughing in anyone's face at the time.'

Eleni's face brightened slightly. 'Thank you, Kirsty,' she said. 'It was terrible to keep picturing my grandmother as a liar. It helps to know, even if Michaelis had been lying to her about the legitimacy of the wedding and the will he'd made for her and my mother.'

'Will?' Kirsty said. 'That's the second time I've heard that mentioned. What will?'

'According to my grandmother's journal, Michaelis had made one and left everything to her and his daughter in case he was killed fighting the Germans. It wasn't with the documents my mother had and Kyria Despina said she sent everything home. So we imagine it was another part of the deception.'

'I don't think so,' Kirsty said, her mind racing as she tried to put together all the pieces.

'So where did you hear about it?' Patrick asked. 'From your friend, Barba Yiorgos, I suppose. That seems to fit.'

'No,' Kirsty replied, trying to keep her faith and deny the huge black cloud of doubt and fear that was beginning to form. 'From Diomidis.'

'Who?' Eleni asked.

'You mean you haven't had the privilege of meeting your jailers' father, Diomidis?' Kirsty replied jauntily. 'Your real kidnapper, the son of the man who gave Marianna to the Germans?'

'No,' Patrick said. 'Only these two, since they trapped us on the way to find Olga. We got lost and stopped at a kafenion to ask for help. Shortly afterwards we met these freaks.'

'I know the place,' Kirsty said.

'Kyria Despina wrote in her letter that my mother should never return and that there was great danger waiting for her and any of her family. I guess I should have paid heed, but thought after all this time the risk would be slight and worth taking.'

'That's because,' Kirsty stated, 'you misjudged the Cretan attitude to vendetta. Some people flee to other countries and are still found and killed. One famous vendetta here started in the nineteen-forties and has left over one hundred and fifty dead so far. A "dish served cold" is the only meal some families will ever share. And if there is money or land involved, I think hell would freeze over before any vendetta stopped.'

Patrick pulled Eleni closer to him.

'We'll get through this,' Kirsty said. 'Besides, if a woman as wise as Kyria Despina hadn't wanted someone to find out the truth and do something about it, she wouldn't have put so much information in the letter she sent.'

Eleni looked uncertain. 'I just hope my father manages to keep the fact he hasn't heard from us, or can't get in touch, from my mother. Or that he doesn't do something rash like coming and joining us in this place for his trouble.'

'Did you meet Olga?' Patrick asked Kirsty.

'Unfortunately, I never got that far,' she sighed. 'But Barba Yiorgos did. He told me just before I was kidnapped, and that he now had all the pieces in place and knew exactly what had happened.'

'I wonder if we'll ever get to find out,' Eleni said, as Panayotis and Leonidas shoved their chairs away from the table and moved towards them.

'We will,' Kirsty assured her, protectively grasping her hand. 'You'll take the truth back to your mother. And it'll be good and pure. Barba Yiorgos will come for us, don't worry. I can feel it.'

'Up, wash,' Panayotis grunted in English.

'Does he mean he wants us to do the dishes?' Kirsty quipped.

'No,' Eleni said. 'This is part of the daily routine around here. Eat, scrub, cell.'

'You first.' Panayotis pulled a huge gun out of his belt and pointed it at Patrick. 'This,' he boasted to Kirsty in Greek, 'is a thirteen-round Heckler and Koch USP 40. It was a present for my last name day.'

'Ooh, nice,' Kirsty cooed. 'And what did Santa bring you for Christmas? A rocket launcher?'

Eleni sniggered.

Panayotis swung the gun barrel and pointed it at Kirsty's crotch. He held it there but, she sensed, without any real intent. She smiled and crossed her legs. 'Move,' he snapped, and led Patrick away. Leonidas appeared in front of them. He was breathing heavily.

'And what did you get for your name day?' Kirsty asked sweetly.

'I'll just bet you got a gun,' Eleni encouraged.

Leonidas looked from woman to woman and began to smile.

He pulled open his waistcoat and exposed a large hand-tooled leather holster. With a gunslinger's speed, he whipped out an odd-looking weapon. He then gave them a display of his formidable dexterity with it. Spinning it, aiming at imaginary targets and sliding it in and out of the holster.

Kirsty wondered, while trying to keep the doubt off her face, how they were going to defeat these two, and how long Barba Yiorgos would survive if he did show up.

'This,' said Leonidas in guttural Greek, pointing the gun at Kirsty, 'is an SR-2 machine pistol. It shoots a special 9x21 Guraza bullet that can pierce body armour. On fully automatic, it can cut someone in half. I know that for a fact. I've tried.'

She could hear that this wasn't a boast.

Panayotis brought Patrick back in.

'Your turn now,' Leonidas said, waving the gun at Eleni. Kirsty didn't wait for her to be led off.

'Oh, great,' Kirsty gushed, getting to her feet as Eleni began to move. '*Our* turn.'

'We'll be able to share toiletries,' Eleni offered, clinging to her hand and heading for the door before the open-mouthed brothers could react.

'He spies on you,' Kirsty informed her as they entered the bathroom.

'I know,' Eleni said. 'I've been giving a bit of a display lately to get him even more wound up.'

Kirsty smiled at her confidence and cunning.

'Well, I'll tell you what,' Kirsty said. 'I'm not in your league. But let's give him a double show.'

'We'll dazzle him,' Eleni teased. 'Drive him crazy.'

'We'd better,' Kirsty said, pulling her T-shirt off as Eleni began to undress.

෨

Kirsty was smirking at how the two of them had hammed it up in the bathroom when another long, jagging bolt of lightning lit the cell. The door opened as she reached five seconds this time and the thunder boomed.

'On your feet, English whore,' Panayotis spat. 'Somebody is coming to visit you.'

He was excited and stared along the tunnel to where his brother was ushering Eleni and Patrick out.

'And then the fun will really begin.'

22.

The table had been laid with a beautiful white linen cloth. Cutlery, plates and wine glasses were in front of each chair. A crystal decanter of red wine sat in the middle. The recently made food was already in place: moussaka, stifado, goat ribs and salads. Kirsty knew the brothers hadn't prepared this and she judged by the grace notes that a woman had been here while they were in their cells and Leonidas and Panayotis were away. The floor looked as if it had been given its first cleaning for an age and the wooden chairs polished.

For what? she asked herself. Did the woman know who she was cooking and cleaning for? Did she care?

Once, a female writer had given a lecture about vendettas. She'd claimed it was solely down to men and yet the women bore and carried the repercussions and scars. Maybe, Kirsty thought, the woman who'd done this had had no choice. But she doubted it. And there was no way she was going to eat with that thought in her mind, even though she was ravenous.

'The last supper,' Eleni said, sounding frightened for the first time.

'Eat,' Panayotis ordered, before Patrick or Kirsty could try to comfort her.

He waited as Patrick filled the wine glasses and Eleni began to put food on the plates. Then he went to join his brother, who was seated in one of those hideous chairs, watching again. But something was different. They were excited. Also, Kirsty saw they'd made an effort to smarten themselves up. Their black clothes looked less dusty and spattered, the leather boots not so caked with goat dung. And their hair and moustaches had definitely been trimmed.

Kirsty pictured the same woman who'd made the meal—maybe even their mother—fussing to get them ready for whatever was coming. Or had they needed to be cleaned up after what they'd done? An image of Barba Yiorgos came to her, beaten and broken. She made a deliberate show of shoving her food away.

'Eat all,' Panayotis called over.

'I'd rather do what you've been doing for years,' she answered in Greek. 'Scrape shit from under a rock and swallow it cold.'

Panayotis was out of his chair and behind Kirsty as if he'd been spring-loaded. He grabbed her hair and yanked her head back. Patrick shoved his chair away and moved to help her. As he did, Leonidas appeared and pointed the SR-2 machine pistol in his face. 'Sit down,' he snarled, 'unless you want me to feed you something else.'

Kirsty kept struggling as Panayotis held her bent backwards over the chair and scooped up a handful of moussaka. She grabbed his wrist. But, if anything, he was stronger than his brother and her resistance was as futile as her fight at the well. She felt his fingers force her lips open and stuff the food so deep into her mouth that she started to gag. Then he clamped her jaws shut and pinched her nose.

She began to convulse as the food went down her throat, more bitter than any poison, unable to breathe as he held her. Kirsty's eyes began to stream. Through a haze she saw Eleni staring in horror at what was happening. Leonidas was smiling and enjoying every moment, and waiting for more. Kirsty felt ashamed and humiliated and stopped resisting. All her life, pride had been vital to her existence. Now she was being force-fed like a foie gras goose in front of the people she had set out to rescue.

Panayotis began to smear her face with food as if making up a clown. He started to push another handful in and probe the inside of her mouth. As he reached the point where, to his pleasure, she began to heave, Eleni moved. Her chair went flying backwards as she grabbed the large bowl of stifado and dumped it over Panayotis's head.

He yelled in pain as the still-steaming liquid cascaded down his face and into his shirt. He released Kirsty and staggered against the wall.

Kirsty saw the look of shock on his face, and an even bigger one on Patrick's. She turned round and looked at Panayotis, who was standing immobilised, the stew bowl still balanced on top of his head. The black knots of his sariki were weeping, not with any mother's tears but with olive oil and a rich, red sauce. The rest of the food was dripping off his moustache and filling his boots.

Kirsty began to laugh, as did Eleni and Patrick. Leonidas was keeping as still as his brother.

Then Panayotis came alive. He tossed his head arrogantly so the bowl flew across the room, hitting another wall and covering it in what remained of the food. Kirsty watched as he began to quiver and his eyes darkened; they looked like portals into his black heart. His lips curled and he howled, a deep pent-up sound that filled the room and mirrored the ones Kirsty had heard coming along the tunnel. All the time he was staring at Eleni. He bent down to his ankle and drew out from its holster a small, curved knife and, brushing Kirsty aside, moved the blade slowly towards Eleni's face.

As he did, Leonidas grabbed his hand and twisted it viciously so the knife hit the floor.

'No,' Leonidas warned. The gun was still pointing at Patrick but his eyes were locked on his brother.

Panayotis appeared more shocked by this than anything else.

'What?' He sounded incredulous. 'You're telling me what to do? I'm the elder, the stronger. I do the telling.'

'You leave her alone. She will not carry your marks on her face. And her death will be mine to give. Not yours.'

Kirsty felt his words fill the air with a foulness, as if a tomb had been opened, and saw Patrick reach out to Eleni as she slumped in her chair.

Panayotis kept glaring at his brother, willing him to back down. Leonidas held his gaze. Kirsty could sense that Panayotis was tensing to attack. It seemed to her that Leonidas was unprepared, almost as if defying his brother and stating his vile claim over Eleni meant the battle was over.

Kirsty watched as Panayotis eased back onto his heels, and knew he was about to leap over the table. She gave a nod to Patrick, whom she judged was also in tune with what was happening. He returned her gesture.

'Get the gun,' she sent him telepathically, over and over. She hoped he was thinking like she was and that Leonidas might drop it in the fight. She tried to beam another message to Panayotis: 'Leap, you bastard. Do it. Do it now.'

Then the door clicked open and their father stepped in.

Diomidis, Kirsty recognised, had transformed himself into the image of his portrait—only, if anything, even more contrived. Though she had no doubt the bullets criss-crossing his chest, the knife in his belt and the huge gun in its shoulder holster were only too real. The one thing spoiling this illusion was the modern briefcase he was carrying. Panayotis and Leonidas crumpled under his contemptuous gaze.

'Clean yourself up, boy,' he snapped.

Panayotis moved even more quickly than when he'd sprung from the chair.

'And, you,' he said looking at Leonidas, 'get that mess off the wall and floor. What the hell are you doing? And put that gun away.'

Diomidis moved over to the counter. He took a spotless white handkerchief from his pocket and soaked it in bottled water.

'Please,' he said to Kirsty, 'clean yourself up.'

Kirsty stared deeply into his lying eyes as he graciously held out the makeshift flannel. As he waited for her to take it, she leant forward, took the hanging edge of the gorgeous tablecloth and slowly, deliberately, messily wiped herself clean. She saw Leonidas wilt and heard the droplets of water fall from Diomidis's hand as he crushed his offering in rage.

'What game are you playing now?' Kirsty asked, as he calmed.

'You're my guests,' he gloated. 'First there were two, now there are three: all enjoying famous Cretan hospitality.'

'Who the hell are you?' Patrick demanded. 'And what do you want?'

'Justice,' Diomidis snapped. 'The honour of my family preserved. All the things you and your treacherous wife are seeking to destroy.'

Diomidis was looking straight at Eleni as he spoke, his face contorted with an expression of hate and disgust.

'Meet Diomidis,' Kirsty gibed. 'Future mayor of Chania. Building contractor and property developer. Son of the great Kapetanios Panayotis. Also a kidnapper, burner of forests and killer of innocent animals, the living legacy of the coward and traitor who bred him.'

Eleni snorted dismissively.

Diomidis grasped his gun, then released it. Panayotis and Leonidas moved behind him.

'I warned you not to listen to that cowardly drunk's lies,' he hissed at Kirsty. 'And incidentally,' he turned to his sons, 'talking of *her* Yiorgos Casanova, how did he enjoy his swim?'

Kirsty had the picture now of them dragging Barba Yiorgos across the sand he loathed, into the sea he feared, then letting him go. She saw him struggling and drowning, then his body floating, his beard and magnificent mane of hair hanging and moving to the will of the currents.

'You bastards,' she spat. 'He's more man than all of you put together. As was his father.'

Diomidis smiled. 'We should be made to face our fears at least once in a lifetime.'

His smile faded as he saw Leonidas staring sheepishly at his brother, willing him to speak.

'He was guarded,' Panayotis spluttered.

'Guarded!' Diomidis bellowed. 'Who would want to guard that worthless piece of shit?'

'When we arrived,' Leonidas said, 'we did just as you told us.'

'Just for a change,' Kirsty mocked.

Leonidas gave her a dangerous look before continuing. 'We got near to his house. The sea was getting wild—perfect for his swim. But there were two vehicles there: large four-by-fours. One was a silver Toyota with a row of spotlights on its roof.'

'We didn't know who it belonged to,' Panayotis added. 'There was also a big Nissan pick-up truck, which we thought might be his son's.'

'He was in the garden,' Leonidas said, 'with two men who had their backs to us. And he had a gun that he was waving around. We heard shots and left.'

'Ran, you mean,' Kirsty taunted, a feeling of relief flooding through her. But she noticed that as the brothers were talking to their father, they were inching towards the table.

'I think he may have been drunk,' Panayotis said, pointing his extra digit at Kirsty, 'like he must be every time he fucks you, bitch.'

'And he was dressed,' Leonidas offered as his father's expression changed to one of anger at the altercation taking place.

Panayotis flashed his brother a warning glance, as if instead of helping him he'd doomed them. But it was too late.

'Dressed! What do you mean dressed?' Diomidis exploded.

'Like you,' Panayotis whispered.

'Exactly the same,' Leonidas said. 'Exactly.'

'Only,' Kirsty goaded, registering the reaction this news was causing, 'I expect his uniform's the genuine thing and he has the right to wear it. Maybe you'll get to see him in it soon. Just like you said: We should all get the chance to face our fears once in a lifetime.'

Diomidis pulled the gun from his belt and, as if signalled, his sons pounced on Patrick. They began dragging him from the table as he fought to break free. Eleni grabbed Panayotis and was carried along. Kirsty didn't hesitate. She threw herself onto Leonidas's back, and the five of them went down in a writhing mass.

A gunshot boomed louder than the thunder that had now passed them and was rumbling high over the mountains. Kirsty felt the breeze of the bullet whistle between them. It hit the door to the cells and tore out a large chunk.

Everyone stopped moving.

'Enough of this,' Diomidis said. The cavernous barrel of his pistol pointed, rock-steady, at Patrick's legs. 'The next bullet will go through his kneecap if you girls don't sit down.'

Kirsty knew that he was about to fire. She took her hands off Leonidas's throat and stood up, gently easing Eleni away at the same time.

'Now get on the bench,' Diomidis ordered. Kirsty saw a look of disappointment in his eyes that he'd not been pressed further.

Panayotis and Leonidas dragged Patrick across the room. They slammed him into one of the enclosed stasidi chairs and Panayotis drew his gun; he shoved it against Patrick's head.

'No,' Eleni sobbed, trying to rise as Diomidis moved and forced her back down.

Kirsty steeled herself for the shot. An image of one of those matter-of-fact executions came into her head. Cold and perfunctory, as recorded on the TV in freeze-frame precision from some distant, uncivilised country. Now she understood it was that simple. The camera hadn't lied. She had. The tin-pot officer who'd fired the shot into the prisoner's head and walked casually away was the truth. The reality of this world of guns and flesh.

Only this time the gun didn't go off.

Instead, Leonidas opened another drawer in the cabinet and took out a tangle of straps and a roll of tape. Kirsty and Eleni watched helplessly as he began to secure Patrick to the chair while Panayotis pushed the pistol against his head. Diomidis paid no attention to what was going on and focused all his attention on Eleni, keeping his weapon aimed at her.

Kirsty realised that the chairs—where once monks would have sat murmuring their prayers to another one-and-only god—had been cleverly modified for another type of crucifixion.

Slots were cut beneath the armrests, so the straps could be threaded through: one place for the wrist, another for the elbow. The same for the legs, thighs and ankles. Each time another strap was secured, she saw a grimace of pain cross Patrick's face as Leonidas stretched it as tight as he could before buckling it in place. But even more harrowing was the look of fear in Patrick's eyes, and she understood it wasn't for himself.

The last strap went around his neck and banged his head against the ancient wood as it was tightened. She heard him wheeze as he struggled to breathe and heard Eleni gulp in air as if she were attempting it for him. Finally, Leonidas cut two lengths of thick tape and placed them on the arms of the chair.

The brothers stared at Patrick, admiring their work. They appeared delighted and looked at their father for his approval. He dismissed them with a nod and pointed at Eleni.

Kirsty waited, dreading seeing Eleni bound next to Patrick as she sat helplessly watching.

Panayotis moved towards their bench and grabbed Kirsty. Eleni moved to help her. 'Back down,' Diomidis warned, swinging the gun towards Patrick, 'or he pays for your courage.'

Eleni did, giving Kirsty a look of regret.

The straps bit into her flesh as Leonidas revelled in tightening them as hard as he could. Kirsty tried not to show her pain and concentrated instead on what Patrick had said as she'd been slammed into the chair. He'd gasped quietly, 'Hold a deep breath and flex your muscles hard. Like Houdini.' Then unbelievably and encouragingly, he'd given her a wink.

The final band went around her throat. Leonidas turned away and she relaxed and was able to exhale. 'Thank you,' she whispered to Patrick.

Kirsty looked at her restraints. They were well used and clearly stained from earlier struggles. She wondered briefly how many people they'd held and where those captives were lying now. She shut it from her mind and concentrated her attention on Eleni.

The three men were facing her. Garish black figures towered above Eleni as she defiantly held their gaze. The oil lights seemed to be forming a golden halo around her beautiful face. And Kirsty whispered a silent prayer.

'Now,' Diomidis spat at Eleni, 'you will pay for your attempts to dishonour and rob our family, by being robbed and dishonoured of everything, as your grandmother was for her sins.'

He gave a signal and his sons moved towards Eleni.

23.

Barba Yiorgos gunned the Brough Superior across the wet sand. The storm had passed but the sea was still raging and drowning out the noise of the 1000 cc V-twin engine. He tried to assure himself that at least it might prevent him from being heard. It was small comfort, though, as the growing panic mounted.

He was lost.

Barba Yiorgos slid the bike to a halt and stared along the single beam of light. He saw four sets of tyre tracks marking the beach and joining his latest one to form a musical stave, and heard exactly what song the other skid-marked notes sang: he'd passed here twice already. He read the time on his father's old Rolex Trench watch. More than a half hour had lapsed since they'd manhandled the bike from the back of Michaelis's Nissan pick-up truck and Barba Yiorgos had ridden off, the hero to the rescue, calling back, 'You just keep to the plan. I'm the only one who can find the way. I've been before.'

But that had been decades ago, during the daytime.

He turned the bike again, searching along the base of the cliff. Nothing. The watch, as it had always done since its mechanical heart started in 1914, ticked its precise message into his veins, pulsing over and over the words he'd stated when synchronising time with Michaelis and Andonis: 'Timing is everything. Timing is everything.'

Now he was going to be late.

Water touched his left foot and nearly made him topple the heavy bike. The last exhalation of the storm was making the tide surge, and he was less than ten metres from the cliff. With a cold shudder, Barba Yiorgos realised he could be cut off.

He spun the Brough Superior so it faced the way he had driven, and confirmed his fears. The sea was already touching the rock face. He didn't know how deep it was, but thought he might be able to get through if he left now. But he knew there was no way back for him. He turned again and switched on the main beam. Twenty metres away, the sea had reached the cliff in front of him.

Another sibilant kiss of water licked its tongue against the shrinking plateau. Barba Yiorgos inched towards the rocks. When he'd driven the bike, for the first time in years, he'd felt young again. Now he felt old.

And this 'Ancient Mariner' hated the sea, and had his own reasons for doing so. The touch of it made him squirm; the sound made him tense. He lived by it as much to deny his nightmares as for any health reasons. But the thought of being held again in its cold clutch—as he had been in two blood-stained war beach landings in Korea—was stultifying. But he had to go on. There were far worse deaths than this one waiting if he ran.

He left the bike leaning on its rest near some dense thorn bushes and gave the machine a gentle farewell pat. He took his long torch from one of the cowboy-style saddlebags and began to search for the opening. A spray of water hit him, and hissed on the bike's hot engine. He started to panic. 'Stay calm, Yiorgi,' said a female voice, drifting in on the waves.

And he heard something whirring in the dark: a bat leaving its lair to hunt blindly in its endless night. Then the smell reached him: a cold subterranean breath sending out a gossamer thread of hope. Barba Yiorgos followed it, forcing open the bushes. He shone his light into the gaping mouth of the tunnel as a wave crashed over his bike, rocking it off its stand and forcing a dying gasp of steam from the hot engine. Its noise melded with another coming from the darkness and seemed to form a voice from the grave.

When his father had shown him this place all those years ago, he'd warned him never to enter. 'It's perilous in there,' he'd stated. 'Full of gas and maybe hidden booby traps left by the Venetians or Turks.' He had sworn he never would.

Barba Yiorgos stepped into the entrance, climbing upwards and away from the chasing waves.

'A small promise broken,' he said, as another bat scythed past his head.

'Bigger ones to keep,' he vowed, moving forward.

❧

'My mother,' Eleni stated calmly, 'was not the daughter of a whore. My grandmother, Marianna, was a woman who fell in love. And when she did, she was willing to give and risk everything. Love is something a man like you couldn't even comprehend.'

Diomidis was getting redder in the face by degrees. Kirsty watched as the mask he wore began to dissolve. The transformation was startling, like Dr Jekyll and Mr Hyde, and just as scary. Only this time she was viewing the real thing, as Diomidis's eyes rolled upwards and, saurian-like, his tongue licked spittle from the corners of his mouth. He started to laugh with a high-pitched cackle. Panayotis and Leonidas lowered their heads, either afraid or ashamed of their father's madness.

Eleni held his stare, her head high and haughty.

'You,' he raged, 'know nothing about it. Your grandmother used her wiles to seduce a weak man away from his wife and children. She brought dishonour to *my* family. On Crete, unlike where you come from, honour is everything.'

'Does that include your father's honourable duty of letting the Germans murder an innocent woman, as well as his comrades?' Kirsty asked, trying to distract him from Eleni. 'And this has everything to do with you getting your hands on Michaelis's will. Or making sure no one is left alive to have any claim on it or to know of its existence. I suppose that's the reason why your father betrayed everyone to the Germans. It seems even they had more honour than him.'

Diomidis stamped over to Kirsty's chair. He slapped her across the face. She recoiled and the strap cut into her throat.

'My father was a great man!' he yelled. 'His legend is sacred. I will not allow anything or anyone to contaminate it. Do you understand?' He raised his hand to hit her again. 'The will is unimportant compared to that. Do you understand?'

'Huh!' Kirsty exclaimed.

'I understand that you've kidnapped us,' Eleni said, before he could strike Kirsty again. 'I can see that you enjoy beating women who are tied up. I know that everyone we talked to about my grandmother and Kapetanios Michaelis spoke of them with love and respect, except you. I also heard, in the voices of those who were willing to talk, that they were desperately afraid of someone. Now I know who it was and why. You're a cowardly thief, interested only in stealing what even your father's treachery couldn't gain.'

Diomidis moved towards his new tormentor. 'It was your slut of a grandmother who was the thief,' he raged. 'A woman who stole a husband from his wife, a father from his sons.'

Diomidis stopped and smiled as if he realised he was being deliberately provoked.

'Besides,' he said, sounding calmer and turning to Kirsty, 'it's your old lover who's sitting on that document, for now.' He gave his sons a contemptuous glance. 'It's he who's kept it hidden, waiting for the right price, no doubt.' He registered the look on Kirsty's face. 'Didn't he bother to mention that little involvement either? You do get led along, don't you?'

Kirsty couldn't reply.

Diomidis laughed. 'And thanks to his little truffle-seeking pig on a lead, I now know who my enemies still are, and what lies they are willing to tell. The cleansing has begun and will continue until only the loyal remain. And when the land is returned to its rightful owner, I'll make sure it's developed in such a way that the whole island will benefit.'

'Amen,' Kirsty said as sarcastically as she could.

Patrick and Eleni laughed as Diomidis's tirade faltered.

This time, Diomidis flew at Kirsty. In a long, scraping motion, he brought one of his boots brutally down her leg. The pain was excruciating; she cried out and felt blood ooze over her foot.

'Stop it, you bastard!' Eleni shouted. 'She's done nothing to you. This is between our families.'

Diomidis moved over to Eleni. 'You have no family,' he stated. 'You have no honour to protect. And soon, I guarantee, you will have even less.'

He strutted to his briefcase and fumbled inside.

'Get over there,' he ordered Eleni, pointing to the area by the two chairs in front of the sofa.

Eleni got up and walked slowly across the room, with Panayotis and Leonidas stalking her like stooping hyenas. She paused and grabbed Patrick's and Kirsty's bound hands. Kirsty managed to give her an encouraging squeeze and noticed that Eleni was cold but not trembling. Eleni let her hand go and turned to face Diomidis. He stood between his sons. He was holding something behind his back.

With a shiver, and a feeling of dread, Kirsty realised what it was.

Diomidis held the red chemise up to his face. He glared over the top of it at Eleni and smiled like some coy lover, wistful behind a veil. His smile became a grimace and he crushed the garment in his hand. 'Put this on,' he suddenly bellowed, making everyone jump. He tossed the chemise and it landed with a whisper and began to unfurl like a red rose.

'What?' Eleni snapped. 'Are you completely deranged?'

'Take your clothes off,' Diomidis shouted. 'All of them. Then put this on.'

'In your dreams.' Eleni gave him the finger as she said it.

Diomidis nodded to Panayotis who moved swiftly. Not, as Kirsty had feared, towards Eleni, but to Patrick instead. He pulled his pistol out and pointed it at Patrick's knee.

'No,' Eleni cried.

'Do what I command, now,' Diomidis growled. 'Do it quickly or Panayotis will start with your husband's legs and work his way up until there's nothing left.'

'Don't, Eleni,' Patrick pleaded. 'I love you. I'm not afraid of these perverts.'

Panayotis clubbed him across the side of his head with his pistol and, as Patrick sagged, aimed the gun back at his thigh and began squeezing the trigger.

'Okay,' Eleni said. She pulled her shirt over her head.

Eleni kept her eyes locked on her husband as she pulled off one boot, then the other. She rolled down the skin-tight white leggings, then stepped gracefully out of them. Kirsty heard Panayotis gasp as she stood there in a thong that matched the bra, transparent green with heavily embroidered purple flowers.

'Everything,' Diomidis ordered. Kirsty could see the revulsion in his face as he looked at the perfect body, trying to deny that his father's enemy could have produced such a grandchild.

Eleni unclipped the bra and let it fall to her feet. Diomidis stared at his sons as they both made exclamations of either approval or desire. A look of doubt crossed his face. Eleni eased her thong off, slowly and provocatively. Kirsty noticed that her eyes were no longer on Patrick but locked on Panayotis.

She put her hands in front of her vulva and lowered her head for the first time. Kirsty could have wept.

'Put that on, you filthy slut,' Diomidis ordered, pointing to the red chemise.

Eleni did, and it fitted perfectly. Eleni raised her head defiantly and put her hands on her hips. 'Turning you on, old man?' she mocked. 'Or are you past it?'

'You turn my stomach!' he bellowed, rushing over to his brief-case. He snatched the journal out of it.

'This,' he opened the book, 'is what your whore of a grand-mother wanted. To wear this while he copulated with her, I imagine. Dangling it seductively under his nose and writing about their fornicating afterwards. I've read her filth and lies . . .'

'Oh,' Kirsty interrupted, mocking him with the mistake he'd made when she'd gone to him, 'was that in "her grandmother's journal that I saw at dinner"?'

'You're so clever,' he hissed. 'But just so your friends know, if you and your senile lover had stayed out of this, they'd be free by now. They might have gone bleating to the police afterwards. To report what? Some fantasy about being kidnapped. But with no ransom note. Unhurt, with no idea of where they'd been and a wrecked vehicle to suggest they might have had reasons for keeping out of sight. This situation is the result of your and that drunken old coward's meddling.'

'Liar,' Kirsty snapped back at him. 'You just wanted to ensnare anyone who might learn about your father's treachery and get in the way of your greed. "Benefit the island"! "Family honour"! You're pathetic.'

Diomidis rushed at Kirsty and kicked her leg more savagely than the first time. As he did, Eleni grabbed his hair and tugged him away. He whipped around and backhanded her across the face so hard she staggered towards the sofa.

'Leave them alone, you little prick,' Patrick shouted. 'Kirsty's right. You have no honour, just guns. And morons for sons.'

'No more blasphemy,' Diomidis raged. 'I've had enough slander.' He motioned to Leonidas. 'Silence them.'

Kirsty noticed that, as Leonidas moved towards them, Panayotis was looking at Eleni with an expression of concern on his face. Leonidas tore a strip of wide tape off Patrick's chair. Patrick turned away, knowing what was going to happen. But it was pointless. Leonidas grasped him and stretched the tape across his mouth from ear to chin, then he did it with the second strip from the opposite direction, making a black cross over most of Patrick's face. Kirsty heard him struggling to breathe.

She needed to speak before being silenced. And, she thought, as she listened to what sounded like a death rattle coming from next to her, probably forever.

'Diomidis,' Kirsty appealed.

Leonidas looked at his father, who held up a stubby finger, telling him to wait.

'Why don't you let Eleni and Patrick go? As you said, no one is going to believe them. Barba Yiorgos and I discovered much more than they did.'

Kirsty hated herself for what she was going to say next but had no choice. 'Especially Barba Yiorgos. He's your real enemy. He has all the pieces. He told me. The ones to bring you to your knees.'

'I know he does,' Diomidis sneered. 'I found the little bird who sang to him. Funny thing was, this little bird couldn't fly.' He laughed again. 'Flutter, flutter all the way to the ground.'

'I don't know what you're talking about,' Kirsty said, trying to remain patient. 'But clearly you have matters well in hand. So why not let them go? You can do what you want to Barba Yiorgos and me. Eleni's mother is dying. Let her go back.'

'Dying?' He stared at Eleni with delight. 'Oh, my day is just getting better and better. So, soon there will be none. All the false claims and fabrications, along with the bodies, buried at last.'

'And he has the will,' Kirsty lied. 'He showed it to me in his house at Kotsiana. I know he would give it to you if you let Eleni and Patrick go.'

'Would he, now? I wonder how well you really know him! But he'll have no choice shortly. But thank you for telling me where he keeps it. I'll mention it to him before he dies and my vendetta is completed.'

'Vendetta?' Kirsty said. 'You have nothing to avenge. Just things to atone for. It's you who should . . .'

The tape cut off the rest of her words.

'Revenge,' Diomidis said as the black cross silenced her, 'will be mine. Now I must read my sons a bedtime story to get them in the right mood.'

Kirsty watched as he grubbed through the pages of the journal like a schoolboy with a smutty magazine, bending its spine and creasing pages.

'Ha ha,' Diomidis trilled, 'I have it. Listen, sons, and look now at the offspring of the whoring witch who wrote such filth: "Hours of passion . . . We made love again . . . Silk chemise fertility charm . . . Wriggled provocatively . . . Dangled it under his nose!"'

Kirsty watched his eyes darting from side to side as he raced through the sentences, finding what he wanted. His Greek translation of what she knew was the diary of a passionate young woman in love was crude and vulgar. But it seemed to be having the desired effect, because Panayotis and Leonidas were beginning to breathe heavily and stare even more intently at Eleni.

Kirsty looked at Eleni to register her reaction. She still stood straight and confident, her hands gently touching the red silk and brushing it against her thighs. A scent of Chanel No. 5 moved in the air.

'Filth,' Diomidis spat, throwing the journal across the room. He aimed it at the large marble basin, hoping, Kirsty imagined, that it would sink in the water, the words washed away forever.

It missed and landed softly near the window. Kirsty strained her head to see it as the moonlight touched the pages.

Diomidis moved angrily towards it.

Eleni spoke and stopped him. Her voice was firm and proud. 'When you reach it, why don't you translate some of the other pages? The ones about how members of your family, under your father's control, treated her. How she bore their insults and petty cruelties. How she forgave, and kept believing in love, until your father sold her to the Germans.'

'Lies,' he yelled. 'She was a worthless little slut like you. She besmirched my family name, as you would do.' Diomidis marched across the room, drawing his gun as he did. He pointed it at Patrick's leg. 'Now get on the sofa, on your knees. Or your husband will lose his.'

Eleni turned and moved as if in a trance. Her eyes met Kirsty's. Kirsty tried to give her a look of reassurance and courage. In truth, all she wanted to do was to be able to open her mouth and shout. To give an almighty ear-shattering bellow of anger, frustration and rage. A cry that would echo into the mountains and, even if no one answered, would linger so someone would listen and know the truth.

Eleni stopped and looked at Patrick. For Kirsty, this was the saddest moment of all. They were saying goodbye. And it was heart-breaking to witness.

'Move,' Diomidis snapped.

Eleni touched Patrick's face and then climbed onto the large, hide-covered sofa.

'On your hands and knees like the animal you are, bitch,' Diomidis hissed.

Eleni looked at the gun, now pointing at Patrick's heart, and did as she was told.

Diomidis spoke to his sons. 'Now, the reward I promised: you can rape this whore to death.'

He watched as Leonidas and Panayotis glowered at each other.

'Together,' he said, 'you will defile her, as her grandmother defiled our family's reputation. And her husband will go to his grave with the true pictures of what he gave his name to imprinted on his brain.'

The brothers began to approach Eleni. Kirsty could feel Patrick straining to break free. She saw blood beginning to run down his wrists and tried to escape herself. But neither of them could move. In fact, it felt to Kirsty as if the restraints had been designed to tighten with every push made against them.

'You will spoil her,' Diomidis raved. 'Fill every hole until you are drained and spent. Then use whatever object you can think of to carry on until she is destroyed. And you will leave the chemise on so it can go soiled to the grave with her.'

They stood next to the sofa, hypnotised by their father's perverted litany. And yet, Kirsty saw, still staring at each other as if neither was willing to risk making the first move.

Please, she prayed, let Eleni's game work.

'Do it,' Diomidis yelled. 'Now.'

Kirsty thought that even though he was shouting, some ineffectual tone had crept into his voice.

But then Leonidas began to unbuckle his belt and, after placing his gun on the cabinet, opened his trousers. He was bulging and slowly pulled down his pants far enough to expose his erect penis. He roughly grasped one of Eleni's thighs and moved onto the sofa until he was poised behind her. Kirsty looked on in agony as Eleni tried to close her legs and he forced them open and began to ease the chemise up.

Patrick was still straining to break free, and there was an expression on his face that Kirsty knew she would carry to *her* grave, along with the depravity she was witnessing.

'Wait,' Diomidis warned, as Leonidas was just inches away from entering Eleni. 'You must wait for your brother.'

Panayotis stared at Leonidas, then at Eleni, who was as inanimate as a blow-up doll.

Kirsty imagined Eleni had decided that to fight was pointless and was trying to blank her mind to what was happening.

Panayotis got up and placed his gun on the cabinet next to his brother's, before pulling his trousers down and climbing on the sofa. He was as hard and swollen as Leonidas. Kirsty noticed that both men's underpants were new, fashionable and, she guessed, bought recently, maybe to try to impress Eleni. The very notion made her want to gag.

'In her mouth,' Diomidis instructed him. 'Get in front of the whore and lift her head.'

He sounded, Kirsty thought, like the director of a porn movie, but she hoped, seeing the look on Panayotis's face, with part of his cast somewhat reluctant.

Her hopes were dashed as Panayotis came alive and threw himself totally into the role.

He crouched so that his legs were either side of Eleni's head, then grabbed her raven-black hair and yanked her up so that his penis was nearly touching her mouth.

Leonidas glanced from his brother to Diomidis, waiting for the signal to begin. Kirsty closed her eyes.

24.

Barba Yiorgos fought to keep moving. He didn't even want to breathe, as every breath he sucked in tasted as if he'd been burrowing through a burial site.

All the adrenaline, and perhaps vanity, was leaving him. He was an old man, crawling with grit in his mouth and the demons of the past in his mind.

He shone the torch into the void, and saw, for his effort, more blackened props straining under their burden, trap-like and waiting for him.

It wasn't long after he had entered the old tunnel that he reached his first cave-in. Just a small part of the roof had fallen. Not enough to seal the passage, but enough to make him dig and move olive wood beams as heavy and solid as those in his house at Kotsiana. As he did, he visualised the men who had cut this tunnel: prisoners harried by the whip and spear, digging not to escape but to allow their captors a portal to bring victims to torture, or to carry bodies away for a sea burial. Barba Yiorgos heard their cries as he moved forward.

A short way on, there was another, larger fall. This time his torch lit up a narrow gap that appeared to stretch away for metres.

He reached it and began to grub his way through, feeling, as he did, a change in the air. Now every breath was drawn through increasing layers of gauze. A band of steel was tightening around his chest. He stopped and listened. The sea noise—which sounded like it was pursuing him—had abated. But what had replaced it was worse. The tunnel was groaning and creaking as if protesting his intrusion. Barba Yiorgos could sense the movement all around him. It felt as if the cliff was working its will to make itself whole again and prevent this latest violation.

He shone his light back the way he'd come, then at his watch. Ten minutes left. Barba Yiorgos began forcing his way through the rest of the blockage with, to aid his strength, a picture of those prisoners at Aptera making their way along a different tunnel into the spotlights of their enemies.

And the man who'd been behind their betrayal.

And what his offspring were perpetrating a short way ahead.

He broke through and began to move upwards, telling himself there was still time: *if* there were no more cave-ins; *if* the door, when he reached it, was unlocked; *if* his 'police officers' had followed their instructions and got their timing right; and *if* there was anyone still left alive to rescue. *If? If? If? If?* The questions echoed along the passage, stronger than any breaking waves, and drove him on.

Then there was another noise, not answering the questions but ending them, as something heavy smashed onto his head and he momentarily blacked out.

Barba Yiorgos came around. He tried to move but couldn't. He reached his hand behind and touched the two large wooden props lying across his back. Like Christ recrucified, he thought, and nearly laughed. The rubble began to fall off him as he strained to break free and find his torch.

261

He did, and it flickered feebly back into life with a dull glow. Then, as its light faded, taking his sense of sight with it, another sense sharpened, and, with it, brought back a memory.

It had been just before he'd shed his bellboy uniform for the Army's version. A woman had handed him her Gucci case to carry and he'd trailed her into the hotel lift like a pet chimp. 'Thirteenth floor,' she ordered.

Her face looked innocent and so angelic she had to be a film star or top model.

But young Yiorgos already knew better. He could see through the disguise.

It was in her eyes. Eyes he'd already met a thousand times in New York. From the worn-out dead-cow ones—'A dollar for a hand-job, mister'—to this: the high-class call girl.

He knew she saw him drooling over her, as the marble- and mirror-clad lift carried them smoothly through another tunnel, this one an orifice of hidden grease, cobwebs, chains and pulleys. The world of the Eloi and Morlocks, the reality of their lives and this building.

She'd just been about to tell him which one he inhabited, when the two worlds collided.

The lift came to a shuddering halt.

Then the lights went off.

Yiorgos had expected her to cry out. Instead, she remained silent, her breathing unchanged, not even bothering to rebuke him or ask what the hell was going on. Nothing.

Then the emergency bulb had come on. It shone with a clinical blue glow.

The woman stared into the mirror, her breathing getting heavier and faster; she began to shake.

'It's okay,' Yiorgos said, trying to reassure her. 'This happens all the time. They'll fix it in a minute and you'll be back on your way to, to . . .' He faltered.

The woman didn't look at him, just at herself in the cold mirror glass. And clearly didn't like what she saw.

She began to panic.

Yiorgos moved to her. 'Take deep, slow breaths,' he coaxed.

'I can't,' she said. 'You don't see what I've just seen waiting for me.' She collapsed into his arms.

He held her quivering body firmly and felt her begin to calm.

She put her head on his shoulder and her long hair fell down over his neck. He caressed her and whispered, 'You're beautiful, and always will be. Nothing can touch you if you keep believing in yourself.'

She went still in his embrace.

The lift began to move back down and the lights came on.

Yiorgos had expected her to leap out of his arms. Instead, she'd clung to him, even after the lift doors had opened.

She moved gently away, took her bag from where it dangled in his hand and looked deeply into his eyes.

'You,' she soughed, 'have the colour of the sea in your eyes and the mountain breeze in your breath.' She kissed him full and long on the lips. 'I will always remember you.'

Then she had left, walking haughtily out of the hotel as if whatever liaison had been arranged no longer mattered. But her taste and perfume had stayed with him. And he could never smell Chanel No. 5 again without being transported back to that lift.

Now it jolted him out of his stupor with a force stronger than smelling salts.

It filled his nostrils as he lay there with what felt like half of Crete on his back and not enough fresh air to keep a cockroach alive. And it wasn't coming from a New York lift. It was drifting along the tunnel. Sensual and evocative. Close. But with a tang of fear and death coating it.

He braced his arms and, like Sampson eyeless in Gaza, began to push against the pillars.

25.

Time had frozen. Kirsty had always believed it was spatial, with clock springs made out of emotion. But this was different. Now it had frozen. The phrase 'pregnant pause' came inappropriately into her mind as she sat, eyes closed, trying to shut her ears to what she knew was about to start the pendulum swinging again: the brutal slapping of flesh against flesh and the grunting and snorting of animal savagery.

Instead, it was Eleni's voice—calm and sexy—that moved time.

'It was only you I wanted, Panayotis,' she said. 'Ever since I saw how easily you beat my husband, I've been longing for you to take me.'

Kirsty opened her eyes, hardly believing what she'd heard.

The scene hadn't changed. Leonidas still had one hand grasping the red silk chemise, while his other hand held his erect penis.

Panayotis was still clutching Eleni's hair, as erect as his brother, inches away from the voluptuous lips that had just spoken.

Kirsty saw both men tense as they prepared to begin their violation of Eleni.

'Now,' Diomidis shouted. 'Do it.'

Leonidas moved, shoving himself viciously into Eleni so she cried out in pain. Kirsty watched Panayotis's eyes go darker than ever. He tossed Eleni sideways before his brother's first thrust was even completed. Eleni crashed against the carved back of the sofa as Panayotis sprang on Leonidas. The black hair hanging from his head and covering his naked body made Panayotis appear more animal than human. He crushed his brother and there was a cracking noise and whoosh of air leaving Leonidas's body. They fell to the floor and began struggling at Patrick's feet.

Panayotis held his bear hug, squeezing so hard Kirsty could see the veins in his arms, pumped up like strands of rope. Leonidas's eyes were bulging and he appeared stunned. Suddenly, though, he recovered from the surprise of his brother's assault and smashed his huge forehead into Panayotis's face, bursting his nose in an explosion of blood. Panayotis carried on squeezing, turning his head away so he was looking at Eleni, who'd sat up and was watching the fight. She had covered herself modestly with one of the hides. Kirsty saw her smile and give Panayotis a look of approval and encouragement. He crushed Leonidas even tighter, snorting blood out of his nostrils like a mad bull.

Kirsty turned away to Diomidis. His mouth was wide open in disbelief, the gun hanging limply by his side.

Her eyes moved back to the battle.

Leonidas tried to butt Panayotis again. This time he missed. Kirsty could see his colour changing and strength fading.

'Fight, you bastard,' she slurred into the tape covering her mouth, not wanting it to end. And not just out of fear for what the victor would believe he had the right to do with Eleni, but for the look on Diomidis's face: that nearly paid for all of this.

Leonidas managed to get his head close to his brother's ear and, for a moment, Kirsty thought he was about to offer his surrender or plead for mercy. But his mouth opened and he locked his teeth on Panayotis's ear, biting and shaking. More blood spilled from Panayotis. He shrieked, let go of his hold and shoved a thumb into

Leonidas's eye. As he did, Leonidas pulled a knife from his belt and slashed it across his brother's chest. Panayotis cried out as the wound burst open. They parted, crouching back on their haunches, bloodied and spent.

'Good,' Diomidis said. 'Now that matter is settled.' His voice sounded tremulous.

But it wasn't, according to one of the players.

'Do it,' Eleni commanded. 'Finish him if you really want me.'

Kirsty saw Eleni's smile, and registered, with a shock, that this could be about more than her survival. She also thought, as she clearly saw Eleni's family resemblance to Barba Yiorgos, that maybe she'd come to do what he and his father had failed to do: avenge her grandmother. And if this was the perfect opportunity, she was capable of forgetting everything else to take it. The thought chilled her as much as the scene she was witnessing.

The brothers rose: Leonidas, one eye closed, Panayotis, blood-soaked. But they were going to continue as another 'Helen' set man against man.

Diomidis tried to stop them. 'Cease this nonsense, you fools. Can't you see this is what she wants? To divide us and cast more shame and dishonour on our family as her grandmother did?'

Neither of them paid him any attention. They were rocking on their feet, still exposed, like two obscene wrestlers preparing to clash.

Then they did, with a shuddering force that moved the floor.

Panayotis brought his knee up into Leonidas's groin so hard his brother left the ground. He came down, buckled, and got another knee in his mouth this time. Leonidas carried on regardless, crashed a rugby punch into Panayotis's already-wrecked nose and, as his head went back, followed it with a punch into his neck.

This, Kirsty realised, was going to be a fight to the death for the prize sitting just feet away.

Diomidis was standing transfixed. Kirsty looked at him, his face contorted in fear and indecision. He was holding his gun and waving it about, aiming it into the air, at his sons' feet, then at Kirsty and Patrick.

One of the oil lamps went flying as the brothers crashed into the cabinet. It burst into a ring of fire and caught them alight. They parted and began stamping out the flames like Anasternarian fire-walkers who'd lost their faith.

Diomidis marched forward as they extinguished the flames and prepared to fight again. This time he was pointing the gun at Eleni and the steel was back in his voice. 'Either of you moves, and I'll blow the little slut's head off.' He looked disgustedly at their bloodied faces. 'I'm even willing to forget and forgive this madness and, if you're still capable, let you have her. But it has to be together or not at all.'

Kirsty watched as they bowed their heads to his will.

'Now shake hands and do your duty.'

They reached out and reluctantly shook hands. Then they turned on Eleni with hunger burning in their eyes and began to move on her.

Lights burst through the windows. Halogen spotlights that froze them in the sudden glare.

A bullhorn bellowed, 'This is the police. We have you surrounded. Put down your weapons and come out with your hands raised.'

Diomidis stared out of the window. 'The police are here,' he said, looking at the uniformed figures, hazy in the distance. 'Leonidas, fire a few shots and take out some of the lights to keep them away, then follow us. Panayotis, get our guests gathered up and we'll go through the tunnel and say our goodbyes to them on the beach. No one knows about this escape passage. Nobody will know who was here.'

A deep voice spoke before anyone moved.

'Someone else does,' it announced, matter-of-factly.

Kirsty looked, as did everyone except Diomidis, who appeared as if he were petrified to acknowledge who'd spoken.

Barba Yiorgos had entered silently and had a gun held at arm's length, pointed at the back of Diomidis's head.

Kirsty felt a rush of relief course through her body. She had to fight not to burst into tears. He looked splendid in his uniform: dusty, but regal.

He quickly and steadily appraised the scene. He approached Diomidis. 'Drop the gun,' Barba Yiorgos ordered, jamming his pistol against Diomidis's neck. He did, and Barba Yiorgos shoved the gun away with one of his heavy black boots. 'Sit down,' he said, pushing Diomidis towards the table. Then he moved into position so he could cover the whole room.

Kirsty saw him glance at the guns on the cabinet and at Panayotis and Leonidas. 'You move away from those pop guns, goat boys,' he jeered. 'And do it very slowly, because I'm a nervous old man who's likely to get trigger happy.'

Kirsty thought he appeared anything but nervous or old. The large pistol, which looked well used, was rock steady, and he was poised like a cat.

'And, boys,' he sneered, 'put those tiny dicks back in your pants; you've given these good people enough of a laugh for one night.'

Barba Yiorgos gave Kirsty and Patrick a reassuring smile.

Then he focused on Eleni. Kirsty watched as their eyes locked. What she witnessed was unmistakable: the same expression, mirrored on their faces.

And it was one that disturbed her.

Barba Yiorgos's normally bright and inviting blue eyes were pale and as cold as ice. As were Eleni's. Some message seemed to be passing between them. Then they nodded their heads as if whatever it was they were communicating had been agreed. Eleni smiled, then stared at Diomidis with a look that chilled Kirsty.

Kirsty knew that Barba Yiorgos couldn't risk turning his back on anyone to release them, and whispered a prayer that his 'police' would arrive. She tried to show him with her eyes the knives the brothers were wearing, and warn him how fast they could move, but his attention was still focused on Eleni.

'You,' he said to Diomidis. 'Pick up Eleni's clothes. Fold them gently and neatly, then carry them over. Place them at the opposite side of the sofa from her, then shuffle your way back here.'

'One of my sons can do it,' Diomidis replied. 'I'm nobody's servant. Especially not that little . . .'

Barba Yiorgos moved forward quickly. He balled his left hand into a fist and smashed it into Diomidis's mouth. He stepped away just as quickly and levelled the gun on Panayotis and Leonidas, who'd reacted as if they'd received the blow.

Diomidis put his hand to his mouth and peered at the back of it. Kirsty could see an even bigger look of shock on his face that there was some of his precious blood on it.

'Now move your worthless arse,' Barba Yiorgos snapped, 'or next time I'll use the pistol barrel on you.'

Diomidis gathered up Eleni's clothes. He tossed them onto the sofa, then moved back. As he did, Diomidis gave a signal to his sons. Kirsty made a long, groaning sound and gestured with her head to Barba Yiorgos, trying to warn him.

Unbelievably, he made his tutting noise as if to scold her for her concern.

Diomidis slumped into his chair and started dabbing at his mouth with the same handkerchief he'd tried to give to Kirsty.

'Now,' Barba Yiorgos said, 'Eleni is going to be allowed the grace to dress herself before the cavalry come charging in. And I'll blind the first fucking son of a bitch who takes even a peep at her. So look this way.'

All heads turned to him, including Kirsty's and Patrick's, as Eleni began to move behind them. Kirsty watched as Barba Yiorgos held their gaze without blinking. She searched his face for the slightest flicker of his vision darting towards Eleni. It did not.

'Finished,' she called to him.

Barba Yiorgos moved slowly to the window, neither his gun nor his attention wavering from the room. He picked up an oil lamp and waved it back and forth.

A few moments later Kirsty heard heavy footsteps running towards the house. The door burst open.

Andonis, the Gorilla, came in first. He still had the bullhorn dangling from his neck and was carrying a large pistol. Michaelis arrived next with a sawn-off shotgun in his hand.

Both men were dressed in police uniforms that Kirsty could see had been bought from one of the carnival shops. They were the type worn by the Keystone Cops, and she smiled at the audacity and improvisation of Barba Yiorgos's plan.

'Release them,' he said to Michaelis. 'Andonis, help keep the goat boys covered.'

Michaelis touched the tape covering Kirsty's mouth. He gave her an apologetic look, then pulled the first strip off quickly. Kirsty felt a wave of pain and water came into her eyes. He removed the next one before she had time to anticipate it.

'Thanks,' she said as he undid her restraints. 'I think.'

He grinned and there was a movement from behind him. He spun and levelled the shotgun at Leonidas.

'I was just shifting my foot,' Leonidas said arrogantly.

'You shift it again, goat boy,' Michaelis promised, 'and I'll blow the fucking thing off.'

Michaelis released Kirsty and then moved to Patrick. Eleni started to rise from the sofa to help.

'Don't,' Andonis warned. 'Stay clear of them and out of the line of fire.'

Kirsty watched the sly look on Panayotis's face fade, and thought of the difference between the normal buffoonery of the Gorilla and the Cretan warrior now present.

Then pins and needles hit her arms and legs, and she felt like she was being devoured by an army of ants. Her neck was aching from the strap and she could hardly swallow. The pain from her kicked legs began to throb and she was certain if she tried to stand she would fall and end up squirming at the feet of her enemies.

Patrick appeared even worse as he was released. The blow from Panayotis's pistol had swollen his already-battered face, and his struggles to reach Eleni had cut his wrists, legs and neck. Kirsty looked at Eleni, who had bent forward and was beginning to shake, and feared she was going into shock.

'You'll be okay now,' Kirsty said to her. 'We all will.'

'You will,' Barba Yiorgos confirmed. 'But now you must leave. Andonis will drive you to my home in Kotsiana—I've given him a map in case you forgot. My cousin, Vassilis, is the best doctor on the island, and he will be called to tend to you. Michaelis is going to fetch the police, as they'll never find this place without his help. I will stay with this scum until they arrive.'

Kirsty saw Diomidis grin.

'No,' she said. 'I'm staying with you. We started out on this together; we'll finish it that way.'

Barba Yiorgos gave her a sad look as if he wished it could be so.

'You must go; Eleni will need you.'

Kirsty stared at Eleni, who was still hunched forward, willing her to tell Barba Yiorgos that she was fine. But Eleni remained silent and started shaking even more violently, as if to confirm what he'd said.

Michaelis pointed his gun at Panayotis and Leonidas, while Andonis helped Patrick and Eleni to get up and move cautiously towards the door.

'Thank you,' Patrick said, passing Barba Yiorgos.

As Eleni got close to Barba Yiorgos, she straightened up and embraced him. Kirsty watched her whispering to him as he held her with one arm, the gun still pointing with the other. Then Eleni turned towards Diomidis and spat in his face. Kirsty was shocked and riveted, as the spittle ran down his face. She felt Andonis, who was helping her out now, tense, and saw Barba Yiorgos's gun twitch slightly.

Diomidis didn't respond. He let the spit snail trail its way down to his lips. 'You think this is over,' he said, not caring that Eleni's saliva was sliding into his mouth. 'But I have a long memory for such tastes as these.'

Eleni's eyes narrowed and she held his gaze. 'I have long memories, too,' she said calmly. 'Ones I've inherited. But unlike yours, they're not sullied by treachery. You're finished.'

Her eyes flashed to Barba Yiorgos as she spoke and he nodded to her. 'Go, child,' he said. 'We'll meet soon. I have something for you. Something I've been guarding for many years.'

'No,' Kirsty heard Diomidis sob.

Eleni followed Patrick out into the cold, misty Cretan night.

'Barba Yiorgos,' Kirsty said as she felt herself being propelled through the door, 'let me stay with you, please.'

He smiled and shook his head.

'Then let your son stay with you. We can send Andonis to fetch the police after we reach your home. There's no need for you to be alone.'

'There is. And you must go. Besides, you need medical attention for your wounds.'

Kirsty glanced back into the room at Diomidis's sons. The blood had dried on their faces, hair and moustaches. It looked like war paint and she could feel them tensing in anticipation of the coming battle.

'Barba Yiorgos,' she pleaded as she felt Andonis moving her away, 'let me stay.'

Then she was dazzled by the rows of spotlights on the roofs of the two 4x4s. For some reason, the memory of Barba Yiorgos in the monastery came to her, when he'd asked her to spend the night on the beach with him. Kirsty saw the army of ghost heroes marching across the sands, and the vision of Barba Yiorgos joining them came to her, colder than the air she was now breathing. She turned, determined to go to him.

Andonis grabbed her arm. 'Kirsty, we must go. Barba Yiorgos knows what he's doing.'

'Does he?' Kirsty said. 'Do any of us? I have terrible feelings.' She pictured the look that had passed between Eleni and Barba Yiorgos and tried to understand what it had been about as she trudged after the other figures fading into the mist.

❧

The moment the door closed, Diomidis started speaking.

'So what do you really want, Yiorgos? The Scottish woman? You need another wife to keep you warm in the winter? Still life in the old dog yet, hey?' He laughed warmly.

Barba Yiorgos didn't reply. He kept his Colt pistol steady, and knew death waited if he was distracted. He longed to hear the vehicles go. For the surgical quality of the spotlights to diminish and leave him in the flickering lights, similar to the one that had danced near Marianna's grave.

'If you really want to give away all of your father's property to foreigners, so be it,' Diomidis continued. 'I'll make sure you have plenty of other land and money to compensate. Kirsty's kafenion could look like a palace by the time my men finished working on it. All of this can be forgotten.'

'I thought you just claimed you had a long memory,' Barba Yiorgos said, looking away from the rest of the room and into Diomidis's eyes.

The instant he did, Panayotis moved. He dropped into a crouch and drew a double-barrelled derringer pistol from its ankle holster. He fired, and the first bullet whistled past Barba Yiorgos's shoulder. The second shot was aimed lower and smashed into his thigh, and sent him staggering backwards. The pain from the .32 bullet was excruciating and burst through him like a red-hot stiletto. But he'd felt worse.

Panayotis charged at him and Barba Yiorgos fired. His first shot hit Panayotis in the chest and took out most of his heart; his second removed the left side of his head, spraying his brother with a fresh coating of blood.

This brought Leonidas to life, and he moved over the collapsing body of his brother, leaping into the air, snatching the two swords off the wall and landing with an elegant Cretan dance step that brought him closer to Diomidis, who was cowering in his chair.

Leonidas began spinning the strange-looking weapons. Their blades were thick and rippled. On either side of their handles were two shorter blades like Neptune's trident. He began to whirr them and made another kicking move to get closer to Barba Yiorgos. They gyrated in his hands like fans, hypnotically, making any chance of a target a confusion of movement.

Barba Yiorgos watched the performance, unable to react.

Then Kirsty screamed from what seemed like a long way off. It snapped him out of his trance as the first of the blades sliced through the hairs of his beard.

He fired, and the .45 dumdum bullet he'd worked on so meticulously blew Leonidas away. He landed backwards. The two blades in his hands clattered on the floor like the wings of some downed harpy. A small entry hole of red marked his breast neatly, while a patch the size of a dinner plate was forming on his back.

He still clung to the swords and appealed, glassy-eyed, to his father for help. Diomidis gestured to him—without any sign of compassion—to continue, and Barba Yiorgos watched as Leonidas rose to the command.

Barba Yiorgos shot him in the testicles. 'For what you were going to do to her,' he hissed. Then put the next round into the man's screaming mouth to finish him off.

Diomidis dropped off the chair and sprawled in some of the blood.

'Spare me,' he sobbed at Barba Yiorgos's feet. 'You have avenged your father. My sons have paid the price. Grant me mercy.'

'As you were going to do?'

Diomidis raised his head and met Barba Yiorgos's eyes with a look of remorse. 'If I'd had your father,' he said, 'instead of mine, *I* would have. Michaelis was a great man; I know that now. You are a true Kapetanios like he was. Show the same grace he did in his life, *Barba* Yiorgos.'

And with those words and the use of that name, decades of pain and doubt seemed to lift.

ॐ

Kirsty reached Andonis's vehicle, where Patrick and Eleni were sitting wrapped in each other's arms in the rear. She stared down through the beams of light and saw the stone house glowing ephemerally in the night, as a shadow she recognised moved across the window. She heard two small shots followed by two much heavier, thudding ones.

Andonis and Michaelis turned to her as another silhouette danced crazily across the window. They were both immobile and she could tell they weren't going to respond quickly enough.

'Don't hurt him,' Kirsty shouted, and began running to the house.

'No,' Andonis yelled. 'Wait. They've got their guns back.'

Kirsty could almost hear the bullets whizzing at her, but didn't care. All she could visualise was Barba Yiorgos lying on the floor. She had to help him. Or at least see him one last time. To cradle him in her arms. To die with him, if necessary. He'd come to rescue her and she wouldn't abandon him.

Another truth came to her, one that had been there, unvoiced, denied even, for some time now—that she'd grown to love him in so many ways. Kirsty felt a desperate longing to tell him this before it was too late.

She shoved the door open and was stunned out of movement or words.

There was blood everywhere. Panayotis and Leonidas—or what remained of them—were lying in ruby lagoons of it, with the yellow glow of the oil lamps flickering on its surface like the flames of their funeral pyre.

But it wasn't this sight that shocked Kirsty out of further action. It was the scene she was witnessing at the other end of the room.

Barba Yiorgos stood, blood streaming from his leg, behind the kneeling figure of Diomidis. Diomidis looked up as Kirsty opened the door and appeared remorseful. Barba Yiorgos placed his hand on the man's shoulder and put the gun back in its holster. The gesture seemed forgiving, almost parental, Kirsty thought. He looked over at Kirsty and smiled.

As he did, there was a sudden swirl of movement. She watched, transfixed as, in a flash, Barba Yiorgos withdrew his long knife. Its blade gleamed, catching all the lights, ancient and modern, as it sliced through the air.

Then everything seemed to happen in slow motion. 'No,' Kirsty heard her voice calling as Barba Yiorgos's knuckles went as white as the dead bones on the handle of the saita knife and, with all of his strength in an endless scimitar arc, he cut Diomidis's neck from one side to the other.

Diomidis kicked wildly, before dropping forward with hardly enough sinew left to hold his head on.

Kirsty screamed. She felt the room begin to spin and collapsed backwards into the arms of Andonis.

26.

Kirsty thought she was drowning in blood. She was in the film she'd seen at the open-air cinema in Chania: Coppola's version of Dracula. The scene where the future vampire curses God, and blood enters the room like a tsunami. She began struggling to escape but could not because she was strapped into a chair again. Only this time, they'd forgotten to gag her and she began shouting to be released.

'Kirsty,' Andonis answered, his arm gently rocking her shoulder, 'wake up.'

Someone put another hand on her other shoulder from behind. 'You were dreaming,' Eleni said. 'You're free. We all are.'

Kirsty opened her eyes and saw a moving nightscape of skeletal trees and a winding road lit by headlights.

'Where are we?' she asked.

'Halfway home,' Andonis replied. 'You passed out and I carried you to the truck.'

Kirsty could taste something metallic and wanted to gag. She hated being sick. The idea of doing it in front of people disgusted her nearly as much as what was tainting her mouth. She tried to swallow, but couldn't. Kirsty just about got the window open in time.

The fresh air felt great, and for a moment, seeing the moonlit trees and rocks, she almost imagined they might have been on their way home from a Cretan celebration and she'd overdone it on too much food and drink. She heard Barba Yiorgos gently tutting away and saying, 'I told you so.'

Only that was just a dream. She was dry-heaving. And all she could taste coming up after this feast was blood.

'Do you want me to stop?' Andonis asked when she got her head back inside.

'I just want to go home,' she whispered.

'We'll be there soon,' he assured her. 'The doctor will be waiting.'

He threw the vehicle, fast and effortlessly, into a hairpin bend. A cliff dropped away to the left and Kirsty saw a twinkling of lights bobbing on a squid-ink sea. She thought of how scared Barba Yiorgos was of the water, and knew that if he'd been alone earlier, the brothers would have dragged him into its cold depths. Eleni would have been gang-raped in every way possible and then killed. They'd have probably done the same to her. Then tortured and murdered Patrick. The three of them would have been buried in a dark, hidden ravine before dawn. All on Diomidis's orders.

She knew he was mad and evil. But witnessing Barba Yiorgos slaughter Diomidis, for what she knew could only be the fulfilment of their vendetta, hadn't only frightened her: it had disgusted her. It seemed to Kirsty that their victory had been sullied by it, and they'd sunk to the level of those they'd been struggling to defeat. No matter how she tried to think of Barba Yiorgos as their saviour and the hero, she couldn't find a way of justifying his final act.

'I want to go home,' Kirsty repeated, louder this time.

And she did want to.

Away from this country of long memories and revenge. Back to Scotland, where disputes were settled with harsh words, fists and the occasional head-butt. Then forgotten and usually pardoned.

'But you can never go back,' a familiar voice whispered. 'And must never run away.'

Kirsty ignored it. 'My house,' she stated.

'Kirsty,' Patrick pleaded. 'Barba Yiorgos said we should stay together. We should wait . . .'

'I'm sure he did,' Kirsty replied, trying to remain calm, 'and for the best of reasons. But at the moment, I want to be alone and try to understand what I've just witnessed. I think you owe me that at least. That's not asking too much, is it?' Kirsty's voice rose alarmingly and she felt the sickness coming again.

'All right,' Andonis said. 'But I still think we should stay together.'

'Please, Kirsty,' Eleni said. '*I* want you to come. I really want . . .'

'I think you've got everything you wanted,' Kirsty voiced loudly. 'All the revenge and vendetta you came for. Every little bloody drop of it. And you made me part of it. And I believe all the right we had on our side just died back there.'

'Kirsty,' Patrick tried to calm her, 'I don't think you know what you're saying. Barba Yiorgos just saved our lives. He's a hero. You've been through a terrible ordeal. Friends should stick together at times like these.'

'Stick together! Then we'll share everything. I'll tell you how this ended: with Diomidis kneeling at Yiorgos's feet, and Panayotis and Leonidas lying dead in pools of blood a short way off.'

'He was a wicked man,' Eleni said. 'His sons were the same.'

'And that,' Kirsty responded, hardly able to voice the words, 'gave Yiorgos the right to cut his head off in cold blood? Is that a shock to you, Eleni? Or did you know he was going to do it? Is that what all the whispering was about?'

'Kirsty,' Andonis said, 'I saw what Barba Yiorgos did. I also saw what Diomidis clutched in his hand as he died.'

'What are you talking about?' In her mind, Kirsty stared back into the room, to the exact moment when the blade had severed Diomidis's neck and she'd fainted in Andonis's arms.

'Diomidis's hands were clasped in front of him, almost as if he were praying for forgiveness.'

'He had a gun, Kirsty,' Andonis stated emphatically. 'A small double-barrelled derringer. The same as the one lying next to Panayotis, that he'd probably shot Barba Yiorgos with as he was trying to protect us. Diomidis must have had it hidden and drew it out as you came in. He died clutching it. Barba Yiorgos knew he meant to kill you.'

Kirsty wanted to believe this more than anything. 'There was no gun,' she sighed. 'Diomidis's hands were empty and Yiorgos executed him. And that's exactly what I'm going to tell the police.'

Andonis shook his head. 'I saw the gun,' he said. 'It will still be in Diomidis's hand when the police arrive.'

'I bet it will. And you're going to back up this fabrication, aren't you?' Kirsty turned and locked eyes with Eleni. 'I expect you sneaked in while I was out cold. Just to make certain that you got all the details clear.'

'No,' Eleni said softly. 'But I did help Michaelis get Barba Yiorgos into his truck. He'd lost a lot of blood and was very grey and weak. His biggest concern, though, was for us, and especially you. Maybe you should think about that.'

Kirsty looked at the rear seat. The journal was resting, along with the red chemise, on Eleni's lap. She was holding Patrick's hand, and one or both of them were trembling so badly that the pages and fabric were moving. Kirsty tried to think of the woman who'd written on the pages and planned, so sexily, to wear the garment. And the terrible thing that had happened to her. It made no difference. 'So now it's over?' Kirsty questioned. 'Or is it? Can hatreds that run so deep ever end?'

'I know this was meant to be,' Patrick replied. 'It was Barba Yiorgos's and Eleni's destiny. And it is over.'

'Well, I hope you're right. Because I don't believe it. The cycle of blood isn't my idea of justice. I'm sorry.' Kirsty turned her head to the side window and stared out into the harsh Cretan night, full of too many shadows and hiding places. All she could think of was her father and the times he'd told her, when describing another crime of violence, 'The pen is mightier than the sword.' As another voice stated that he was dead, murdered if she was right, without any justice or revenge to soften his passing.

☙

Kirsty had drifted off several times on her sofa. Each time, she'd been jarred awake by shocking flashbacks of Barba Yiorgos cutting Diomidis's throat. Now, as dawn arrived, she was afraid to close her eyes.

Ever since Andonis had dropped her off and she'd walked away, ignoring their pleas for her to stay, not even returning their goodbyes, she'd been waiting for the police to arrive. Or for the phone to ring, wondering if she would answer it, knowing she would. And hoping that Barba Yiorgos would be on the other end, checking on her. She wanted to ask him, 'Do you remember Telemachus shining his light into the places of darkness? His dreams of reconciliation?' Then listen, as he gave a glimmer of something to follow back from the darkness now engulfing her. But there was nothing except the solitary chirping of some lovelorn cricket and the sea's whispered harmony to its song.

෴

Andonis pulled up just after Kirsty had opened the kafenion. She was dusting some of the outside tables and hoped he was going to lift up his bullhorn and shout out, 'Wake up, Kirsty, it's just been a dream. You're back in Kansas now.'

'They're safe,' he said, sagging onto a chair.

Kirsty could see that he'd had even less sleep than she had. For a moment, a terrible image of him and Michaelis, working like two ghouls to hide the remains and evidence of Barba Yiorgos's butchery, flashed across her mind. Then it passed, as she saw a look of genuine concern and sadness on his normally mischievous face.

'I'll get us some coffee,' Kirsty said. 'Then you can tell me what's going on.'

She fetched the drinks, praying that no early-morning Germans on their way to storm the beach would arrive, demanding beer and hotdogs.

'After I brought you home,' Andonis began, 'I took Eleni and Patrick to Kotsiana. Barba Yiorgos, his cousin Vasillis the doctor and Michaelis were already there. Barba Yiorgos had only a flesh wound in his leg, though he'd lost a lot of blood. Vasillis thought he should go to the hospital for a transfusion, but he refused, saying a bottle of Mythos and a few shots of tsikoudia were all he needed!'

In spite of herself, Kirsty couldn't help smiling.

'Patrick had some broken ribs and other injuries, but nothing too serious,' he continued. 'But it was Eleni who took it the worst.'

'What?' Kirsty exclaimed. 'She told me that up until last night the brothers had left her alone.'

Kirsty felt a chill at the thought that maybe Eleni had been lying to stop her from being afraid, and that all manner of atrocities had taken place without Diomidis knowing. Or even Patrick.

'I think they had, physically at least. Eleni insisted, when we reached the village house, that the first thing she had to do was call her parents. She was desperate to let them know they were safe, and very worried about what the recent silence may have done to Athena's already-fading health.

'Eleni used Barba Yiorgos's upstairs phone and was on it for ages. Then she came down and told Patrick that her parents had been frantic and just longed to have them home.

'Then she broke down. I've never heard sobbing like it, and never want to again. Nothing could console her and she clung to Barba Yiorgos like her life depended on him. In the end the doctor sedated her and they put her to bed. I can't imagine what that girl's been through. Or how she stood up to it.'

'And where are all the heroes now?' Kirsty asked, cutting him off.

'Barba Yiorgos wanted to be taken to his beach house. Eleni and Patrick are staying at the village, under doctor's orders to relax and recover before they travel back to England. He's going to check on them this morning, and I'll get a car to them and . . .'

'What about the police?' Kirsty interrupted. 'And the small matter of the pile of bodies we left in our wake? Or have they already disappeared without trace?'

'Michaelis is on his way to the police now. He left Barba Yiorgos's house at the same time as I did. The doctor said that none of the victims were in a fit state to be questioned last night and insisted that we wait until morning. Michaelis will take the police to the scene, and I imagine we'll be interviewed, maybe arrested or even charged. I guess it depends on who says what to them and how it's interpreted.'

'You mean the truth versus lies?' Kirsty snapped. 'Is this your latest mission, to soften me up? Or to brief me on what to say? Is that what Yiorgos sent you for?'

'No. He wanted me to check that you were coping and to tell you the police would be coming. Followed closely, once this gets out, by the press and media—including the international media, as it involves foreigners. And also to let you know you have friends who are still there for you.'

'Not brave enough to call himself?'

'He wanted to, but I think he's unsure that you would want to hear from him, after Eleni told him what you said on the way home. But he asked me to tell you that you're wrong. He did some of what he did out of honour and duty, but the end was not of his choosing. Though he doesn't expect you to understand everything.'

'Why? Because I'm an "English woman"? A Frank? And only Cretans have the God-given right to commit murder and dress it up as honour?'

Andonis looked sheepish. A group of red-faced, white-legged British tourists arrived and he got up.

'Do you want Vasillis to come and examine you?'

'I'm fine,' Kirsty replied. Though in truth, her legs were hurting like hell and she'd had to plaster her face in make-up to try to hide the bruising. 'I can take care of myself.'

He touched her gently. 'I'll be back,' he said, and fled before she could tell him not to bother.

༖

A police car arrived for Kirsty early that afternoon. Two police officers, who normally mooched free drinks, acted like they'd never seen her before. She was requested, loudly, in her kafenion full of gossipy ex-pats and tourists, to accompany them to the station. As they reached the car, the owner of Cristos's taverna stepped out and pointed his video camera at her.

'Get used to it,' Kirsty told herself as they drove off. She felt everyone staring and heard tongues already beginning to wag.

'Am I being arrested?' she asked the taciturn officers as they sped through the chaotic streets of Chania. 'Don't you have to caution me or have a warrant?'

'That'll be up to the investigating detective,' one replied.

'At the moment,' the other added, 'you're assisting us with our enquiries.'

And she did, for the next three hours. They seemed to believe everything she was saying and kept complimenting her on her courage and ingenuity.

All the time, Kirsty was watching the tape machine turning two tapes, counting down to the final scene, probably the final question, knowing that when the words were out they could never be retrieved.

'So you ran back in,' the younger detective encouraged. 'That was very brave.'

Kirsty pictured herself as she charged along those beams of light, and recalled what had been in her heart at that moment. Then what had been waiting when she'd arrived.

'I suppose it was. Though I wish I hadn't now.'

'No,' the older one said. 'I was one of the first officers to reach the scene. No wonder you fainted!'

'And you threw open the door,' the young one continued as she drifted away, imagining Eleni, Patrick and Barba Yiorgos recounting their tale, supported by Michaelis and Andonis.

'When I heard the guns go off, I thought they'd shot Yiorgos . . .'

'Which they had,' the elder officer stated.

'I needed to help him. I don't know. It was all happening so fast. To try to rescue him, I guess.'

'As he had done for you. For all of you, in truth,' he butted in again.

This wasn't coming out how Kirsty had planned it. In fact, she felt herself getting more tongue-tied with every word. 'I needed to see him anyway,' she blurted, the tears beginning to well up in her eyes, and she knew that if she didn't hurry this, she was going to break down. 'There was so much blood, flesh and bits of brain.'

Kirsty began to shake.

'It's all right,' the older officer soothed. 'You've done brilliantly. I've just one final question, then we'll get you down to the hospital for a check-up.'

Kirsty tensed, preparing herself for the question and its only answer.

'Now, did you actually see Diomidis aim the gun at you before Yiorgos stopped him firing? Or did he just get his hand to it as you started to black out?'

I'm doing this under protest, Kirsty told herself, and will never fully forgive Barba Yiorgos for what he did. 'It happened so quickly,' she lied, seeing in her mind the slow-motion arc of the knife, 'but I'm certain he had it pointed at me.'

The tape machine went off and both men sighed heavily.

'That's exactly what Yiorgos told us. Well, I think we've got everything we need at the moment. We may have to contact you again as the enquiry continues. But nothing like this—just some minor points, perhaps.

'I'll tell you something, off the record, that may make you feel even prouder of what you've achieved. Diomidis was an evil and corrupt man. He thought, like a lot of these types, that he had the police in his pocket and could get away with anything. But we had an arrest warrant out that day and were searching for him.

'In what seemed like a totally unconnected incident, we were on a murder investigation. We'd been led to the body of an old lady. Every bone in her body had been broken, her skull caved in, and then she'd been set on fire. A witness—one of Diomidis's family—came forward and betrayed him. She'd seen him arrive, heard a scuffle and cries, watched him carry a lamp back into the house. She tried to go in and help after Diomidis had gone, but the flames were too fierce, and she's an old lady herself. I think it was her guilt over this, or the fact she hadn't tried earlier, that made her turn on him. Or the fact, as she told us, that he was laughing as he left.

'When Yiorgos gave us his full statement, it all fell into place. The woman's name was Olga. She was apparently the last person in your quest. Only I don't think you met her.'

'No,' Kirsty replied. 'I lost the faith, you might say. Only Yiorgos kept going to the end. But then, I guess he always knew where he was heading.'

'He's an honourable man,' the older officer stated.

Kirsty had seen elephants once, charging down the main road through the centre of Chania. She'd been sitting enjoying an ice-cold beer with Andonis outside the market hall at the time.

'Look! Elephants!' he'd suddenly said.

'Pink ones, I suppose,' Kirsty replied, before turning round to look. And there they were—three of them, huge and prehistoric, thundering their way through the lanes of vehicles. As the elephants got closer, the bull raised his trunk and bellowed. The noise drowned out the traffic and made Kirsty nearly jump out of her seat. The creatures picked up speed and began racing along the crowded road. Cars swerved to get out of the way, or hit their brakes as drivers and passengers cowered. The ground shook and ripples of disturbance spread out across the surface of Kirsty's beer.

'Andonis . . .' Kirsty started to say, then stopped as the bull let out another roar at a group of tourists crossing the road.

'The circus,' he informed Kirsty, returning to his beer and their conversation as if nothing out of the unusual had occurred.

Now, another circus had come to town, this one a pack of jackals and wolves, more dangerous than any rogue elephants. And Kirsty seemed to be right in their path.

Eleni and Patrick had left Crete as the story really began to gather momentum.

They'd called in to see her as the 'Heroic Rescue' headlines started to turn into a search for the more lurid details seeping out—of gang rape, vendetta and German brutality.

A posh Mazda had pulled up outside the kafenion just as she was opening. Kirsty got ready to deliver her usual 'No comment' before showing them the door.

Then Eleni was in Kirsty's arms almost before she'd recognised her. The tears had flowed just as quickly. Kirsty didn't even notice the camera pointing from the taverna opposite as she hugged Eleni. The photo would be in the next day's papers: 'Kidnap victims embrace as the real hero recuperates.'

She'd not seen or spoken to Eleni or Patrick since they'd left her on the night of their escape. Kirsty had been waiting for this moment, rehearsing her lines. Hearing them in her mind thanking her for her lies. One word about it, she'd sworn, and she'd give them some truths to swallow.

But there was no mention of it. Just a genuine sharing of emotions, relief and humour.

'Did you see that photograph of Barba Yiorgos,' Eleni asked, 'naked-chested in his braces with a bottle of beer in his hand?'

Kirsty had, and its caption: 'Zorba the Second recovers from injury.'

'We went with him to visit Marianna's grave,' Patrick said. 'We had to half-carry him, as he refused to use the walking stick the doctor gave him.'

'We also went to his father's grave,' Eleni continued, 'where he's laid to rest next to Barba Yiorgos's mother. Do you know, it was the first time Barba Yiorgos had visited it? He said while we were there, "That's another wrong I'm going to right before I'm gone."'

Kirsty felt herself choking a little but still couldn't clear the image from her mind of the man she'd seen killing Diomidis.

'I had two men in here last night with a lass nearly as pretty as you,' Kirsty told Eleni, trying to change the subject. 'They said they were tourists and started asking lots of seemingly innocent questions. Then another three men came in. "Ha, so *The Sun* is still not setting," one of them said. "No," the girl replied. "Nor *The Star* declining." Then they all had a good laugh together, while watching my every move and pretending to get drunk.'

'Barba Yiorgos is lapping it up,' Eleni stated. 'He even asked if they didn't think it would make a good movie!'

'All a big joke to him,' Kirsty sneered. 'Or another Greek myth in the making.'

'Kirsty.' Patrick held her hand. 'It's not. Barba Yiorgos is suffering and looks to have aged overnight. I think he's hamming it up for the media to try to keep them off our backs as much as possible.'

'I know he's desperate to see you,' Eleni said.

Kirsty pulled away from them. 'I don't think I ever want to see or speak to him again. I see him in my dreams, or nightmares, and that's enough. I'm delighted you're safe, but I wish you'd never come.'

'We're leaving today,' Eleni said, sounding sad. 'I'd like to think we could return one day under different circumstances, but somehow I doubt it.'

Kirsty nodded. 'I'm thinking of leaving myself.'

'But there is one thing,' Eleni continued, seeming not to have heard. 'Barba Yiorgos wanted us to tell you what Olga said. The woman we were looking for, the one Diomidis murdered.'

Kirsty cut her off. 'I don't want to hear,' she warned.

'But, Kirsty,' Eleni pleaded. 'It explains so much, justifies so much.'

'Nothing will ever justify what I saw in that room at the end. And I don't want to know. I have enough guilt to deal with. I don't need any more. So let's part friends, shall we?'

'Can we at least stay in touch?' Patrick asked as the women tried to stare each other down. 'Maybe you'd even like to visit our home one day.'

'Of course,' Kirsty said, her stock reply to most tourists. 'Are you leaving straight away?'

'My mother,' Eleni said. 'She's getting worse and I must hurry back.'

Eleni kissed Kirsty on both cheeks and turned away. Patrick did the same and followed his wife out.

Kirsty remembered Kyria Despina's gift. She rushed to the door. 'Wait!' she commanded as the car began to move. 'I have something for you.' She hurried down the road to her house as they stopped.

When she returned, they were standing outside the car holding hands and enjoying the late autumnal sun. They looked just as beautiful and handsome as the first time she'd set eyes on them. Momentarily, it felt as if they'd just arrived and she was about to greet them and welcome them to her kafenion and this 'dream island'.

Then the sunlight hit the phial, and the golden liquid inside changed to blood red. The shadows from the pollarded eucalyptus trees seemed to gather around them, deformed and grotesque. Eleni looked at the ugliest of them and smiled, pleased with whatever she saw in its form. Kirsty reached them and the shadows faded. 'Kyria Despina sent this for you to give to your mother.'

Eleni took it and kissed her again.

27.

Christmas in Scotland had been terrible for Kirsty. Her mother's acerbic nature was usually bad enough to deal with, but far worse—as with any of the old friends Kirsty met—was her mother's obsession with the story.

Her mother had collected many newspaper articles and pasted them into a scrapbook. Kirsty did her best to indulge her, sitting next to her and leafing through the grey pages.

'She's so beautiful,' her mother sighed. 'Just like a movie star.'

'Yes, she is,' Kirsty agreed, looking at a photograph of Eleni, back in England, fully restored and stunning.

'Her husband is dashing, and very brave.'

'He is.'

'And the older man. He was the hero, wasn't he? And it says he won medals when he was younger.'

'Yes, Mother. They're going to erect a statue of him, I expect.' Right outside my fucking kafenion, she'd nearly added. She saw for the first time the picture of Barba Yiorgos outside the courtroom and the headline: 'Korean war hero exonerated, praised for courage.' Kirsty saw her mother staring at him, with his neatly trimmed beard, dressed in traditional clothes and wearing his medals, and knew what she was longing to ask.

'No, Mother,' she pre-empted her. 'The stories in the papers are romantic nonsense. We're not getting married. We're not lovers. We're not even friends anymore.'

'You always look so dour in your pictures,' she said, staring at one of Kirsty trying to avoid the cameras.

'Thank you, Mother,' Kirsty replied. 'It was not, as the press stated, "a great adventure". It was a nightmare.'

'Well, then, look at this,' her mother sneered. 'This will cheer even you up.'

Kirsty stared at a photograph of her ex-husband next to an ideal of the bonnie Scottish lass. 'Classical guitarist marries whisky brewer's daughter,' the caption read.

'He didn't even tell me,' Kirsty said.

'Well, why would he, my dear?' her mother stated with relish. 'You don't live here. This isn't your home anymore.'

The vague thought she'd had of trying to sell her kafenion and returning to Scotland vanished, and she counted the seconds until she could leave her mother's house.

Kirsty visited her father's grave the day before she left and was shocked to see a small clump of wild flowers growing above his remains, despite the harsh Scottish weather. Their colour and shape made her instantly recall the ones she'd seen growing in the threshing circle on her visit to Gavdos. The windflower, growing red from the blood of Adonis. And with that image, words she'd heard from another mouth spilled out of hers, making a vow without knowing how she would fulfil it. 'I will right this wrong one day, Father. I swear, I will.'

Kirsty lay in her bed, exhausted after the long journey back to Crete, but feeling euphoric. The sound of the sea came in through the open window; scents of jasmine and thyme filled her room. And Kirsty began to laugh for the first time in a long while. Tears ran down her face, but different from all the rest she'd recently wept: these were tears of joy.

'Tomorrow,' she told the empty house, 'I'm going to have my hair done. Then I'll cook up a storm and give a drink on the house to anyone who welcomes me home.'

'Yes,' she stated out loud, 'this is my home. And I was homesick.' For some reason, memories of Barba Yiorgos came to her. The day he'd slapped her butt, and the time she'd shooed his precious chicken off.

The thought of his chickens stopped her tittering for a moment. 'I'll get him some more,' she decided as she fell asleep. 'I'll send them anonymously as a belated Christmas present.'

Don't write a letter or make decisions late at night. One of her mother's good pieces of advice. *Wait until the cold light of day shines on your thoughts.*

In the morning, Kirsty knew she'd never send the birds. And could still find no way to forgive Barba Yiorgos. But the feeling of lightness remained. She went to her kafenion to wait for someone, anyone to share it with.

'Merry Christmas,' a familiar voice called into the kitchen as she was stirring her favourite cake mix.

Valentinos stood by the bar. 'Here's your Christmas present,' he said, and handed her a box.

Kirsty felt something move inside.

'Oh, Valentinos,' Kirsty gushed, as she opened the box and saw the most gorgeous, long-haired black kitten staring up at her with emerald green eyes.

'He's the only one that survived out of a litter some cruel bastard dumped in the skip. I tried to nurse them all but they were too weak; or maybe it's just that this little guy was tougher. A real Scottish fighter.'

Kirsty put the box on the counter and hugged Valentinos. 'Thank you,' she said. 'You're such a kind man.' The thoughts of how she'd doubted him touched her briefly to taint the moment.

'What will you name him?' Valentinos asked.

'Sam.'

'Sam! What sort of name is that for a cat?'

'My sort, with my own reasons.'

He shrugged as a loud, metallic-sounding voice boomed across the square. 'And what would a black cat be without a white dog to keep it company?'

Andonis stormed in from where he must have been hiding, as Kirsty had heard no one pull up. In his arms he had a West Highland White Terrier puppy. 'Merry Christmas,' he said. 'She's a top pedigree and cost me a fortune. But for you, anything.'

Kirsty went over to him and saw the look of doubt on his face. She took the puppy, then kissed Andonis full on the lips.

'I'm so glad to be home,' she said. 'And so pleased to have you two back. How long have you crafty Greeks been planning this little surprise? And whose brilliant idea was it?'

Kirsty saw a guilty look pass between the men. She stared hard at Andonis, then Valentinos, but couldn't read anything from their expressions.

'Well, you've both made my Christmas. And before you ask, her name's going to be Becky.'

Kirsty saw Andonis roll his eyes at Valentinos in despair at her human name for an animal. 'Now we're going to share a bottle of champagne to celebrate,' she announced.

Later, after they'd left, Kirsty sat watching the two sleeping animals, curled up in front of the kafenion bookcase. They already looked at home, and she was about to start snuffling again when a small motorcycle pulled up.

Tasos the postman arrived, carrying a package. He was smiling his wicked smile, the one he normally reserved for the handing over of bills. 'A parcel for you,' he boomed, 'and from England.'

'Three presents in one day,' Kirsty cooed, pouring him his customary shot of tsikoudia from the bottle she kept in the freezer.

Kirsty handed him his drink and placed her delivery on the counter. There was a fancy-looking envelope attached to it. She recognised neither the handwriting nor the postmark.

'My aunty,' she bluffed, determined not to open it in front of Tasos, a man renowned for being one of the biggest gossips in Chania. She had the strongest feeling that whatever it contained was for her eyes only. 'More Scottish teabags, I expect.'

'Ah,' Tasos exclaimed. 'The cup that cheers.' He threw the shot of tsikoudia down in a gulp.

Kirsty could see that he didn't believe a word.

'I like the new members of the household,' he said, getting up. 'Shame about the rest of the kittens, though.'

'Tasos,' Kirsty said, 'is there anything that goes on around here that you don't know about? I bet you even know how much Andonis paid for my puppy!'

'Who?' he asked, sounding genuinely puzzled. 'The Gorilla? He couldn't have found that dog in a hundred years.'

Kirsty watched him drive off, shouting greetings at everyone he saw, and tried to figure out what he'd meant. She waited until the sound of his bike had faded and shut her mind to what she was thinking.

'Please,' she prayed, sitting down to open her parcel. 'No customers for a while.'

The letter inside the envelope had been written on violet-coloured paper in blue ink. Kirsty didn't need to read the embossed name at the top of the page to know that it was from Eleni.

❦

Dearest Kirsty,

I hope you are well. You have been so much in my thoughts and prayers that I had to write, even though I suspect you are trying to forget me and all the pain and disturbance I brought. Patrick told me I should give it more time, but I could not.

I wanted to phone you several times. But I couldn't find the words or courage to do it. Then, Barba Yiorgos told me you were back in the UK for Christmas.

Kirsty looked across at Valentinos's kitten. 'Still got your spies working, Barba Yiorgos,' she said to the sleeping animals.

I kept hoping you were going to call and say you wanted to come and visit. I pictured the two of us Christmas shopping or just doing some 'girly' things together.

I prayed that you would get to see my mother before it was too late. She was longing to meet you and thank you for all you had done for Patrick and me. And, of course, for her.

Mother died just after the New Year. Not easily nor without pain, but at least now she is at peace. She was more content than I'd ever known her before. It felt as if a burden had been taken away and she was at last free to leave. My mother told me just before she died that she was immensely proud of what Barba Yiorgos had done and believed that her mother and father were in heaven together now, united through his courage.

I can imagine what's going through that splendid, kind, prag-matic Scottish mind, if you've read this far: 'Like mother; like daughter. Both blood-thirsty Greeks wanting their dish of vengeance served cold.'

I won't deny it. Or try to justify it. But I will tell you this: It was meant to be. It was my fate. As it was Barba Yiorgos's.

I've known this since I was old enough to understand what was written in my grandmother's journal and Kyria Despina's letter. The thread had been woven and could not be cut. This had to happen. There was a tear in history that needed mending before the future could continue with any chance of purity.

You're not convinced, I'm sure. But it's my truth.

Or maybe it was in my genes. I told Barba Yiorgos the last time we were together, just before we kissed goodbye, 'You know, the same blood is flowing through our veins.'

'Huh,' he grunted, 'you're just another English woman who is hell-bent on pissing me off.' (I'm Scottish, Kirsty whispered, a lump beginning to form in her throat.) *But he held me far too long and hard for me to believe him.*

Inside the parcel you'll find my grandmother's journal and Kyria Despina's letter, which my mother wanted you to have. She felt that you needed to read them and that it would help. I hope you will and that it does. The last pages are in a different hand. Mine. It's our story with my feelings, and some of my mother's, laid bare. It also contains all that Barba Yiorgos learnt, including Olga's confession, which I know you didn't want to hear. But I think you should look at it and see if it clarifies things. I hope so, as I would hate to think that you will never forgive me or, more especially, Barba Yiorgos.

Anyway, that's all the heavy bits. Now the slightly lighter ones.

The potion you gave me from Kyria Despina for my mother was a miracle drug. As was the news that her 'yiayia' was still alive and thinking of her. Every time Mother took a sip of the elixir, she drifted out of pain and back to the days she'd spent on Gavdos with Kyria Despina. She told me that she could hear a voice, sweet and strong, telling her not to be afraid. And she wasn't.

My mother took her last drink just before she died and let the bottle fall and shatter. Breaking glass, Patrick told me, is an omen of death in Ireland. What does it mean on Crete?

'Tell my yiayia that I have never forgotten her and can't wait to meet again,' she said, smiling and radiant, before passing away.

I asked Barba Yiorgos to inform Kyria Despina and he promised he would, but he suspected she already knew. Having met her, I imagine he was right.

So did Kirsty.

Barba Yiorgos came to England for my mother's funeral. I even had it in my heart that you were going to turn up and that I would see you standing next to him. He looked absolutely splendid in his Cretan clothes, with a neatly shaved beard and plaited ponytail. He sang a Cretan song at the end of the service and had us all in tears.

'Determined to do a good PR job, aren't you?' Kirsty said aloud, trying to deny what she was feeling.

Now, the best bit for last. There must have been something magical in that Cretan honey and village wine, because I'm pregnant. And Patrick and I know the exact night it happened. I told Barba Yiorgos when we last spoke on the phone and the cheeky old goat said so did he! He even claimed to have sent us a good luck gift at the moment of conception! Can you believe it?

It made me think of something Andonis told me about him just before we left: 'The devil reformed is still the devil.' But I love him.

Anyway, if we have a girl, it's going to be named Marianna Kirsty. And we would love you to be a godparent.

If it's a boy? Well, I leave you to guess that one.
So, I'll say goodbye for now and beg you to read the journal. Then
shine your light where you think it should go.

All my love,
Eleni xx.

∽

Kirsty opened the package. Inside there was a leather-bound journal and a letter written in Greek on parchment with what appeared to be an English translation attached to it. Also, the red silk chemise and a photograph of Eleni and a woman who could only be her mother.

Kirsty started to read the journal. Reluctantly, at first. But then avidly, with the passion it inspired.

The intensity of the love it portrayed, both in sketches and words, burned with such a flame that she found herself bathed in its afterglow for days and needed to look and read again, before the darkness came and killed the light.

The birth of Athena had been a joy for Marianna. The sketches had caught Athena's future beauty and made Kirsty long to see Eleni again. The dreams Marianna dreamt for her daughter made Kirsty detest whoever could have brought them to an end.

Then, as Kirsty read on, something she didn't want to name began to burn even more fiercely inside her.

Marianna had done watercolours of her husband, Michaelis, as well as Athena. He looked just as handsome as Barba Yiorgos had in the photograph he'd once shown her. She'd also done paintings of her little house and garden, so vibrant that Kirsty could almost smell the flowers. And another that was clearly of a younger Kyria

Despina, smiling and holding Athena. Plus glimpses of village life: all light, all colour.

Then, suddenly, things changed.

Marianna began to record the abuses and try to justify them. *But I'm sure she was only joking.* Or, *It must be because my Greek is so bad that they refuse to serve me.*

Always, she managed to find acts of kindness by Kyria Despina, her sister and Kapetanios Rossos to offset these.

But the insults were there, and beginning to mount.

In one place she tried to write off some malicious comments shouted out from the taverna as she passed. *They are young men back from fighting and letting off steam. They didn't mean what they called me. It was just drunkenness. I will make them like me for my husband's and child's sakes. And for the children we're still going to have. It's only this awful war that makes people suspicious of all foreigners.*

Even when the flower arrangement she'd laboured on for hours and sneaked into the church for the next day's celebration had been torn to pieces and thrown at her doorstep, she'd put it down to village yobs. *I know the priest scowls at me,* she'd written, *and makes the sign to ward off the evil eye whenever our paths cross, but he would never have done or allowed this.*

Then, towards the end of the journal, as Kirsty became more familiar with it and learnt to read between the lines, a cloud of darkness, like the one floating in the distance over the mountains, began to gather. Marianna caught it in one of the last small paintings she had created.

In this, a storm was brewing over the wedding-cake frosting of snow covering the Lefka Ori. It felt, to Kirsty, as if the artist had sensed it was advancing with an inevitable, unstoppable descent towards her.

Names of people began to appear, some of whom Kirsty had met. Others she had not, though they became familiar through the pages. All, it seemed, had one thing in common: they were good or evil.

Kyria Despina put in an appearance, giving—in an almost identical action to the one she would perform decades later—a herbal potion to Athena, who'd suddenly become ill. Along with the picture came words that chilled Kirsty every time she reread them. *Be very wary of whose children you let near your baby from now on, my child. Some of them carry diseases that Athena may not be immune to.*

Marianna had sketched the lady she described as the 'white witch' holding Athena close to her and staring into the baby's eyes as the golden medicine flowed from its phial.

And her following words: *Do you understand what I'm telling you?*

Kyria Despina had shaken her head sadly at Marianna's reply, *That Athena needs more time to build up her immunity?*

As Kirsty had read the journal on the last occasion, it seemed to her like watching a Hitchcock movie, or opening a great thriller for the tenth time. One knew exactly what was going to happen and wanted desperately to reach into the screen or onto the page and change the ending, but was as helpless as the victim. What made this worse was that Kirsty knew that every image and word was the truth.

Marianna had known something evil was coming and that she had no escape. Within all her optimism and joy, love and hope, there was the clear understanding of her fate.

Kirsty reached the ending again, recording Michaelis's surprise visit, Marianna's passionate description of their lovemaking and their final, short time together, her desire to become pregnant and her excitement over the gift she'd received from the most unlikely of neighbours. And the last terrible entry: *One thing that will not fade, however, were his parting words. He started to say— after all the goodbyes and sweet love promises—something strange. He said . . .*

'What?' she asked aloud, every time. 'What did he say to you?'

Kyria Despina's letter tore at Kirsty's emotions. It not only recorded the death of Marianna and voiced her suspicions about who'd been responsible for it, but included pages about how she had loved and raised Athena on Gavdos, including when she'd let her go.

And the warning: *Athena must never return. Death waits for her here.*

At the end of the parchment lay a promise: *There is someone here who can right this wrong. I don't know when, but I see it in my visions and know it will come to pass.*

For a final time, Kirsty read Olga's tragic confession, as she clutched the red chemise in her hand.

Her hands began to tingle. She pictured the German parachutist whom the material may once have carried down from the sky, hanging dead under its red canopy. 'Good,' she snarled. 'And I hope it was Michaelis who shot you.'

The tingling stopped. A warmth entered her body, and a coldness flooded her mind.

'Yes,' she said, 'souls can cry out for revenge. And I could hate for what was done to these people.'

Kirsty let the garment drop, gossamer soft, another sigh of death falling onto the blood-sodden earth of Crete.

As it did, she saw the final moments of Diomidis's death run through her mind again. But differently for the first time. Barba Yiorgos was still standing behind Diomidis. He smiled at her and she saw him relax slightly. Diomidis reacted and his hand snaked out to his ankle and a gun appeared as if by magic. It began to rise and aim at her before a different curtain of red fell and closed the scene.

'Oh my God.' Kirsty clasped her hands to her face. 'What have I done?'

28.

May 17th, 2005, Kissamou, Kirsty and Barba Yiorgos

The two 4x4s crawled quietly along the beach towards Barba Yiorgos's house. Both drivers parked a short way off and killed the engines. It was the middle of the night and no moon rippled on the darkling sea. The two people in each of the vehicles didn't speak or smoke as they awaited their moment.

Kirsty sat in the first one with Michaelis. Andonis and Valentinos were in the other vehicle following them and towing a loaded trailer. Andonis, she figured, was still sulking over the fact she'd insisted he leave his bullhorn in her kafenion. There was no way she was going to have him ruin her planned surprise by bellowing into Barba Yiorgos's dreams.

As it was, Kirsty had her doubts about being able to keep the three men under any sort of control. They'd insisted, against her wishes, on bringing two large jugs of village wine. And she could feel the excitement oozing from Michaelis and the men behind them. Twice, the Gorilla had driven so close he'd actually touched their bumper. When they'd first reached the beach, he'd shot down the sands and splashed the Nissan through the surf. Now, in the silence, she could feel the men, young and old, tensed to do something exuberant.

'What is it,' Kirsty asked herself as they waited, 'that makes the Cretans turn everything into a game or adventure? Or treat the most mundane task as if it was the first time it had ever been done? A joy of life, a denial of death?' Kirsty pictured Anthony Quinn in *Zorba* telling the stiff Alan Bates, 'Grab it with both hands.'

'Michaelis,' she asked, 'you and Andonis were acting very mysterious in the kafenion before we left. And I noticed the spades in the back of your truck were as filthy as is the floor of your vehicle. Not your usual style. What's been going on?'

'Grave robbing,' Michaelis whispered. 'You'll have to ask my father, though, or he'll bite my head off.'

'Michaelis?'

Barba Yiorgos's lights went out and the men began moving before she could probe any more.

They began working immediately. Valentinos was in charge, as he claimed to have built many such things before.

Each set of staging planks that Andonis and Michaelis had made over the last few weeks under Valentinos's supervision clicked into place like the pieces of a jigsaw puzzle. The rubber mallets Michaelis had suggested were driving the restraining pegs in with relative silence. As each muffled blow echoed back from the bay, they still sounded to Kirsty like the explosions of a distant battle. With each one, she stared at the house in dread of lights coming on, the door opening, her plan ruined.

Once, a light did go on and everyone got down low and froze. Kirsty watched as a figure moved behind the curtains, then a long minute passed and the light went off.

Kirsty let out a deep sigh.

'Taking a piss,' Michaelis said, then tittered mischievously.

'Old man's disease,' Andonis added.

'He's not that old,' Kirsty said.

'Barba Yiorgos has gone downhill a lot lately,' Valentinos warned her, brushing a hand through her hair.

Kirsty thought of Eleni's letter and her description of Barba Yiorgos at Athena's funeral. Please, she prayed, don't let me have left this too long. But it had to be now.

'Can we get on with this?' she snapped at the men. 'Or we'll never get finished.'

'Best let him have a little time to fall asleep,' Valentinos advised. 'Andonis, fetch some wine while we wait.'

ᘖᘙ

Finally, just as dawn began to break over the distant Rodopou Peninsula and turn the sea into a shifting mirage of mercury, they were finished. Kirsty stood with the men, looking from Barba Yiorgos's garden gate along the new gangway, until the final piece they'd laid touched and moved in rhythm with the lapping sea.

'Perfect,' Kirsty whispered.

It was. A ruler-straight walkway across the beach, risen from the ashes that those evil men had left in its place. Kirsty pictured Barba Yiorgos tutting as family and friends ran back and forth, then imagined him seeing again the shadows of those who'd once traversed the original. She even saw herself, and maybe Eleni, skipping down it one day. A bridge to span the sands of time.

'Right, boys,' Kirsty ordered. 'Time for you to go.'

She'd been expecting some resistance at this point, for them to insist on staying. Or at least to be allowed to park a short way off and witness his surprise. But they didn't. In fact, the men seemed more delighted with this part of her idea than the rest.

'Good luck,' each of them said, hugging and kissing her goodbye.

Kirsty watched them drive off as she stood on the beach with her bag and equipment, like someone marooned.

The sky had started to brighten. It was going to be the glorious day she'd been wishing for. Kirsty paused for a moment, looking at the rebirth of the sun as Zeus's child, Apollo, awoke.

Kirsty placed everything on the end of the gangway and began to undress. When she was naked, she glanced back at the house, half-expecting Barba Yiorgos to have arisen and be observing her. She was pleased to see that he slumbered on, blind to this nymph. Kirsty waded into the sea, carefully, over the first barrier of rocks, before her feet touched the sand and she plunged into the waves. The shock of the early season's water temperature hit her, but did nothing to quell her excitement about what today, and especially tonight, might bring.

Kirsty began to swim powerfully, then stopped and cavorted in the sea as she hit a warm patch of water. She did a handstand, kicking her legs wildly, before diving under and ploughing on again.

By the time she returned to the shore and stood on the cedar boards, Kirsty felt cleansed in body as well as mind. She dried and took a carefully folded dress from her bag, the one she'd worn the day of the visit to the Monastery of the Golden Step. Had the step turned golden that day? she wondered. She felt certain that if she trod on it now, it would.

Finally, with her long hair brushed, dress on, and the mataki back on its chain around her neck, she sat down and waited, determined not to move until she heard the sound of Barba Yiorgos's door opening. At her side, a bowl of sea water warmed gently under the rising sun.

Barba Yiorgos had slept badly. He'd had another terrible dream. In this one, a variation on the many others, Diomidis had him tied to a stasidi chair and forced him to watch as he'd raped Kirsty. He awoke, with his usual feeling of loneliness and self-loathing at what she'd believed him capable of, and repeated helplessly, 'That would have happened to you if I hadn't saved you.' He pulled his trousers on and sat at the table. 'He would have killed you, even though he'd lost. I was the hero, not the villain.'

Barba Yiorgos looked at the two photographs that were lying there. First, the repaired image of Michaelis and Marianna, who both seemed to be smiling at him now. Then, next to it, the one of him and Eleni taken a few months before at Athena's funeral. Eleni was embracing him firmly. She was radiant, proud and as beautiful as the woman who had bewitched his father.

He recalled their last evening together, when she'd told him how much what he had done had meant to her mother at the end. And how it had made him feel at the time.

Since then, there'd been no such moments. Or just one, which had turned out to be a fool's hope.

Valentinos had turned up for his usual weekly game of Tavli. As they'd played, Valentinos said casually, above the castanet-clicking of the game, 'Oh, something strange happened yesterday. I went to Kirsty's kafenion.'

Barba Yiorgos had rolled a double six and pretended not to react to the fact this was the first time in months her name had been mentioned.

'She was reading that journal again and hardly bothered to serve me. Then suddenly she put it down and asked about you.'

'What?' Barba Yiorgos demanded, getting to his feet and tipping the board over. He grabbed Valentinos and shook him. 'What did she ask?'

'She just wanted to know how you were. If you were well.'

Barba Yiorgos let him go. He'd felt like dancing. 'Did Kirsty say anything else?' he asked, ignoring Valentinos's smirk at his reaction.

'She asked me if you ever mentioned her.'

'What did you tell her?'

'I told her that she should phone you, or visit.'

'And?'

'She said, "We'll see."'

'"We'll see"?'

'That's what she said. And I think I was winning that game.'

'Maybe I'm winning mine,' Barba Yiorgos replied, hoping in his heart it was so.

But there'd been nothing. Each time the phone had rung, he'd thought he might hear her voice. Every car that had pulled up or passed made his heart race. But she was never there.

Twice, when the frustration had become too much, he'd gone to Chania, determined to march into her kafenion. On each occasion he'd baulked.

Especially the second time, when he'd seen Kirsty. She'd been sitting alone in the kafenion reading, and he'd hidden in Valentinos's carport watching her. Barba Yiorgos thought she looked wonderful and content. He'd wanted more than anything to go in and join her. Then, before he could move, he saw her expression the day he had killed Diomidis.

Finally, after sitting alone day after day, he'd decided for the second time in his life that he would end it. He went and found his other gun—the police had confiscated the first one, but like all true Cretans he had a spare. He'd placed the Luger on the table and begun a farewell letter to Kirsty, when the phone rang.

'Fate?' he whispered, and decided to answer it.

It had been Eleni. It had been a long conversation, and she'd finished by saying, 'Don't forget, you've promised to be my baby's godfather. And you're going to have a big surprise at who's just written to say she's going to be the godmother!'

He'd put the pistol back in its hiding place and torn up the letter.

He thought of it now as the nightmare began to fade, and he saw instead a christening ceremony with Kirsty by his side and the baby's beauty mirroring Marianna, Athena and Eleni: blue-eyed in wonder at life. His suicide could not be allowed to mar that.

Barba Yiorgos got up and took his coffee out to the terrace. It was time to get some more chickens, he decided. Maybe he would train another to lay his morning egg, and when Kirsty came again she could take a kick at it.

He was still smiling at his fantasy as he opened the door and looked out to sea.

Then realised he was still dreaming and sat down resignedly, waiting for whatever torment was coming next.

A figure seated at the end of the new cedar-wood walkway was beginning to rise.

It was a woman with a mass of glistening auburn hair. She was wearing a flowing white dress. The bright sun was shining through the material and exposing her long legs and shapely figure. The light was too bright for him to make out her features. But he knew exactly where he'd seen her before and who she was.

'Wake up!' he ordered himself as she picked up a bowl and began to walk ethereally along the scented wood that he could actually smell in this dream. 'Wake up,' he repeated, dreading the moment when the flames would burst into life and choke his breathing with ash. Or when the sweetly smiling, forgiving Kirsty would change into some monstrous apparition—a gorgon,

313

hair writhing with snakes that turned him to stone—and the clear water in the bowl would become blood that she heaved into his face.

Kirsty stood, real, at the bottom of his steps. Barba Yiorgos began to shake.

'Kali mera, Barba Yiorgos,' Kirsty said, smiling cheekily at him. 'Do you like what the fairies did in the night?'

'I like the queen of them, who just walked over what can't be there,' he said. 'And if you're going to do what you once threatened, and pour that over my head, could you wait a little while? Because this isn't a dream I want to wake up from.'

'This isn't for your head,' Kirsty said, climbing the steps. 'It's for your feet.'

She squatted next to him and gently rolled up his trousers. Then she placed his feet in the sea water. He made no attempt to resist as she began to massage his toes.

'Feel good?' Kirsty asked, trying to keep the expression of shock from her face: Barba Yiorgos *had* aged badly from when she'd last seen him.

'Kirsty,' Barba Yiorgos replied, 'I've missed you and wanted so much to . . .'

'I'm the one who needs to do the explaining and apologise.'

'Apologise? For what?'

'For seeing what I wanted to see. For believing what I wanted to believe. Maybe because you did what I once failed to do and saw things through to their end. And with honour.'

'You did more than me.'

'He had a gun and would have killed me if you hadn't saved me, wouldn't he?'

'He'd probably have missed. And I'd probably have killed him anyway. You better believe it.'

Barba Yiorgos's face broke into the wicked smile Kirsty remembered so fondly. 'Besides, you were too busy making eyes at me to notice that little snake!'

'You better believe it,' Kirsty replied, hurrying to embrace Barba Yiorgos as he stood and opened his arms.

'Sit,' he told her. 'I have something to show you.'

Barba Yiorgos fetched out the restored picture of his father and Marianna.

'Such a beautiful couple. Such a terrible waste.'

Barba Yiorgos nodded in agreement. 'He used to carry that in his pack. Turn it over.'

Kirsty did. She knew what the paper inside the frame was, without removing it. 'The will!' she exclaimed. 'I thought you were going to give it to Eleni. That your father had left it for Marianna!'

'Tut tut tut,' Barba Yiorgos was smiling. 'You doubting me again? Of course I gave it to Eleni to take home to her mother. But she wanted me to keep it. As did her daughter. They trusted that I would do the best thing with it. Don't you?'

'Of course. I was only . . .'

'You've only been back five minutes and you're already starting to . . .'

'Piss you off! I know. But not too much, I hope, because we've got a date.'

'A date?'

'One I've been waiting patiently for. It's May the seventeenth. You asked this lady to spend the night on a beach with you. Have you forgotten?'

'Ah,' Barba Yiorgos said mysteriously. 'So it has come at last. No, not forgotten. Just more running away, you might say.'

'What?' Kirsty looked perplexed.

'Nothing. I'm just surprised you remembered, that's all.'

'But you still want to go?' Kirsty asked.

'Of course. It's my fate. How can anyone escape from that?'

29.

May 17th, 2005, Frangokastello, Kirsty and Barba Yiorgos

Barba Yiorgos transmogrified, becoming more satyr-like, as their day together progressed. Kirsty wanted to believe it was because she'd come back into his space, but sensed it was not, and that he was recharging his batteries for a coming challenge she had no part of.

Before she'd finished her coffee—sitting outside admiring her night's work—the old dishevelled man who'd greeted her had done his quick-change routine once again. He stepped out, spectacular in a white shirt, leather jacket and blue canvas trousers. His beard and hair were perfect and a musky scent of aftershave came off him.

'Nice,' Kirsty said.

'Me or the coffee?' Barba Yiorgos winked, and Kirsty saw the familiar blue flame in his eyes begin to burn again.

'You, of course!'

'Ha! For that,' he said, 'I'll buy you dinner. We'll stop on the way, at this place I know. They do the best goat ribs on the island. But first, I must fetch some provisions for our night under the stars.'

He shot inside before she could move, then came out with two leather panniers. 'You can load,' he said, and left her again.

A minute later he returned with two bottles of wine, another of tsikoudia, and plastic containers of olives, cheese and cured meats.

'Did you know I was coming?' Kirsty asked, seeing how well everything had been prepared. 'Wasn't it a surprise?'

'Don't be so suspicious,' he said, not meeting her eye. 'Anyway, it's my turn to surprise you.'

'What?' Kirsty asked as she began packing the bags.

'I saw you the first day you came here, staring at my Brough Superior.'

Kirsty recalled it and smiled to think of how she'd imagined him asleep at the top of his stairs.

'You fell in love with it, didn't you? Love at first sight?'

'Yes,' Kirsty admitted. 'My father was a fanatic about vintage bikes.'

'Good, then you'll be pleased to know that I've left the Brough to you in my will.'

'What? I thought you abandoned it on the beach.'

'Abandoned! I don't abandon friends.' He stared hard at her. 'I thought you, of all people, knew that much about me.'

Kirsty blushed.

'Michaelis went and got it. It's back and in pristine condition. It will be yours, along with some other things, one day.'

'Oh, Barba Yiorgos,' Kirsty said. 'I don't know what you're talking about. Besides, by the time I get it, I'll be too old to drive the beast.'

'You better believe it,' he said. 'Now, the next surprise: I'm taking you to the beach. And on the back of that bike.'

Kirsty smiled, thinking of how much she had loved to be driven by her father. 'Why not?' she said teasingly. 'You only live once.'

'Do you really think so?' Barba Yiorgos replied. 'You may have another surprise coming today then. But first: eat and drink. We'll stop on the way to pick up some bread at an old fourno I know. They do . . .'

'Let me guess,' Kirsty interrupted, trying to lighten the mood, 'the "best bread on the island".'

Barba Yiorgos raised his hand. 'Do you remember what happened here the last time you spoke to me in this fashion?'

'Yeah,' Kirsty replied saucily. 'I pissed you off and got my arse slapped!'

'And don't use words like those,' he said, smiling and moving off to fetch the bike. 'You're a lady.'

ᗡᐤ

Kirsty clung to Barba Yiorgos, loving every sensation of the journey. She had never driven so fast and couldn't believe how he handled the bike.

They pulled up at his chosen taverna.

'Wow!' she cried. 'Where did you learn to drive like that?'

'Army telegraph, New York courier, Wall of Death rider, Los Angeles Circus. You better believe it,' he said, springing away from her like someone reborn.

The goat ribs were excellent and Kirsty watched in amazement as Barba Yiorgos ordered a second plate and more wine.

'Hungry?' she quizzed. 'Must be all that digging you did the night before last.'

'Ha,' he said. 'My son has a big mouth.'

'You moved Marianna's body, didn't you?'

'No.' He ate another rib as if she hadn't asked anything significant. 'Barba Yiorgos?'

'I moved my father. He's sleeping next to the one he loved.'

Kirsty reached across the table and touched his hand.

'I've agreed to be the godfather of Eleni's baby,' he said, before Kirsty could speak. 'That's if I live long enough. If not, I will always be there in spirit.'

'You'll live long enough,' Kirsty assured him. 'I'll make sure of it, as I'm going to be her godmother.'

'Her? It will be a boy. All good Cretan women want to produce a man-child. Something strong for the island's future.' Barba Yiorgos threw a shot of tsikoudia down and glared challengingly at Kirsty.

'Well,' she replied glowering back just as hard, 'I'd say, going by the examples of Marianna, Athena and Eleni, there was a pretty strong female line produced from somewhere. What do you say to that?'

'I say, pray the gods better help some poor man in the future if there's another of this matriarchal clan to contend with!'

ॐ

At Frangokastello, Barba Yiorgos became even more rejuvenated. He gave Kirsty a guided tour of the fortress that she could barely keep up with.

Startled visitors looked on as he virtually re-enacted the battle for her. Kirsty already knew the tourist version of the story, but now she was getting it through Cretan eyes. It was no longer the tale of the wild adventurer, Hadzimichalis Dalianis, and his band of men, making the mistake of trying to defend the castle instead of fleeing into the hills. Rather, it was a heroic stand against the Turkish conquerors that would become an inspiration in all battles for the liberation of Crete.

Kirsty had visited the place before and been unimpressed by it. 'Huh,' she'd scoffed at the time to her friend as they looked at the disappointing ruin. 'So this is the great fort of Frangokastello!'

Now she felt its power and tragedy.

The feelings emanating from the place were still with her as Barba Yiorgos drove them along the beach and picked the exact spot he wanted. Kirsty watched the castle's silhouette as the sun began to set and Barba Yiorgos prepared their camp. The fort seemed to be reborn and, mirage-like, regain its former glory. Kirsty turned to Barba Yiorgos, who was staring at it, and felt the fear or apprehension she had sensed in him earlier intensify.

'Why are we here?' she asked, as he carried on gazing, hypnotised.

'My father, Michaelis, came here once on this date.'

'With Marianna?'

'No, a long time after she'd died. Too long, as it turned out.'

'And what happened? He saw the Dewy Ones?'

Barba Yiorgos reacted as if struck. 'The Drosoulites? You know about them?'

'The story's in all the guidebooks. The ghosts of Dalianis's army marching from the castle at dawn, black-armoured, carrying their swords and wearing helmets. Vanishing if anyone approached them.'

'What do books know?' he replied, irritated, as if she'd spoiled his surprise.

'Is that what your father told you he saw? Is this why you brought me: to see ghosts?'

'You don't believe in dolphins. Now you're telling me you don't believe in ghosts either?'

Kirsty watched him smile and felt his spirits lift as he looked away from the fort.

'If you'd grown up in Scotland,' she said, 'and visited as many "haunted" castles as I have, you might be a little sceptical.'

'This isn't Scotland,' he stated. 'This is Crete. Its mysteries run deep. There was a culture here when your people were dressed in animal skins, living in caves.'

'Hold on a wee minute—I thought we were talking about your father, not the Minoan culture.'

'I'll tell you all about him in the morning. Now, I'm going to bank up the fire, drink some wine, put on the little cassette player I've brought and we'll dance.'

'Dance?'

'Of course. I'm Cretan. We always dance.'

'I can't. Well, only a little that I learnt from my dance lesson evenings.'

Barba Yiorgos brushed Kirsty's hair back from her lowered head. 'Don't worry,' he said. 'I'll give you a real lesson. If that fraud Anthony Quinn can get some tight-arsed English pen-pusher to move, what do you think the real thing can achieve?'

So they danced. The lyra music swirled out and made even the flames of the fire sway to its rhythm. Step by step, arm in arm, she moved with Barba Yiorgos. Slowly and tentatively at first, then with an energy and intensity that began to take control so that her body seemed to move of its own accord.

Kirsty suddenly became afraid. She let go of Barba Yiorgos and hurried to the comfort of the fire.

She turned, expecting him to be trailing after her. Instead, it appeared that he'd not even noticed. Barba Yiorgos drifted, as Kirsty watched, into a trance and no longer appeared to be dancing to the music she was hearing.

His feet were pounding the ground as if they were stamping down every spadeful of blood that Kazantzakis had written about. His hands and arms writhed in the air, as though they were trying to touch the pain and agony that had spilled it. Barba Yiorgos's eyes rolled back into his head and he seemed blind to reality. Kirsty felt the island take him in its grasp and she wanted to set him free.

'Barba Yiorgos,' she called softly, switching the music off. She called again as he carried on, oblivious to her.

This time there was a reaction. He made a few additional gentle, graceful movements, then stopped. He walked over slowly, threw a few logs on the fire and took a long drink from a bottle of wine.

'You could become a good dancer if you learnt to let go,' Barba Yiorgos said, offering her the bottle.

Kirsty took it. 'I will,' she promised. 'Next time I'll really cut up the sand rug with you.'

'So, there'll be a next time with me? More dancing and wine on the beach?'

'I'd like to think so,' Kirsty replied, taking the plate of food he'd prepared.

'Okay then, it's a deal. Same place, same date.'

∾

Barba Yiorgos was sleeping.

He and Kirsty had been talking non-stop since the dance, getting merrily drunk together and swapping stories about their lives and families. Both of them, Kirsty sensed, needing to keep everything light. All the time, though, she'd seen him staring towards the castle with an expression that was anything but light.

Then, just as the first rays of morning arrived, a bird started singing. 'It's a nightingale,' Kirsty cried. 'Our "Piper at the Gates of Dawn". How appropriate that the music of Pan should end our night.'

But Barba Yiorgos wasn't listening or sitting up anymore. He was curled up in a foetal position on the blanket. Kirsty smiled as she looked at him and a gentle snore reached her. 'Been talking to myself,' she whispered as the bird sang on.

Their fire was dying and she decided to put a blanket over Barba Yiorgos before doing the same for herself. Then suddenly she couldn't move. The temperature plummeted and a heavy mist began to form.

Kirsty looked at the fort and saw a host of figures moving from it. Tourists, she assured herself. A couple of coachloads of English, or more likely, at this time of day, Germans, come on some 'Dewy Ones' excursion!

'Barba Yiorgos,' she called, 'rouse yourself. Company's arriving.'

He didn't respond and slept on.

Kirsty turned back to the fort. The people were getting closer but were still too vaporous to define.

Then she began to see them clearly. Her mouth opened and the hairs on her body became erect.

'Barba Yiorgos,' she pleaded, 'wake up.'

A black-clad, weapon-carrying, helmeted army of men were marching in orderly fashion. And they were coming straight towards her. The mist was acting like stage curtains, making sure only she saw this play.

'Barba Yiorgos,' she tried again, the words hardly able to leave her mouth. 'They've come.'

Kirsty watched as the men assembled in front of her. None of them looked wounded or even blemished by battle. They were, she saw, at their moment of triumph, and had left their resting place to state it.

Finally, after they had formed a precise semi-circle in front of her, the warriors stopped moving. Every dark eye, staring through the visors of their armour, was directed solely at the prostrate figure of Barba Yiorgos.

A man moved from their ranks. Kirsty knew it was their leader, Dalianis. A power and charisma emanated from him with a tangible force as his form became more solid than the rest of the men. He lifted his helmet and Kirsty looked at his face, which was hard and unforgiving.

He began to approach. Each high, black-booted step seemed to take an eternity to fall and made the sand explode in bursts of ancient dust that released a scent of decay. With each one, a new question formed in Kirsty's mind. Is this what your father, Michaelis, told you he'd seen? Is this why you came? Or are you keeping the truth from me again?

But suddenly none of her questions mattered, because Dalianis arrived, and in her heart she knew all the answers.

He studied Kirsty: it felt as if he was staring mercilessly into and through her. Then the darkness faded from his eyes and a familiar Cretan blue sparkle entered them. His expression softened and a slight smile crossed his face. For a moment, Kirsty thought she could be seeing Barba Yiorgos, or even Eleni. Then it passed, as he turned and concentrated on the sleeping figure next to her.

Dalianis moved to Barba Yiorgos and towered above him. He drew his sword with a speed that made the air part. As he did, every warrior on the beach did the same. The sound was like waves breaking. Dalianis raised his sword high into the air and his men followed suit. All the blades turned golden and reached ruler-straight upwards, so that they appeared to touch the mist hovering above and stretch into infinity.

'We come to honour and reward you, Kapetanios Yiorgos,' Dalianis said. His voice was soft and yet, to Kirsty, deafening.

She wanted to tell him to stop, but couldn't speak.

His ghost legion cheered and banged their swords on their shields.

'You have earned this right,' Dalianis said. He lowered his sword and made the sign of a cross over Barba Yiorgos's heart. Then he turned and, without giving Kirsty another glance, marched back to his men.

Kirsty watched, still transfixed, as they began to move back into the mist and towards the castle, like the smoke of a genie sucked slowly back into its lamp.

She heard the gate begin to grind open, and the chains that had held her were released. Kirsty let out a long, slow sob, then spoke. 'Barba Yiorgos, wake up. Wake up or you'll miss them. Please.'

She reached over to him to give him a gentle shake. Her hands touched his ice-cold and stiff arm.

'No,' Kirsty sobbed, kneeling next to his body so her hair was brushing his neck and cheeks. 'This isn't fair. He deserves more time. We deserve more time.'

She heard a song answering her plea. Kirsty stared at the sea. It was perfectly still for a moment, a limpid black mirror, denying the sky above. As the voice sang its sweet elegy, a beam of sunlight struck the surface and a blue wave exploded into the air. It held for a moment like a rainbow and Kirsty saw Kyria Despina within it. She stood on the edge of a cliff, her long hair loose and blowing in the wind, her hands held out. She smiled at Kirsty just before a wave broke on the beach and the image and sound disappeared.

Kirsty turned to witness the Dewy Ones, who were entering the castle's gate. She looked for Barba Yiorgos amongst them. 'No,' she cried. 'You're not going to take him. I defy you.'

She rushed to the Brough motorcycle, kicked it into life and raced across the sand in pursuit of the retreating legion of the dead.

The gate was slowly beginning to close as she got near. All the men except two had entered. She recognised Dalianis easily, but not the figure next to him. Then suddenly a single ray of light cut through the fading mist from a long way off and bathed the other man in its radiance. Kirsty skidded the bike to a halt as she saw who it was: Barba Yiorgos, transformed into the man in the photograph he'd shown her at his house that day, young and dashing again, freed from the constraints of the aging body he'd so despised.

Dalianis followed his men and Barba Yiorgos turned to her. He waved and blew her a kiss, and said something that she couldn't hear.

He entered the portal and the gate boomed in a defiant closing.

'Don't forget,' Kirsty yelled as the mirage of the fortress evaporated into its former ruin. 'We have a date. Same time, same place, next year.'

She turned the bike and rode it into the blood-red eye of the rising sun.

ACKNOWLEDGEMENTS

I find it a surprise that in this lonely 'craft and sullen art', one ends up with so many good people to thank. However . . .

I would like to thank The Arts Council England; The Oppenheim-John Downes Memorial Trust; and The Royal Literary Fund for their belief and support. Deepest gratitude.

A short story that became the genesis of this novel appeared in the *Ellery Queen Mystery Magazine*: my thanks to the editor and her team.

A big thank you to the team at Amazon for making it all so seamless and professional; Emilie, Sana, Serra, Jennifer, Lori and Neil: you are the best.

I am proud to give my thanks, trust, and confidence to my literary uber-agent Jon Elek and his super-efficient assistant Millie Hoskins at United Agents London.

Muchas gracias to my ideal first reader, Neil William Nelson, for his gentle wisdom and support. Madrid this year!

And finally, for my best friend, first reader, greatest advocate, harshest critic, proof-reader, lover, and the real force behind all of the writings, my wife, Lisa. The novel is dedicated to her; this author is in awe of her.

ABOUT THE AUTHOR

Neil Grimmett was born in Birmingham. After being expelled from school at 14, he spent the next decade on the road and in recording studios playing the drums with various rock bands. He also worked making high explosives at a top secret establishment for the Ministry of Defence; as a gamekeeper for minor aristocracy; as a professional handler of show dogs; and as a teacher of creative literature.

He published more than 85 short stories in anthologies and journals including *London Magazine, Strand, The Yale Review*, and *Ellery Queen Mystery Magazine*, as well as online at *Blackbird, Web Del Sol*, and *The Dublin Quarterly*, to name just a few.

He won seven Oppenheim John Downes awards, five major British Arts Council awards, a Royal Society of Authors award, and the Write On poetry award. His work made the South Million Writers Notable Short Story list for the last three years.

Sadly Neil passed away in November 2015.

Printed in Great Britain
by Amazon

60881381R00210